Second Class

DEDICATION

Thank you to all of those that thought us worthy enough to pledge support on Kickstarter to make this book possible including: Sarah Lahue, Kevin Flahaut, Gwen Fischer, Hameed Mohammed, Carl Hancock, Richard Wawrzyniak, David Smith, Elliott Neumeister, Greg Murphy, Sandy Adams, Stephen Barber, Mark Ferrer, Nancy L. Wood, Gael Knowles, Andrea Knight, Jordan Pires, Johanna Faith, Lauren Mader, Carly Lanthier, Kel Schwab, and Mark Wood.

CONTENTS

CHAPTER 1

The chill spring breeze pushed through her thin sweater, causing her clammy skin to cover itself in goosebumps which increased her already extreme discomfort. Kya looked at her phone, studying the picture displayed on it. She reviewed the endless faces in the crowd and tried to find his face in the moving torrent of people outside the busy restaurant where they were supposed to meet.

As the crowd thickened, people began to bump into Kya, pushing her around, and causing her anxiety to shoot upwards. After being pushed and bouncing off another person without an apology, she glanced down at her hands, frustrated at the lack of respect. She could see herself, so presumably so could they, but the crowd continued to walk into her as though she was not worth noticing. She rolled her eyes and imagined having telekinesis. With it she would push all of the people away, giving herself a comfortable bubble of personal space.

"Keea?" A male voice said from above.

As she looked up, she saw a man hovering in the air,

just above the tallest of the people walking by, and her mouth dropped open. The crowd parted slightly, and her date's feet touched the ground. He had a practiced, charming grin plastered onto his face and reached out to take her hand. Kya's head came only to about the bottom of his nose. His noticeably toned body was covered in a full black suit complete with a striking royal blue tie, which contrasted with the paleness of his sharp blue eyes. His light brown hair was meticulously styled, sitting perfectly in place. As her heart quickened, she couldn't help but think about how his online profile didn't prepare her for his grand entrance or how attractive he was. Suddenly, Kya felt underdressed in her 'fancy' dark wash jeans and a deep red silk top.

"Um, it's actually Kya," she said with a nervous smile. "Like 'Hi-yah!'" Kya made a chopping gesture with her hand and then waited for a few seconds for him to laugh. "But with a K", she continued when he didn't. She tried to come up with a witty retort, something funny, something interesting, but then blurted out, "and, you're Keen, right?"

"My name is Ken."

The deadpan, serious tone of his response let Kya know that he did not appreciate her joke, and she was in for a long night. The butterflies in her stomach that she had felt while waiting for him flapped harder after their initial interactions.

Inside the restaurant, Ken placed his hand on a podium by the front door and a green light flashed. A server appeared from nowhere and gestured for them to follow. Passing by a long line of waiting people, they were led to a private booth with gold accents, plush seating, and silk napkins. A crystal chandelier hung just above the table providing a dim glow to their surroundings.

"I almost feel sorry for the Normals in line. I bet they had to reserve months in advance," Ken said as he slid into the booth.

As the person that had seated them turned to leave, two other servers appeared with a bottle of wine, and two plates overflowing with food.

Ken directed the waiters with large gestures. "I'm glad I pre-ordered. The slow service here is the only negative thing about this place."

"Yeah, who would want to stay here all night?" Kya said with a smile, still hoping to salvage the evening. She picked up her utensils that were wrapped in a rich burgundy napkin and noticed not only the swirling design woven through the silk but also the weight of the cutlery. In her mind, she mused at how much it would cost to furnish and stock this restaurant. She couldn't help but imagine that it would cost her more than a week's wages just to buy a four place setting of the cutlery. She placed the knife, forks, and spoon back on the table and spread the napkin across her lap.

"So..." Ken said while he swirled the freshly poured glass of red wine. His brow furrowed as he studied the viscous liquid that sloshed around the near flawless crystal glass.

"So?" Kya replied. She made a conscious effort to smile as she said it, as she still wanted to appear friendly, despite the feeling that the date was quickly sinking.

Ken put down his drink and leaned his elbows on the table over his steak. The large slab of pink meat, with its bloody juices pooling and mixing with the melting butter, drenched the pile of carrots, green beans, and red peppers on his plate. It was almost enough to turn Kya's stomach. Her steak, with the black seared lines, and consistent dark colour, sat separately from her pile of delicious looking vegetables was inviting by comparison. She could never understand how anyone would want to eat a piece of a cow that looked like it had just stopped 'mooing'.

"So, what do you do for a living, Kya?"

She cringed a bit as he confidently, but incorrectly spat her name out, putting far too much emphasis on the 'ah'. 'Seriously,' she thought, 'how hard is Kya to pronounce? K-eye-uh.'

"Well, I guess you could say I'm..." She cleared her throat and took a moment to think how she wanted to approach the topic. "I'm a robotic arm. I work..."

"Oh! That's so cool!" Ken cut in, his whole face came alive. "You get to program robotics, then?"

"Um, no." Kya picked up her knife and the smaller of the two forks, turning her attention to her meal. "I work shift work at Starlife Technologies."

"You work for SLT?" Ken grinned wider and put down his drink. "Do you know Don Georgetown personally?"

"He's my boss." Kya looked around the restaurant. The windows were large, with beautiful stained glass imagery, surrounded by thick black iron, and draped with thick curtains with gold stitching. Unique, intricate chandeliers hung over every table. The overall ambiance was one of extravagant wealth. She watched as a man at a nearby table sat with his hands folded in front of a bowl of salad and mouthfuls of food floated effortlessly from the bowl into his awaiting mouth. Kya couldn't help but smile. "This place is pretty spectacular, don't you think?"

"Mr. Georgetown seems like he'd be a great guy to work for. Is he?" Ken continued to talk as he filled his mouth with his nearly raw meat. "I hear he's got four Supers now. That's pretty impressive for an I.T. Director."

The smile fell from her face. "I've only seen two."

Kya picked the napkin up from her lap and fiddled with the edge of it, she glanced around the restaurant, counted four exit signs but could not think of a way to escape talking about her less than impressive job or boss. She placed the napkin back in her lap, leaned forward with her left elbow on the table resting her head on her thumb and first two fingers. With her fork in her other hand, she pushed a circle of carrot around her gold-rimmed plate.

"Anyways, I manage the data backup systems there, mostly doing overnights. I remove the full hard drives and replace them with blank ones so that the company can continue to backup its data. It doesn't take long to do, and it's not hard. Most companies have long since switched to a robotic system to swap out hard drives, and I could easily be replaced by a robotic arm tomorrow." She smiled, hoping Ken would get her earlier attempt at a joke of being a robotic arm.

Ken slumped back in his chair, his eyes glazing over and his face became nearly expressionless.

"Get it? Robotic-" She half chuckled and trailed off as it

seemed to be Ken's turn to count the exits. "What do you do?" Despite the obvious physical attraction she had felt, Kya couldn't muster much enthusiasm in asking even this simple question.

"I market Supers to people like your boss."

The computerized beeping startled Kya. She blinked, stretched and shook herself awake. As her eyes adjusted to the darkened room, she struggled to lift her stiff, but average-sized frame from the black task chair where she spent her eight-hour shifts. She looked at the bank of displays monitoring the backup system, only to be nearly blinded by the flashing red and orange colours letting her know that it was time to do her job.

"What I wouldn't give for just one Super." She mumbled as reached out her hand and imagined herself directing the drives to swap themselves without her having to move any more than she already was. Unsurprisingly, nothing happened, so she pulled the first full hard drive and swapped it for the first blank one she had already set out at the start of her shift. The office was empty, as it always was during her overnight shifts, and every sound bounced off of the sea of cubicles. She counted out the forty drives she had to replace, making sure to label each one that she took out before setting them aside. With millions of files being archived on each one, Kya was cautious with the drives, though not as careful as her employers probably would have wanted. She scooped them all into a large plastic basket before quickly tossing them into slots on the long floor to ceiling rack storage shelves.

Kya made audible whirring and buzzing noises as she

moved her arm slowly and precisely, as she pretended to be nothing more than a robotic arm. She giggled to herself as she completed filing away the hard drives.

Kya jumped slightly as her phone vibrated in her pocket. While continuing to toss drives in their proper spots along the wall, she checked the time as she grabbed it from the back pocket of her jeans. She glanced at the alert that included a small picture of a blonde woman in a wedding dress. "Mattie, what are you doing up so late?" She said quietly to herself, reading a text from her friend.

>How was it? Were you out all night? Was he as awesome as his profile? Was he hot? Too many questions?

Kya rolled her eyes and responded.

>Sheesh, woman! I thought the world had ended! You're awake at 1:30 am?!

>Meh. It's Saturday night, and Rory has some friends over for beer and video games... I can't sleep.

>Must be torture for an old lady like you!

Kya smirked as she typed.

>Shut your face miss three months younger than me. NOW tell me about your date!

Kya looked around at the drives. She knew full well that none would need to be changed for at least four hours, but she still searched for an orange flash before responding. All green, signaling they were ready to go.

>*It was…*

He called me Keea.

>*Ouch! I guess he didn't read far enough through your profile to see that's one of your pet peeves. Never a good start. Guess that answers question 2.*

>*It was the only thing I had listed in that section. So, yeah, another early night for yours truly.*

And I read his whole profile. It made me think he had a personality! This dude… Nah. I think he had a bigger crush on old Donnie or even a glass of wine than on me!

>*Lol!*

Was he as hot as his pics though?

Kya twirled around in her chair for a moment, watching the ceiling tiles spin and thought about that.

>*If you'd asked me that at 8 pm when he wasn't there yet I'd say no. If you'd asked me when he finally showed up using Flight at quarter after, I'd have said WAY HOTTER!*

>*He's a Super? Cool! And also a little weird, no offense.*

>*None taken.*

The date went the way of the Titanic so quick, and his personality or to be more precise: lack thereof took ALL the hotness away.

>*You and those pesky personalities! lol*

>*I doubt you are literally laughing out loud.*

>Add it to your pet peeves.

Kya smiled at the message from her friend.

>I'm so glad you get me.

He actually asked if we should go to his place or mine after what had to be one of the worst first dates in the history of the world.

>Think he's just doing the online dating thing to score? Like he thinks Normals are desperate or something?

>You know, Mattea, you might be onto something there! Have you ever thought of becoming a detective?

I have to admit, I am still kind of half considering a second date.

>What? Why would you do that??

Kya smiled at getting the kind of response she had hoped for. Even just typing the words, and accepting the truth behind them had made her skin crawl. Her smile faded as she drafted her response.

>I could get a Super if I stay with him.

>Don't do that! There's plenty more fish in the sea. There has to be one out there who will find your wit endearing. Supers or not.

>Well the sea of online dating can keep its fish.

>Oh :-(

Kya clenched her teeth for a moment and took a long drawn out breath.

>No :-(needed, I'm cool with being single. And two more years

at SLT, and I'll be able to afford a Super without a guy.

>You know I just want you to be as happy as I am.

Kya's thumbs hovered above her keypad, ready to type a response when Mattie sent her final message:

>Oh! Rory and his bros are done. I'm going to bed. Nighty night.

She replaced her phone in her pocket without responding and the long wait set in for her next hard drive swap. Donning her headphones, Kya fell into her chair, spun it back towards the status monitors and began to listen to the most energetic tracks available on her Song Feed station. She checked her bank balance more out of habit than necessity and confirmed that if she was able to continue saving the way she had been, and if the prices didn't jump again, she could get her first Super in two more years. It seemed like a terribly long time to stay in this job, but it also seemed better than the alternative if the only alternative was Ken.

With the beat of the music providing her with a second wind, she opened her web browser, and pulled up her account on Flash Fiction Fan Favourites, a website with thousands of independent writers, and began reviewing fiction written by writers from around the world. Her editor profile had dozens of submissions in the queue, and she couldn't help but smile.

"You push me without touching me, but I'll use my hands to shove!" Kya sang her heart out as she closed her web browser and made the rounds to swap the hard drives once again. She lifted one of the empty drives near her lips and continued to belt out the rhythmic lyrics. "Maybe I can't fly like you, but I can rise above!"

Twenty minutes of work every few hours was all the babysitting that the machines needed. A light tap on her shoulder cut Kya off mid-chorus and startled her. With her heart racing, she turned and saw a tall, lanky man, her relief.

"Leonard! Don't sneak up on me like that!"

"Don't you know by now you shouldn't be listening to music at work? And anyways, I'm not sneaking around here."

Leonard walked past Kya and put his briefcase on the desk closer to the window. She turned to look at her co-worker and noted that he was dressed in full business attire, with pressed black dress pants, an ironed button up shirt, and a dark green checkered tie in a meticulous Windsor knot. Despite his pale skin, dark eyes, and thin frame, the suit fit him well, making him look older than Kya knew he was.

"Nice threads," she said. "New tie?"

"Yes. I got it yesterday." He squinted a bit as he took in Kya's appearance. "What does your shirt say?"

Kya looked down at her black t-shirt. Above a purple circle, it had words written. "It says 'When I was your age, Pluto was a planet.'"

"Charming," Leonard said, his nose turned up slightly.

"Don't you think it's a bit silly to dress up for a job swapping out hard drives? Seems a bit overkill to me." Kya blurted.

"Ugh, Kya!"

"I know what you're going to say," Kya said. She dropped her tone of voice to sound more masculine. "'Not only do we have a dress code, but you should dress for the job you want."

Leonard straightened his tie. "And judging by your sweat pants, some people might assume you want-"

"Anyways..." She cut him off. "Nothing of interest happened last night. I swapped two sets, placed them in the library. The third set is being chewed through right now. Gotta go catch my bus."

As Kya collected her stuff, Leonard inspected the logs slowly and carefully before signing off on the changeover.

"I don't know why you do that. No one ever checks the log book."

"I do it because it's procedure."

"Well, you have fun with that," Kya said with a mocking grin and a wave. Humming the tune of the last song she listened to, she quickly turned and pushed her way through the double doors exiting the Information Technology section of Starlife Technologies. Out in the main pavilion, the smile melted from her face, and her shoulders slumped as the weight of another boring night slammed into her.

A few of the information technology staff were coming in as Kya left, their eyes still red, coffees in hand, frowns etched on their faces, but they were all dressed up in professional clothing, something that Kya dreaded having to wear on her upcoming week of day shifts.

Kya made eye contact with someone she recognized from her department, and he smiled at her. He stood the same height as Kya and wore a suit that looked older than she was.

"Hey, Kya," he said.

"Heyah," Kya said back, uncertain of his name.

"I hope you are going to be ready for your day shifts. I'll be working in the desk next to yours, and I'll need you to be on your toes swapping drives for me as I run some tests." The older man paused, seeming to wait for Kya's answer, and just as the silence lingered on for a little too long, he continued, "I heard they only give you data management folks twenty-four hours to switch from nights to days."

"Yeah, it's rough. I feel like I'm sleepwalking my way out of here most days."

"I don't think I could do shift work ever again. I did it when I was in my twenties, but we were given a week off between major changes like that."

"Yeah. I don't know why Don won't let anyone have just full days or full nights." Kya said as she pulled her hair back from her face with both hands.

"Oh! Is the purple new? I could have sworn you had orange in your hair."

"Yeah. I did it a couple days ago." Kya was surprised he'd remembered her orange streaks. She kept her brightly coloured streaks of hair mostly hidden under the top layer of natural brown.

"Don't let Don see!" The man beamed back and winked.

Stifling a yawn, she responded. "Nah. I'll keep it down and professional for dear old Don. Like always."

"Good plan. Good plan." He said, patting her on the shoulder as he started to walk past her. "Speaking of Don, I don't want to be late. Can you imagine what he'd do? I'll see you the day after tomorrow. Bright and early!"

"Bright and early," she repeated less than enthusiastically, as she walked towards the big glass doors to the outside world.

A weight was lifted from her shoulders as a light breeze hit her face. She closed her eyes for a moment, which stopped them from burning, before heading to the bus stop. Time dragged on as she waited for her bus that would take her from the wasteland of factories and offices that was the industrial section of the city to her apartment near the downtown core. She closed her eyes again, quickly falling into a daydream about being able to fly home, over the buildings, and right onto the balcony of her apartment.

The bus stopped at a large transfer point, one of the few in the city where both buses and the light rail system met up. The building that served as the hub was two stories tall, and the center area was a large glass dome, open to both. The lower level served bus terminals and was an entry point for all passengers while the train platforms lined the upper level. A glass and metal staircase led down from the trains into the open pavilion.

Kya watched as one of the large trains, only accessible by Supers, pulled into the station on the far side. She walked closer to the staircase trying to glimpse inside the train while staying close enough that she could see her next bus when it came. A gate at the top of the stairs prevented unauthorized individuals from accessing the trains.

"She was my wife!" A loud voice boomed. Kya quickly craned her neck to try to see where the voice had come from. A horde of people began moving chaotically through the station, clearing a line of sight for her to see the situation. She watched as a man, likely no older than herself, drew a large gun from his billowing jacket, and aimed it at the chest of a slightly older man in a suit who had just descended the stairs.

CHAPTER 2

Kya's heart skipped a beat. With the two men only a matter of feet away from her, she instinctively shrank back. Her hands found her ears and covered them.

Quick to react, a young lady, near the two men, projected a large semi-transparent wall that stretched wide and high. Kya stood on the same side of the barrier as the intended victim and the woman. Frozen in place as she witnessed everything that was happening, her heart raced as the endless barrage of bullets continued to fall to the ground in small piles. The enraged man swung the gun wildly, trying to spray death everywhere.

An older man pointed his finger at the gunman, and his weapon changed from cold black to blazing red, causing him to let out a cry and drop it.

Kya felt the entire crowd breathe a sigh of relief as the weapon deformed on the ground. The gunman, now defeated, glared at those around him. He held his burned hand, and tears streamed down his face.

A young man, maybe eighteen, who had been watching the whole situation unfold, put his arm out, palm towards the gunman. Clenching his fist, the gunman crumpled to the ground, and much like his weapon, he was deformed.

The silence was deafening. The body laid crumpled and lifeless on the ground. Those waiting to board the train walked around the body and proceeded up the stairs. In the distance, sirens started to ring out. A few police officers were already pushing through the crowd. One reached out and shook the hand of the teen who had taken down the gunman while another approached the woman who had erected the forcefield.

Kya's jaw ached as she realized it had been opened as wide as her mouth could go. 'Well, that's why you need Supers!' Kya thought as she watched the Supers, confident that they did the right thing, board the nearby train.

After being assessed with a small handheld device, the nearby police officers directed Kya and the others around her to line up along one of the walls of the station. She watched as officers waved a few people past, who then proceeded to head up to the train platform.

"Wait, what about the trains?" A woman asked, her hair rippling with shades of red.

"Trains will continue running on schedule." The officer closest to her responded. "It's only the buses that will be held."

Kya took her place in the line and waited to be questioned while crews began cleaning up the area. The large screens showed maps of which transit lines were affected by the incident. All of the buses in the city were halted, appearing red on the screen, while the trains were all green. Kya imagined being on one of the trains heading home. Her heart was still pounding in her ears, and she was thankful for the security precautions ensuring that when she was free to leave she would be safe from further threat.

An officer who looked to be about fifty called Kya forward with the wave of a gloved hand. His expression seemed tired or perhaps bored.

"How long before the buses start running again?"

Kya turned around to see who was asking, it was a very tired looking pregnant woman standing three people behind Kya in line.

"Wait your turn!" The officer snapped.

"They'll run when we've cleared the area." Another younger officer explained as he paced the line with his gun at the ready.

Kya's mouth went dry.

The older officer took a handheld tablet from his pocket and began tapping on the screen.

"Name?" He asked.

"Kya Roberts."

"Where are you headed?"

"Home. I live in an apartment complex in the core."

The officer raised an eyebrow. "The core, eh? Where do you work?"

"Starlife Technologies"

He tapped on the screen some more, and Kya assumed he was taking notes based on her answers. He asked her a few more questions about what she had seen and then got her contact information before dismissing her.

She checked the nearest screen and saw that none of the buses were moving yet. There were still roughly a hundred people to be questioned and she knew that they wouldn't let the buses move until they were all questioned, so Kya decided to walk home.

As she walked, she replayed the scene at the station. She imagined being the woman who had erected the forcefield to save the man's life.

An hour of walking and daydreaming later, Kya entered her apartment and set her keys down on the table by the front door. She could see Sam, her roommate, sitting at the kitchen table, breakfast bagel in one hand, and tablet computer next to his plate.

"What took you so long?" Sam asked without looking up from the tablet.

"There was an incident at the Hub Station."

"Anyone get hurt?" Sam looked at Kya, and she could see the concern in his eyes.

"This guy tried to shoot another guy, but three Supers took down the shooter."

"Did they hurt him? Was the shooter a Normal?"

"I guess so, I mean he wasn't moving at the end of it. And yeah, he was a Normal."

A shadow seemed to cross Sam's face.

"But they protected a lot of people! If they hadn't been there, who knows what would have happened."

"What about the intended victim? I guess he wasn't a Normal."

"I don't think so. He was heading towards the stairs."

"So Supers protected another Super from potentially being murdered by potentially murdering a Normal."

"When you spin it like that it sounds horrible. But a lady with Forcefield used it to protect a whole bunch of us."

Sam shrugged.

"Anyways," Kya said after a tense moment, "whatcha doing?"

"Oh, just reading news on Myles Redwood."

"You still reading that celebrity gossip crap?" Kya walked around and looked over Sam's shoulder.

"Yep. Because no matter how messed up I feel like my life is, these guys make me feel normal." Sam tipped the tablet towards Kya.

A SUPER Happy Birthday for Myles Redwood

If you don't know who Myles Redwood is, where have you been for the last three years? The Internet phenomenon turned multi-billionaire teen heartthrob/singer/dancer/actor turned eighteen today, officially making him Age of Procedure. To celebrate finally achieving this milestone, it seems he has done what all teenagers dream of doing.

This evening, Redwood was seen leaving the head offices of Enhance, presumably after undergoing his first Super procedure.

Speculations are being made over what ability he would have chosen as his first, but in the next few days I'm sure the world will know. I can't see Mr. Redwood keeping it a secret for long...

Sam shook his head. "I'm not sure I want to live in a world where that kid has even one Super."

"Haha, no kidding!"

Sam swiped to different pages, and each time it flashed a similar headline on the screen.

With a sullen look, Kya sighed, "But imagine what you could do with a couple Supers..."

"In the wrong hands, though..." Sam said still staring down at the screen. He tapped the screen again, and it brought up a picture of Myles Redwood with a date from just a few weeks earlier. He was being escorted out of a club by two large bouncers, and a mischievous grin was plastered over Myles' face.

Sam swallowed the last of his bagel, flicked the power switch on his tablet and stood up to leave. "Well, I better get going."

Kya smiled at Sam as he walked past her and put on his long wool coat.

"It isn't cold out," she said.

Sam turned and looked at Kya, his thick eyebrows raised high on his head and his lips tight, as he began buttoning up the coat.

"Right... You're a reptile." Kya winked.

"Gotta hold onto what heat I have. I can't make more."

"Sounds like an anti-Super."

Sam rolled his eyes. "I can't wait for summer." He wrapped a thin red scarf around his neck.

Kya giggled lightly and thought to the thousand times Sam had complained about the temperature. "You definitely live in the wrong country."

"Only in the winter," he said as he opened the door.

"It's April!"

"Yeah... Winter!"

Kya could hear Sam echoing her laughter as he closed the door and went off to work.

Without the diversion of Sam's presence, Kya looked around the apartment. The place was decorated in a palette of crisp greys and sophisticated neutrals. In front of her was the door to the hall of the building that Sam had just left through, and to the left of that the coat closet. Next to the closet was the kitchen, and then the dining table where Sam had been sitting just moments before. The black leather couch with a grey and black decorative throw blanket perfectly folded and placed along the back sat on an angle partitioning the living room from the kitchen and dining area. To the left of the couch was a matching oversized armchair that Sam had long ago claimed at his spot in the living room. Behind his chair was the door to his room. Between the chair and the large television was the door to the balcony. Kya noticed that Sam had already closed the blinds, darkening the living room. She took out her phone and set a reminder.

>*Thank Sam for being so considerate.*

She slipped her phone into her pocket and turned back toward the front door. She slid her shoes off her feet. Her foot flailed wildly as she attempted to kick the shoes towards the front entrance. The door to her bedroom just to the right of the front door less than a dozen steps away seemed too far away. She turned, and her eyes settled on the couch.

"Do I sleep or stay up?" It was a question that Kya always had to ask herself switching between night shifts and day shifts. As if in response, a reminder buzzed on her phone. *Have a nap! The day's a total write off when you don't.* She cleared the message without reading it. She knew what it said; she had read it countless times before. Heavy fatigue hit and her eyes were dry, needing to close.

As she stumbled towards the couch, Kya set an alarm on her phone for two hours. She told herself aloud, as a self-affirmation, "I will not oversleep. I will make use of my day off."

She let herself flop backwards, landing on the couch behind her. The chill of the leather passed into her body. She pulled a blanket over herself and shut her eyes. For a moment, she thought about turning on the television to have some background noise, but before she could even grab the remote, she drifted off.

In what felt to Kya like an instant, the alarm noise blared through the apartment. She looked at her phone and noticed that she had, without really waking up, set the alarm to snooze twice already. She groaned, slowly lifting her still heavy body from the couch. The warmth of the couch and blanket beckoned her back into their embrace, but Kya knew if she slept any longer, she wouldn't be able to sleep that night.

Her phone buzzed, right as she shut her alarm off, letting her know she had received a text message.

>Hey K, want to come see me at work?

Kya didn't even need to look up who the message was from, as only one person called her "K", it was Amelia.

Kya struggled to get her body to move and type out her response.

>Ya, see you soon.

Rubbing her eyes, she looked across the living room at

her bedroom door. Her first attempt to stand failed, and she fell back into the warmth of the couch. She hesitated to try again, thinking instead that she should just message Amelia and say, "Decided to sleep." Amelia would understand, and a quick battle back and forth raged in Kya's mind. The winning side pushed her up and towards her bedroom and through to her bathroom to start her zombie-like day.

The bathroom light nearly blinded Kya as its glow illuminated the small room. The mirror reflected back large dark circles around her bloodshot eyes. "Well, this sucks," she said as she stripped off her clothes and turned on the shower. The dark green bath mat on the pale tile floor was soft and warm on her bare feet, and the steam poured from over top of the shower curtain as Kya waited for the shower to reach the perfect temperature.

The water pressure blasted her as she stepped inside, but she felt both more awake, and calm. 'I could stay in here all day,' she thought. She imagined the water blasting off all of her negativity, frustration with work, and the horrible date she recently had.

The blinds in Kya's room were open, letting in the daylight. Her clothes strewn about in the laundry basket on the floor and on her unmade bed, it took a minute to select an outfit. She decided to wear her 'comfy' blue jeans, and a t-shirt she had purchased from the Internet with characters from her favourite web video show, they both fit her loosely. She dressed as quickly as her energy would allow. Just as she was walking out her bedroom door, she decided to grab a grey zip-up hoodie because although it wasn't cold enough for Sam's coat, she knew there was still a crispness to the air.

She threw the top waves her mostly light brown hair up into a loose ponytail bun, allowing the purple streaks to shine for all to see. She glanced in the living room mirror to confirm the bun had had the desired effect and grinned.

Kya locked the door as she left the apartment and began to walk down the dreary hallway towards the elevator. She watched as the lights announced which floor it was on, and just before it arrived on her floor, the fifth floor, Kya tapped her back pocket. "Shoot, my phone!"

She ran back towards the apartment, slammed the key into the lock, and threw the door open. Snatching her phone from the bathroom, she turned and bounded back out of the apartment towards the elevator. Kya arrived just as the doors slammed shut. Turning on her phone, she realized that she only had three minutes before the next bus came. She grumbled. "I wonder if there's a Super to fix forgetfulness?"

She typed out a text to Amelia as she pushed through the nearby doors to the stairwell.

>*I might be a bit later than I thought. Trying to make the bus. I'll let you know.*

Kya knew that Amelia wouldn't be able to answer until her next break.

Holding both rails in the narrow stairwell and barely touching the stairs as she ran down, she burst forth from the building into an alleyway. Winded, she continued to will her body to move quickly towards the bus stop at the front of her building. "Why do I always cut this so close?" She chided herself arriving just as the bus was closing its doors. Kya tapped on the doors and pleaded with the driver using her eyes.

The door swung open. She grinned, thanked the driver and sat down, extra exhausted and took a deep breath. She could smell the bitter aroma of coffee from another person on the bus, only a few seats away, and felt her mouth water. Her mind fixated on the warm beverage. She began to count down the minutes until she could drink the coffee that Amelia's shop served.

She threw on her headphones and let the music and the smell of coffee carry her away. Kya appreciated the views of new construction mixed with long forgotten buildings. As always, she was mesmerized by the beautiful graffiti murals on the old buildings their brilliant colours and intricate designs breathing life into the urban wasteland. Many showed scenes of shadowed figures amidst the bright colours of city life.

Kya arrived at the Uptown Centre, the largest shopping mall in the city, and was surprised at the number of security guards hanging about. They were pacing back and forth at each of the doors. Despite not having done anything herself, Kya felt guilty. She quickly made a beeline to Noble Brew, the cafe where Amelia worked and lined up in the queue. Decorated in royal blues and gold, the coffee shop had long earned its ostentatious brand.

On a T.V. screen, mounted high on the wall behind the baristas, Kya read through menu items while a ticker tape scrolled the bottom of the screen with the latest headlines.

Classroom ratio now 15 students to 1 teacher, Education

Minister quite pleased. Supers procedures now fastest growing industry nation-wide. Myles Redwood to discuss Supers selection tonight. Latest census shows 25% drop in children requiring foster care over the past 10 years.

"I'll have a large black coffee." The man in front of Kya said to Amelia.

"So a tall..." Amelia began and then grinned. "Or do you mean the extra tall?"

The man stood with his mouth agape. Kya could see that he was having a difficult time processing what was being said to him as his eyes scanned around, his gaze avoiding Amelia behind the counter.

"You see we don't exactly have a 'large' coffee." The corner of Amelia's mouth was curled in a controlled smile as she talked.

Kya knew Amelia well enough to know what was coming next, and she turned her attention to the man as Amelia kept talking. The man had closed his mouth. Muscles tightened and twitched along his jaw. His dark and tired eyes were now staring directly at Amelia.

With a chipper, presentation tone, Amelia continued, "If you'll turn your attention to our wonderful menu boards, sir, you'll see we have five sizes: extra short, short, regular, tall, and extra tall."

"With all due respect, *barista*," he spat the last word like it tasted horrible in his mouth. "It's a quarter to nine in the morning. I have to be at work by nine. I have a headache, and all I want is my damn coffee!" As he spoke his voice got louder until, by the end, he was yelling, and steam was rising from his clenched fists.

Amelia winked at Kya and picked up two cups. "With all due respect, sir, I simply want to ensure you get the perfect beverage. Could you maybe point to which size you would like?" Amelia held up the cups to eye level.

The man pointed to the larger of the two cups.

"The extra tall." Amelia grinned again. "I'm glad I asked."

After she had finished with that customer, it was Kya's turn to order. "An extra tall coffee," she said, needing as much caffeine as possible.

"So that's an extra tall vanilla-hazelnut latte with extra espresso?" Amelia said, with a wink in a deadpanned voice. It was one of the most expensive drinks on the menu. As Amelia punched some buttons, the words *extra short brewed*, the least expensive thing they sold, appeared on the Point of Sale display.

"Lia," Kya whispered without the slightest hint of surprise, "you don't have to."

"I know." Amelia whispered back and rang through the extra short coffee.

A few moments later, Amelia handed Kya her drink. *My break is at 11:15* was written on the side of the cup inside a heart.

Kya left the cafe with an extra tall vanilla-hazelnut latte in hand. She wasn't too fussy for the fancy espresso drinks that

Noble Brew sold at way too high a price. She would never have ordered this drink for herself, but as she sipped it, the warm frothy milk mingled with the sweet vanilla, nutty notes and the bitter coffee balanced perfectly in her mouth and tasted like she wanted more.

After walking around for a while, Kya decided to sit by the marble water fountain in the middle of the mall. The mall was built with a hub and spoke system, and five hallways all lead straight to the fountain in the middle. From there, she could see all four levels of the shopping complex. The bottom level was where the pool of the fountain was, and that floor contained all of the discount stores. It wasn't lost on most people that the nicest thing on that level was the fountain. The next level was where the essentials, like groceries, could be found. The smell of fresh produce and bread wafted through the entire level, and it was rare Kya could escape without getting a pecan butter tart or freshly baked blueberry muffin. The third level was where Kya was sitting, it was the only level, to the best of Kya's knowledge, that had seats near the fountain.

The water from the fountain was blasted in the air past the third floor and arced up to the fourth before raining back down. It gave an interesting effect of seeming to rain both up and down. She could also see that there were lasers on the floor of the fourth level that projected images into the water in all sorts of wonderful colours. The third floor had higher end stores and sold things that were nice, but not essential, such as the extra tall vanilla-hazelnut latte in Kya's hand. Kya had no idea what kind of stores were contained within the walls of the fourth floor. Unlike the areas between the other floors, there were no stairs, escalators or elevators leading up to it, and only the extremely privileged had access to it.

Kya had heard rumours that those that were able to shop up there, never had to pay for anything. Kya closed her eyes and imagined flying up through the water and landing gracefully on the floor above her, finally seeing what it was like to be one of the upper-class elite.

CHAPTER 3

As alarms started ringing all around her, Kya jumped and stifled a scream. Her latte sloshed wildly around in its biodegradable and heavily branded cup and nearly spilled over the rim.

A young man ran by her carrying something black wrapped in his arms. He screamed loudly as he passed. "I need it for my family!" He bounded onto one of the seats near the fountain and stepped out onto the ledge. Huffing and puffing, he paused and looked back at the police officers following him. They slowed as they came closer to him.

Two officers flashed into existence right next to Kya, and they began to speak to the man. "Now son, you can't escape." The older of the two officers said with his hand open, palm facing out towards the shoplifter on the ledge.

The thief faced Kya and the officers, tears streaming down his young face and fear in his eyes. He turned and aimed himself towards the stairs leading down to the second from the third took a deep breath and jumped, the black bundle still clutched in his arms. As he fell over twenty feet, the musky sour aroma of sweat caught Kya off guard as it filled the air. Before the young man could make contact with the stairs below and escape, he was tackled by three police officers who materialized within feet of where he landed. The black package opened, and an array of pastries flew out and scattered along the stairs. A fourth officer, a lady around the same age as Kya, took a running jump from the third floor and hit the platform of the stairs effortlessly.

Kya looked around to see a crowd forming on every level, interested to see the commotion. The police quickly controlled the man, but he continued yelling as they dragged him away. Security guards from the mall walked onto the scene and frantically began to try and disperse the crowds making a path for the police.

"What happened?" A middle-aged man from the crowd asked Kya.

"I think it was a shoplifter," Kya replied.

"Stupid kid." The man sighed. "Normals always get caught."

Just as fast as they appeared, all the police officers had left, and the security guards instantly seemed to calm.

Amelia was still behind the counter when Kya returned. She saw Kya, quickly waved, and then turned to say something to her co-worker. Kya couldn't remember his name, so after taking a moment to wander through her mind, she decided that it should be Julian.

Amelia took off her apron, popped into the back room, and emerged seconds later with her black leather handbag. As she walked around the counter, Kya noticed Amelia was wearing a fitted white button down short sleeved shirt with black stitch work details, a black pleated skirt that came to about mid-thigh, and cute black flats. Technically, it was within the dress code for the cafe, though she was pushing the edge of how revealing her clothes were allowed to be. She had her straight black hair pulled back into a pristine French roll, with a few wisps purposely left down to soften the look.

Kya smirked, *'typical Amelia'*. As Leonard would say, Amelia was dressing for the job she wanted, which was definitely not the one she had.

"Hey K," Amelia said as she wrapped Kya in a hug.

"Hey Lia," Kya said, returning the embrace. "How's the shift treating you? Nearly given anyone else an aneurysm?"

"You mean like the guy in front of you this morning?"

Kya nodded, and they started walking towards the food court.

"Nah. Can you believe that guy, though? I mean, we are *the* cafe used in movies. You can't open a magazine without seeing pictures of the rich, famous and Super walking around holding a Noble Brew coffee cup. Our sizes are part of our brand. They're common knowledge."

Kya could see fire and energy emanating from Amelia's eyes as she finished speaking about her work.

"I love how passionate you can be about it," Kya said.

"Oh, do you mind if we eat at that restaurant at the far end with the patio?" Amelia said with an air of affected apathy.

"Coliseum? Sure. But only because we never seem to be able to hang out lately." Kya said playing along.

"Yeah, between your shifts and mine, you'd think they'd line up more often."

Rows of small, fast food restaurants lined both sides of the hallway. The various smells wafted and mixed together in unpleasing ways, and Kya tried not to focus on it.

She noticed a change in Amelia as they approached the end of the hallway where a doorman in a suit stood ready, waiting to open the door for anyone wanting to enter Coliseum. Amelia took earrings, rings, bracelets and a necklace out of her handbag and put them all on. She then freshened her lipstick and touched up her eyes without missing a step.

"No matter how many times I see you do that," Kya said, "I am always still amazed."

"Gotta look my best. You never know when the future Mr. Bronsen will show up."

Kya chuckled and shook her head. The doorman pulled the tinted glass doors open, and Amelia entered followed closely by Kya.

Kya was glad to see that the normally busy Coliseum wasn't too full to seat them immediately.

"Isn't it fabulous in here?" Amelia said following a young

man as they sauntered to a booth over to one corner.

The ambiance of the restaurant was darker, more intimate, than the bright coloured LED lights of the mall. The rich red and gold fabrics of the seat cushions and draperies were complimented nicely by the dark wood moldings and marble columns. Sliding into the booth, Kya noticed the table rippled various colours where her arms, hands and fingers touched the surface.

"Amelia, nice to see you again. You know what to do. Enjoy your meal." The young man said as he winked and excused himself.

Amelia smiled at Kya and tapped out their order on the table. Without asking Kya what she wanted, the order was submitted.

"So… You come here that often that they all recognize you?" Kya said smiling back at her friend.

"Just a second," Amelia said gesturing with her index finger at Kya to wait one moment.

Quickly, both food and drink arrived, and Amelia, after a polite smile and nod at the waiter and taking a deep breath, finally looked ready to chat.

"So, how are you, K?" Amelia asked over her chicken Greek salad.

"I'm alright," Kya replied, stifling a yawn. "Tired. Shift work is hell."

"You wanna talk shift work hell? How about this?

Yesterday I opened. Today I'm closing. Tomorrow I'm closing and Monday I'm opening again."

"I thought you couldn't work an open after a close."

"Actually," Amelia smiled. There was an air of excitement in her expression. "The rule is that you have to have a minimum of eight hours between shifts and since the mall closes early on Sundays..."

Kya knew where Amelia was heading and interjected, "so there's your eight hours."

"Exactly." Amelia took a sip of her carbonated mineral water. "You had Friday off for that big date, right?"

"Yeah, but don't ask how it went. I would have been better to stay home and do laundry."

"That sucks!" Amelia said with a laugh. "So, changing subjects... Did you see the commotion today? I heard the alarms."

Kya shrugged and took a gulp of her regular ice water, then she picked up her chopsticks and shoved a piece of a Red Dragon roll in her mouth. Amelia had ordered her six sashimi, four pieces of the Red Dragon roll, miso soup and an avocado salad. Kya loved Japanese food but rarely ordered it for herself because of the price. She gave her friend a closed mouth grin and chewed the roll.

Amelia seemed to get the hint. "Well then... How's work going? Did you see what Jacob was wearing today?"

"Jacob! That's his name! I could have sworn it was

Julian. Um, an apron?"

Amelia laughed. "I swear, I'd love to take the boy to get some real clothes. He's such a cute thing. But it looks like everything he wears comes from Level One."

"Well, that *is* economical." Kya said and then sipped her soup.

"Anyways, as I was asking? How's your work? You getting along with Mr. Georgetown yet?"

Kya rolled her eyes. "You are *so* going to wish you hadn't asked that!"

"That well, eh?"

"Oh, Mr. Georgetown isn't even all the problem! You know Leonard?"

Amelia nodded. "Only what I've heard from you."

"He has to cause frustration on every shift. I try to be nice, you know, compliment him on his suits and whatever, but he takes a look at me and implies I dress like a hobo. What is that?"

"Well, a hobo is someone that..." Amelia said with a mischievous glint in her eye.

Kya shot a glare at her friend and then they both erupted into laughter.

"But yeah, Don walks around looking at everyone like we're monkeys. Now that he's got the cash for multiple supers... It's just hell."

"I'm so glad I don't have to deal with that office crap." Amelia sighed wistfully. "I love working at Noble Brew. If only they'd pay me just a *little* bit more."

"You mean a *LOTtle* bit."

"Yep."

Kya nodded. "Me too."

They ate and chatted for the next fifteen minutes, and then it was time for Amelia to go back to work. When the bill arrived, Kya reached into her pocket to take out her cell phone to pay using the debit app.

"No, no, K, it's on me. Please."

Kya sighed and accepted her friend's generosity. "Next time, it's one me."

"Sure."

As they walked back to the Noble Brew, they continued to discuss work, their mutual friends, family, world news, and window shopped. The crowds of people were getting thicker as the day wore on, and Kya was once again feeling exhausted. Amelia took off her jewelry and stashed it carefully back in her bag, looking once again like the barista that Kya had picked up a little more than a half an hour ago.

"You still enjoying living in the apartment with Sam?"

"Yeah, after a year and a half we're still going strong," Amelia said.

"Sheesh! Has it been that long?"

"Yeppers. He's so considerate. When I got home, all the blinds were closed so I could easily sleep."

"Wow!" Amelia took a deep breath. "Do you know if he's got a girlfriend?"

Kya laughed. "You know, I never pictured him with a girlfriend! I guess it is possible, though."

Amelia stepped behind the counter, waving back at Kya as she clocked back in.

"See you later," Kya said with the knowledge that she likely wouldn't see her friend again for a few weeks.

As she turned back into the hall, all of the advertisement billboards unfurled along the hallway, covering the store window displays and sprang to life with the same commercial: Enhance promoting their Super procedure.

The commercial started with a small group of five young people from various ethnic backgrounds walking along a crowded street and having issues getting through the sea of people all walking in the opposite direction. While the voiceover calmly exclaimed, "Do you ever feel like you can't move forward in life? Do you ever wish you could rise above all of your challenges and roadblocks?"

Kya watched, entranced by the advertisement as it continued.

The well-dressed, dark haired and fair skinned young

man in the group floated up above his cohorts and raced over the tide of people below, smiling confidently.

The scene quickly changed, and the advertisement was now focused on an older couple. A white-haired lady was kneeling beside her noticeably injured friend or husband, a bald man holding his leg.

"Ever get hurt, and feel like it would be forever before you could get up again?"

The camera showed an animated sequence of the inside of the old man's leg repairing itself in seconds before returning to the bald man picking himself up and dusting his pants off. A look of relief spread across the woman's face as he did so.

The last vignette showed a young man in a medical centre, a nurse injecting his arm with a needle.

The announcer voice continued, "Stop by today and get the Supers of your dreams!"

The young man in the commercial looked directly at the camera, his eyes now glowing white. A message appeared at the bottom of the advertisement stating *results are not typical, expect seven days before the presentation of Supers. Do not purchase Supers if pregnant or planning to be pregnant.*

The camera zoomed in close, and he spoke confidently, "who would ever want to be normal?"

Ending the commercial, it ran quickly through a list of side effects.

Kya had long since known all the limitations of getting

Supers and the biggest one, the one they spent the most time on at the end of each and every commercial, was the fact that each person could only have five Supers.

Taking up most of the screen, the price flashed in bright white numbers. "Sixty-five thousand dollars!" She squeaked out louder than she had intended. She made a quick mental note that the price was increasing by as much as a thousand dollars per month. Kya also noted that the cost was now double what she earned in a year and increasing faster than her savings.

The screens along the hallways all rolled away, and the store windows were no longer covered, many people had continued walking during the entire presentation, as it was played every few hours in most malls across the country. Kya stopped each and every time it played, imagining herself inside the commercial, receiving her own Supers, but now the dream of that life was feeling further away than it ever had before.

CHAPTER 4

Kya opened her eyes and stretched. "Hmm?" was all that managed to come out in response to the very gentle knock on her open door.

"Hey," Sam said in not much more than a whisper, as he opened her door a crack, "you told me to wake you if you were sleeping before eight."

"True." She groaned, rolled slowly off her bed and looked at Sam. "I'm hungry."

"Want to go out and get a bite to eat?"

"Shawarma?"

"Of course," Sam replied with a raised eyebrow and a smile that crinkled his eyes.

Kya stretched her arms into the air and grabbed her phone. A short five-minute walk later, they both had wraps in hand, and Kya was feeling energized. On the way back to the apartment, her phone buzzed an alert.

"Wait here a second. I'll be right back." She quickly popped into the convenience store and emerged moments later with a king-sized package of peanut butter cups.

Sam raised his eyebrows with a questioning glance.

A grin plastered on her face; Kya handed him the chocolate. "For always being so awesome," she explained.

"You know, I'm not," Sam said with a chuckle as he humbly took the treat.

Laughing lightly, they walked back to the apartment without needing to say another word.

When they got in, the chill of the air conditioner hit Kya. It was refreshing, and she knew that as much as Sam wasn't ready for it to be running, he was always going above and beyond to make her feel welcome and at home.

"Thanks for that," Kya said as she took off her shoes on the gleaming hardwood floors.

"My pleasure." Sam dropped his keys into the painted glass dish on the small table by the front door.

Nearly everything in the common areas of the apartment was Sam's, and his sense of style, while not what Kya would choose, was modern, sleek and modestly elegant. Kya watched as Sam sauntered into the living room to grab his tablet computer from the coffee table.

"So, what's new in the world?" Kya asked.

Gesturing all over the small screen, as he did almost every time he returned home, Sam sighed. "Just checking in with the news and my usual dose of celeb gossip."

"I still don't get your fascination with that stuff."

"Myles Redwood's Super hasn't manifested yet." He nodded with a hint of relief on his face. "Not surprising, it should take three or four more days."

Kya nodded.

Sam's brow furrowed though he kept his voice casual and conversational. "It looks like he has set an appointment for a second."

"That's a little fast." She said and started to move to her room. "I think I'm going to go chill with some tunes on."

"That's cool," Sam said with his eyes glued to his screen. "Too much money and power given too freely," He mumbled.

In her room, Kya switched on her music, then pulled out her own tablet to check her e-mail. Her social media accounts automatically logged her in when the tablet came to life, and a split second later she got a message notification. The avatar of a plump blonde woman grinning in her wedding gown let Kya know that it was Mattie.

>Kya, How's life?

>Not bad just grabbed food with Sam.

You do realize that your avatar picture is over a year old, right?

Kya's picture changed every time she changed her

hairstyle. Currently, it was of her with pigtails to show off the purple streaks, and her face scrunched up and tongue sticking out.

>Yeah, I know… but I look so awesome in that pic. I just can't bring myself to change it.

>Fair enough.

So, what's up?

>Just kind of needing a friend.

>I think I can do that. Wanna tell me what's up?

>Rory and I had a fight.

>That sucks. You ok?

>I will be…

We found out that we can't have kids the "normal" way.

Kya sighed, not knowing how to respond. She stood up and looked around her bedroom. The bed she slept in alone every night, the photos of her and her friends in frames on her shelf and tucked into the edge of her mirror, graphic tees, and single concert stubs were scattered around her room. Who was she to give relationship advice? Let alone advice on fertility.

>That is terrible! I don't know what to say.

>It's actually becoming frighteningly common, Kya. My doctor said he has seen women and even men every day regarding fertility issues. It sounds like there are better odds that we'd win the lottery twice than us having a kid.

Kya swallowed hard and paced her room. She didn't feel like she was the right friend for Mattie to turn to. Kya had never thought much of being a parent. She had often thought that if her own parents had to plan on having children, they never would have had any. She shook her head and typed.

>*You must be devastated.*

>*Yeah. It's weird because I always thought I'd be a mom, and I guessed I always assumed it would come easy. Even before we got married and started "trying" I was reading pregnancy websites and frequenting forums. And now it looks like it might never happen.*

Mattie continued.

But Rory and I have been saving up… you know… for something big.

>*Supers?*

>*That had been the plan, and we have almost enough.*

Kya felt jealousy rise up within her. It wasn't often that she was envious of her friends, but at this moment it was tangible. She typed with shaky fingers.

>*Wow.*

>*Not so "wow"*

Rory and I are at odds. We were planning on using the money to get Supers so we could offer our kids a better life… And now it looks like we won't be able to have kids unless we spend that money on fertility treatments.

>Why not have kids and then get Supers, I mean you've saved the money once already...

> It wasn't that easy. A lot of the money was gifted for our wedding. Plus, kids are expensive... Even after they are born. Diapers, food, clothing, education.

Plus, the price of Supers is only going up.

If we didn't use this money on Supers, we likely wouldn't be able to save this much again. You know how hard it is.

Kya knew that Mattie didn't intend the last bit as a jab, but the reality of it still stung.

>Ok, how about just getting the Supers now and waiting a few years before having kids?

>I started doing research on it a while back, and I'm actually not convinced that it's safe to have kids once you've had Supers. Even the ads discuss that it might not be a good idea. >I never gave it much thought.

>Well, anyways, even without that, the price for fertility treatments are doubling every few months. It's already more than we have set aside... The longer we wait, the further it is from our grasp.

I told Rory we should take out a loan and do the fertility.

>Have you checked out the interest rates on loans?

>Yeah... He thinks we just shouldn't have kids. Hence the fight.

Kya tried to put herself in Mattea's situation and considered what she would do. Children were never something she had considered part of her future, but she could empathize with wanting something that seemed out of reach.

>*I don't know what to tell you...*

>*I know. I just needed to vent. I'm sure we'll figure it out.*

>*I know how much you've always wanted a family. That's really tough.*

Kya waited for a few minutes, but her friend said nothing else. She stared at her screen blankly trying to remember what she was about to do before talking to Mattea. "E-mail," Kya said to herself with a snap of her fingers. She shook her head trying to erase the clouds that had formed in her mind during her conversation with Mattea.

Sure enough, there were some e-mails about changes and tests going on at work that week, and one with Internal Promotions Update as the subject line. With interest, Kya opened that one first.

To All Staff of SLT – Starlife Technologies

We have had another amazing quarter and due to our success we will be opening up new positions as we expand our company. We will be looking to promote from within first, so if you are interested, please contact your Human Resources representative.

Attached was a list of job promotions available. Each job had the potential to double Kya's annual income, but each job also had a minimum of one Super listed as a prerequisite. She knew that more than education, having a Super was quickly becoming a non-negotiable part of getting a higher paying job. Kya huffed and closed the app without looking at the rest of her emails.

Kya ranted to the walls around her, "How can I get a job that makes a good money if it costs more than I make to get that job?"

She opened her bank account summary, hoping her frugal month would result in good news, but she was in the red, her statement showing a negative balance of $205.68 in her main account, and no growth in her savings.

Kya put her tablet on her bedside table, laid down in bed with the comforter pulled up to her neck and closing her eyes repeated without pause, "It's not that bad. It will get better," until she fell asleep.

Kya slowly opened her eyes and groaned. She silenced her alarm, but even after the noise had stopped, she could still feel it pulsing in her ears. She rolled and stretched, feeling every stiff muscle in her body. Looking outside through the slits in her blinds, she saw the still dark city streets. The sky near the horizon glowed pink and orange as the sun was readying its final push to start the day. Kya knew it would be much easier to simply go back to sleep than to get ready for work, but digging deep, she was able to shake off the lure of her warm blankets.

A quick look at the clock on her phone and she was mortified to see that she had slept for ten hours. Even worse, she still felt like her internal energy stores were empty. A checklist played out of order in her mind, 'cell phone, brush teeth, grab lunch, get dressed, keys, and bus pass'. She pushed her body from her bed, tossing her thick duvet towards the side pressed against the wall. As she avoided looking into the mirror; she grabbed her clothes that were sitting, already chosen, on her dresser. Kya thanked the version of herself from the night before for being so forward thinking. Her morning brain still slowly processed the things she needed to get done before catching the bus.

As she reached the door, she did one last mental check and realized that she had completely forgotten about food. Her belly made a slight rumble, as though it had just been reminded that it was empty. Kya grabbed her lunch from the refrigerator and a granola bar from the cupboard.

She arrived at the bus stop moments before the bus. Swinging open its door, the bus driver smiled at Kya. "A rare day when you beat me to the stop, isn't it?"

Kya nodded and forced a grin. Taking her regular seat at the back, she closed her still burning eyes and waited to arrive at work.

The bus, using its own roads through the city, had the advantage of missing the inevitable gridlock of cars during the rush hour commute. Kya couldn't imagine sitting behind the wheel of a car, lurching forward little by little as the time ticked away. She looked at her phone and knew that, even with the efficiency afforded to public transit, she was going to arrive very close to the start of her shift. A familiar rumble cut its way through Kya's music and the flicker of motion outside her window caught her attention. Her eyes shifted quickly as she tried to catch a glimpse inside the train as it rushed by. She imagined another version of herself glancing out the window of the train and feeling sorry for the poor Normals stuck on the bus.

As the bus arrived, Kya hastily jumped off and walked briskly towards the large towering building. Entering Starlife Technologies' front hall, she found her will to rush vanished, and her pace slowed to a crawl. Kya consciously pushed her shoulders back and squared her chin, keeping her gaze focused towards the IT department trying not to make eye contact through the busy corridors. Even still, she could feel the eyes of strangers on her and considered that if she could hear their thoughts, she'd know that they were thinking things like 'who is this weird girl?' and 'she doesn't belong here'. If it hadn't been for her staff badge, Kya felt she would have been stopped by security long before arriving at the IT department offices.

"Well, if it isn't Kara." A familiar voice boomed.

"Kya." She corrected in a frustrated but controlled small voice that no one besides her could likely hear.

"You are late." The menacing, booming voice came from an open doorway to her left. Kya knew right away who it was. Don Georgetown stepped from his office, his wide frame taking up most of the doorway despite his shorter than average stature. Each step made a loud clacking noise as his over polished dress shoes slammed into the ceramic tiled floor.

Kya impulsively looked at her phone, and she noted that she still had two minutes before the official start of her shift. Feigning innocence, she responded, "I was sure I'm on the day shift this week. Aren't I?"

A deep rumbling groan emanated from Kya's boss. He smoothed down the few thin hairs he had left to try and hide his balding scalp. "The policy states that *all employees* are to be here ten minutes before their shift to have the proper amount of handover time between employees. Are *you* an employee of Starlife Technologies?" As he said the name of the company, Don grinned and lifted his arms to gesture at the building around him, and he drifted closer to Kya. His mouth fixed into a grin intended to show as many teeth as possible and his deep-set eyes glinted as he scrunched the corners of them in what Kya assumed was a failed attempt to make his large grin reach his eyes. "Do you wish to remain an employee of Starlife Technologies? If not, such a thing can be arranged."

When he finished speaking, he was only about three inches from Kya's face. A wave of Mr. Georgetown's pungent cologne wafted into her nose, burning it as it entered.

Kya stifled a cough as she thought about a million things she wanted to say, things she knew would make her boss livid, but instead, she swallowed those impulses and looked down at the floor. After taking a few quick, deep breaths, she looked straight into Mr. Georgetown's eyes. With a mildly insincere tone to her voice, Kya responded, "Sorry, sir."

"Seriously," his voice boomed as Kya walked away towards her desk, "who hired such an undisciplined... No team spirit!" His shoes clacked against the floor as he made his way back to the door that he had come through. When he reached it, he turned back to face the department and hollered so the whole room could hear him. "I'd be better off replacing all of you worthless idiot Normals with machines!"

Kya gave her head a little shake and imagined Mr. Georgetown's words as drops of water, beading on her skin the way she had seen water bead of the feathers of ducks when she used to feed them in her youth. She smiled and approached her desk by the bank of hard drives.

"Wow, he's extra friendly this morning," she said to the co-worker that she was to relieve.

He rolled his eyes and tossed the logbook at her before turning to leave.

Kya scanned it quickly before signing it. She opened the bottom drawer in the desk and gently tossed her lunch bag inside then sat down, leaning back in her task chair. "Just another day at the office."

The man at the desk next to her stifled an audible chuckle and Kya looked over to see the older man who had greeted her at the end of her last shift. His nameplate was the only personalized item in his otherwise plain cubicle and with deeply engraved white letters it said, *Elliot Shepherd*. Kya remembered working alongside Elliot once before, but it was rare that the other departments, including other groups in the IT department, interacted with personnel in Computer Operations, like Kya.

With his receding hairline, and the mostly salt of his salt and pepper hair, Elliot seemed slightly out of place among the sea of young faces that made up the department. His light grey suit swam on his waif-like frame. As he turned to look at Kya, his eyes brightened.

"Glad to see there is still fire in your belly," he whispered, and winked.

Kya let the corners of her mouth curl into a smile. "It'll take more than that to break me."

"If I didn't know better I'd think there was granite coursing through your veins." He turned back to his monitor, and his shoulders slumped, and his eyes showed a strong sense of doubt and frustration as he stared deeply into his monitor. "Never lose that."

Kya nodded at him and returned her attention to her work. The trays next to her desk were filled with different hard drives. Some needed to be mounted for the testing that had to be done for a new software update. Other drives were part of the normal daytime routine and were just blank drives that needed swapping so backups of company data could continue.

Kya's attention returned to Elliot when she overheard another coworker greet him.

"Hey, Shepherd. You still not retired yet, huh?" A younger man slapped Elliot on the back in a friendly manner. "I haven't seen you in days."

Elliot shook his head and forced a noticeably fake chuckle. "Our days off must have overlapped. I haven't gone anywhere."

The newcomer sat at the computer next to Elliot and logged in. "Jeez, man. Did you happen to see the email last night about the promotions?" His eyes were glued to the screen "I mean speaking of retirement and all."

"You know, Gavin, I did see it," Elliot said with a sigh. "Hey Kya, did you see it?"

"Yeah," Kya said with a note of surprise at being included in the conversation.

Elliot raised his eyebrows in a manner that insisted she continue.

"Well... Um, it kind of bugged me."

"Yeah! It's supposed to!" Gavin said as he adjusted his tie. He wasn't as pompously put together as Leonard, but Kya could tell he was another one who was dressing for the job he wanted, and something in his demeanour told her that it just might be working. "They want us to know there's no room for Normals in the nursing home." He pushed a few strands of his longer, but neatly coiffed, dirty blond hair behind his ear and smiled at Elliot.

"As much as you joke about me retiring, it is something I would actually like to do. But you're right." Elliot hesitated and began typing and clicking madly for a few moments before continuing. "There doesn't seem to be any room for Normals in the nursing home, or nearly anywhere in this society anymore. Guess I'll just have to buy myself a Super or two." He grinned first at Kya then at Gavin.

"Like what?" Gavin asked. "Is there a Super for anti-aging?"

Elliot broke out into a hearty laugh. "I sure hope so!"

Kya felt a wave of awkward energy being projected through Elliot's laugh. It was a little too loud, and all three of them took the hint and didn't speak another word.

Kya watched as Elliot turned his full attention back to his computer screen. She witnessed all of the positive energy melt from his face, and Elliot's sorrow filled eyes returned. It looked as though he was two seconds from crying, and Kya wished she could make him feel better.

Don Georgetown's imposing frame loomed overhead holding a hard drive in his hand. "Can someone tell me why this drive was stored incorrectly last night?"

With a slight startle, Kya turned and looked at her boss. "I wasn't here last night. That was Tom."

"Maya!"

Kya held her mouth firmly closed, pinching in the corners, at least it rhymed.

"Always trying to avoid blame. Typical." He came around the cubicle walls and stood right beside her. He was close enough that she could see the beads of sweat on his brow. The smell his musky cologne didn't fully mask his unique smell. She wished she could conjure a forcefield with him outside her bubble of personal space. Kya wondered how often he was able to intimidate people by standing so close.

"Well, I am sure if you bring it up with the person responsible, he'll be able to explain what happened," Kya said glancing back at her monitor and keeping a calm and even tone.

"You signed the logbook this morning, right?" Don paused and looked around the room for a moment. "That makes you responsible for the mistake." He took the logbook from the table and pointed at the drive identification code. "Right here, you signed that this drive was used as a scratch drive for the finance department during last night's test."

Kya knew he was just trying to make her angry, and as his voice got louder, it took more and more energy not to give in to the sparks of anger within her. "What was it used for instead?" She asked gently, staring her boss in the eye.

"It's blank!"

Kya glanced around quickly to see that everyone close enough to hear had turned to peek in on the interaction between Kya and Don.

"Blank! Strange, I wonder *how* that happened." He lifted his hand, bringing attention to the hard drive in it, and clenched his fist. The metal frame of the drive had made a horrible high pitched whine before it began to bend, much like a tin can. A noise, which sounded like that of glass breaking, let everyone know that the platters inside had shattered. With seemingly no effort on his part, Mr. Georgetown had destroyed the hard drive. He dropped the pieces of the twisted metal, plastic, and shattered ceramic on to the floor by Kya's desk.

Raising her eyebrows at the show of strength, Kya knew that she just saw the third of Don Georgetown's powers. Previously, he had shown the staff his ability to memorize anything he read since getting his powers, and another time, he had a friend drive a car into him in the parking lot, and he was uninjured. A chill shot down Kya's spine as she recalled Sam's words, 'too much money and power given too freely.'

Walking away from Kya's desk, Don yelled to the whole office, "Clean that up, Kiva."

Kya could feel heat coming from her face as she swallowed hard to suppress her rage. Her ears were buzzing, her fists clenched. She was used to a little bullying from her boss but never had she felt so much of his wrath focused on her alone.

Lunch couldn't come quickly enough. As soon as the clock on her monitor showed noon, she pulled her lunch out of the drawer and got up to leave.

"Oh, Kya, may I join you?" Elliot asked, placing his hands on his arm rests to push himself up to standing. There was definitely effort required as his knees made an audible crackling noise as he stood erect.

Kya looked at him blankly for a brief moment then smiled and nodded.

Elliot walked a few paces behind Kya as they made their way through the corporate building. Various prints of paintings of natural landscapes, focusing on calming and picturesque locales were hung in the common halls. Kya always found them boring, and their strong blue tones almost blended into the light blue walls around them.

The cafeteria was a small, dimly lit room with multiple vending machines lining one wall, half a dozen microwaves on the opposite wall and four long bench style tables in between.

Painted in a light grey with furnishings in white, the cafeteria was not very inviting.

Elliot moved over to the drink dispensary and typed in a code. Black coffee spurted from the machine, filling two cups. "I hope you don't mind, I got you one too. With the morning you had, I think you deserve it. How do you like it?"

"Thank you. Cream and sugar, please."

Kya and Elliot sat across from each other. Everything in the room seemed crafted to minimize comfort, and the hard wooden chairs felt like they were instantly cutting off circulation to her legs as she sat down. Pins and needles pulsed through her thighs, causing her to shift herself to the edge of the seat to relieve them and making it impossible to receive any back support.

A wave of silence went through the cafeteria as a boisterous laugh filled the room. Kya and likely everyone else could hear people laughing in the executive dining hall next door. She had previously seen through a crack in the door as one of the precious elite was walking through, and she knew that the lounge seating and padded dining chairs were more than a small step up from what she was sitting in.

"Can you believe Gavin?" Elliot said, bringing her attention back to the present moment. Elliot chuckled and shook his head. "That guy. He thinks he knows everything, but I swear he just does favours for our boss. If you know what I mean." He winked multiple times for effect.

Kya couldn't help but burst out laughing.

"My suit is older than that kid." He continued. "Next

time he comes around, you should deal with him. You seem to be good at handling idiots."

With uncontrollable tears streaming down her face, Kya tried to take deep breaths to compose herself. "I have my own problem people to deal with."

As she opened her lunch, Elliot did the same. The conversation continued, only stopping for brief moments of chewing. The remaining twenty minutes of their lunch break rushed by in an instant and then it was time to head back to their cubicles.

Elliot held the door open for Kya as they exited. "We should do this again sometime."

Kya nodded, surprised at how much she enjoyed spending time with a co-worker.

The week flew by in a tiring frenzy, with each day draining both her energy reserves and patience a little more. Kya was eager for her night shifts to return so that she no longer had to deal with Mr. Georgetown, who was continuing to target her with his fury. Thankfully, she found her continuing lunches with Elliot were the bright spot of each day.

Monday was the end of Kya's eight daytime shifts. After returning from lunch, she sat back at her desk ready for more of the routine, filled with verbal assaults from her fearless leader, but as she focused on the screen an unexpected, yet recognizable, voice came from Mr. Georgetown's office and turned her stomach.

"And so if you purchase both of them, I can give you a twenty percent discount. Fifty if you are interested in purchasing any for your wife or children."

Kya slouched in her black task chair as the door opened, hoping she could blend into her surroundings. "Please don't let it be him. Anyone but him." She whispered.

Kya turned and saw Ken a few steps ahead of Don Georgetown. Both of them were leaving his office with smiles on their faces. Kya couldn't remember the last time she saw her boss smile so genuinely, but she didn't feel comforted by it.

"Keea, is that you?" Ken said pointing right at her, a plastic grin stuck on his face. His black, pin-striped suit held tight to his frame, accentuated his physique. His entire appearance and the way he held himself was a testament to the quality of salesperson that he was.

She could feel her face begin to burn red, Kya intentionally rolled her shoulders back and spoke clearly with her own plastic smile. "Yes, Keen, it's me."

"It's Ken actually. Sorry I never called you. I was looking for someone a little easier." He said, his brow slightly furrowed, and a slight pout on his lips but his eyes glinting with mockery.

Kya fought the urge to roll her eyes. Instead she kept her face expressionless, not wanting to give Ken the satisfaction of a reaction.

Mr. Georgetown looked a bit confused before connecting the pieces together. "You two know each other? Is this the girl you were telling me about? That date, you said she was a cold fish." Don started laughing as he looked down his nose at Kya.

"Yeah, that's the one," Ken said joining Kya's boss in laughter.

Kya wanted to turn invisible. Her heart was beating in her ears and her eyes scanned the room for exits. She could feel her entire body warming, but she refused to react. Beside her Elliot seemed to be very interested in his screen where nothing was happening. Kya took a deep breath. "Wow!" She said, still smiling. "I didn't know you could laugh, *Keen*"

"If you were actually as funny as you think you are, you would have heard me laugh last week," Ken said, quite loudly. Then he turned his attention back to Mr. Georgetown. They both could see he was earning points with Kya's boss with each insult. "Instead I just laughed when I got home imagining what kind of hell it would have been spending more time with her!"

Mr. Georgetown laughed heartily, including himself in their exchange. "Or any Normal, really." He winked at Kya. "But especially a Normal girl who wastes her time in Computer Operations." He spat out the last words like they tasted terrible in his mouth.

Ken sighed. "Ugh, Normals! I know it is horrible, but you'd be amazed what they'd do for the promise of a Super, though."

Kya could feel her skin crawl at the thought of what she had considered doing with Ken for a Super. Bile caught in her throat and burned a little.

"You know, Ken, I think I will take you up on that offer. Sign me up for two. And Molly will love one for her birthday."

Don said, grinning.

"Right, Don. One for the Missus. We can conclude all the paperwork junk on the course tomorrow, and get you set-up right away. You'll love our treatment centre."

The two men shook hands and Kya groaned. She was happy for the reprieve and to go back to being unnoticed, but she knew that two more Supers would make Mr. Georgetown ten times more unbearable.

Kya was extremely relieved when her shift ended, and she was able to escape before Leonard had a chance to say more than two words to her. She got on the bus with her headphones already on and zoned out listening to music. Her head leaned against the chilled glass and her eyes randomly focusing on things as they passed by. She wanted nothing more than to pretend the recent week at work had never happened, but pent up frustration ate at her.

Her pocket buzzed, and she took out her phone to see a text from Amelia. Just seeing her friend's name improved Kya's mood as she opened the message.

>Switched shifts with Jacob today, free this evening! Wanna chill?

>Sure, but can we do it at my place? I'm kind of beat from this week of hell.

>Will Sam be there?

>I don't know.

Why?

Is my presence not enough?

>Now that you mention it... lol

Kya smiled and stored her phone back in her shoulder bag. It shifted and slowly sunk down amongst the rest of the random things she carried.

About half way home, Kya passed a school that had closed in recent years. Windows broken, rusted metal scattered about, and overgrown bushes were retaking the area. A large rubble-filled field surrounded the dilapidated school, with stone foundations still in place, a sign of a subdivision that had probably once housed a bustling community of families. On the side of the old gymnasium was her favorite piece of graffiti. It was a beautifully painted young girl in a field full of blooming flowers. Beside her, on either side, were two adult sized silhouettes. On her left, one of the blackened shapes was sowing seeds. The seeds were black marks in a random pattern that led the eye to the start of the blooming flowers. On the other side of the girl was another adult shaped patch of black paint with a watering can in hand, tilted to release water on the waiting mounds of planted dirt. The girl and the flowers around her were painted in iridescent, color changing paint that gave it the appearance of motion. The girl seemed to be dancing, with the wind in her hair and a dress that changed from blue to orange then to purple and finally to green as the bus drove by. It reminded Kya of her own, ever changing hair. The first time she had seen the urban painting she had claimed it as her own. She couldn't explain why, but she just felt a strong connection to the image.

When Kya got home, Sam was sitting in the living room still in his work clothes, his tie loosened, and beer open on the table beside him. He had a stack of tablets in front of him and a stylus in his right hand, but his attention was intently focused on his tablet in his left hand.

"Hey," Kya said as she dropped her keys in the dish, "just so you know, Amelia's going to come over, okay?"

"Yeah, sure, that's fine," he replied without looking up.

"Umm... There's also been an invasion of mutant alien cats."

"Mmm. That's good."

"They have the president," she said.

"Okay."

"Sam!" Kya said sternly.

Sam pulled his eyes away from his screen and looked at her innocently.

"You haven't heard a word I've said."

"Yeah, I did. Amelia's coming over, mutant cats, no more president." Sam grinned.

Kya rolled her eyes. "You sure are something special."

"You love it."

She walked into her room. It wasn't the cleanest the

room had ever been, as various pieces of clothing were scattered about on the floor. Tucking a dressy shirt back into her drawer, she closed it and took a quick look around. In her mind, she made a list of everything she would have to do to clean her room to Amelia's standard. By the time the list was compiled, it felt like Kya had done all the work and she was even more exhausted. Tossing off her work clothes, and changing into something more comfortable, she took a few seconds to kick everything on the floor under the bed.

Amelia arrived bearing gifts. Her arms were nearly buckling as they brimmed with fresh fruit, a large bowl of salad and another bowl of pasta.

"Nice spread!" Sam said looking towards her with a nod. "But you didn't have to do that. We have tons of food here."

"I know I didn't have to," Amelia said with a smile. She barely paid Kya any attention as Kya started unloading the bounty of groceries onto the counter.

"You made the pasta?" Kya asked though she knew she was right.

Amelia nodded. "It needs to be warmed up, though."

Kya helped Amelia ready the food and set the table while Sam got some of his marking done. The smell of fresh pasta, tomato, garlic, basil and an assortment of other spices filled the apartment as each person went to the kitchen and loaded their plates in turn.

"Hey, Sam," Amelia said as they all sat down to eat.

"What's that you were doing?"

"Marking math tests," Sam replied, scooping up a mouthful of pasta.

"Oh, that's so wonderful," Amelia said with a grin.

Sam raised his eyebrows, a look of confusion spreading across his face. "How are math tests wonderful?"

"I mean," Amelia blushed, "if you're marking tests, doesn't that mean you have a class now?"

"Yeah!" Kya said a little too loudly. "My Sammy's growing up! He's no longer just a supply teacher."

"At least not until September. I'm covering a maternity leave. It's super lucky, getting in on a long coverage like this. There are more teachers than jobs it seems and long-term absences of teachers in classrooms are rare." Sam shrugged and turned his attention back to his meal.

"Amelia, this is really good," he said after finishing a good portion of his pasta.

"Why thank you," Amelia said with a little bow of her head. "There's more good stuff where that came from." She punctuated her sentence with a raised eyebrow and a sultry stare.

Kya cleared her throat. "So, anyway." She stirred her food on her plate trying to figure out what to say. "Good old Donnie is getting two more supers. I -"

"Two? At once?" Sam asked, his eyes as wide as saucers. "Man! He's almost as bad as Myles Redwood."

"What?" Amelia asked.

"Myles capped out on Supers this week! His first just manifested within the past day or so, and he has gone four more times, each at different facilities to have treatments. I guess the painful injections weren't enough to dissuade him from doing it." Sam took a long swig of his beer, emptying the remnants of the bottle he had started before Kya had arrived home.

"Can you imagine?" Kya said, staring off into space as she thought about the Supers she would get. "Having the money to buy not just one but five Supers all at once."

"Tell me about it!" Amelia said with a grin.

"Yeah, I can imagine," Sam said with an edge to his voice. "Just starting to realize what life is going to be like with one Super. You have absolutely no control over it and then four more about to manifest in the next week. It's insane!"

"It can't be that bad," Amelia said with a nonchalant shrug.

"Yeah, it's fast, but..." Kya trailed off. Her brow knit together, and she closed her mouth, unsure of what to say next.

"It's a recipe for disaster," Sam said in a dismissive tone, halting further conversation.

Finally breaking five minutes of quiet, Amelia spoke up, directing her question at Kya. "If your boss has another two Supers, does that cap him out?"

"Yep," Kya replied, pushing the last of her noodles

across her plate. "Strength, Invulnerability, some kind of super Memory... And then two more. He'll probably spread them out, though. He likes lording them over us, and I can't see him wanting to stop that."

"Well," Amelia interjected. "He can always swap one out."

Sam stood and pulled his plate up quickly, knocking the edge of it on the table and causing his fork to fall to the floor. Without a word, he grabbed Kya's plate and let it smack on top of his own. Leaning over the table he huffed as he loudly added Amelia's plate to the stack and then kicked his fork, which was still on the floor, towards the kitchen and walked off in that direction.

"What a gentleman!" Amelia said with an extra wide grin and a flip of her hair.

Kya rolled her eyes and hoped neither of them saw.

"I can't even imagine getting sick of a Super and wanting to switch it out," she said, directing her attention to Amelia.

"Oh, I can," Amelia said. "I mean, I'd probably like telepathy for a while, but I'd get sick of it. But I'd probably enjoy it for a few months."

"I don't think you'd like it at all. Besides, I hear the extraction process is even more painful." Sam said from the kitchen.

Amelia laughed. "Okay, probably not. But even just having any power and being able to see what's on the fourth floor of the Uptown Center."

Kya laughed, "Yeah! Or how about getting to ride the train for once!"

"Or getting to see a doctor at the hospital right away if you're sick," Amelia said.

"Forget that! Super Healing... Hello?"

With his face turning a little red, Sam finally walked back over to the table. "It's not all sunshine and lollipops, ladies!" He said. "It's a potentially life-threatening choice that you are putting yourself through."

"Life threatening? No *sane* person would attempt to get more than the maximum. They're pretty clear that it could result in death." Amelia said twirling her hair.

"I didn't mean getting more than five. There is risk in even just controlling one power." Sam said.

Kya raised her eyebrows and leaned on the table, gesturing for Sam to sit back down.

He complied and sat down with a heavy sigh. "Accidents happen, Amelia."

As he said her name, Amelia took in a deep breath and fought to keep her composure, but a shaky smile crept across her face. Kya lifted her hand to her forehead, embarrassed for her friend.

"Yes, accidents happen," Kya said. "But accidents happen to Normals too."

Sam bit his lip and shrugged.

"Sure," Amelia said, "you could get hit by a bus tomorrow. If you were a super, though, you could use your Flight, Invulnerability, Strength or something and survive."

"You could be a Super and still get hurt by the bus," Kya said with a little laugh. "Telepathy, Invisibility, Memory or something like that won't save you."

Sam rolled his eyes and folded his arms in front of himself.

"You ok?" Kya asked.

"Yeah," he said, "I'm fine." He unfolded his arms and forced a smile, but the tension still radiated off of him in nearly visible waves. "You girls want anything to drink? And what say we move this to the living room instead?"

"Sure." The two girls said in unison. Moving to the longer sofa, Amelia left the spot next to her free.

Sam joined them in the living room a moment later with three drinks balanced in his two hands. Placing the drinks clumsily on the black rectangular table between the various seating options, he took a deep breath.

"Telekinesis would make it easier for you to get all those glasses in here," Amelia said.

"But it might not save you from the bus," Kya added causing Amelia and her to both laugh.

Sam handed out the drinks, then sat in his spot, a black leather recliner that faced towards the couch, and picked up his tablet from the table beside him. "I wasn't actually talking about that type of accident," he said, turning on the tablet and tapping.

"Oh?" Amelia said.

"Let's take our dear friend Myles," Sam said in what Kya recognized as his teacher's voice. "His first Super to manifest was Size. Today alone, he has been photographed at his Normal height of about six feet tall." Sam turned the tablet to show the girls, and swiped to corresponding photos as he spoke. "Ten feet tall, twelve feet tall and then he was walking down the street, a good fifteen feet tall, hit his head on this overpass... and all the pictures since then are like this, between one and two feet tall." Sam turned the tablet back to himself. "He can't control it."

"Well, yeah," Amelia said. "He's eighteen. He's a kid."

"A kid who is going to find himself dangerously overwhelmed by his abilities, I'm telling you," Sam said. His eyebrows raised in concern and he shook his head.

"You're talking like Supers are a bad thing," Amelia said.

"Any power in the wrong hands is a bad thing," Kya said, thinking about Don Georgetown and even Leonard at work.

"Not just the wrong hands," Sam said with a sigh. "You could have the best intentions in the world. Hope to be a Superhero, and still end up causing more harm than good." He tapped his tablet some more. "There are countless documented cases of Super accidents."

Kya took a gulp of her drink. "Wow, Sam. You're just a

barrel of sunshine today."

"So, I guess you wouldn't want a Super even if you could get one?" Amelia asked sadly.

Sam cracked a slight smile. "No."

He began gathering the tablets and his stylus. "Thank you for a wonderful dinner, Amelia." Nodding his head, he continued, "But, ladies, I'm afraid I have to turn in. These tests won't mark themselves, and I need my beauty sleep." He smiled kindly though Kya noted that his eyes looked distant, and Sam walked to his room, shutting the door behind him.

"He's so cute when he overreacts," Amelia said, grinning at the closed door to Sam's room. After a moment, she continued. "Hey, K, is Sam ok?"

"Um, yeah. I don't know; I guess work must be getting to him." Kya responded, pondering Sam's reaction.

"K, do you know much about First-Gen Supers or the Black Market for Supers?" Amelia asked in a hushed tone.

"Not much," Kya admitted. "You know, I paid a lot more attention in English, computer science and even Math classes than I did in any of that historical or political stuff."

"I don't think it was ever really discussed in school. I've been doing a bit of research. It's pretty cool." Amelia whispered, and leaned in closer to Kya. "Most of it isn't common knowledge, but it seems there might be other ways of getting Supers." She grinned.

"Really?"

"Yup. I'm going to look into it more, but if I find any good leads, you want me to share?"

"Oh, Lia, yes please!" Kya said, her words echoing in the living room.

Amelia brought her index finger up to her mouth. "Shhh, I don't want everyone knowing." Grinning wildly, Amelia continued, "Imagine us shopping on the fourth floor. Riding the train, great apartments in the best neighbourhood with no need for roommates."

In a more subdued but still excited tone, Kya continued her friend's thoughts, "Access to medicine. Better schools."

Amelia and Kya talked for a short while longer, laughing and coming up with various ideas before finally calling it a night. After Amelia had left, Kya started getting ready for bed. She felt like the weight of the week had been lifted off of her shoulders just by having contact with her friends and couldn't contain her excitement at the idea that maybe Supers could be accessible to her as well. The thoughts rolled around in her mind, keeping her awake until the sky started changing colours back towards dawn.

CHAPTER 5

Kya's eyes shot open. Her heart was thumping fiercely inside her chest. She knew something was wrong, and though she couldn't quite place it, she knew there was a noise that had awoken her. She held her breath, waiting for another noise to help her pinpoint if it was just Sam, or something more. As she focused, it was though she could hear everything. There was a slight hum of electricity, air moving through the ventilation system, and the traffic from the roads outside of her building. She waited, her imagination growing wild, filling the apartment with all sorts of horrible possibilities.

Less than a minute went by before there was another bang and crash. It sounded like breaking glass that came from the living room and was followed by two low muffled voices. Kya knew then that it wasn't Sam, and that things weren't right. Slowly, she rolled out of bed and stepped gingerly onto the floor of her room. The area rug dampened the noise from her footfall. She could hear her pulse in her ears, and fought to control her breathing.

Another small noise came from the living room.

All of the things that Kya had imagined coalesced into one clear image: they were being robbed. She took a deep breath and summoned all of the bravery within her as she twisted the cold metal door handle, quietly opening her door.

Two shadowy figures which Kya knew shouldn't exist in the apartment, froze in place. She could see a glint off of the eyes of the closer of the two and realized they were likely both men and were definitely both taller than her.

Before Kya could get a word out, the two men darted towards the door, arms crossed over their torsos. She knew they were taking things from the apartment - her things.

Without thinking, she leapt towards the door, trying to block the men from leaving. The three of them collided, in a flurry of elbows, knees and shoulders. One hand, not her own, held her hair tightly. Kya cried out as her feet left the ground, and she fell onto her back.

The two men stumbled over her, through the door and out into the hallway. Kya's head bounced off the tile floor, and she felt pain ring through her entire body.

Everything was distorted, and the room still dark, but as her eyes regained focus, she saw Sam exiting his bedroom.

Rage fueled her body with energy, Kya flipped around, and pushed herself back on her feet, ready to pursue the intruders.

Sam yelled as he rushed towards the door. "Kya, don't! It isn't worth it."

As she ran out into the hallway, Kya noticed that the doors of her neighbors were open, and many of them were peering out into the hall, most in pyjamas, but all of them witnessing the commotion. Chasing after the two figures, Kya watched as the emergency exit doors slammed shut. Her energy waning, and her head spinning, she gave up the chase.

She turned back and looked at the few people still watching, mouth agape. "Why didn't any of you stop them?" She said, out of breath and slightly confused. "I know that some of you have to be Supers, and most of you are healthy and strong." She looked at each face in turn, wanting to burn each of them with her gaze. Her words were small, barely more than a whisper, as she tried to catch her breath. "Some of you could have easily stopped them."

As she stepped slowly back to her apartment door, she began to feel pain in her right knee and hip, presumably from her collision with the robbers and impact with the floor and throbbing in the back of her head. Eyes of her neighbours were still on her, and a new emotion, one of disgust, bubbled up inside her. Her voice echoed in her head as she yelled at the onlookers. "What is wrong with you people? I needed help!"

Sam came along side her and wrapped his arm around her. "Let's go back to the apartment."

Energy slipped from Kya's body as the adrenaline drained away, she leaned on Sam, and he propped her up. She couldn't help but note the broken door lock as they slipped back into their still darkened apartment. Her mind reeled over what had happened. Kya couldn't focus on anything as Sam let go of her in front of the sofa. She fell backwards into it with a thud, and as her pulse slowed, she began to feel more aches and pains from her experience. Her entire body felt like it was on fire, her ears were still ringing, and sweat found its way into her eye. But the stinging from sweat was the least of her worries.

Sam picked up the broken pieces of glass and frame that until that night had proudly displayed a candid shot of a young Sam blowing out six candles on a birthday cake and two people Kya assumed were his parents grinning behind him.

Kya stood, grabbed her phone and paced the living room as she dialled.

"What are you doing?" Sam asked standing up with the pieces of the picture frame in one hand and turning on the floor lamp next to his chair with the other. The illumination did little to make things feel brighter or better.

"Calling the police," Kya replied, placing the phone to her ear. It was an odd sensation having to wait for someone to pick up as each ring chimed through the device. Impatiently, she waited and realized that she couldn't remember the last time she had used her phone for its classic feature.

A woman's voice answered in a calm but detached tone. "Please state the nature of the emergency."

"I'd like to report a robbery," Kya said in the most authoritative voice she could muster.

"Describe the perpetrators, please?"

"Two men, about six foot-"

"Supers or Normals?" The woman interrupted.

"Well, I didn't see them use any Supers, but-"

"Describe the victims."

"My roommate and me-"

"Supers or Normals?" The woman interrupted again.

"Normals."

"I'm sorry," the woman said in a patronizing tone, "we are unable to assist you at this time."

The line went dead.

Kya felt anger shake her body once again. Her muscles tensed, and waves of pain and nausea flooded through her. "What do you mean you won't do anything about it?" She yelled into her phone at no one. "What about justice? They came into our home! Took our things!" Her voice got faster and more high pitched as she spoke.

If it were anyone else, Kya would have recoiled, but as Sam calmly sat next to her and put his arm around her shoulder, she felt comforted. "Stuff is stuff, Kya. You and I are safe, and that's what matters."

Kya snorted, "Safe. Safe? How are we safe?"

Sam took an audible deep breath and shifted in his seat. His head swiveled, surveying the entirety of the apartment. "Looks like they took my laptop and tablet, eh?" He sighed lightly and leaned against Kya. "It's going to be okay. I can buy a new one. And we can replace whatever you're missing too."

A sick crawling feeling covered her, making it hard to sit still. It was as though worms were making their way through her skin, causing her muscles to twitch with a strong feeling of general unease. She kept replaying her conversation with the police officer, her blood pressure throbbing strongly through her whole body. It felt as though someone was pounding on a drum set right inside of her head.

"I want to go to the police station," she said. "They should fingerprint the apartment, or at least try to run some kind of leads. Doesn't our building have a camera system monitoring the front entrance?" Focused on the idea of fixing the problem, Kya felt a sense of calm and purpose, and her pulse slowed.

"We could do that. Let me deal with this," he nodded at the broken glass, wood and photo still in his hand, "and grab your coat." Sam said almost too calmly, as he got up and walked to the kitchen.

It seemed to take an eternity for Sam to drive them there, but as soon as they arrived at the Police station, Kya made a beeline towards the front counter and Sam followed closely behind.

A young officer sat behind the counter, his head propped up by his arms and a look of boredom covered his face.

"Excuse me, can you help us?" Kya asked.

The office perked up slightly, looking at Kya. His gaze started at the top of her head, moved down towards her chest, where it paused for too long before it continued to follow down to her legs. "What do you want?" He said in a voice sounding more like a sigh than a proper question. His eyes shifted to Sam, starting at the top of his head and quickly moving down.

Kya tried to keep her aggravation in check. "We were robbed. We called the police, but no one came. We were hoping you would do something to uphold the law?"

Sam put his hand on Kya's shoulder, and it helped steady her as she waited for the officer's response.

"Were you robbed by a Super?" The officer replied. There was something about his reply that was dismissive, as though he already knew the answer.

"I don't think so. No. They didn't seem to be. But what does that have to do with anything?" Kya said. She tried to recall the events of the evening, but the details were already fading like a bad dream from many nights ago.

Sam quickly interjected, "My name is Sam. Samson Hart."

The young man behind the counter stood up and took notice. His entire presence changed. It was like lightning had hit him, energizing his body and giving life to his face.

Kya turned her attention to Sam, her brow furrowed in confusion, she opened her mouth to question him but decided instead to stay quiet.

"Just a second, sir." The officer said before disappearing outside the view of the small window in the counter.

A blue and white door with metal framing and cross beams opened on the left-hand side of the hallway and the officer approached. "Stick out your hand please, sir." He gestured towards Sam and Sam complied. A small silver device hovered over his hand and started to blink red after a few seconds.

The officer burst into a light laugh. "Some Hart you are. Stop wasting my time." He swung around on his toes and turned his back to the pair. Before either of them could get another word in, the officer disappeared back through the door, slamming it closed behind him.

"What was that all about?" Kya demanded, still looking up at Sam.

"It's a long story for another time, but I don't think they are going to help us," he said.

Sam's assertion was proven right when a hand pulled down a thick metal sheet in front of the window where they had previously talked to the officer.

Kya felt like the entire hallway was closing in from all sides, and she could hear laughter coming from behind the metal as Sam helped guide her from the building. Her anger was boiling over once again, and Kya wiped a bead of sweat from her brow. "Are they seriously laughing at us?"

"It's going to be okay," Sam said opening the passenger door to his car. "Get in, and let's go back home. I'll get us a new lock in the morning, and some extra security." Sam watched the road and spoke in a calm, even tone as if reciting a grocery list. "I'll also pick up a new computer and tablet, and everything will go back to normal." He turned his attention towards Kya with a tiny smile. "You'll see."

His words were little comfort to Kya as they drove back home. She focused on her breathing, trying to calm herself down, constantly willing tears to not fall from her eyes. All the while, she felt spikes of rage and fear ripple through her as she reflected on different points of her night.

"They wouldn't have treated us that way if we were Supers," Kya said, breaking the long period of silence as Sam parked the car.

"I know," Sam said heavily.

CHAPTER 6

Kya tossed and turned in her bed. She willed her eyes to stay shut, but they kept opening. Every sound that used to be familiar and comforting now made her jump or flinch. She tried breathing deeply and counted down her breaths.

'One hundred, ninety-nine, ninety-eight...'

For the first time that she could remember she made it all the way to zero without falling asleep or losing count. She opened her eyes, and turned on her phone, according to the display, only a few minutes had passed since she last checked.

Turning on her music to a nice, soothing classical playlist, and closing her eyes again, she tried to focus all of her attention on more positive memories. She could feel herself calming and looked forward to getting some sleep before having to start working overnights again.

Kya found herself at work, with stacks of hard drives surrounding her in high columns from the floor to the ceiling. They reminded her of strange prison bars. Everywhere she looked, they were isolating her from the rest of the room. Grunting as she slammed her shoulder into one stack, she tried to push them over, but they wouldn't give an inch. Beyond the drives, she could see Don Georgetown looking larger than life. He stood ten feet tall and was looking down on her. The stacks of drives shook slightly, and a metallic chatter echoed with increasing volume as though they were afraid of Kya's boss. A strange green light from an unknown source emanated from below his chin, highlighting his double chin and jowls, his crooked nose, heavy brow. It made him look even more evil than normal. Two shadowy figures loomed behind Kya's boss, the light reflecting off office furniture scattered throughout the never-ending room, but none of it seemed to touch the two of them. It was as though the two shadowy figures absorbed the light. Their almond shaped eyes glowed slightly red in the darkness of their silhouette, and a chill raced down Kya's back. Her boss pointed directly at her and began to laugh.

A glowing apparition of Kya slowly tore itself away from her, and started moving towards her maniacal boss. Don grabbed the glowing echo out of the air and crushed it with his fist before tossing it in his mouth, swallowing it whole. The eyes of the shadow figures began to glow a bright red. The red light was so bright and piercing that Kya felt it begin to burn her skin. She turned away, hoping to shield herself. She couldn't help but notice a distant sustained scream, but as she gasped for breath, she realized the screams were her own. She ran towards the bars of hard drives away from her boss and the two figures. As she slammed into them, the hard drives fell to the ground, shattering loudly.

Kya gasped and opened her eyes in the darkness. It took a moment for them to adjust as she sat up. She looked around her room and pulled her blankets up around her. She was alone, and it was still completely dark outside.

"Calm down, Kya," she said to herself. "You're not five. It was just a dream." She pushed her covers back down, and glanced around her room, attempting to regain her composure. Beads of sweat all over her body left her feeling a little gross, but she couldn't muster the courage to leave her bed. Falling backward into her sheets, and exhaling sharply, she tried to settle her mind once again to fall back asleep.

With dawn breaking, Kya's eyes were burning. Every time she began to doze, her sleep was constantly ruined by either a small noise or her imagination of a noise. She found her thoughts were moving like molasses through her mind as she considered a day in bed.

Kya jumped and let out a gasp as her phone vibrated on her bedside table. It was Mattea.

>Hey Kya, want to hang out with me today?

>No. I haven't really slept.

>Why not? You were on days this week weren't you?

>Yeah, but we got robbed last night.

>Oh sweetie that's terrible!

>You're telling me!

I hate how helpless I feel. I'm so jumpy!

It's like I can see the guys everywhere!

>How many? Did you see who did it? Did you go to the police?

Kya could feel her blood pressure rising. Her hands shook, and she could feel the heat in her cheeks. She took a deep breath and began composing her response.

>You know, Mattie... I don't think I can talk about it yet.

I'm still trying to process.

>Okay. I get it.

As long as you're alright...?

>I'll be fine.

Kya powered her phone off, and immediately felt disconnected. It was as though she had cut off one of her hands. She hoped for a feeling of relief but felt none as she rolled over to face her bedroom wall, in the fetal position, hugging her knees.

Exhausted and half awake, Kya rose from her bed slowly the next morning. Stabilizing herself with one arm firmly pressed into her bed, she wiped the crusts from her eyes. She looked at the door and felt like it was a million miles away.

"I think today is a party in bed day." She said yawning.

Kya turned on her phone, and it immediately alerted her to a dozen new messages. There was something both comforting and annoying by the number. She decided to ignore them, and loaded up the local food delivery app and ordered herself a pepperoni pizza, a large bottle of pop, a bag of her favourite sour cream and onion chips and a chocolate cake. It was an expensive way to shop, but Kya felt justified after the previous evening's stress. With everything arriving in an hour, she took inventory of herself and decided that before her food arrived, she would need to shower and change out of her pyjamas that felt less than fresh after another stressful and sleepless night.

Kya could hear Sam moving around in the kitchen, and for a brief moment she thought about asking him if he wanted to share in her huge bounty of food that was on the way, but she couldn't even bring herself to open the door. Slightly ashamed, she turned away from it and sat at the edge of her bed looking out through her window.

After a few moments of contemplation, she looked around the room, feeling some relief that her life within these four walls hadn't been ransacked. Kya used the remote control app on her phone and set the large display, which sat on top of her dresser, to the local celebrity gossip station. She surprised herself by laughing out loud as outlandish graphics covered her screen, letting her know the importance of the latest celebrity wardrobe malfunction. Kya shook her head slightly. "Nothing like the junk food of television to keep my mind off things I suppose."

The television blared loudly as a special report took over the broadcast.

This Just In, Myles Redwood, murderer?

The abrupt change in tone caught Kya's attention.

The reporter on screen was a young, blond woman,

with big over-whitened teeth. Kya thought she could almost see the reflection of the camera man in the reporter's teeth. The woman looked slightly hysterical, as she stood in front of a police line near a heavily damaged red brick wall. A blue glow pulsed behind her slightly distorting the image. Her giant fake smile faded to a more serious look as she inhaled in preparation to speak.

Her tone was low and kurt as she began. "We are here in front of the Gambit Club where Myles Redwood's party last night came to a tragic end."

The camera panned slightly, and the glowing purple logo of the Gambit Club could be seen. Police tape covered everything, and various officers were walking around the area.

"It seems Mr. Redwood was intoxicated when he exited the club, and several witnesses saw him become quite angry with the paparazzi following him around."

The camera returned to the face of the reporter.

"According to witnesses, one young man named Newton Wilson, a photographer for the Uptown Press, got too close to Myles, and was struck by Mr. Redwood's superhuman strength. This Super seems to have manifested only a few short hours before the incident. Mr. Wilson flew, as you can see, over twenty-five feet and into this nearby brick wall."

Pausing, for effect, the reporter turned and gestured with her outstretched hand, the camera panned and zoomed towards the wall. The bricks were smashed in a slightly oval shape, and a thick, red substance coated the affected area. Kya recognized it as blood and found her hand jump to her mouth in surprise.

"The Police have put up a protection field, quarantining the area until their investigation is complete. They've taken Myles Redwood to a holding cell pending a trial. For more information on the health of Mr. Wilson, we turn now to Jason Lu at the Merciful Redeemer Hospital. Jason?"

The scene on the display changed to show a new reporter, Jason Lu. A lanky man with black hair and almond-shaped eyes. He seemed younger than the previous reporter, but also more calm and collected. He was standing outside the Normals emergency entrance at the hospital. The area was dark, with room for a single ambulance to pull up. Kya knew that if the camera panned to the left, just a tiny bit, she would be able to see the entrance to the Supers ER with spaces for half a dozen ambulances, and a brighter, cleaner exterior. Kya thought back to the last time she had to wait in the Normals emergency room, spending nearly twenty hours with a broken arm before receiving any service and she shuddered to think what Newton Wilson was going through.

"Thanks, Lana," Jason said with a smile and nod to the camera. "I am here at Merciful Redeemer Hospital, where Newton Wilson was admitted just moments ago. His condition is quite serious. There are even, unconfirmed, reports that he was dead upon arrival. A source from inside the hospital told us that his spinal column was shattered upon impact with the building, and he has suffered severe internal injuries."

Kya shook her head, her eyes stayed glued to the screen. The camera zoomed out to show the emergency sign above the entrance, and only the letters "E" and "M" were lit up while the rest of the sign was dark.

"Mr. Wilson was hit by Myles Redwood's Super Strength Ability early this morning." Jason continued. "Myles gained all of his Supers within a one week period of time, which is in direct violation of the Best Practices Act. All five of his supers have since manifested. The first was Size, followed by Voice, which, for those unfamiliar with this ability, is the super amplification of vocalizations. There is evidence of this Super's manifestation as early as Monday evening." From the way his eyes rapidly flicked from side to side, Kya could tell that Jason was reading off a teleprompter. "Less than twenty-four hours later, Myles demonstrated his Flight Super, and we have also seen, since his incarceration, that he seems to be immune to injury using a Super known as Imperviousness."

The female reporter's disembodied voice broke in. "Any news on the paparazzo's family? Have they been informed of what happened to Mr. Wilson? Do we know anything about them?"

Jason perked up and stood at attention, his voice dripped with excitement. "Yes Lana, we have. Newton's wife, Liz, and three-year-old daughter, Melody, arrived at the hospital just seconds after his ambulance got here, and they had no comment at that time. They have been asked by the hospital administration to hold a press conference about the event later today. We will continue to cover this story as it unfolds."

"I am sure this will spark quite the discussion. Supers have been known on rare occasions to spark the onslaught of underlying psychoses." Lana's voice said again.

The image changed to a still shot of a very angry looking Myles Redwood, and Lana continued, "So, what do you, the people, think of this incident? Was it an accident or something else?"

Tapping the screen of her phone, Kya shut off the broadcast. She grabbed some clean clothes and slipped into her shower. Her food arrived just as she finished putting on her clothing. With a towel still wrapped up in her hair, she opened the door.

On the other side was a young man wearing a uniform that hung off of him like it was two sizes too large. He was holding a box filled with food and drink. "Kia Robbers?" Kya blinked, and let out an involuntary and cold chuckle. She cleared her throat. "It is Kya. Kya Roberts, actually." She made sure to pronounce clearly the T in her last name.

The delivery boy clumsily passed the package to Kya and nodded slightly before quickly turning on his heels and departing down the hallway back towards the elevators.

Kya groaned as she closed the door and walked back toward her room. She glanced around and noticed that Sam's door was open. She could hear the sounds of a news report echoing out into the common area. Once she was back in her room, Kya shut the door, and turned her television back on, queuing up a random comedy movie. Before she knew it, she had eaten all of the food, and the movie she had selected was over. Kya threw herself back into her bed, surrounded by the debris of her feast and quickly fell asleep.

Nearly two hours later, she woke up to the sound of her alarm and picked up her phone. The screen flashed a reminder message noting that it was time to get ready for work. Kya obeyed and grabbed everything she needed for her overnight shift.

When she left her room, Sam was sitting on the couch, staring intensely at his phone.

"Hey, Kya, how are you feeling?" He asked without looking up from the screen.

"Rough," she said, her voice coming out a little like gravel. "I couldn't really sleep."

"You've seen the news too, then?"

"Um, yeah." She paused, not sure where Sam was going with his comment.

"See? These Supers!" Sam tossed his phone on the couch and turned to Kya. She could see there was a little sadness in his eyes. "It's insane. No wonder you can't sleep. How can anyone feel secure when we live in a world where rich children have the power to end your life in a fit of rage?"

"You mean Myles? I was feeling rough before all that."

"Oh? How come?"

"Sam! We were robbed! Strangers... Criminals came to our home. Broke our things, took our stuff."

"I've looked into it, and I'll be getting the updated version of my tablet and laptop today, I bought a new frame for that picture. There are also a few of your movies missing. I've transferred money to your account to replace them, or get new ones if you'd like." Sam's head tilted slightly as he continued. "Stuff is just that: stuff. It can be replaced. People. Life." He paused with each word, letting them hang in the air, the weight of them pressed down upon Kya as Sam tried to drive his point home. "Now, those things can't be replaced." Sam picked up his phone again. "Newton." He paused searching for the man's full name, looking like he wanted to burn it into his mind. "Newton Wilson is dead. Liz and Melody... They have truly lost. And Myles..."

Kya interjected, her patience gone, her frustration overwhelming her. "Sam! He's a Super. All that stuff? That's not our real life. Our life is here and now. There are criminals walking around out there with our stuff!" Tears started welling up in Kya's eyes, and she tried to hold them back as she continued. "They broke into our home! The police don't care. The world doesn't care. Are you saying we shouldn't care?"

Sam looked at Kya and raised an eyebrow.

His non-reaction only fuelling her rage, Kya felt her fingers tingling like she was touching electricity. Unable to look at Sam any longer, she turned. "I'm going to work." A heavy march of footsteps echoed in the hall before she slammed the door closed behind her.

Kya hugged herself tightly as she walked from the apartment entrance to the bus station. As her anger dissipated, she was filled with new emotion. She felt twitchy and constantly felt the irresistible urge to look over her shoulders. Waves of unease began to drown out all of the rational thoughts in her mind. *What if they think I saw their faces? What if they come back to make sure I can't talk to the police?*

CHAPTER 7

Kya's overnights passed by in a blur of progressively less emotionally strained trips to and from work. Her concern about the robbers trying to silence her quickly felt like nothing more than a silly idea that Kya once had a long time ago. The time between hard drive swapping was wasted on websites chronicling Myles Redwood's downward spiral or listening to upbeat music and the days were spent mostly alone in her room, sleeping, eating or trying to relax.

On the last day of Kya's overnight shifts, the news about Myles Redwood had changed from the sad death of Newton Wilson and discussion as to whether or not the manifestation of his Supers had sparked underlying psychoses, to the forced removal of Myles' Strength Super. The Internet was buzzing with reports, images, statistics and videos relating to the court sentence. Kya's curiosity got the better of her, and she decided to watch the live streaming footage of the Extraction process. Between drive changes, Kya loaded up the video of the forced removal.

Myles screamed, and the sound was distorted no doubt by the power of his Voice Super, as they strapped him to a large metal chair. He was crying and flailing as the judge read out his sentence. "Myles Redwood, you are to be stripped of your Strength. You will never be allowed to possess this Super again, and you will serve a five-year prison sentence for your crime."

A large metal pad came down and covered Myles' bare chest. At first, nothing happened, but after a few moments, Kya could see small, bright blue streaks under Myles' skin slowly inching along his veins towards the metal pad. Kya had heard the extraction process was uniquely painful, but she had never witnessed one before. As the lines continued to move slowly, Myles shook uncontrollably, and writhed in the chair, unable to move beyond his restraints.

His voice was wavering wildly as the machine continued its work, sweat soaking his body, Myles screamed out in agony once more, pleading for the procedure to stop. The noise of his cries echoed outwards, the plexiglass walls vibrated, and the microphone squealed before the audio cut out completely. Kya could see the veins in his neck extending outwards, strained, and his wide open mouth still belting out his suffering.

Kya wanted to turn away from the screen but felt compelled to continue watching. She paused the video and glanced around to make sure none of her work needed her attention. Then, without an excuse to stop, she resumed watching as Myles Redwood's Super was extracted.

After another three minutes of watching and waiting, a trickle of dark red blood slowly dripped down from the center of the metal pad along Myles' chest and down his belly. Myles Redwood's entire body went limp as he passed out, and Kya knew the Super had been removed.

Doctors and nurses rushed to his side, and the extraction tool was lifted away. The video feed ended, and Kya found her jaw slightly aching as she opened her mouth.

As she left work, the sound of the celebrity singer's scream still echoed in her mind. I never want to go through that, she thought.

With her day off spent sleeping, Kya arrived just in time for the handoff from Leonard at her first-day shift on Monday.

"There's no point even saying anything, is there?" Leonard said in greeting.

"Nope," Kya admitted without looking directly at him.

She looked at the desk next to hers, but Elliot was not there. A rather young girl was sitting at the desk. Kya estimated she was maybe a year or two older than Kya. The girl had black, pixie-cut hair and wore elegant makeup that subtly played up her eyes. She was wearing a white blouse with blue and purple pinstripes. The blouse tied in a loose bow below a lace collar. A matching blue pencil skirt that came to just above her knees and black heels completed the provocative but professional outfit. She also had earrings and a matching bracelet that complimented the purple in her clothes.

"Hi." The girl said when she noticed Kya staring. "Can I help you?"

"Um, yeah - No." Kya stammered. "I was just hoping to

see someone else."

The girl rolled her eyes and focussed her attention back to her screen.

Kya signed off on the logbook and loaded up her e-mail.

"Leonard, you can go. I've got this." She said, realizing that Leonard had yet to vacate their area.

"Actually, I'm waiting for Mr. Georgetown. He told me he needed to talk to me.

As if on cue, Don Georgetown's door opened and he stepped out, grinning. "Hello, my minions!" He boomed with an almost happy sounding laugh. "Today is a special day for one of you." He was walking towards the robotic arm cubicle where Computer Operations staff spent their shifts.

Kya closed her eyes and willed herself to become invisible. She knew it wasn't working because when she opened them Leonard was looking right at her and grinning.

"Leonard, here, has shown himself to be a wonderfully skilled and organized employee. He follows the letter of the rules and has quite an eye for detail." Don raised the tone of his voice, overemphasized the last words in a playful tone and then winked at Leonard.

Leonard bowed his head slightly in what Kya decided was mock humility, but he also maintained eye contact and raised his eyebrows at Kya.

"Leonard, I am very happy to announce to the I.T. team that you have been promoted to the Database Administration group! And as all of you know, in our most recent memo about promotions, it was noted that higher up positions need at least one Super."

Kya seethed as Don continued to pause for effect, making his announcement seem like it was taking forever. Wishing that she was in a dream, she began to grind her teeth as her boss continued.

"Leonard, to put you on the same level as everyone else in your new department, Starlife Technologies will be providing you with your first Super."

Don Georgetown turned to Leonard and spoke directly to him, placing a hand on his shoulder. "I'll talk with you personally later to discuss the details."

"Thank you, Sir." Leonard said turning his attention fully towards his boss, but talking loudly enough for the whole department to hear. "I am truly honoured for the opportunity to grow within this amazing company."

Kya's mouth hung open, and her ears were ringing. She slumped back in her chair and stared at the screen unable to muster the energy to move. She wished she was working an overnight shift so that she could text Amelia or Mattea without anyone noticing.

Kya had one of the worst work days she could remember. All anyone would talk about was Leonard, his promotion and his company sponsored Super. The girl at the desk beside Kya's was so unfriendly through the day, it only served to make Kya miss Elliot even more. About an hour before the end of her shift an urgent email came through about pay cuts.

To All Information Technology Staff of Starlife Technologies - As you will note on your upcoming pay stub, your salaries have been reduced by twenty percent. This is to pay for overages in expenditures. Our choice was difficult, but it came down to either reducing our staff by five people or making this sacrifice. If anyone has any issues with this change, please contact me during office hours.

Don Georgetown

Vice President of Information Services

Kya knew the message wasn't about any overages in expenses other than the personal expenses that Don Georgetown himself had been adding to the company's bottom line. She had overheard her boss talking to another person in the management team about how both his wife and child had finally been able to use their Supers. The whole situation only infuriated Kya even more, but a sense of futility also overwhelmed her.

When it was finally time to leave work, Kya couldn't get away fast enough. She threw her hair in a messy ponytail even before she left the building, showing off her, now fading, purple streaks that were in direct violation of the Starlife Technologies dress code. She then pulled her phone out of her purse to text her friends. Before she could send a message out, she noticed that she had one waiting for her from Amelia.

>Hey K. Great news! I found out some stuff about the BMS. Text

me when you can. Hugs!

Kya quickly scanned her memory to try and decode what BMS could mean, and after some consideration, she concluded it must be Black Market Supers.

Kya fought the urge to growl. She clenched her teeth and held her phone tightly. Tapping the on-screen keyboard, she crafted a response.

>Seriously??? Leonard's getting a Super... You're getting a Super... This is crap. Today is crap.

But instead of hitting Send, Kya deleted the message and wrote a friendlier response.

>Hey Lia, I think I know what BMS means, but...

It only took Amelia a moment to respond.

>I knew you would. But let's keep it on the DL. Wanna swing by my work? I'm done in 15.

Kya sighed as she considered her friend's question. She didn't really want to go and felt it would be a waste of a bus token. It didn't help that she also felt that she was in way too terrible a mood to be good company.

>Ok. See you in 15.

WARNING: I'm not feeling all sunshine and lollipops.

>Awesome! See you soon!

The bus was half empty, as Kya got on and took her normal seat. Tossing on her headphones, she started playing some music. Before the first song had completed, the bus came to an abrupt stop. Flashing blue and red lights ahead caught Kya's eye, and she watched as four officers approached the bus.

The driver checked his rear mirror, watching the passengers as he opened his door, and Kya could tell he was nervous. "Can I help you, officers?" He said as two officers, an older man and a younger woman, boarded.

The older man held two devices and stepped near the driver. "We are looking for a woman, a fugitive Super, hiding among Normals. Have you seen her?" Displaying an image on his phone, he turned it towards the driver.

Kya couldn't make out any details.

The woman officer rolled her eyes and nudged him on to continue the investigation. Her hands gripping her weapon tightly in its holster, she fixed her gaze on each of the passengers in turn.

Despite not having done anything, Kya felt her pulse quicken. She tried to focus on her frustrating day at work, and not the meeting with Amelia she was heading to. If either of them have Telepathy, can they arrest me for thinking about black market Supers? The thought popped into her mind before she could do anything about it.

The older officer walked down the aisle and waved around a small scanning device while the woman withdrew her weapon and pointed it at each woman being scanned.

As they approached Kya, she winced slightly. The younger police officer moved in closer with her gun pointed at Kya's head. The older officer waved the scanning device over

Kya, and the light continued to blink red. "It's okay; it isn't her."

"Didn't you have a picture of her?" Kya stammered.

The older officer responded in a calm and even tone while using both hands to gesture slowly. "We do, but she has the Polymorph Super."

The female officer clenched her jaw and cleared her throat.

"So she could look like anyone?" Kya asked in a small voice.

The man maintained eye contact with Kya. "Her ability is limited to female shapes only, but otherwise, yes. Now please, stay calm and in your seat until we are finished."

His partner cleared her throat again.

"Young people these days. So impatient! We were all born Normal, you know." He said the last part with a laugh, but as he said it is eyes darted quickly around the bus.

Then they moved on. The male officer smiled politely at various people as the two officers continued sweeping through the bus. His partner never let her scowl lift. None of the travellers were found to be Supers, and the police vacated quickly. Just before completely exiting, the male officer turned back and smiled one more time. "Thank you, everyone, for your patience and understanding. Have a great night."

With that, he exited, and the bus was waved through the checkpoint. Kya finally let herself breathe a sigh of relief, glad they were unable to feel her anxiety regarding the black market Supers.

Kya was at the Noble Brew when Amelia got off work. The coffee house was mostly empty, and many of Amelia's co-workers were standing around, talking. Instead of joining them, Amelia quickly clocked out, grabbing her stuff and pulling Kya from the storefront into the hallway. No smiles and no goodbyes.

"You feeling alright?" Kya asked as soon as she had the chance. As they walked down the mall corridor, the advertisement for Supers came on, covering all the windows of the stores.

"Ugh, I just have so much to do!" Amelia said, striding briskly towards the bus station.

Kya fought herself to maintain her focus on Amelia. "You going to fill me in? You wanted to meet up with me."

"Yeah, I didn't want to text about it... I mean it's not exactly," she hesitated, but they both knew the unspoken word was "legal."

Kya raised her eyebrows and nodded slightly. "True."

"I'm just not sure I want a record of it on my phone."

"You want to slow down a smidge so we can talk about it?" Kya said nearly jogging to keep up with her friend.

Amelia complied and slowed her pace.

"So, you found out how to get Supers from the Black Market?" Kya said in a tone just above a whisper.

"Yes." Amelia matched her tone. "I found a guy. Five Supers for five thousand dollars."

"That's a thousand a Super," Kya said.

"Well... yes, Captain Obvious, it is. It's also five Supers for less than one-tenth the price of one through one of those government approved clinics." She gestured to one of the screens where the Supers advertisement was just ending.

"Okay, Amelia, but is it safe? I mean, like Sam always says, there are a lot of risks to getting Supers."

"I've done my research, K," Amelia said in a tone a little harder than Kya was used to.

Kya nodded. "Alright." She put her hand on her friend's arm.

Amelia turned and stared eye to eye with Kya.

"Just be careful," Kya said.

CHAPTER 8

Kya arrived back at her apartment, and her pent-up emotions drained her of her energy. Her concern for her friend, coupled with jealousy that Amelia could have Supers while she was still stuck as a Normal, both weighed on Kya's thoughts. Sometimes, Kya was surprised that she didn't lose her mind.

She removed her key from the lock and pushed open the door. She could smell pizza, something that she knew Sam reserved for days when he was feeling down. Before putting down her purse, she spoke loudly towards the slumped mass scarfing down a slice, "What's wrong?"

The apartment was darker than normal, as the blinds were all closed, and Kya noticed the light of Sam's new tablet reflecting off of his eyes. Sam looked at Kya, his face sagging slightly and his lips drooped at the corners. "You'll never believe this," he said his shoulders slumped. "They are going to release Myles. He'll only be in prison for five days."

Kya couldn't hold in her shock. She had expected something worse, something that actually had some bearing on

Sam's life, and on her life. She had to process each of the words in her mind, repeating them in sequence over and over before they had any meaning. After a wave of understanding finally hit her, the whole situation still confused her. "Wait. What?" She squeaked in a tone loud enough to echo through the entrance way.

"His lawyer convinced the government that he would be unsafe in the prison system and that he has cultural value to the country." Sam's words dripped with annoyance, and he sighed deeply before continuing, sounding like his teeth were clenched. "Myles posted his bail, of course. Twenty million, can you believe it? What a pile of... Kya, our world is broken. How can we teach kids right and wrong when this is what they have to look up to?"

Kya slipped off her shoes and placed her purse down. Walking over slowly, she sat next to Sam on the large couch, and Sam turned to look at the slice of pizza in his hand. Kya wanted to tell Sam something to improve his mood, but she couldn't think of anything that didn't sound like a weak platitude, and worse, she actually agreed with him: The world was broken.

Taking a large bite of his pizza, Sam turned his tablet to face Kya. On the screen was an article discussing the merits of releasing a celebrity like Myles Redwood because it was an accidental manslaughter and not murder. "Where's the justice? Can you believe that?" Sam's voice sounded colder to Kya somehow.

"No, I really can't," Kya said trying to keep her tone even, supportive and without her own emotional baggage.

Sam dropped his pizza back into the open box sitting on his coffee table. "Supers get away with more and more each day, don't they?"

"Well, it isn't just Supers. What about those thieves who robbed us?" Kya paused, making sure her thought was coherent. "They got away with it, and they weren't Supers."

Sam turned slightly to be able to face Kya better. "They got away with it because Supers only care about issues relating to Supers. If we had been Supers, we would have gotten the service we deserved."

Kya's mouth fell open in shock that Sam was expounding the virtues of having a Super. She listened intently.

"Supers make the laws, Supers are protected, and Supers get to do whatever they want. I sometimes feel like the whole world is set-up against Normals."

"Yeah, at the mall a couple of weeks back, there was a Normal trying to steal food for his family." Kya felt her pulse quicken slightly as she told Sam about the man leaping from the ledge, only to be caught by the Police.

"See the difference?" Sam said.

Kya shook her head. "No. The difference between what?"

"The guy at the mall and the jerks who robbed us." He continued before Kya could respond. "He was stealing from the system. The same system that puts Supers above us. They made an example of him, Kya. They said to everyone else in the mall that there is no sense in trying to get anything for free."

Kya nodded. "I got that message loud and clear."

"But when the guys robbed us?"

"The system gained," Kya said completing his sentence.

"Exactly! What did I do? I went and bought more stuff." Sam nodded and tossed his tablet onto the couch beside him in disgust.

"Yeah." Kya sighed. "Hey, they were searching for a Super on the bus today. I wonder what she did to get that kind of attention..."

"Well, it wouldn't matter if she were famous." Sam shuddered. "Friggin' five days! A woman is a widow, and a child will grow up without her father, and that brat gets five days!"

"It's just about the almighty dollar," Kya concluded.

She and Sam sat in silence for a while, the pizza going cold on the table.

 Kya didn't know how long they were sitting there when her phone buzzed. She took a deep breath before glancing at the screen. She had a feeling that it was going to be Amelia, and her phone confirmed it.

> *I did it*

Kya's mind processed the short message, and she felt too exhausted to respond. She turned to Sam and forced a grin. "I have to hit the sack. I'm exhausted. This day felt five times longer than normal."

"Only five?"

Kya stood up, stretched her arms towards the ceiling and yawned loudly. She caught Sam trying to stifle a laugh and felt a real smile cross her face.

"Hey, Kya?"

"Hmm?"

"Thanks for the talk."

As Kya's hand touched her bed, her whole body gave in, and she fell flat on top of her messy covers. With a bunch of pillows, some for decoration, and others for comfort on her bed, Kya stretched out, tossing them all onto the floor. She turned over and stared up at the ceiling. It wasn't long before she felt her eyes burning, and her mind wandering endlessly. Unable to focus, she closed her eyes to rest.

The next morning, Kya flipped over and tapped the button on her phone to turn off the alarm. Her cell beeped loudly letting her know it that it was running out of charge.

"Shoot! I forgot to plug it in." She said, speaking to herself and placing her right palm on her forehead.

"What's wrong?" Sam replied, peeking his head into her open doorway, seeming not to have heard the full statement.

"Nothing, I just forgot to charge my phone last night."

"Alrighty."

Kya looked down at her previous day's clothing and felt both uncomfortable and dirty. She trudged to the washroom feeling like a zombie. Stripping down, she jumped in the shower and tried to fortify herself for the day ahead. She knew that it was likely that Don and Leonard would both be in the office, and as much as she dreaded seeing them, she hoped that Elliot would be there as well. She thought about her conversation with Sam the previous night and basked in how nice it felt to be on the same page as her roommate again.

When Kya got out of the shower and back in her room, she noticed a message waiting for her on her phone.

>*K! I think it worked. We need to talk.*

Kya sent Amelia a quick text as she rushed out the door to work.

>*I'm on days this week, remember? I will try and call after work.*

Kya daydreamed of the Supers she could have all the way to work. She felt so frustrated that Amelia had done what she hadn't had the guts to even consider. On top of that, Leonard was on his way to being a Super too.

With mixed emotions, Kya arrived at the office. It was a quiet day at work as Mr. Georgetown had gone on vacation, Leonard was nowhere to be seen, and the young woman from the day before was still at the desk beside her and not saying a word. Unfortunately, Elliot was also nowhere to be seen.

Over her lunch, Kya asked a few random workers about Elliot, but no one had seen him since the middle of the previous week. A small pit of concern formed in her stomach as she thought about the old man who had befriended her so easily.

The rest of the afternoon, Kya mindlessly worked through her monotonous tasks, craving her evening shifts for the chance to wear comfortable clothes, listen to music, and just relax.

Just as she was getting ready to leave for the day, she received an urgent e-mail from Don Georgetown's secretary.

All Departments - Effective Immediately:

With the reduction in the Information Technology budget mentioned previously, and the recent restructuring, the Computer Operations department will now only be operational from 6 AM until 6 PM. The two staff in the department will be assigned mornings or afternoon shifts on a weekly rotation from here on out. Please adjust all of your data needs accordingly.

Kya sighed deeply, her elbows propped on either side of her keyboard she let her head slump into her hands. "Damn."

"I'm telling you, K," Amelia whispered to Kya over her dinner of salad at Coliseum, her favourite restaurant. She leaned forward and stared Kya right in the eyes. "I can feel it, coursing through my veins. Changing me."

Kya nodded, unsure of what - if anything - to say.

Amelia had texted her seven times throughout the day, insisting that they meet up, and discuss the BMS procedure that Amelia had gone through.

Kya's mind reeled, swaying from fear to hope, from

envy to excitement. She fought with herself about whether or not to meet up with her friend, and in the end it was curiosity that swayed her heart.

Amelia's eyes blazed with energy. Kya couldn't decide if it was passion or mania, but whatever it was it made Kya's stomach cold. She pushed her sushi around her plate with her chopsticks.

"It's amazing, K. I can't wait to hook you up." Amelia continued. "My powers," She whispered even quieter as she glanced around and then leaned in closer, "should all manifest within a week."

Kya glanced around and still didn't speak. Her mind drifted to the images she had seen of Myles after his first Super had manifested, and then each of the subsequent four and a quick flash of the wall where the paparazzi man, Newton Wilson's, life had ended.

"You have been saving for yours, right, K?"

"Hmm?" Kya raised her eyebrows, and returned to the moment, sitting in the Coliseum restaurant with one of her best friends. "Oh, yeah... I have some cash set aside." She pushed a smile across her face. *'Myles is a kid. We're adults. Lia and I will be fine,'* she told herself. She repeated it inside her mind and tried hard to believe it before taking a deep breath to calm herself.

"Don't worry, I'm going to wait for you, you know." Amelia continued, leaning back a bit and taking on a calmer demeanour.

"Wait for me?"

"Yeah. I'm going to wait for your Supers to manifest before I, you know, check out the fourth floor or ride the train. All those fun Super's privileges. We're going to do them together."

She sounded like the same old Amelia. Kya smiled genuinely at her friend, and the knot in her stomach seemed to loosen a bit. "Thanks, Lia."

Kya pushed the trepidation out of her mind and allowed herself to dream like the same old Kya that Amelia knew so well.

They sat and talked losing all track of time while discussing all the ways their lives would soon be better. They pulled up information on various Supers on their phones and weighed the advantages of one Super over another. Kya felt like she used to as a child in the weeks leading up to Christmas.

When she got back to the apartment, Sam was sleeping on the couch. She quietly covered him with the throw he had as decoration on his couch, and went into her room. She was relieved that he was asleep because she had no idea how to break the news about Amelia's Supers, and she didn't know if she could keep it a secret from him.

As the week wore on, Kya started to come to terms with the fact that her overnights were gone. She grieved the loss of that time, as she trudged through the monotony of her job and the politics of the office.

Elliot never showed up, and the more she asked around, the less comfortable she felt with his absence. She wished that she had someone else there to talk to about him, but she didn't like any of her other co-workers.

Having access to all of the data backups, Kya started digging through the available files to see if she could uncover any information on where Elliot had gone and why.

Friday came before Kya even had a chance to realize the week was ending. She barely spoke to anyone and spent her time at home researching Supers to figure out which five to pick. She also checked her bank account frequently to make sure her small sum of savings was still there. The balance of her savings account was in the black, stating $2875.78 was available. She knew that she could do some financial juggling to come up with the rest of the funds needed for the Black Market Supers, and that money was no longer going to be a barrier for her.

>Hey Kya, Mattea texted her on Friday just as she was leaving work. *I'd love to hang out soon. I feel like it has been a million years since I saw your face.*

>*I know Mattie.*

Work has been... Weird. No more overnights.

>*Oh, hey! That's awesome!*

Welcome back to the real world.

>*Not so awesome. You know how much I like people!*

>*Haha no doubt! I guess there will be a learning curve for you.*

But it means you'll have more evening time for the people who really matter.

>Like you?

>Well yes!

Kya chuckled to herself as she boarded the bus. It had been way too long since she had last spent time with Mattie. With everything else that had been going on lately, Kya knew she hadn't been giving nearly enough time to her friend.

>How are you and Rory doing?

>A lot better!

After doing research into Supers and pregnancy, I'm so glad we agreed to do Fertility before Supers.

Even if we end up having to live as Normals forever, it'll be better than the complications that could happen by doing Supers first.

Kya exited the messenger on her phone to throw on some tunes before texting back.

>I didn't know there could be complications.

>Yeah. It's scary! If you even do a quick search on the Net, it's shocking what you'll find.

Kya shrugged and looked out the window on the bus. She'd never seen herself as a potential mother, and it had never seemed relevant to research Supers and pregnancy.

>So, can we make plans to meet up sometime? Mattie asked.

Before Kya could respond her phone buzzed alerting her to another text message. It was Amelia.

>*It went wrong, K.*

Kya stared at the message. She didn't know how to respond. Amelia messaged again.

>*I swear!*

I think I'm dying!

Or maybe going crazy? This was a mistake!

The bus stopped at Kya's apartment. She got off, and her phone buzzed again. It was Mattea.

>*You still there?*

>*Yeah. Sorry. Amelia started texting me too.*

>*Okay. Well, I'm going to pencil you in for Monday night.*

>*OK*

Kya responded without even thinking. The image of the smashed wall from the news report on Myles Redwood and Newton Wilson flashed through her mind as well as Myles' scream during the extraction. She walked towards her apartment building.

>*Lia, what's wrong?*

>*It's too much.*

Help me!

CHAPTER 9

Kya thought about calling Amelia, but she knew that Amelia tended to overreact. She remembered the time Amelia was convinced that the guy walking down the street behind her was stalking her. She ended up walking half an hour away from her house to throw him off because she didn't want him to know where she lived. Then had she Kya meet her at the closest Noble Brew where Kya spent an hour convincing her that she was likely safe. But on the other hand, Kya knew that Amelia did just get five Supers.

Kya slowly dialed the numbers, and made the phone call.

"K?" Amelia answered immediately. It was obvious that she was trying to stifle her crying as her breathing lacked a normal rhythm, and there was something not quite right in her tone.

Kya spoke, keeping her voice even and calm. "Yeah. You okay?"

"No! I can't control any of them!"

"They're manifesting all at once?"

"Yeah. I don't know what to do!"

"You got five, Lia. It'll take time to manage them." Kya was standing outside her apartment as people streamed past her in both directions. She tried to decide what direction to walk. Standing still felt awkward.

"I don't know, K." Amelia sobbed, and her voice squeaked.

"Do you remember the time you had the hiccups and they wouldn't stop? You thought you had been poisoned. We tried a bunch of home remedies until they just randomly stopped."

"Yeah."

"Well, you survived that." Kya shuffled quickly through her memories. "How about that time you thought the guy was following you home?"

"Yeah." Amelia sounded like she was somewhere between laughing and crying.

"Or the time we went and saw that horror movie, and you were convinced it was predicting your future."

"Well, she did have black hair and worked in a coffee shop."

They both made a little laugh. Kya walked away from her building, not wanting to go up to her apartment and risk having this conversation in front of Sam.

"But, Kya, I feel like I'm going insane!" Amelia said.

"Did the guy you got these powers from say anything about the side effects?"

"He gave me some sedatives, told me to take them as I need them, and he said that the manifestation could be really intense." Amelia sniffed as she spoke.

"Have you taken them?"

"No. You know I don't like drugs."

They both gave a small, awkward laugh again.

Although she had seen evidence of it, Kya hadn't considered that there would ever be consequences to getting Supers and in her mind she chided her friend for getting so many all at once. "Amelia, you are impossible!" Kya started. "But, I think you'll be fine."

A stranger, a man older than Kya, walking along the sidewalk gave her a large amount of space as he passed. It was as though he was worried the drama, that he could likely hear, would spread to him like a disease if he got too close.

"You sure?" Amelia said. She still sounded rough.

"Well, yeah. You're a big girl. You can take care of yourself."

"How?"

"Okay. Do some deep breathing. Try and relax. You have

four options that I can see." Kya began in a calm tone, hoping she could help her friend find peace of mind. "You can go to the hospital and admit to obtaining Black Market Supers, you can take the sedatives and see if they help, you can try to distract yourself with a book or movie or meditation or something, or I can come over, and we can try to work out another solution."

"What do you think I should do?" Amelia's voice barely came through the speaker on the phone, sounding more like a scared child.

"Take the sedatives, and text me throughout the night. If I don't hear from you for like twenty minutes, I'll come by." Kya had walked around the block and was nearing the entrance to her building.

She didn't want to rush over to her friends place, but she also knew if things were reversed, she might want Amelia to come and help her. She took a moment to reflect on the changes that were happening in her life. It felt like the only safe thing, the only unchanging thing, was the tall apartment complex that she called home.

"Okay, Kya. Thanks." Amelia said after a long pause.

"Think you'll be okay?"

"Yeah. I think so."

"Hey, roomie!" Sam said, opening the door before Kya could put her key in the lock.

"What? How did you?" Kya replied with a questioning

glance.

"You have a distinctive way of jingling your keys." Sam smiled and extended his arm to grab her purse. "I made dinner for us."

Kya walked past slowly setting down her purse. "Hmm?"

"Spaghetti." He said and gestured towards the table that had already been set. "And salad."

"Very nice," Kya said, returning a smile. "But why?"

"Well, I know things have been rough lately, and I just thought it would be nice." He shrugged.

"Thanks." Kya sighed as she sat in her usual spot, and she suddenly felt exhausted and starved.

"You look like you need it," Sam said with a nod as he sat in his usual seat. "Long week?"

"You could say that." Kya served herself a generous helping of spaghetti and then loaded it with parmesan. "How is school going?"

"I'm getting my performance appraisal at the end of next week. Pretty nervous about that. But I really love my class. They have come a long way since I started with them in November. The school is also amazing. I hope I get a permanent placement there in September."

"That's awesome." Kya nodded.

Kya's pocket buzzed, and she took out her phone. The

message was from Amelia.

>*Feeling better. Thanks.*

Kya sighed then smiled and returned her phone to her pocket.

"Everything okay?" Sam asked.

"Yeah, Amelia's just going through some stuff."

Kya and Sam had a good visit over the rest of their dinner. Neither one of them mentioned Supers in any capacity. They talked about their jobs and life in general. They each told some jokes and just enjoyed each other's company. Every so often, Amelia would check in, which Kya appreciated.

After cleaning up from dinner, Kya and Sam sat in the living room together, music on, and both quietly locked their attention onto their electronic devices. Kya was surfing the Net and trying to decide if she wanted to see what a search for pregnancy and Supers brought up. The idea of motherhood had never really been in Kya's long term plan. She had hoped to maybe find a husband at some point in her life, but beyond that, her attention was focused on her friends and getting Supers.

Every so often, Amelia would text, and Kya would stop what she was doing and respond.

>*You know, I haven't taken those sedatives.*

I'm not taking them unless it's absolutely necessary.

>*Probably a wise choice.*

What did you end up doing to calm down?

>*I had a bottle of wine, put on classical music super loud through my headphones, and covered every mirror in my apartment.*

The music drowns out the voices.

The last text hit Kya hard, and a cold chill ran up her spine.

"Amelia, what did you do?" Kya whispered.

"Sorry?" Sam questioned and looked up from his tablet.

"Nothing," Kya replied with what she hoped was a casual smile.

As the evening wound down, Kya excused herself and returned to her room. Turning on her display, she programmed her on demand video service to play through random science fiction shows that had been released in the last five years. Kya felt that it was great background noise, as she rested on her bed.

After only moments of relaxation, her cell phone rang, instead of the normal text vibration that she was used to. She expected it to be a call from Amelia but was surprised when Mattie's face appeared on the display. "Oh, hey Mattie. What's up?"

"I just wanted to confirm we are still on for dinner on Monday. I said I'd pencil you in, did you pencil me in?"

Kya checked her calendar. The phone highlighted the current date, and she noticed that it was Friday. Tapping on

Monday, she then typed in *Dinner with Mattie*.

"Is there a problem?" Mattie said breaking the silence.

"Nope, I'm good. I just forgot which day it was today."

"You never change!" Mattie said, her grin showing through her voice.

"I hope that's a good thing."

Laughing, they both said their goodbyes and Kya turned her attention back to the movie playing. Before an entire scene had played through, Kya's phone buzzed again, and this time it was a text from Amelia.

>We should get together tomorrow. I think I have this figured out.

>Will do. Say around three?

>Perfect, see you then!

Kya got ready for bed, and as she thought about her day, she smiled. Her dinner with Sam lifted her mood, and for once, she didn't feel as anxious to get a Super.

The next morning, Kya got ready and wore her favourite geeky printed t-shirt. She waved at Sam, who was sitting on the couch, as usual, and she rushed out the door without a word.

She gave herself over two hours to get to the park and decided to walk instead of taking the bus. It would mean going to the edge of the city, a less than safe place to be, but she enjoyed the change of pace. Her headphones covered her ears, and the bass shook her eardrums as she basked in the melodies of her favourite walking songs. Kya couldn't remember the last time she just stopped everything and went for a long walk. The entire world was quiet, relaxing, and the occasional late spring breeze felt nice against Kya's sun-kissed skin.

As she walked, she took in the sights around her, and she was once again mesmerized by the graffiti of the silhouettes against vibrantly coloured scapes. She took her phone out and snapped a picture of one. It was an intense image. Painted as if the observer was looking over the shoulder of a silhouetted man. A distorted cityscape stretched out in front and below him. The depth of the image almost gave Kya the slightest vertigo, as she scanned the details with her eyes. The shadowed man was reaching out, his arms entwined with a more detailed figure, saved from his potential death. Kya was hypnotized by the seeming motion of the city caused by the iridescent paint, and she was drawn into the artistry of the man's face. Whoever painted this mural managed to capture both fear and immense gratitude in the face of the man as he looked upon his silhouetted saviour.

Looking at the screen of her phone, Kya was disappointed but not at all surprised that the image she had taken did not capture the magic of the mural in front of her.

Arriving at the park, Kya could see why Amelia had picked it, as there was no one around. The play structures were overgrown, and the paint had mostly peeled from the equipment. The grass hadn't been cut in a long time, and the sign, which once was where the city put its own rules and regulations, had been long since covered over with a sign by the corporation that had purchased the park. Rust, weeds, and cracked pavement were all that were left in the abandoned section of town.

Taking off her headphones and turning her music off, she looked around for her friend.

"Hey K, over here!" Amelia shouted, standing near the last two swings still in a reasonable state of repair. With nearly a street block of distance between them, Kya couldn't make out all of Amelia's features. She knew her friend looked a little different, but couldn't put her finger on what it was. In a blink, the distance between them was gone, and Amelia was nearly standing on Kya's toes. Her eyes were blazing in excitement. Kya stumbled but caught her footing. She almost fell backwards as her personal space was invaded.

"Isn't it great? I can teleport!" Amelia grinned wildly.

"That's awesome!" Kya said, regaining her composure. In her mind, she was wished Amelia would back off just a bit.

"Yeah, I guess I'm still having issues with things, but it is getting a lot better." She shook her head slightly stepping backwards two paces as she continued. "You know, I didn't mean to teleport so close. Sorry, K."

Kya opened her mouth to respond.

"I haven't actually done it much." Amelia started laughing lightly, "I'm still trying to figure it out." She took a deep breath and continued, her eyebrows knit together slightly. "Yes, I am trying to be careful."

Together they walked toward the swings.

Kya made a noise that would have started a word, but Amelia cut in again. "Oh, yeah. I have Telepathy as well. And Teleportation, as you saw, and Water Breathing."

Kya moved the hair from her face and pushed it behind her ear. Amelia followed suit, mirroring her movements. Amelia's hair changed, and the strands that were touched looked exactly like Kya's hair, right down to the faded purple streaks.

"What was that?" Kya exclaimed, forgetting about Amelia's mind-reading abilities for a moment.

"Oops, I don't have the best control yet. The other two powers I have are Body Manipulation, which is how I was able to mimic your hair and one called Adomopathy." Amelia's speech raced as she continued to explain. "I hadn't heard of it before either, but apparently I can copy any move or action I see. If I see someone pour a perfect leaf design on a latte, I can pour one the exact same way."

Kya listened intently as they approached the swing set, she turned and sat down on one of the old swings. While they were rather uncomfortable, she noted that they were also the only thing around to sit on that wasn't dirty or rusted, and that made them the best option.

Amelia continued with her examples without missing a beat. "If someone does ballet, and I see it, then I can do it too. I've always wanted to learn to play the guitar, and now I can. I just have to watch some videos online, and I'll know how to do it. Isn't that awesome?"

Kya smiled at her friend, and a little fear entered her mind. *Are all Supers so manic when they first get their powers?* Kya thought to herself.

"I don't know." Amelia responded. A look of fear entering her eyes.

"Please don't do that..."

Amelia deflated slightly. "Sorry. I am not really in full control of my abilities yet." Amelia was moving around slightly in the seat, next to Kya. The chains of the swing vibrated and squeaked loudly. "This is just so amazing. I feel like I can do anything."

Kya looked off at the edge of the park, where a tall tree was blowing in the wind and wondered, *how far could she teleport?*

In a split second, without a warning, the swing next to Kya was empty, and standing next to the tree was Amelia, waving back franticly. Standing up, Kya slowly lifted her hand to wave back at Amelia, but before she had waved once, her friend was back by the seat of the swing.

"I don't know how far I can go," Amelia said.

"Oh? How many times have you done that?"

"Maybe half a dozen now. I think I can go as far as I can see, though the guy that did this said that some people with both Teleportation and Telepathy can travel as far as friends or family they can focus on in their mind."

"That's really amazing. Is that why you picked those two powers? And that Adomo-thingy..." Kya was itching to ask what the procedure was like, and where she went, but she also wanted to give Amelia time to revel in and share the experience, instead of just focusing on her own selfish desires.

Amelia locked eyes with her and nodded graciously with her mouth closed. She took a deep breath through her nose and then smiled. "This place is wonderful, isn't it?" She sighed. "It's so quiet here."

Kya and Amelia sat on the swings without speaking for a few minutes. Birds sang in the trees and planes passed overhead.

"So..." Kya began, her heart racing slightly in anticipation of the change in subject.

"Nah, it wasn't so bad. Not that scary. It felt cold."

"Lia, please! Can you let me ask some questions? That's how a conversation goes." Kya said in a tone louder and sharper than either of them was used to.

"Yeah. Sorry," Amelia said with a kind smile. "I don't even realize I'm doing it sometimes. It is like I hear you say things without you moving your lips."

Kya nodded and looked at the grass by her feet. She kicked slightly, and the swing rocked.

"Let's try again." Amelia suggested and began pumping her legs to start swinging. "Anything you'd like to know, K?"

"Um, yeah." Kya began pushing her swing backwards and forwards more with her feet, but still keeping them planted on the dusty ground beneath her. "What was it like, you know, getting Supers?"

Amelia stopped pumping and stretched out straight as she continued to swing, she stared off into the sky, and Kya waited with baited breath as her friend seemed to be trying to put her own thoughts into words. "It wasn't too bad. I found the guy by doing some research online and emailed him to make an appointment. We met up, and he was a pretty big guy. He was over six feet tall, bald, and wore jeans, a t-shirt, and a suit jacket. At first, I was a little confused because he had me meet him near a grocery store at this end of town. He led me into a back entrance and moved a shelf. There was a hidden door behind it. Inside were two younger guys, sitting in big office chairs on computers."

Kya looked around at the desolation. Abandoned buildings surrounded them. "Were you scared?"

"Not really, no. I mean, everyone was friendly and nice, and the place was, well, clean." Amelia took a deep breath, her voice getting ever more excited. "Then he had me sit on an exam chair and locked my wrists in leather restraints. I think it was only because I wanted Supers so badly that I sat as still as I did when he injected me."

Kya didn't realize her mouth was hanging open until she started to talk. "Wow! Man! Amelia! What did it feel like?"

"The injection was cold. They stuck the needle in my chest - did you see Myles Redwood's extraction?"

"Yeah." Kya tried to block the image from coming into her mind.

"Well, that's where the needle goes in. It was like ice pumping through my heart." Amelia popped into being directly in front of Kya, causing her to jump. The swing empty and still moving, Amelia was grinning and hugging herself. "But a comfortable, pleasant ice. I could see my veins changing colour, and the iciness turned into a tingling, and I felt full of power." Amelia ran her fingers from the opposite shoulder down each arm. She seemed to be vibrating energy as she spoke, and Kya noticed her veins rippling with blue hues.

Kya's eyes widened at the sight, she dug her feet into the ground and stopped swinging.

"Oh, Body Manipulation," Amelia explained with a shrug.

"Was it one injection or five?" Kya asked as she leaned forward. She could feel her excitement rising.

"Five." Amelia said it lightly and continued. "But it didn't hurt, and each one was a new bunch of colours. It was amazing." She spun in a circle and appeared back on the swing. She started pumping her legs to keep swinging.

Kya sat and stared open-mouthed at her friend.

"Remember that freak out I had?"

"You mean, last night? Yeah, I think I might remember." Kya raised an eyebrow, and the right corner of her lips twitched as she tried to maintain a serious expression.

"I think that was just a little hiccough. The whole thing has been pretty easy except for that and of course, the constant noise of people thinking." Amelia sped through the last half of her sentence with a sigh.

Kya raised an eyebrow.

"I'll figure it out." Amelia smiled. "I can't wait to tell my sister about all thi-"

Amelia vanished. Kya looked all around the park, but her friend was nowhere to be seen. She got off the swing and walked more to the center of the park to get a clearer view. She turned in a circle and took in the sight of the old forgotten park in this old forgotten piece of the town, where she was suddenly all alone with the shadows getting longer as evening approached. Her pocket buzzed, and Kya took out her phone.

>So... I'm at my sister's. Sorry!

Kya breathed a sigh of relief, happy that her friend was okay. She contemplated how far Amelia had teleported. From here to her sister's is more than an hour drive away! Kya thought to herself as she pondered the best way home.

Kya's heart was racing as she started her long walk. With the closest public transportation station over halfway home and the excitement of her meeting energizing her body, she decided to walk the same way she had come.

Thoughts of having her own Supers rolled around in her mind, crushing every other thought that tried to enter. A pang of hunger was replaced by the thought of getting a Super that stopped her from needing to eat. Her legs began to tire as she sped through the seedy area back towards home, but the aching only made her long for a Super that would allow her to get home faster, or easier. As darkness washed over the area, Kya thought about Supers that provided better sight and night vision.

Occasionally she would get the sense that someone was following her, but when she would glance around, no one was there. She shook off the sensation and continued wandering in her fantasies of Supers.

Kya came home to a dark and empty apartment. She hummed a tune to herself as she took off her shoes, placed her keys in the bowl by the door, threw her purse into her room, grabbed her laptop and flopped comfortably onto the couch. She opened up her Internet browser and searched *popular Supers* as well as *list available Supers* in separate tabs. The results brought up various company pages discussing the merits of Supers, how the procedure worked, and the costs. She also found a few places that listed the available supers. Kya went through each one, and in a file to herself, she wrote out ones that interested her.

"Flight, Invulnerability, Telekinesis, no wonder people have trouble just picking five." Kya typed out several Supers from the list, including ones she had seen before - *Body Manipulation, Strength, Electricity, Size*. The list quickly ballooned to over a dozen different options. Some worked well together, but others were just flights of fancy with little use to her everyday life. There wasn't any rhyme or reason to her selections, but Kya felt more and more invigorated with each set of choices available to her.

Her excitement turned to daydreams, and soon her imagination drifted and Kya found herself fighting to remain awake. With her mind and body exhausted from the long day of walking, she closed her laptop, leaned over, stretched herself out on the couch and passed out.

CHAPTER 10

Sunday morning, Kya found herself back at work. Thankfully, most of the staff didn't have to work weekends, and it reminded her of the overnight shifts that she had lost. With her hair a little less cared for, and her more comfortable clothing, everything felt more relaxed than she had recently experienced. The day moved quickly as no one needed specific drives, so she was mostly on autopilot, making sure the server backups ran as required. Kya continued to research the various options available to her for Supers and felt her excitement rising as she imagined her life with them. It felt like she had been waiting her whole life to join a special club that was finally going to allow her membership.

Checking her bank account, one more time, she noted that she still had over two thousand dollars saved. While she wasn't going to be able to afford a full set of five Supers like Amelia, she didn't want to wait any longer to get her first ones. She about Amelia's manic behaviour and the video clips she had seen of Myles Redwood. She shook her head, two would be a good place to start.

She texted Amelia, her fingers stumbling over her phone's keyboard as she nervously typed.

>*I think I'm ready to meet your friend.*

Kya felt phantom phone vibrations in her pocket as she went about her day. She checked it religiously, awaiting a message from Amelia, but by the time she was packing up for home, none had come.

Kya arrived home, ate a small dinner, and turned in early. She tried not to get mentally hung up on her friend's lack of communication, but she perseverated on it for several hours before finally passing out.

In the morning, Kya woke up and immediately checked her phone again. Resending the message from the previous day, she wondered if she had been too vague and felt as though her dreams of a new life were slipping through her fingers. Feeling a tinge of worry, she grumbled and spoke softly to the universe as she prepared for another day at work, "I hope you haven't forgotten about me, Amelia."

As soon as Kya arrived at work, she wished she could turn around and leave. Leonard was at his new cubicle, dressed in his fancy attire, beaming about his Super procedure.

"I chose Electricity, just like Greg Stone. I figured since Starlife Technologies has been so great to me, why not model myself off of the President of our wonderful company?" Leonard spoke to a small group of people gathered near his cubicle, but he made sure to speak loud enough for the whole department to hear. "I can't wait for it to manifest. I'll be able to turn off all the power in the building just by thinking about it, and I'll never have to worry about a dead cell phone battery. The best part, if someone messes with me, I'll electrocute them like a human taser." He grinned.

Kya gritted her teeth and tried to tune Leonard out as she took her seat without anyone noticing and checked the logbook.

"Hey, Backups girl." A slightly shrill voice crawled over the walls of the cubicle and climbed into Kya's ear, causing her to convulse slightly. "You know if he's single?"

"Sorry?" Kya said, standing up to more easily see her neighbour. There was a nameplate on her desk: JADE LIU, the woman who had taken Elliot's seat. Her appearance was almost unchanged from the first time Kya saw her, not a hair out of place, nor a blemish to be seen. But today she wore a tight fitting, royal blue silk blouse over a low-cut, black lace camisole, her A-line skirt hit about mid-thigh, and with her legs crossed, Kya could see the top of her thigh-high stockings. Blue stilettos completed her outfit.

Jade nodded her head towards Leonard's cubicle. "You used to work with him, right? Leonard, is he single?" She popped open the top button of her blouse, and Kya, as well as anyone else that was taller or stood above her, could now easily see down her shirt.

Kya fought to maintain a neutral expression as her insides crawled with revulsion and her body tensed up. Swallowing hard to dissuade herself from heaving, Kya replied in as polite a tone as she could muster, "I'm not sure. I've never taken much interest in him or his love life."

Sitting back into her task chair, Kya hoped the conversation was over. She placed her elbows on her desk, and rested her head in her hands, sighing deeply.

"That's understandable. He is out of your league."

Kya slammed her eyes shut and tried to focus on her breathing in hopes of calming herself down, but instead of tranquility, she saw an image of herself pulling a chunk of straight black hair from the head of the annoying woman that she was learning to detest in ever greater amounts.

"Do you happen to know what happened to the person that was sitting there before you?" Kya asked, hoping that Elliot would return any moment.

"Yeah, I heard he quit."

Kya leapt from her chair and leaned over the cubicle wall. "What? Who told you that?" She spat out in confusion.

"I don't know. I didn't really care."

"It's just..." Kya stumbled over how to phrase her words and sat back down. "Why wouldn't he have told me?"

"Why *would* he tell you?" She could almost hear Jade rolling her eyes as she spoke.

Kya ignored the question and spoke more to herself than to her co-worker. "He was trying to save up for retirement. Why would he quit? It just doesn't fit. Plus, I thought we were friends..." She shook her head and stared at her screen. Thoughts of their lunches together hit her like a tidal wave, and she instantly had a hard time holding back tears.

"Whatever. He was old." Jade said, and it surprised Kya that she still thought they were conversing. "Old people rarely make sense. If you'll excuse me." Jade pushed her chair back, stood with no difficulty in her massive heels and strutted towards Leonard's cubicle.

"You're excused," Kya mumbled to her screen. Her stomach turned in knots of worry for Elliot, and she checked some old backups for any information on Elliot's resignation.

"Leah!" Don Georgetown hollered as he threw open his office door.

Kya rolled her eyes drew in a deep breath and pushed her chair away from her desk to better see her boss. "Yes?" She asked, ignoring the fact that he got her name wrong again.

"We have been looking for a way to cut back our Computer Operations department," he said as he walked to the edge of Kya's cubicle.

She groaned involuntarily as she noticed that attention was being drawn from Leonard's group towards her conversation.

"I know, I know, it's sad to see anyone go," he said with obvious mock sympathy. "But today is your lucky day!" He grinned.

Kya raised her eyebrows. "Oh?"

"You see, Tom has decided to move on to-" He took a deep breath, "other opportunities." He smiled, but it failed to meet his cold eyes. "So you are fortunate enough to keep your job." He tapped the edge of her desk, and spoke in an only slightly lower voice, "you know, if it weren't for this little bit of luck, it would have been you out the door." Then he began walking towards Leonard. "And how is our Golden Boy! Having a *shockingly* good day?"

Laughter erupted around Leonard and Kya turned her attention to the blinking orange lights with a sigh. She swapped the backups like the robotic arm she knew could someday replace her.

The cloud that loomed above Kya's head as she left work matched the dark clouds rolling around violently above her as she waited for the bus. It amused her slightly that her emotions matched the weather as so rarely happens. Just as the rain started pouring heavily, the bus arrived. She sat down, in her usual spot, and took out her phone to listen to some energetic music to raise her mood. It was only when she saw a text waiting from Mattie that she remembered their plans.

>*Hey Kya, is it okay if we meet at the Roseburg Cabin at King and 7? It's half way between us, and their rotisserie chicken is so yummy, and their secret sauce. Mmmm.*

Kya wasn't surprised Mattea would choose the family restaurant chain, and it had been her favourite place to eat for as long as Kya could remember. And it made it easy that there happened to be three in their city alone. Kya sent back a quick response.

>*Cool. I'm on my way. I'll be there in about 20 minutes.*

The phone buzzed only a moment later with Mattie's response.

>*Excellent! I'll leave now too. I should be about 25 minutes.*

Kya donned her headphones, put on her tunes and watched the scenery go by until she arrived at the transit station where she had to switch to the bus to take her to King Street and 7th Avenue.

At the station there were small groups of people, around fifty in total, huddled around the flat panel displays that hung from the ceiling every fifteen feet down the platform. On the screen were images of Myles Redwood, grinning as he was escorted from the jail. The word Live flashing on the screen took Kya by surprise as she quickly counted backwards to the evening Sam had told her of Myles' planned release.

The screens were all showing the same news station, and the announcer was midway through a speech about what had landed Myles in jail and his sentence of five days incarceration. Kya half listened, as she turned her attention to the display on the wall showing the status of the buses. The next bus she would need to take was on-time and would be there in two minutes. Kya walked over to the part of the platform where her specific bus would stop and leaned against the wall. She glanced around and from what she could see it seemed that the screens in the train station for Supers were displaying the same broadcast. She turned her attention to her phone.

"It wasn't fair, you know." A teenaged girl's voice was projected from the screen above Kya's head. "It's not like he could've killed the guy without the Super."

Kya refused to look up at the screen. Kya blocked out images in her mind of the crushed brick wall with blood still on it, and the trickle of blood down Myles' chest after the extraction. A fleeting thought of Amelia entered her mind, but a sudden shrill noise pulled her attention back into the station.

"We love you, Myles!" It sounded like a group of girls screaming as the shouts of praise overlapped each other.

"Really," This time it was the deep voice of a man, but Kya still refused to look up. "The paparazzi and all Normals should flat out avoid contact with Supers! That man caused his death by being in the wrong place at the wrong time."

Kya was extremely relieved to see her bus arrive. She shook her head at the commotion and got on, finding her way to her usual spot at the back.

As she arrived at the Roseburg Cabin, Kya's nose filled immediately with the smell of slow roasted, rotisserie chicken. She got a table for two near the window, and looked over the menu, even though she knew she was going to go for the white meat rotisserie chicken dinner with fries. She ordered an iced tea and waited for Mattea.

It didn't take long for a familiar face to appear in her peripheral vision as Kya sipped her icy beverage. Waving, Mattea noticed her and began to approach. The grin that spread across Mattea's face emphasized the roundness of her cheeks, her large green eyes sparkled with a friendly happiness as she raised her eyebrows in recognition of Kya.

Mattie's blond hair was cut in shoulder length layers that were meant to enhance her natural waves, but she always brushed them out, making it look more bushy and uncontrolled. It had been a long running joke that Mattie had mom hair, despite not having any children and being only a few months older than Kya. She wore little makeup, sensible flats, tan capri pants, and a purple collared tee shirt. Her large navy purse hanging from her left shoulder reminded Kya of the number of times that Mattie was able to produce nearly anything needed at any time, as though the bag had a magically unlimited supply of goods hidden away in it.

Kya slid out of the booth and Mattie opened her arms for a hug.

Kya slipped her arms around her friend.

"Don't squeeze too tightly," Mattie said causing Kya to loosen her grip.

"You not feeling well?" Kya replied stepping back and sliding back into the booth.

Mattie joined her and sat across from Kya, smiling wide, as she set her purse on the bench seat beside her. "Well, you know Rory and I have decided to focus on having kids. I was at the doctor's the other day." She paused as if getting ready to say something important. "I found out that the treatment looks good, so I could be pregnant right now." She grinned and gently touched her stomach under the table.

"Wow. That's great." Kya said with a noticeable lack of excitement in her voice. As she processed the information, a wave hit her. It was as though her lips had replied before her brain had understood the weight of the news spoken to her. "I mean, that's great!" She squealed. "Congratulations!"

Pausing again, her anxieties about being a parent caused Kya's mouth to completely dry out. She took another sip of her drink, and nearly finished the half a glass that had remained when Mattie arrived.

Before Mattie could respond, the waiter returned, and took her drink order, and asked if Kya wanted a refill. She nodded. When he left, the two friends looked at each other, and a smile crept along Kya's lips.

"We are so excited!" Mattie grinned. "It was expensive, but it's only getting more expensive, and you know I've wanted to be a mom for a long time." She sighed. "Rory finally gave in, admitting we'd never truly be ready, and that there wouldn't be a better opportunity than we have right now."

Kya's phone buzzed. She could tell that it was a phone call and was glad she had it on silent. She tried to discreetly pull it out to check who would be calling. It was unusual for her to receive phone calls.

Mattie raised her eyebrows in a questioning glance.

"Sorry." Kya shrugged as she tapped her phone to ignore the incoming call from her mom before putting it back in her pocket.

The rest of their visit progressed easily, and Kya realized how much she missed her friend. It was hard to say goodbye at the end of the night. Kya walked Mattie to her generic gray four-door car.

"Kya, it was so great seeing you again," Mattie said as she wrapped her in another hug. "Please, let's not wait another month between visits." She chuckled slightly, but Kya could hear the sincerity in her words.

"Well, hey," Kya began, not sure what she was about to say. "Want to come by tomorrow night for dinner with Sam and me?"

"Um, I'll have to clear it with Rory, but if he's good with it, I'd really like that."

"Oh, uh, you could invite him too," Kya said. It wasn't that she disliked Rory, but she could never think of anything to say to him.

"Maybe I will," Mattie said, though her tone told Kya, *'Maybe I won't'*.

Mattie got into her car, and Kya walked to the bus stop. On the way, she took out her phone to listen to the waiting voicemail.

"Hi Kya, it's mom. I was just calling to see how you were doing. Your brother, Ben, is graduating from University, with honours, in a couple of weeks, and I don't know if you remembered or if you're planning to go, but it might be nice to see you there. Dad says 'hi' too." Kya heard her dad grumble in the background. "Anyways, I'd better go."

The automated voice came on asking Kya what she wanted to do with the message. She pressed the option to save it though she was unsure she'd listen to it again, or even if she'd call her mother back to respond.

Tuesday night arrived in a blur. Kya sat slouched on the couch in the living room of her apartment with Sam and Mattie, worn down from her day at work. With a few finger foods placed out on trays, and drinks already poured, Kya raced through a rant about work, how her hours had changed, and life with Super Leonard.

"Why don't you just quit?" Mattea asked. "You are better than the crap you have to deal with from Don and now Leonard too."

"I wish I could!" Kya laughed. "But, sadly, I need the cash. The job pays well, especially considering it's a Normal job. Plus, Sam's a nice guy-"

Sam raised a questioning eyebrow at her which interrupted Kya's train of thought.

Continuing, she stuttered slightly. "But I don't think he really wants to carry me financially."

Sam tipped his glass to her and gave a half smile. The pint of pale golden beer sloshed around and foamed slightly as he took a small sip and held it firmly on his knee.

"I just have to stick it out there long enough to get Supers." Kya finished.

"That's ridiculous." Sam blurted out.

"Pardon me?" Kya asked. Her eyebrows were high on her forehead, and her voice was a touch higher than usual.

"Sorry, it's just Supers." Sam paused as if he were searching for the right words to use. "Everybody acts like Supers are the be all and the end all. Like they're the answer to every problem. It's ridiculous." He placed his glass on a cork coaster near the edge of the table and frowned, looking down at his half empty drink.

"Well, they do make things easier." Kya replied unsure of why Supers were always such a touchy subject for Sam. "I feel like we've had this conversation a million times."

"Okay," Mattea cut in turning on her motherly voice. "So let's change it up a bit. Why not focus on current events."

"Oh, here we go!" Kya said with a grin. "Myles Redwood was released yesterday."

"Yeah Kya, and we've never talked about him before!" Sam said with a friendly laugh.

"I saw a news report where people were giving their opinions on his release and his punishment. It seems that most people think that because his Strength is gone he's safe to be in the world. It was the Strength that killed that photographer."

"Newton," Sam said with his eyes closed. He took a deep breath and his face tightened.

Kya leaned in and wondered what he was going to say next.

After two short seconds, Sam opened his eyes wide, and with a look of determination on his face he spoke solemnly, "Newton Wilson."

Mattea leaned forward. "Sam, why do you remember his name?"

"It's important to me," he replied. "He was a victim of a senseless act that should never have been allowed to happen."

A breeze passed through the apartment causing Mattie to shiver visibly. Her choice in clothing was more suited for a bright, warm day than an evening in an air conditioned apartment.

Kya smiled as she noticed Sam turn on his phone to adjust the temperature of the apartment up a few degrees.

"It shouldn't have been allowed, you're right," Kya said. "But Myles is only just old enough to get Supers. He got all five of them from different companies."

"Exactly," Sam said.

"I'm not sure I get it," Mattea admitted.

"Myles cheated the system." Kya continued, "he secretly went to five different companies to get the Supers, and then he was overwhelmed by them. There was no way for any of the companies to-"

Sam cut in, stopping Kya from completing her thought. "Each and every company missed the mark with him." He continued, calmly but clearly. "If any one of them had done a simple Internet search they'd have found that he'd been to other clinics. The system failed him."

Taking a loud deep breath, Mattea caught Kya's attention. "I think Myles could have chosen to be responsible, instead of cheating the system that is in place to regulate these things."

"Supers are dangerous," Sam said. "How and where can Super Strength *not* be a dangerous weapon?"

Kya opened her mouth to respond.

"It's a rhetorical question," Sam said.

"So," Mattea began with a small smile on her face, accentuating her round rosy cheeks, "you don't think that Myles was to blame?"

"That's not what I'm saying!" Sam said. "If a person is shot, the person who pulled the trigger on the gun is guilty, not the gun itself." He opened his hands wide, and Kya noted his tone and gestures had become more professorial in nature. "But if the gun was never in the person's hands..."

"No one would have been shot," Mattie said finishing his thought with a nod.

Kya stood, as she took the last sip of her drink and contemplated Sam's words. "Can I get either of you a refill?"

"More water would be wonderful!" Mattea said with a good-natured smile. "Thanks."

Sam shook his head 'no' then turned his attention to Mattea. "No wine? I think we have a Zinfandel, you like that stuff, right?"

Grabbing Mattie's cup, Kya went into the kitchen and began to pour the drinks, but thankfully she could still see and hear her friends.

"I do," Mattie nodded, "But Rory and I are trying to have a baby."

"Oh, that's cool," Sam said. "A test-tube baby?"

"Sam!" Kya scolded from the kitchen. Her head swiveled and her eyes locked on Sam. Distracted, Kya continued to pour the water, and as it streamed onto the floor over the sides of the glass, she mentally chided herself.

With a calming smile, Mattea responded. "You could say that, yes."

Kya came back into the room with a glass of Zinfandel filled nearly to the brim and a still overflowing glass of water. Passing the water to her friend, she took her seat back on the couch, a full cushion away from Sam.

"Hey, Mattie," Sam said leaning his elbows on his knees. "Do you mind if we talk about genetics?"

"You mean, genetic modifications to the embryos?" Mattea clarified.

"Just so you know where I'm coming from, I mean no disrespect, I just want to understand better. You see, I'm not sure I'm comfortable with the whole idea of designing a perfect child the way they advertise it. Some of the things you can modify, like personality traits. Why not just let your kids decide if they like music or sports or books or math? I feel like it's weird to choose that stuff for them, isn't it? Or am I out of place in thinking that?"

"Well," Mattea shrugged, "Selecting specific personality traits doesn't guarantee they'll like those things, but it does kind of lead them in those directions. We didn't do that. We agreed that we wanted our kids to gravitate to whatever is natural for them."

"The idea of picking what they look like is interesting,"

Kya said, taking a sip of her drink.

"I think I'd rather see a natural mishmash of me and my lover in my kids," Sam said.

"You have a lover?" Kya said with a grin and a wink.

Sam threw a small pillow at her in a knowingly playful way, and they both laughed.

"Rory and I thought the same thing as you, Sam," Mattea said, ignoring the exchange between Sam and Kya. "In fact, the only gene manipulation we did was to filter out diseases."

"See, that part is cool," Sam said. "Did you filter out the fertility problem?"

"No," Mattea said. "They don't know enough about what is causing it to be able to filter it out."

"That is so weird to me." Sam's brow furrowed and he ran his hands through his hair, taking a deep breath before continuing. "I have spent a lot of time thinking about this. I have a class of fifteen kids, the media presents it as a good thing," Sam changed his voice to try and sound like a news broadcaster, "smaller class sizes mean a greater quality of education." He cleared his throat and continued in his natural voice. "stuff like that. But even with smaller class sizes we have an absolute surplus of teachers, and each year schools are closing without new one's opening. None of the kids in my class have siblings, none. And I have talked to other friends of mine who are teachers, and it is rare to have two kids from the same family in the school. Maternity leaves are a rarity too."

"But education isn't the female dominated industry it used to be." Kya cut in.

"I know, I'm proof of that," Sam said with a smile. "But think of how few pregnant women you see just around on the street."

Mattea nodded knowingly, but Kya simply shrugged.

"One could argue that priorities change, and more and more women are choosing the working professional route, and not opting to start families," Mattea said, raising an eyebrow.

"Yes." Sam leaned toward Mattea. "But don't most women have that internal clock that tells them they *need* to have children?"

Kya thought for a moment while her friends continued the conversation.

"You know that I do." Mattea laughed and put a hand on her belly.

Sam turned his attention to Kya.

"I haven't thought about it," Kya said with a shrug. "I mean I haven't exactly shut the door on being a mother, but it just hasn't really been a priority for me."

Both girls stared at Sam and waited for him to continue.

"Well, isn't it weird that we can give people the ability to fly? We can make them invisible; we can engineer a child to be a tall, blond, astrophysicist, surfer, who is immune to most diseases, but we can't figure out how to fix whatever has taken away our ability or maybe even just our desire to replicate naturally?" He polished off his drink.

Kya and Mattie both shrugged. Unsure of what to say, Kya popped several small squares of Swiss cheese into her mouth.

CHAPTER 11

The alarm surprised her as she rolled over and placed her palm on her phone. The conversation at dinner with Mattie and Sam still danced around in her mind a week later. As she slid the phone towards her face, she half opened her eyes. She noticed the time, 5:30 am, and a dozen notifications listed.

"Amelia?' Kya gasped as she sat up and began reading through the thirteen text messages Amelia had sent since midnight.

>Kya, I can't do it. I've tried, but it is TOO MUCH!

They won't shut up!

Shut up!

Seriously... I need help... You don't know. You don't want to know.

Kya, where are you? I need you to, like, talk me down or something...

Help!

Help me!

I'm calling you.

Why the hell didn't you answer?

I can't even focus my Teleport, I've been all over the place!

Can't even stay in bed.

You know what, K? I can handle this. I've got an idea. It's all good. Don't worry.

Don't worry.

After reading the messages, Kya leaped out of her bed. As she grabbed some fresh clothing, her mind raced. She knew she wanted to find Amelia, but didn't even know where to start.

Frustrated, she looked at the time again and felt like each minute was dragging her further from being able to help her friend. The blinking notification reminded her of the waiting voicemail.

She pushed frantically on the screen and retrieved the message. It started with a sniff, and then words broke through, "Kya?" Amelia's voice pleaded. "I can't control my body, I can't control how I look. I keep jumping all over the place... But worst is the voices. All those thoughts, all that misery, all the criticism. I tried to drown myself... I found myself on the beach, and well you know how I can't swim? I walked out as far as I could, then walked farther... I totally submerged. But this stupid Water Breathing! I couldn't even drown!" Amelia's voice sounded like she was trying to force a laugh, but instead it turned into small sobs. "Kya. I made a huge mistake, and I don't know what to do."

The message ended abruptly, and the automated voice prompted Kya to choose what to do with the message, but she just hung up without choosing any of the available options. Kya stopped her frantic preparations to leave, sat on the small throw rug beside her bed, pulled her knees up to her chest and tried to breathe deeply.

She opened the text messaging application on her phone and began crafting her series of messages in hopes that Amelia's panic attack had once again passed.

>Amelia, are you okay?

I just saw all your texts and heard your voicemail.

I'm so sorry I wasn't there for you. I guess my phone was on silent.

Kya waited for a response, but none came. She stood up and started getting ready to leave. After she was dressed, she checked her phone again and was frustrated to see there was still no response.

>Amelia, please respond. I am so sorry I wasn't there.

I understand if you're angry and don't want to talk to me.

Please just tell me you're okay.

As Kya walked to the bus station, she checked her phone again and noted that there was still no response. She tried calling her friend, and it went directly to voicemail.

"Amelia, it's Kya. Please, let me know where you are and how you're doing." She sighed deeply, pausing slightly before continuing. "I'm really worried about you."

A city bus rushed around the corner and slowed near Kya. As it stopped inches from her feet, she was hit with the realization that she had to go to work. The bus that would bring her to Amelia's apartment wouldn't arrive for another ten minutes, and by that time, she would be late for work. As she looked at the bus driver, through the open door, she sniffled, trying to hold back her emotions.

"Coming on?"

Kya struggled to lift her foot and placed it heavily on the first step of the bus. Pulling herself onto the bus took a Herculean effort as she slid one foot in front of the other until she sat in her regular spot. As soon as the door slammed shut, she felt like she was further abandoning her friend, but a selfish voice inside her mind reminded her that she would lose her job if she called in at the last minute.

The bus stopped, and a loud, manly voice pushed Kya from her persistent worry about Amelia. "Ma'am, this is your stop, isn't it?"

Standing, and shuffling towards the door, Kya nodded slightly at the bus driver. Without a word, she dropped down onto the sidewalk, and the bus quickly sped away. She didn't know if she wanted to turn around and jump on another bus to get her to Amelia's, or enter into the large glass and steel building in front of her.

The conflict between her desire to try to help Amelia and her need to continue to earn an income battled inside her, and Kya took out her phone and dialed her friend's number again. When, after a single ring, the voicemail message began to play, Kya dropped the call and stared angrily at her phone. She wondered if Amelia was angry at her for not being around in her time of need and felt a little of her anger begin to mix in with her worry. Kya decided to go to work, she would search for Amelia after.

Her cubicle was a mess, as papers were strewn about. It was as disorganized as she had left it during her previous shift. Hard drives were in various piles, and a note she had left herself on her keyboard reminded Kya that she needed to put an extra drive in place for the Accounting department.

She sighed and slumped into her chair she decided to check a few things on her computer before searching for the drive she needed.

"Oh, hey backups girl," Jade said in an overly sweet tone from the desk next to Kya's.

"What's up?" Kya responded in a flat and unimpressed tone.

Jade came to stand over Kya's desk; she was wearing a beige pencil skirt, pink stilettos, and a matching pink wrapped cardigan that tied up around the waist over a black camisole. Kya looked at her own gray pants, her green button up blouse and her sensible black shoes. Kya had her hair pulled back in a low ponytail that hid her purple streaks, and she wore no makeup. Although she didn't usually care about how she looked, working next to Jade made Kya feel like maybe she should.

"I'm going to need you to do something computery for me. I have to run some tests today, and I'm going to need a free drive to play with."

"That might not be possible, the accounting department," Kya pointed to the note she had written herself, "is needing an extra drive today. I'm already going to have to shuffle some stuff around."

"Look, your job is not rocket science, and I know you don't actually care about any of it." All of the sweetness had drained out of Jade's voice. "But I do care. Don has asked me to do this work, and I expect you to make it happen for me."

Kya shrugged and stared at her screen and opened her email.

Jade snapped her fingers twice, and Kya could feel her cheeks get warm as anger and stress bubbled inside of her.

"Seriously, Backups-"

"My name is Kya!" She snapped. "How hard is that? Seriously, it's ridiculous! I have worked here for three years!"

"If you wanted to be taken seriously," Jade snapped back, "You should have started taking your job seriously three years ago."

Kya could feel the eyes of everyone else in her department on her and Jade.

She grabbed a blank drive from her desk drawer and placed it on the pile. Taking a sticky note, she affixed it to the drive and wrote in block letters, ROCKET SCIENCE. "There! You have a drive."

Kya turned to watch Jade slither back into her chair and took a deep breath. She tried to calm herself as she pulled up the file listings from the security database for entries and exits over the last few weeks. She queried Elliot's entrances into the building and found the last time he had come to work.

The file listing also included the security cameras that captured his entrance, and the time codes relating to the files. Kya grabbed the hard drives related to the security feeds and placed them into the hot-swappable drive slots in her desk. She queued up the files and before pushing play, stood up and looked around. Everyone had stopped focusing on the Computer Operations area and was going about their business normally. Despite the lack of trust towards Computer Operations, Kya felt that she had a moment of opportunity to look through the files she had queued up.

Kya sat and pressed play. The first file showed Elliot arriving and parking his car in the underground parking lot before following him into the building. She scrubbed through the video quickly, watching events play out at five times their normal speed. It wasn't long until she saw herself in the video having lunch with Elliot, both of them laughing and smiling as they took the time to reinforce their friendship while working at a job they both disliked. It was moments like that which Kya missed so deeply.

The video continued to speed forward, and Kya watched as Elliot toiled away at his desk. The hours passed by in minutes until the office began to darken. Late in the evening, no one was left in the video feed, other than the now exhausted looking Elliot.

Kya gasped as the obese form of Don Georgetown entered the frame. She slowed the playback to its normal speed, her eyes glued to the screen. Don pointed at Elliot, and he looked less than pleased. As Don grabbed Elliot's chair, a look of fear crossed Elliot's face. Don pulled the chair out from under Elliot and tossed it backward.

Elliot fell slightly out of frame before standing up and turning to face his boss. The behemoth of a man filled most of the frame of the video. The lack of audio meant Kya couldn't hear their exchange, but she could tell it was heated. Even Elliot, who had seemed rather meek in previous confrontations, seemed to have his back up and, by the look of strain on his face, seemed to be shouting at Don. The argument continued for several minutes before Don reached out and grabbed Elliot by the neck. Just as his sausage fingers lifted the small aged man off the ground, the video stopped.

As she stood up, Kya checked to make sure no one was watching her. Shock and confusion raced through her mind. She sat down and tried to load up alternate angles of the scene she had just witnessed, only to find the recordings missing. She decided next to check the secondary backups from that evening, only to find those drives all completely blank. She was used to such roadblocks and ran the data recovery software on her computer. She sighed as it came back with a response of *zero files recovered*.

Changing tactics, Kya loaded up the video covering Don Georgetown. Scrubbing through the video at ten times the normal speed, she watched her boss go through his day. Just as the scene with Elliot began, the video cut out once again.

Kya's frustration bubbled as she wracked her brain for a workable solution. Checking the logs, she noticed that Don Georgetown checked out of the building soon after, while Elliot did not. Changing to the underground parking, Kya watched Elliot's car. The hours ticked by, the image unchanging, until the next morning. A tow truck came, hooked up the aging car, and dragged it from the underground lot using Don's security access card.

A terrifying conclusion hit Kya like a ton of bricks. *Elliot was dead, and Don Georgetown killed him.*

CHAPTER 12

Kya closed all of the open programs on her computer and scrubbed clean her file history. She spent the rest of her day focusing on the drives. She kept her interactions with her coworkers to a minimum and was painfully aware of the lack of vibrations from her phone. She made sure she had everything set up for tomorrow and left as soon as the minute ticked over for the end of her shift.

She called Amelia as soon as she was through the door to her department. It went straight to voicemail.

"Listen, Amelia, I have had pretty much one of the worst days of my life. I'm really freaking out here, and I need to know that you're okay. If I don't hear from you, I am going to the police. I mean, I already have to go there anyways. I wish I could talk to you about it." Kya paused and reflected on what she had witnessed. "No joke, my friend. I swear, call me now or I'm going to tell the cops that you're missing."

Kya ended the call and could feel her body shaking. Her mouth was dry, and she couldn't stand still as she waited for the bus. She silently berated herself for never getting her license. The bus couldn't come fast enough. She kept looking behind her for fear that she had been followed, that someone had caught onto what she was planning to do.

The bus arrived after what felt like days, and Kya tried to act as normal as possible as she took her normal seat. She hugged her backpack and stared blankly out the window, her knees bouncing uncontrollably.

Kya checked her phone as she got off the bus near the police station and saw that there were still no new messages. With thoughts of Elliot's presumed murder, and Amelia's disappearance, a wave of nausea and tension washed over her as she walked up the stairs towards the door.

"I need to report a crime," Kya announced with a shaky voice as she walked through the entrance to the police station. It was the same station she and Sam had been in nearly three weeks ago to report the break-in at their apartment.

The officer at the desk, thankfully, not the same one as before, looked up and raised his eyebrows. "Oh?"

"Yeah." Kya swallowed and licked her dry lips, not sure of how to continue.

The officer stared at her for a moment and then, looking disinterested, he returned his attention to his computer screen.

"A murder." Kya blurted loudly. "I work in computer operations at Star-"

"A murder?" The officer interrupted, with a still disinterested tone, his eyes still focused on the screen. "Was a Super involved?"

"Yes!" Kya said, frustrated at the interruption. "I work at-"

"You saw the murder?" He glanced back at her.

"Yes. Well, no. Well, kind of. I-"

"Listen, I have a lot of work to do, and I don't have time for games."

"If you would just let me speak!" Kya's brazenness surprised her.

The man folded his hands, placed them on the counter between them and stared at her with a blank expression. "You do realize I could arrest you."

"What?" Kya realized her approach was getting her nowhere and took a deep, calming breath. "Sorry."

"Okay." He sighed with slight smugness. "Now I'll listen to you, but make it quick."

"I work at Starlife Technologies. In-"

"Computer operations." The officer smirked, his hands still folded on the counter. "Yes. Continue."

"Do you want to take down some notes?"

"No."

Kya shrugged, she could feel her temperature and pulse

rising again. "My boss is Don Georgetown."

She waited, but the officer did not react to the name.

"Anyways, a friend of mine, Elliot Shepherd, went missing..." Kya proceeded to tell the officer about Elliot's disappearance and the videos.

"So, you didn't actually see the alleged murder. And you have no evidence that it happened."

"No."

"Nothing we can do then," he said with a cold smile.

"Please, listen to me." Kya could feel tears welling in her eyes and her throat tightening. "Bad things are happening." She took a deep breath. "My best friend, Amelia Bronsen, she's gone missing too."

"So your boss killed her too?" He said with a raised eyebrow.

"Um, no." Kya gritted her teeth and tried to explain. "Amelia has nothing to do with what happened at work."

"Okay then, were Supers involved?" The officer asked with a yawn, making no effort to hide his annoyance.

"I think she went to get Black Market-"

The man's face turned hard as stone and stopped Kya from continuing. He forcefully pointed to the door behind Kya.

"Get out," he growled.

"Pardon me?" Kya whispered.

"If you don't leave, I'll call the Psychs and have you locked up. Did you forget to take your meds?"

Kya couldn't help but sob deeply and slowly. Like a cold wave, the realization that she was alone, and half the people she cared about were missing crashed over her. "I'm not crazy, my friends are gone. I need help."

"Okay, look... If your friend was stupid enough to go to the Black Market, she's probably already dead. But if she's not and we find her, I assure you, worse things will happen to her." The officer said his voice quieter than before. "But, if you stop crying and transfer ten thousand dollars into my account, I'll open an investigation into your friend. Eli was it?"

"Elliot Shepherd." Kya fought to regain control of her voice and her emotions. "He worked at Starlife with me. I can get you the logs and files that show he didn't leave and that his car was towed and that my boss -"

"Just transfer the money and I'll start writing the report."

"I don't have that kind of money, but I really need your help. I don't know what else to do."

The officer pushed a button, and the window blacked out. All the sounds from beyond the glass pane became muffled.

Kya couldn't see anything through the window. She felt like slamming her fist into something, anything, but knew that it would only serve to get her locked up for harassing the police.

As she exited the police station, heat bubbled inside her. Her heart pounded, and she felt like she could explode. Kya looked up into the sky and released a visceral scream in hopes of quenching her anger. It barely helped. Her heart pounded in her chest, and her throat felt like razor blades had sliced it.

She walked over to the bus station and noticed a small computerized sign blinking. A message scrolled across the screen: *bus service suspended until further notice.*

Kya kicked the base of the bus shelter as hard as she could. Her foot immediately sparked with pain, like electricity shooting up her leg, and numbness caused her foot to feel as though her toes were missing. It felt like steam was coming from her ears as she clenched her jaw and began to shuffle slowly towards her apartment. With over an hour walk ahead of her, Kya hoped that the time would be both therapeutic and beneficial. However, as each step caused a refreshed pain, her anger only grew.

She crossed half a dozen blocks with no memory of how she got there. Looking up, she noticed that the street was lined with active displays. A voiceless news reporter mouthed her report while an emergency message was scrolling along the bottom. Kya continued walking as she read the report being repeated on dozens of screens along the street as it cycled back to the beginning. A picture of a young, thin, brown-haired man wearing what looked like a suit jacket, dress shirt and tie took up a quarter of the screen with the word *fugitive* above his head.

All bus transportation services have been suspended while police look for a fugitive. A Super by the name of Reggie Vanbeek. He is to be avoided at all costs and is extremely dangerous. Those taking the trains today...

Kya knew the reporter would discuss how extra precautions were being taken on the trains, and that all Supers would get home without delay, as usual. Her eyes fell towards the sidewalk as she continued her painful march home.

She couldn't stop her mind from racing, despite her foot trying to distract her as it throbbed from the kick of the bus shelter followed by the long walk home. Even while lying down in her bed and putting it up on some pillows, the aching was endless. The towel-wrapped ice pack was mostly melted after an hour of balancing on the end of her foot and the painkillers she had taken barely touched the overall ache.

Thoughts of Amelia and Elliot weighed heavily on her mind. Kya worried that they were both dead and that there was nothing she could do. She tried, with some difficulty, to push such negative thoughts from her mind, and formulate a plan. She knew at best they were either trapped or injured. Unsure of where they were, or what state they were in, she knew she had to think her way through to a solution.

Kya tapped bullet point notes into her phone. It's light illuminated her otherwise dark bedroom. She knew that she was not going to be respected by the authorities unless she found a way to get Supers. She knew that if she could get Supers, she could use them to find a way to help Amelia and Elliot. She also knew that getting time off work would make things easier. Writing a simple plan in her phone, she immediately felt better, and it calmed her enough that she could finally fall asleep.

As she arrived at work, Kya felt confident that her plan from the previous night was going to work and that she was going to be able to help Elliot and Amelia. She took her phone out of her pocket, still disappointed that there was no response from Amelia, and she sent her friend a quick text.

>*Hey Lia, hope everything is alright. I miss you. I have a plan... So, text me if you don't need my help. Text me if you do. Just text me, okay?*

She closed the application and looked at the notes on her phone. She made a mental note to read over her plan whenever her resolve would waver, but immediately, upon seeing Don out of his office, she felt nervous that he knew she had been digging through the security files. Kya kept her head down and moved quickly, trying to slink by the crowd that included Don, Leonard, Jade and a few others from the IT department.

"Hey everyone, look who it is." Leonard pointed at Kya with a mischievous grin on his face and everyone turned and looked. A spark shot from a nearby socket and hit Kya in the hand.

Kya's hand went numb as the spark dissipated, and a faint whiff of burning flesh wafted up and into her nose. Turning, she glared at Leonard.

Leonard resumed his attack on Kya. He stood straighter, continuing to boast, "I remember when I was that useless. Thankfully, for me, it was only a temporary state of being."

The crowd roared with laughter, and Jade, who had been standing so close to Leonard that her hand occasionally brushed his, smiled. She wrapped her arms around Leonard's shoulders and leaned into him.

The display was enough to turn Kya's stomach. She sat in her task chair and opened her e-mail. She typed furiously.

Dear HR,

I am requesting a sick leave of two days, tomorrow and the day after, to deal with some health concerns. Please confirm that this is okay.

Thanks,

Kya Roberts

Computer Operations

Kya exhaled deeply and closed the email application. She checked her drive bays for orange lights, but there were none. The drives weren't used overnight, and it would still be several hours before the machines needed someone to tend to them.

"Hey, Kira!" Leonard called as he turned her computer screen off and on from across the room.

"You know my name is Kya," she whispered to herself before turning to acknowledge Leonard.

"Don wants to see you!" Leonard said, with the same mischievous grin he had when Kya had been shocked.

As Kya was about to stand she got an email alert, and

she decided to take a moment to read the response to her request. Her heart had sunk before she had even opened the message, as the reply came from Don Georgetown. Opening the message, it said nothing other than, *Request Denied.*

"Come on, Cara. We all know you don't have any pressing work to do right now."

Kya stood and walked over to the group of people.

Don grinned at her as she stopped at the far edge of the circle of people. With Don at one side and Kya at the other, half a dozen people on either side were primed for their exchange. "I have a special project for you, and I will need you to be here two hours early tomorrow."

Kya nodded, her mouth dry. "What is it?"

"Too much to go into right now, I am a busy man, you know." Don Georgetown boomed. "Just be here early tomorrow. Now back to work with you!" He said, swatting his hand at Kya like she was an annoying bug.

Returning to her desk, she checked her cell phone and noticed there was still no messages awaiting her. Opening up the messaging application on the phone, she typed to Mattea.

>*Hey Mattie, please contact me. I know you're still working, but as soon as you're done, please. I'm having a really rough time right now, and I could really use a friend.*

The rest of the day went off without a hitch, despite Kya's nerves that it would not. She ate her lunch in her cubicle, and only moved to switch around the hard drives in the massive arrays. She became slightly paranoid about attracting attention, especially more attention from her boss. Her brain crafted various scenarios. Some of her imaginings even had her being killed by Don in some horrible way.

As she left the building, a large weight seemed to lift from her shoulders. Her muscles ached from being so tightly wound, and she wiped a bead of sweat from her brow. The fresh air chilled her, and she was anxious to get home. She tried to mentally focus on finishing her week at work and then carrying out her plan.

The next morning, Kya arrived early for her shift. Yawning, she noticed that the only other person present, in the department, was her boss, and he had a smarmy grin plastered on his face.

"So, the new project is waiting for you in your area. Go and have a look."

Kya walked around the corner and saw a large metallic object moving around in front of the drive bays. It was a large, robotic arm. It was nearly silent as it moved, picked up a blank drive and placed it in an open slot. A screen next to the drive bays showed the request and its fulfillment.

"State of the art. We had it installed last night. We wanted to make sure we had a backup for the machine's first day, but after that, we won't need you anymore." Don gestured towards Kya's cubicle. His words dripped with contempt. "You'll find a small severance envelope on your desk. Not that you deserve it."

CHAPTER 13

Kya stared at Don open mouthed and in shock. She blinked slowly, three times, as her boss ran his hand through his thin hair smoothing down his comb over. His lips were slightly upturned; he grinned at her victoriously.

"You want me to watch over the machine that's replacing me?" She asked in a flat tone.

Don Georgetown nodded, his grin turning into a full, toothy smile.

Kya could smell the bitter, burned coffee on Don's breath as she thought through her current situation. "What if I decide just to break it?" Kya asked.

"We both know you won't do that." Mr. Georgetown replied in a calm voice, but Kya noticed a definite malicious energy emanating from his eyes.

Images of his hands around Elliot's throat flashed in Kya's mind, and she nodded her agreement to his statement.

Kya took her seat at her desk and set about watching over the shiny new robotic arm.

Leonard came in amidst a rush of others. Kya knew the train must have just dropped them all off. He came walking towards her, and she felt her spine stiffen as she prepared for his assault.

"Hey, Kya," he said in a gentle tone, just above a whisper.

Kya turned to stare at him, unsure of how to respond. If she didn't know better, she would have sworn he looked sad.

"I'm sorry things turned out this way." He took a deep breath, closed his mouth and exhaled through his nose before continuing. "But that's the game." He shook his head as he spoke, glanced around quickly and then leaned in closer to look Kya straight in the eyes.

She was confused by Leonard's behaviour, but she tried to maintain a hard expression. She stared him in the eyes, even though she would have much rather looked away.

"You are smart and talented, and I hope you find out how to help yourself succeed," he continued.

The words hit Kya and rang in her ears. She couldn't remember the last time someone had said such positive things to her and it bothered her that Leonard was the one saying them. She wanted to say *if you knew that, why have you been such a jerk for the past three years*, but instead she stayed silent.

He patted her on the shoulder and said loudly. "See ya, Keea! Ha! It rhymes!" And he turned from her to walk away.

Kya felt the heat of rage flare up within her. "What the hell was that about?" She said in a rough tone.

Leonard turned around, laughing. He waved at her and allowed lightning to spark between his fingers. "You really are painfully clueless!"

As Leonard walked away laughing, Kya opened up a browser on her computer and began to search for a new job.

It wasn't shocking to Kya that most businesses now required someone to have a Super for anything more than manual labour. It had been slowly changing over the course of a few years. She thought back to when only military and high ranking government officials were given Supers, and then how it slowly spread throughout society. The genetic manipulation split the world into two classes, and Kya was sitting on the wrong side of that divide.

After five hours of looking at entry level service and maid positions while watching a robotic machine perform her normal tasks without a flaw or delay, it was time for Kya to head home. She couldn't feel more thankful that her day was done. Grabbing the certified check from her desk, and sliding the few personal items she kept in her cubicle into her purse, she got up to leave.

The stress of being unemployed slowly pressed down on Kya, and though the time she wanted to search for Amelia and Elliot was now available, something was still holding her back.

Don Georgetown was standing near the entrance to the department, his hand outstretched, and palm facing up. "I'll need your security badge."

"Of course." Kya responded curtly as she removed the lanyard and placed the badge in his hand. "Anything else?"

"That'll be all. I don't expect I'll be seeing you again."

Kya exited the department, mumbling under her breath, "I hope not."

As she neared the front door of the building a familiar and entirely unwanted figure loomed in front of her.

"Well, hello there!" He said with a slimy smile.

"Ken," Kya said in a flat tone, her expression equally flat.

"Don told me he was implementing a new system for backups." Ken raised an eyebrow at Kya.

"Yup," Kya said, glancing at the door.

"I guess that means you're looking for a fresh start," Ken said with a chuckle.

Kya didn't respond.

"What do you say you and I meet up for dinner tonight, and we discuss your options for coming out on top." He reached out and touched her arm as he licked his lips.

Kya pulled back, her stomach seethed with revulsion.

"My life could completely fall apart, and I could hit rock bottom and I could still not sink low enough to entertain your offer. Not even if you could offer me a full five Supers. Why don't you go get yourself a good Super woman?" She paused, but he did not answer. "That's right, they're too good for you. And so am I."

Kya stepped around Ken and despite her heart pounding and the rapidness of her breaths, she left Starlife Technologies with her shoulders back and her head held high.

Arriving back at the apartment, Kya immediately noticed that Sam wasn't home. A flashing green light drew her attention. It was Sam's tablet on the dining room table. Kya went over and tapped the power button, and a message appeared. *On a trip with friends, be back in a day or two.*

Kya exhaled and a groan escaped unintentionally as she sat, folded her arms on the table and allowed her head to rest on them. She closed her eyes. Half of her was relieved that she didn't have to explain to Sam about her job, but the other half was sad that he wasn't there to help her through it. She let her mind wander over all of the stresses in her life, and tears flowed from her closed eyes though inside she felt cold and devoid of emotions.

Kya was pulled out of her moment of distraught by her phone alerting her to a call. She reached her hand into her pocket and pulled out her cell, keeping the other arm and her head firmly planted on the table. She opened her eyes to glance at the display; it was Mattie.

"Hey," Kya said in a rough tone that she barely

recognized as her own voice.

"Wow!" Mattie responded with a giggle. "You sound like you've been hit by a bus!"

"Just about," Kya said hollowly, lifting her head from the table.

"What's going on?" Mattie asked, her voice suddenly full of concern. "I got your message yesterday, but I totally forgot to call, I had a busy night with a doctor's appointment and then dinner with Rory's parents. I am so sorry. How can I help?"

"I don't know. Everything alright with you?"

"Yep, all is well with me. Now, what's going on?"

Kya didn't know where to begin or what to say. She opened her mouth, unsure of what would come out. She took a deep breath and then spoke. "Amelia's missing. I think my boss killed my friend Elliot at work. I got replaced by a machine. Sam's gone."

"Wait. Slow down. First, what happened to Amelia?"

Kya told Mattea about Amelia's texts and her connection to the Black Market, and then about Elliot's disappearance, and her visit to the police station. She finished up with a recount of her final day of work. Mattea listened and prodded Kya on when necessary.

"Man, Kya!" Mattea said when Kya had finished. "That is all so terrible. Do you think Mr. Georgetown replaced you because you'd been snooping through the videos?"

"Nope." Kya rolled her eyes. "I think he replaced me because I was replaceable. He'd been threatening to for a long time." She thought of her interaction with Leonard that morning. "I never really played the game. I made myself replaceable." As Kya said the words, she knew they were true, and it felt like a knife twisted in her gut. "But," she said after a considerable silence, "at least this gives me time to search for my friends."

"Way to look on the bright side," Mattea said. "I want to help you out in any way I can. If you want me to come over tonight..."

"It's okay," Kya said, knowing it would be a long trek for Mattie to make on a work night.

"Well then, after work tomorrow I can help you. Rory's supposed to take the car to his basketball game with friends, but I can drop him off, then come see you."

"Yeah, maybe," Kya said though she was fairly certain that wouldn't work out.

After their conversation, Kya dragged herself to the couch and threw on a romantic comedy. It wasn't what she normally watched, but she wanted something easy on her mind and heart as she tried to unwind.

Though she never felt the need to live alone, having the apartment to herself was a rare treat. The air conditioner sprang to life, and she wrapped herself tightly in the blanket hanging over the back of the couch, more for a feeling of comfort than for warmth.

The next morning, Kya woke up feeling disoriented. A beam of sunlight was on her face, and the brightness and heat were uncomfortable. She wiped her eyes and tried to block out the light as she sat up and realized she was still in the living room. The blanket was crumpled up on the floor, and her clothes were wrinkled from sleeping in them. Kya stretched her arms and legs, following with a loud yawn.

A thought quickly crept into the forefront of her mind; *I am unemployed, and I need to find my friends and get a new job before I run out of money.* Pulling herself up and off of the couch, she rose unsteadily as she tried to force her body to move and wake up completely. Stumbling into her bedroom, she grabbed some clothing from her clean, but not folded or put away, laundry basket and jumped into the shower.

Feeling a bit more awake, Kya grabbed her keys and phone. Checking her phone, she saw that there were no new messages, and instantly wanted to throw the seemingly useless device away. With a calmer mind prevailing, she slid it into her pocket and left her building. The bus came after several minutes, and it brought her to the mall, the closer of the two places that Kya was planning on going in search of Amelia.

She hoped that Amelia had just lost her phone and that she would find her friend working away behind the counter at Noble Brew, serving special caffeinated beverages in her own sassy way. She imagined the discussion that would occur between them as the bus arrived, and she made her way into the mall. The idea that the two of them would laugh off the misunderstanding, and that Amelia would help in the search for Elliot was almost enough to raise her spirits and made her excited to get to the coffee shop as quickly as possible.

The crowd was a little thin in the Uptown Centre as Kya made her way towards Noble Brew. With glass windows lining the entry, she could see inside long before she entered and was disheartened when she didn't immediately see her friend behind the counter. Thinking about the last time she saw Amelia at her work brought a nervous smile to her face. *I hope you are just on a break,* she thought as she entered and stood in the short line that was in front of the wall to wall counter.

After several minutes of waiting for people to spit out their overly complex orders, it was finally Kya's turn to talk to the barista.

"How can I help you today?" A young woman said with an overly chipper voice.

"Hi, I'm looking for Amelia. Is she working?"

"Amelia?"

"Yeah, she works here."

"Sorry, I'm new. Just a second and I'll get my manager."

Kya sat on a nearby loveseat. Her concern slowly rose as the seconds ticked by. She tried to distract herself by looking at the people around her, but most of them were focused solely on one piece of technology or another.

The manager, a short, heavy-set, young woman, walked over with a hard expression on her face. "You Amelia's friend?"

"Yeah," Kya said.

"Well, I haven't seen her in almost a week. She stopped showing up for shifts five days ago."

Kya opened her mouth to speak, but no words came out. She could feel her blood pulsing through her body and began to feel lightheaded.

"If you see her, tell her she's fired." The manager said as she turned and walked away.

Kya sunk into the loveseat, her mouth hanging open, processing this new information as the world continued moving around her. After five minutes of staring and blinking, she stood up slowly and left the shop.

She continued, like a zombie, moving without thinking or paying attention to her surroundings, and found herself somehow back on a bus heading towards Amelia's apartment before she regained any sense of awareness. She couldn't help but wonder what she was supposed to do next if she couldn't find Amelia at her apartment.

As she arrived, she noticed that the building looked older and more worn down than the buildings around it. Advertisements relating to million dollar condominiums were plastered on displays all over the street. It was like Amelia's apartment building was untouched by progress. An older four storey brownstone with no computerized displays, automated doors, or digital directory was what stood in front of her. Air conditioner units hung precariously outside of the windows of most units, and black spray painted words and pictures covered most of the stone on the first storey, they were not at all beautiful like the graffiti murals elsewhere in the city.

Kya realized that she had never been invited over to Amelia's place before. They had always met at Noble Brew or some fancy club, bar or restaurant. She had always pictured Amelia living in some amazing apartment on her own, with high-end appeal. Now she understood why Amelia had never invited her over. Kya could feel eyes on her though the street was empty. She hurried to enter Amelia's building.

Kya climbed the stairs to the fourth floor where the listing on her cell phone told her Amelia's apartment was. She walked down the dimly lit hallway with a brown carpet that appeared to be about forty years old. Amelia's door, number 417, was at the end of the hall. Kya knocked on the door, and there was no response. The metal number seven on the door rattled as she knocked again. Pressing her ear to the door, she heard nothing. She gently twisted the doorknob, but it was locked.

"Amelia?" She called as she knocked again. "It's me, please let me in!"

No response.

Kya jiggled the handle frantically and pushed on the door, unsure of what to do next, but she was surprised when the door jerked open with a loud creak. Suddenly, she wasn't sure she wanted to go in. She stood at the door, and a stale smell hit her like the air hadn't been circulating for a few days.

"Amelia?" She said again nervously, as she walked in. What little light came through the open door behind her was enough for Kya to find her way to a table lamp beside the couch. The windows looked like they were blacked out with thick, satin backed curtains. Kya turned on the lamp and in its light she saw Amelia's cell phone on the couch, its screen face down, next to a round imprint in the fabric, as if someone had just gotten up, or as if Amelia had just teleported away.

Kya laughed involuntarily. "Amelia, you are so scatterbrained!" She reached out and picked up the phone. "Always losing your stuff." She shook her head and laughed again.

Then the smile fell from her face as she realized that Amelia had been without her phone for five days. She surely should have come back to her apartment in that time, no matter how far she had teleported.

Kya turned on the cell phone and tears welled up in her eyes as she scrolled through countless alerts from her, Amelia's work, her landlord, and her sister. Kya blinked, and the tears poured down onto her face. She flopped onto the couch, her elbows on her knees she rested her forehead on her hands both still holding the cell phone.

"Oh, Amelia," she sobbed. "What do I do now?

As she scrolled through the messages again, with a more watchful eye, Kya noticed one from another person, Frank B. She clicked on the message from Frank, and the full conversation stream between them was displayed. Her pulse quickened, and she saw information about meeting up and the injection. There wasn't any direct mention of Supers or the Black Market, but Kya was certain that she had found the person who had given Amelia her Supers and potentially caused whatever situation she was in now. A simple question started forming in her mind. *What if this Frank guy killed Amelia?*

The last message from Frank was an address. She burned it into her mind. Either way, Kya knew that she had to find him and confront him and that the longer she waited, the more she might lose her nerve.

Kya slipped Amelia's phone into her purse. It felt wrong to take it. She felt a little like she was stealing, but it was also the easiest way, just in case she needed more information from the phone. She made a mental note to get in contact with Amelia's sister if Frank was a dead end.

It was only half a dozen blocks between Amelia's apartment and the address in her phone. It lead Kya to a nightclub that had dozens of motorcycles sitting in front of it, even though it was the early afternoon. The sign out front wasn't turned on, and the stench of alcohol seeped out into the street.

A tingling sensation rushed through her as she tried to focus on the task at hand. The door of the bar seemed farther and farther away from Kya as her steps got shorter each time she put her foot forward to approach. Breaking out in a cold sweat, when she finally reached it, she battled internally to push through the door. The voice inside her mind screamed at her to run away, but she conquered it and entered. Instantly, she was met with a dimly lit pool hall, filled with smoke, and the noise of an aging stereo system. The light of the outside world caused Kya to be the center of attention, and half dozen people looked at her as the door shut behind her. The yellow glow of the ancient light bulbs barely lit the pool tables below them, and the bar was awash in a dark red glow.

Kya walked up to the bar, feeling like she was in over her head. Most of the people had turned back to drinking, shooting pool, or otherwise entertaining themselves, but she still felt like a watchful eye was focused on her, and curious about her intent. It felt like a burning sensation at the back of her neck and caused her throat to feel tight.

A gruff voice, filled with the rumble of boulders being smashed, came from behind the bar. "What can I help you with, little one?"

Kya turned and was face to face with the bartender, an older gentleman, wearing a tank top that only served to expose his full sleeves of tattoos that climbed from the knuckles of his hands, all the way to his ears. Some looked faded, and others looked fresh. A nearly naked woman of inhuman proportions caught Kya's eye.

The assessment of the barkeep must have taken too long as he spoke once again, in a louder, but still gravelly voice. "You need something?"

"I'm looking for a Frank?" Kya said, her entire body trembling. She tried to fortify herself and feign confidence, but she knew her comment had come out as a squeaky question.

"Are you sure?" The bartender responded.

"Sorry?"

"Sounded like you didn't know." He grabbed a glass, opened a bottle and poured it until it was half full. Slamming back the entire half glass full of what Kya assumed was alcohol, the bartender put his hand out on the bar. "We don't really ask for names around here."

Confused at what was happening, and why the bartender had his hand outstretched, Kya spent half of her concentration focused on quieting the voice inside her mind that was telling her to run away and never return. After several tense seconds, she moved from staring at the open hands to the bartender's face, and finally realized what she needed to do.

Kya opened her purse and pulled out her bank card. She placed it in the opening on the bar and the bartender grinned slightly. A small display near the opening was glowing, Kya made out the numbers and saw that a transaction of nearly two hundred dollars was being charged to her account. She felt like she needed a shot of whatever the bartender had drank as the wind was knocked from her sails.

"A nice lady like you could find any kind of Steve she wants," he said as Kya put her card back into her purse.

"Frank. Frank B." Kya spat out, feeling her frustration push away any feelings of inadequacy. The near theft of her money caused her to have the guts to speak louder and clearly.

"Right, Frank. He's not here."

"Where is he?"

"He'll be back. Two days. He'll sit over there." The bartender pointed to a round booth in the back corner. A pair of fuzzy dice hung from the small light fixture over the table. "You want me to tell him you came?"

Kya could feel that she was starting to draw attention, and her body was tensing up, preparing for trouble. Her flight instinct was so strong that the muscles in her legs started to twitch as though she was already running. Turning towards the door, she felt she'd accomplished something and needed to leave with the information she had, rather than press her luck.

As she walked to the closest bus stop, she could not shrug her uneasy feeling. No matter how many times she turned and looked around the empty streets to confirm what she already knew, Kya could not shake the feeling that she was being followed.

Back at home, Kya was lying on her bed listening to music with her eyes closed, trying to find a moment of peace, while her feet twitched uncontrollably. She heard a noise like a key in the lock. Her eyes snapped open, *or someone breaking in* the thought had entered her mind causing uncalled for panic. Her heart boomed in her ears as she sat up and scanned the room for something she could use as a weapon. She heard the door open, and she made herself stand up. She wished that she had a baseball bat or a trophy or something, but the closest thing she could find to a weapon was a shoe. She picked it up, determined that she was going to fight to the last.

She crept to her bedroom door and had a clear line of sight to the front door of the apartment. A man, wearing a gray hoodie, was crouched by the door, opening a large backpack. His hood was pulled over his head, and a shadow was covering his face.

Kya stayed in her doorway clutching her shoe, waiting to see what the man would do. Her nose started to run and caused her to sniffle. Pulling back into her room slightly she hoped whoever it was hadn't heard her. She focused intently and watched as he pulled a small tablet computer out of the bag and lifted his head.

"Why is it so cold in here?" He asked, looking straight at Kya with a grin on his face.

Kya exhaled deeply and started to laugh uncontrollably. "You don't know how glad I am to see you!"

"You look terrible!" Sam said with an immediate look of concern crossing his face. "Kya, what happened? And why are you holding a shoe?

Kya dropped the shoe and walked over to Sam. "We should sit down. This will probably take a while." .

CHAPTER 14

Sam set his tablet down on the dining room table and joined Kya in the living room. He turned off the air conditioner before sitting at the opposite end of the couch from her.

Kya caught Sam up on the news about Amelia and Elliot. She found herself going off on tangents to explain the stories, as she attempted to convey what was happening in her life with as much clarity as possible. He nodded as she spoke, his attention focused solely on her and his eyebrows knitted in concern. Once she had finished, she took a breath and twisted her fingers around each other, playing for time as she tried to figure out how to tell him about her job.

"Kya, what's wrong?" He asked, leaning forward. "I mean, what else is wrong? I know something more is bugging you."

The ease at which Sam could read Kya was something she had never experienced with anyone but him. "It's just." She bit her lip and tried to maintain her composure. "I lost my job."

"What?"

"I'm sorry. I know. I know I should have taken it more seriously. Don fired me. He replaced me with a machine."

"Oh, Kya."

"I know." She stammered. "I'm looking for work... When I'm not trying to-"

"Help your friends." His tone was conclusive.

"Yeah."

"No, Kya." Sam stared deeply into Kya's eyes, and she did the same in return. She noticed the bright gray hues in his stood out amidst their clear whites. His eyebrows turned upwards with concern. "Help your friends."

"Sam, we both know that we need the money."

"No." Sam shook his head and looked around the apartment. "Kya, we don't."

She followed his gaze, looking at the beautiful furniture, the large media shelving, and then stared at him in confusion.

"I can carry this place. It's not a problem."

"How? You're just a teacher."

Sam stood up, walked over to the counter and picked up his tablet while Kya stayed planted firmly on the couch. With his tablet in hand, he walked back over to the black leather couch and sat down.

"I'm not just a teacher. I am also Samson Hart." He said

and unlocked the tablet before handing it to Kya. "Here. Do a search for me." His tone sounded sad.

Kya took the tablet from him but did not look at it.

"Do you remember the email I sent you about moving in here? I gave you all the details you would need to search me out online and understand who I am, my full name, my age. I really expected you to look me up. I searched for you. That was part of why I picked you." Sam grinned slightly as he continued. "Did you know that you have almost no online presence? Well, except that blog you started when you first moved away from home. And your profile on that creative writing site, what's it called?"

"Flash Fiction Fan Favourites"

"Yeah, and that I found by your email, not your name. You're the only person I've met with such little info online. I was kind of impressed." Sam shrugged and for a moment his tone seemed lighter.

Kya blinked. It had never occurred to her to search out a potential roommate online before moving in, but now she wished she had, as Sam suddenly seemed like a complete stranger.

He tapped his finger on the edge of the tablet in Kya's hands, and it sprung to life. The screen illuminating both their faces as they sat closer to each other. "Search for," he said pausing for a moment, "Samson Hart."

Kya opened up the web browser application and slowly typed in Sam's full name. As she typed in each letter, the results were automatically whittled down until the screen filled with links to articles with titles like *Hart Family Tragedy*, *Quest for Supers Raizes Hart Dynasty*, *Multi-Billionaire Widower Disowns Son*, *Samson Hart Granted $98,000,000 in Court Battle with Family*.

Kya stared at the screen unable to process what she was reading. The room somehow felt darker, and everything more distant. The couch felt uncomfortable, and Kya shifted in her seat. She tried to figure out what she was supposed to do with the new information in front of her. She hesitated, not sure if she was supposed to click on an article to read more. Her bedroom was beckoning to her, and she had to fight to remain where she was. The memories started to loop around and around as she thought about every interaction with Sam she had ever had.

Sam cleared his throat, and Kya flinched involuntarily. She had forgotten he was there.

"What is this?" Kya pulled her gaze from the screen and focused on Sam. "Who are you?" She could feel the heat rising in her cheeks, her muscles tensing as an overwhelming emotion filled her, though she was unsure what the emotion was. It felt a bit like fear, or rage, or jealousy.

"I didn't want to talk about it. I expected you to find out for yourself." Sam shrugged. "But you never did."

Kya handed the tablet back to Sam and folded her arms. She stared out the window, unable to look at him.

"You know, for someone as brilliant as you are, I'm surprised how often you lack curiosity."

"Wait! You're rich!" Kya blurted out. "You could have

bought us *both* Supers at any time without your bank account even feeling it."

"I don't want-"

"Why the hell did you take me in as your roommate?" Kya was nearly screaming, as she stood up and walked over to the window, still unable to look at the man sitting on the couch.

"I wanted-"

"What am I? Your personal pet charity case?"

"Kya." His voice was low, quiet and somber.

"No. Sam, I don't want to hear it! I don't need your pity!"

"Kya, It wasn't pity."

"Sure!" She laughed sarcastically and clutched her stomach as it churned.

In the reflection from the window, Kya saw Sam place the tablet on the coffee table as he stood up. He walked towards her. Kya turned to face him, and heat burned in her chest. Her lungs felt constricted. Her heart raced, and each beat sent near boiling blood racing through her body. She felt as though opening her mouth would let loose a torrent of fire.

"I thought I knew you." She said in a rough tone and shook her head.

"I never wanted to hide this from you. I thought you'd figure it out."

"So now I'm not *just* your charity case, I'm your *stupid* charity case!"

Kya pushed past Sam and ran towards her room. She wanted to hit something, destroy something. Blinded by rage, she slammed her door, leaned against it and slid down to the floor, her legs giving way beneath her.

She gasped for breath as her emotions overtook her. She had always assumed that she and Sam were equals, that they were both struggling to get by in a world set against them and that he was anti-Supers because he knew how out of reach they were. Reading those headlines, Kya had realized that so much of what she knew of Sam had been simple assumptions and so far from the truth.

Her room was dark, chilled and quiet. Her body ached as she sat pressed against the solid door, her legs pulled in as tight to her chest as they could go causing it to ache slightly.

There was a deeper hurt in her chest. She felt exposed. Sam had searched her out, and had learned about her without her knowing. He'd read a blog she had intended only for family and that she had given up on when she realized that her family didn't care enough to read it. Sam had snuck into her past, and she had kept herself out of his past without even realizing it.

A sob escaped Kya's mouth, and she raised her hand to her face to find her cheeks covered in tears. She had spent so much of her time since she moved into this apartment stressing that if she couldn't give Sam her seven hundred dollars in rent by the first of the month that she or they would be out on the street. She had said as much to him many times, and he had never said a word. Why did he wait so long before letting her know the truth? Why couldn't he have told her on his own? Why make her read it off a screen?

If Sam had all this money, why didn't he get Supers? She thought, her mind slowly calming.

Daylight streamed through Kya's window, as she became aware of the hard floor beneath her. She stretched and felt the door behind her. As she slowly woke, she realized she had fallen asleep on the floor, too exhausted to even make it across the room to her bed.

Kya wiped her face and stood up. Every muscle in her body ached. She walked over to her bed and then back to the door. She took a deep breath and let her mind wander, remembering her fight with Sam. She wondered what she would have to do to get Sam to agree to help her get Supers. If she could only convince him that with Supers she would be able to find and help Amelia and Elliot. She touched the handle of the door, thinking that she would go out and talk to him again, but she was suddenly struck with a fresh wave of rage.

As she turned the handle, Kya was stopped suddenly by her phone buzzing in her pocket. She took it out and answered the call without even checking to see who it was.

"What?" She yelled into the phone.

"Kya?" Mattea asked in a small voice. "You okay?"

"No!" Kya's heart was pounding in her ears. She didn't want to take her feelings out on Mattea, but she couldn't find a way to control them either.

"So, you've been watching the news then?"

"What?" Kya rolled her eyes. "Listen, Mattie. I'm not in the mood for guessing games."

"Your friend from work. Was his name Elliot Shepherd?"

"Yes." Kya said, and a wave of icy fear washed away the fire of her rage. "Why?"

"I'm going to send you something that you have to see."

Kya dropped her phone on her bed and grabbed her laptop. Opening it up, it sprang to life instantly. A notification appeared at the top right corner of the screen. A new message had been received, and it contained a link to a local news broadcaster website. She clicked the link, her web browser opened, and a video started to play.

A middle-aged news reporter appeared, with a bright blue background behind him. His sandy brown hair perfectly swept across his forehead to cover a receding hairline, and his eyes gleaming in the studio lights.

Kya thought she noticed a tear forming in his eye and felt her own face follow suit. Nervously, she waited for the report to begin.

"This evening, the body of a middle-aged man was found just outside Drayton Park. It was found by a young couple at three this afternoon at the bottom of the cliffs at the south end. The body has been identified as that of Elliot Shepard, who was reported missing earlier this week."

Her ears began to ring with a deafening tone. Kya tapped repeatedly and paused the video. She wanted to throw up. Picking up her phone, she felt weak, dizzy, and stiff.

Stuttering, she forced words from her shaky lips, "I don't think I can watch this right now."

"I know it is hard, but I really think you should listen to the whole thing. Did you want me to come over?"

Without responding, Kya took a deep breath and resumed the video. Pictures of the cliffs and police vehicles appeared to the right of the news anchor, and a photo of Elliot appeared to the left.

"Initial police reports say that Shepherd committed suicide. Many of his bones were broken in the fall, and his body was found drenched in alcohol. A bottle of prescription antidepressants prescribed to the deceased was also found at the scene. The police retrieved a message, stored on his phone, relating to his dissatisfaction at not being able to afford Supers. Elliot Shepherd was sixty-three years old, and was, until recently, an employee of Starlife Technologies. More on this as we receive it."

Kya took a deep breath and stared at the now still image on the screen.

"Kya?"

She held the phone to her ear but said nothing.

"Kya, I'm so sorry," Mattie spoke slowly and softly. "Are you okay?"

"How can I be okay?" Kya blurted, maniacally, almost laughing.

"Kya." Mattie tried to soothe her.

"Elliot's dead. Like, really dead! Don Georgetown killed him!"

"They said it looked like a suicide."

"It's a cover-up." Kya stood up and started pacing. "I saw the videos from work. I know Don killed him. Don even left a convenient message on his phone as a motive for suicide."

"Listen, I'll come by."

"No. Don't. I'm fine."

It was Mattea's turn to almost laugh. "You are not fine. We both know that."

Kya looked around her room for her jacket, purse and a pair of shoes. "The cops don't believe me. but I know I'm right, Mattie."

"Okay, Kya. Maybe I can try and help you talk to the cops."

"I don't have any evidence except what I saw with my own eyes. That's not good enough for the cops."

"So what are you going to do?"

Kya put her jacket on, and set her purse on the bed, sifting through it to find her wallet, keys, and phone. The phone was in her hand, and she rolled her eyes at how long it took her to realize that. She shook her purse and didn't hear the telltale rattle of her keys.

"Kya?" Mattie said.

"Hmm?" Kya scanned her room, ready to destroy it in search for her keys before she remembered that they were in the bowl by the door of the apartment.

"What are you going to do?"

"People don't take Normals seriously."

"Kya." Mattie's voice took on a parental tone.

"I'm going to find Amelia's Black Market contact."

Kya put on her left shoe but was still looking for the right. It was the shoe she had picked up as a weapon only a few short hours earlier.

"What? No." Mattie whispered. "There are a million other ways to handle this."

"No," Kya replied, annoyed at her friend's motherly way of speaking. "There's not. I've tried, Mattie. I have tried to play by the rules. It doesn't work. I'm going to make the rules now."

"This is a bad idea! You don't know what you're doing."

"I'm a big girl, and I can handle this." She found her right shoe and slipped her foot inside.

"Really? And Where's Amelia?" Mattie asked, and Kya could hear the desperation in her voice.

"Wrong question." Kya said, and she could feel the

coldness in her words. "I'm going to get off the phone now."

"Take care of you!" Kya heard Mattie say before she hit *End*.

CHAPTER 15

As Kya arrived at the nightclub, it looked busier than it had been before. She knew that Amelia's contact, Frank B. was supposed to be there that evening under the fuzzy dice, but she didn't expect the club to be so packed. From the entrance, she couldn't even see to the back tables. As dozens of bikers were dancing, playing pool, and drinking beer, a small shoving match was occurring near the bar. Security was quick to respond, waving in Kya and then attending to the two large men pushing each other while a thin, heavily tattooed lady tried to step between them.

The whole atmosphere was so far outside Kya's regular existence that it felt like she had entered a strange movie. Her heart was pounding as she pushed through the crowd and made her way towards the seating area in the back. The thick smoke caused her eyes to water heavily, and her lungs to feel constricted.

The music was so loud that Kya felt could feel it more than she could hear it and an older man brushed up against her.

He was flailing wildly on the small dance floor halfway between the pool tables and the lounge-like area. He turned and saw Kya, and began to smile.

She felt a little wave of disgust as the old man's chest moved independently of his aged, thin frame; it reminded her a bit of a woman jogging without a bra. She hadn't seen someone so old move so lively before. His skin hung off his bones, his muscles were no longer firm, and his tattoos were long since faded. A scar across his face caught her attention, and Kya stumbled backward. Without saying a word, the man recognized her disinterest and immediately seemed content to continue dancing alone, wildly flailing his arms, completely carefree.

Kya noticed that three people were sitting in the far left booth with the fuzzy dice. A thirty-something man, with short dark hair and a square jaw, sat with a confident look on his face. His thick, suit jacket covered arms stretched around two young women, sitting on either side of him. His clean shaven face showed little wear or stress, and a pair of prescription glasses sat in front of him on the table. Next to the eyewear, a dozen empty bottles and glasses were strewn about the circular table. A laptop computer sat open to one side; it's light illuminating the thin, young scantily clad woman to his right.

Approaching, Kya felt her throat nearly closing up. She couldn't decide if it was due to anxiety relating to the situation she was forcing herself into, or if the smoke was so thick that she really couldn't breathe.

"Can I help you, beautiful?" The man said an instant grin plastered on his face.

Kya felt frustrated at his cavalier attitude. The anger over Elliot's death and Amelia's unknown situation hit her like a sledgehammer, and she wanted to wield that hammer and smash the grin off of his face. "I need to find Amelia," she said. Her tone was curt, and it seemed to have caught the man off guard. "You are Frank, aren't you?"

The man looked at each of the women with him. He gestured, and they quickly slid from the booth and disappeared into the crowd. "Yeah, I'm Frank. And if you want to talk business, you'll have to follow me."

Kya's heart was racing, the drumming of it began to deafen her. The music in the club, which originally seemed fast, now felt like it was at one-tenth its normal speed and volume.

Frank closed the laptop and placed it within a shoulder bag. He grabbed his glasses and put them on as he slid easily from the table. As he stood up, he hit the fuzzy dice hanging from the light. They went flying around sporadically, and then quickly slowed to a gentle sway. He gestured towards Kya and began to walk towards a metal door nearby on the wall.

Exiting, Kya found herself in the alleyway between the club and a two storey red brick building. There were a few lights along the alley, and Kya was able to see Frank with more detail than she had in the club. She noted that he stood only a few inches taller than herself, quite shorter than she thought he would be. His frame was less opposing now, as his suit clad body looked rather thin, except for this thick neck and broad shoulders.

"So, you're looking for Amelia, are ya? I don't know what to tell you."

"You know who I am talking about, though? I think you gave her Supers."

"Look, your friend did get Supers from me. She went against my advice, and she couldn't handle them. I tried to help her, but it was all her choice."

"What do you mean, her choice? What did you do?"

Leaning against the wall to the club, Frank grinned, but the light exposed something Kya wasn't expecting, sorrow filled eyes. "I could show you if you want."

"Show me what?" Kya said.

Frank slowly put his arm out at shoulder level. His palm face down. He nodded slightly, and then shrugged. "Touch my hand and you'll see."

Stepping in close to Frank, Kya felt like she was going to explode. She wanted to hit him. She felt confused, angry and frustrated, but she also wanted answers. Reaching out, she touched the tip of Frank's fingers with her own and instantly felt a fog wash over her.

"Frank!" Amelia shouted as she stumbled towards Kya.

Kya looked around and saw Frank right beside her. She realized that she hadn't moved and was in the same spot she was in before the fog. Kya tried to speak, but there was no sound to her words. Frank stared in the direction Amelia was coming from.

Amelia looked terrible. Her hair was a mess of knots and

tangles and appeared to be changing colour and length at random. Her blue blouse was buttoned askew, her gray sweat pants were wrinkled and looked like she had spilled coffee on them. Amelia twitched her head around, trying to see in all directions, as though she was paranoid, or going insane. As she got closer, Kya could see dark circles around Amelia's eyes, and it didn't seem like she was wearing any makeup either.

"Hey, beautiful," Frank said with a smooth tone as he took in Amelia's haggard appearance. "Rough day?"

"Frank, you gotta help me." Amelia was standing directly in front of Kya now, and her bloodshot eyes appeared full of fear as they darted left and right, seemingly unable to focus on anything.

"You want me to remove a Super or two?" Frank asked with his arms folded in front of his chest.

"Yes," Amelia whispered.

"I told you." Frank's voice took on a tone similar to a parent lecturing a young child, and he shook his finger at Amelia. "I *told* you not to get all five at once. Too much to handle, isn't it?"

"Yes." Amelia whispered again, and tears welled up in her eyes. "I need all the voices to stop." She sobbed, raising her hands to her head and pulling at her ever-changing hair.

"It'll cost ten thousand to extract the Telepathy," Frank said as he brushed a piece of green hair out of Amelia's eyes. "More if you want to get rid of some others as well."

"I don't have ten thousand dollars!" Amelia said, and

she began to shake.

"I don't know what to tell you then," Frank said, scrunching up his face in a sort of grimace.

"Please." Amelia's voice was so soft it was barely audible. "I'm desperate."

"I can see that," Frank said with a tiny laugh. He took a deep breath and stared at Amelia for a moment in silence as if calculating what to do.

Amelia mouthed the word *"please"* again, but no sound came out.

"Listen, beautiful. I can give you another Super to help you control the rest."

"Really?" Amelia asked, her face seemed to brighten with hope.

"Four little letters that mean a lot. W-I-L-L."

"Will?" Amelia asked.

"Yup. The power to control your existence, and in the same vein, the Will to control your five other Supers.

"I'll take it!" Amelia smiled.

"Well, wait." Frank sucked in air between his teeth before continuing. "This isn't an easy process. It's super risky."

"How much will it cost?"

"Are you listening to me, kid?" Frank leaned closer to Amelia and spoke slowly and directly. "It's dangerous. There's a reason the people in charge of Supers put a limit of five out there. Six... Well, it can really mess you up."

"Look at me, Frank." Amelia said, and Kya could see a glimmer of the strong-willed friend she knew. "I'm already messed up. How much will it cost?"

"It could kill you."

"I'd rather die than live like this. How much will it cost?"

Frank's tone was low. He looked at the ground as he spoke. "A thousand."

"I can do that." Amelia nodded emphatically.

"Amelia," Frank said, and Kya was shocked to hear him use her friend's name. "Make sure you're using your listening ears, sweetheart. You could *die*. A sixth power, even Will, can seriously mess you up."

Kya reached out and tried to grab her friend's hand, but they passed right through each other. She tried to yell at Amelia, hoping her words of advice could be heard, but there was no sound, no notice of Kya's efforts.

Amelia shook uncontrollably, and her features continued to change at will. "I get it, Frank." Kya knew her short and curt tone meant Amelia was angry. "I'll be back with the money."

Amelia took her phone out of her pocket and started texting as she walked away. Kya couldn't explain how, but she knew that Amelia was sending her that last text. *You know what, K? I can handle this. I've got an idea. It's all good. Don't worry. Don't worry.* A shiver ran down Kya's back, and she tried to chase her friend, but the alleyway around her began to get dark, and all of the details faded away.

It only took a moment for her perception of the world around her to begin to brighten again and for everything to come back into focus. Kya was still in the alleyway that was now illuminated with morning light. Amelia had just materialized about twenty feet away. Frank was still to Kya's right. He leaned against the brick wall behind him, cleaning his glasses. His clothes had changed from the previous scene. His dress pants were now jeans, and his suit jacket was far less formal looking. Despite the change in clothes, he looked tired. Frank stared over his right shoulder at Amelia as she walked towards him.

"Frank! What is going on?" Kya tried to yell at him for answers, but again her voice made no sound. Neither Frank nor Amelia acknowledged her presence and Kya felt the all too familiar bubbling of anger inside her. She noticed a few garbage cans just down the alley, she walked over and reached for the lid of one of them, intending to throw it at Frank. "Great!" She screamed silently as her hand passed through it. She tried to kick the can, but her foot passed through. Kya gave up and turned her attention back to Amelia and Frank.

Amelia's face was gray, as she stood a foot away from Frank holding out an envelope. Her hair still changing at random, her eyes twitching, but she stared at him with her lips pursed in what Kya recognized as an attempt at her *'brave face'* which she reserved for times when she was most afraid. Kya could feel a piece of her own heart breaking for her friend.

Frank took the envelope and nodded. He bounced it

between his fingers and without opening it, he grinned for a moment, but it didn't reach his eyes. "Right then." Frank said, his voice rough and lacking all the vibrancy he had used earlier. "One last chance to back out."

"No," Amelia said. Kya noticed a maniacal fire seemed to burn behind her eyes.

"I can offer you a payment plan for the extraction," Frank said with his eyebrows raised.

"No." Amelia said again, and as she said it, her hair turned short and red, as did her eyebrows, making her take on a demonic aura.

Frank closed his eyes and bowed his head. "Right." He took a deep breath. "Then, come on. We'll see my boys."

The world faded again, and then once the fog was lifted, they were near a small grocery store. Kya wondered if it was the place where Amelia had talked about getting her Supers. She walked with Amelia and Frank as they went around to the delivery entrance to the building. The blue metal doors swung open, and it looked like a generic store room. There was an exit to the rest of the grocery store. On metal wire, rack shelves along all of the walls, a variety of goods were stored. Near a fully laden shelf of beverages, Frank waved his hand, and slowly the rack twisted open, the wall moving with it.

Behind the opening, were two younger men sitting behind desks. Their computer displays illuminating their faces as they peaked over, quickly looking at Amelia and Frank as they entered.

"Relax guys, it's just me. This little lady is looking to get a sixth Super." Frank said. His tone was one of confidence and command. He walked with more of a noticeable swagger as he entered the hidden room.

"I knew this place was here. I knew it!" Amelia said more to herself than to anyone else. Then to Frank she said, "What do these guys do, just sit on their computers all day? I swear they were in the exact same positions last time."

"My dear, they are here to make sure no one sees this place unless I want them to. They are paid handsomely to make this room imperceptible, especially to the Supers on the police force. The twins have such amazing talents, and I couldn't do any of this without them." Frank was glowing as he passed the two guards.

"So, is that why I couldn't get in here on my own? Why I couldn't find the place?"

"Yes, lovely. It's safer for everyone that way."

Kya noticed one of "the twins" twitch a small smile as Frank spoke."Right," Frank said. "You know the drill."

"Do I have to be strapped down again?"

"That's the drill," Frank said with a shrug.

Amelia walked over to the table, climbed and laid down. Frank walked slowly behind her and strapped down her ankles and wrists. He shot Amelia a disarming smile. He walked over to a mirrored cabinet on the wall that looked like a regular household medicine cabinet and took out a vial of deep blood red liquid, and a needle. He attached the two as he walked back over to Amelia.

Amelia's features were still morphing at random, and she still twitched from side to side. "Man! Guys! Could you shut up!" She yelled. It took Kya a few seconds to realize that she must have been talking about their thoughts.

"The twins have to keep their minds active. I'm sorry they're so noisy. Here, how about some music?"

The twin on the left looked over at Frank, then they both nodded, and music began playing throughout the room.

"Alright, sweetie, I need you to do me a solid. Can you concentrate on being just you for a minute? This is gonna be hard enough without your veins going all over the place with the shape-shifting." He grinned at Amelia.

"Ok." She closed her eyes and breathed deeply. Kya watched as her skin took on its normal porcelain complexion, and her hair returned to its normal black colour. Kya felt a pain in her chest as she stared at her old friend.

Frank gently grabbed Amelia's left wrist to hold her arm still as he stuck the needle inside her arm just below her elbow. The blue vein that the needle entered immediately began to glow dark red, and Amelia's breaths quickened. The red pulsated and flickered like fire or lava as it flowed outward through Amelia's body, and every vein and artery could be seen deep red. Kya felt her heart quicken, and though she wanted to, she could not pull her eyes away from the painful but mesmerizing scene before her.

When the procedure was done, Amelia was still twitchy and not in control of her appearance.

"Thanks, Frank," She said and suddenly disappeared.

"Teleport." Frank said to the twins, and they both nodded.

The scene changed again. Kya and Frank were at his booth in the tavern, fuzzy dice overhead. Frank was in a suit again, and Amelia burst into being directly in front of the table. She looked worse than Kya had ever seen her. She looked around and began mimicking the dance moves of the people around her. Her skin being marked with tattoos that faded in and out. She smacked the dice and sent them twirling.

"That's right, Frank. You're doing business with me *right now!*" Amelia yelled, and several people turned their attention toward her.

"Amelia," Frank began and put his hand on her left arm.

"What the hell did you do to me?" She screamed, pulling her arm from his grasp.

Frank slowly stood. "Let's go to my office."

"The alley?" Amelia screamed. "No!" She pulled back her right arm, hand clenched in a fist and punched Frank square in the face. Then she disappeared as quickly as she had appeared.

Kya took a deep breath as she found herself standing back in the alleyway. She felt dizzy, and would have fallen if Frank hadn't reached out to catch her.

"What-" Kya heard her voice and was taken aback. She began again. "What was that?"

Frank gently held Kya's shoulders until she regained her balance. He stared into her eyes with a concerned expression.

"Well, that was my memories. Everything I know about Amelia after she obtained her first five Supers."

"Why should I believe you?" Kya asked, her voice ragged.

"What reason do I have to lie?"

Kya looked around the alley. It looked the same as it had in the flashbacks - if that's what they were. Frank was wearing the same suit he had been when she first met him at his booth in the back of the tavern. More than anything, the fact that he could hear her and touch her made her believe that they were back in the present. She pushed his hands away and stood on her own merit.

"You gave her five Supers all at once!"

"I told her not to. I told her it would be a lot to handle, and that it could make her go crazy. Especially the telepathy. I could show you that too."

"No! You knew she'd go crazy, and you gave her five supers all at once anyway?" Kya's voice was shrill and reminded her a bit of her mother, but she didn't care.

"I only knew it *might* happen. She might have been okay. Some people have a strong enough sense of self and pick Supers so complimentary to their own personality that it all just works perfectly."

"Did you think Amelia's powers were complimentary to her personality?"

"How was I to know? I didn't know her any better than I know you." Frank's voice took on a defensive tone.

"Then why did you give her five Supers all at once?"

"She insisted."

"So?"

"So?" Frank raised his eyebrows and stared at Kya. "So, I run a business. Money talks. She insisted it was all or nothing. Even Robin Hood has to have money to run his business."

"So you're Robin Hood, now?" Kya asked with a sarcastic laugh.

Frank shrugged.

"What would have happened if you'd given her Will first."

"Now, sweetie, it's not good to dwell on *what if's*," Frank said, staring down the alley past Kya.

"Why didn't you give her Will first?"

"She didn't want it," He said, still not looking at Kya, but folding his arms across his chest. "She didn't even want to hear about it. I don't blame her. It's not a spectacular power. Not many people would take it as one of their five. It doesn't show as a power." Frank tapped three of the fingers on his right hand

and a look of joy spread across his face. "Heck, I can count on one hand how many people have taken Will since I started doing this."

"So what happened to Amelia after she hit you?"

"I don't know."

"How can you not know?"

"Do you know where she is? You're her friend."

"Don't you throw that in my face. I didn't give her Supers!" Kya fumed. "You gave her a sixth Super that might have killed her!"

"You saw - You heard. I offered to extract one or more of her Supers."

"For ten times the price of a sixth! If she could have afforded that much for an extraction why wouldn't she have gone to a real clinic in the first place? Plus, we have all seen how well that Myles kid dealt with an extraction! Who would voluntarily pay for that!"

Frank stood, stone-faced and stared at Kya as she yelled. His arms still crossed in front of his chest. "Are you done?" He asked.

"No!" Kya yelled. "You took money from an innocent girl and then left her for dead."

"That is not..." Frank's eyes were wide, and his tone was firm.

"Lies!" Kya yelled. "You don't care about the wellbeing

of your clients! Money talks. You said it yourself!" As she said the last words, her hands seemed to act on their own accord, and she shoved Frank hard against the wall behind him. She heard him exhale as his back slammed into it, generating a very dull thud.

As if by reflex, Frank punched Kya in the stomach. With the wind knocked out of Kya, her vision became spotty. She doubled over, unable to suck in any air. Panic quickly set in as she gasped and wheezed, but before she blacked out, she saw a look of shock on Frank's face before he turned and ran away.

Kya heard soft footsteps approaching and forced open her eyes to see a shadowed figure coming towards her. As he left the shadows in favour of the diffused light of the dim alleyway, she noticed that the man approaching her wore the strangest clothing she had ever seen.

From head to toe, he was covered in various dark gray fabrics. Blackened leather bound his torso while a silkier material was wrapped around his arms and legs. A woolen hood arched over his head and shadowed the majority of his face. A thin scarf, wrapped loosely around the neck, covered up the remainder, from his chin to just below the bridge of his nose. While the materials were all different, Kya noticed that the dark gray colour was nearly uniform. The clothing suited the man, and most of it was relatively form fitting and showed off his physique. She also couldn't help but notice that the garments were endowed with a great deal of detailed stitching, button work, and clasps and she couldn't think of a single store that sold anything even close to the outfit of the figure in front of her.

A gloved hand reached down towards Kya, and there was a slight sheen to it. The material that had covered his arms twisted down, separated and wrapping each, individual finger, it covered his entire hand.

"Here," A gentle voice came out from under the hood. "Let me help you up."

Kya hesitated for a moment, uneasy about trusting a person that she could not see.

"Please," He continued. "I only want to help."

"Why?" Kya rasped. It hurt her chest to speak.

"When the world is full of such evil, it's rebellious to be good." The man said, and from his light tone, Kya imagined he was smiling. "I saw what happened to you." His voice becoming more serious again. "You're not the first I have seen hurt here. But you are the first I have heard ask questions." He offered her his hand again. "Please, let me help you."

Kya took the man's hand, and he helped her up. Her body ached from the hit she had received from Frank, and it was difficult for her to straighten up. She took as deep of a breath as she could muster, and exhaled quickly when it felt like her rib was cutting into her lung. She couldn't help but let it out in an unintentional sob. "My best friend is probably dead! Frank... That Frank..." She wept.

"Shhh." The man soothed as he gently rubbed her back. "I know. I know."

CHAPTER 16

Kya tried to catch her breath and stop herself from crying. The mysterious man in gray continued to rub her back and soothe her. After a moment, Kya wiped her face and tried to stand up straight. She clutched her middle as it still ached, but she wanted to appear strong, despite feeling so confused and alone.

"You will probably be sore for a while." The man said as he stepped in front of her and watched her struggle with the pain. "I don't think anything's broken, though." He shook his head quickly as he spoke.

"Oh?" Kya groaned. "You have much experience with broken bones and people getting hit."

The man chuckled. "I guess you could say it's an occupational hazard."

The man's voice was smooth and gentle. It wasn't too low, or too high in pitch or volume either. It was warm, caring, but also strong and masculine. The fabric of the scarf, across the lower half of his face, was made of a thin enough material that it didn't seem to muffle his voice, and as Kya could not see his face, nor any of his skin, she only had his voice to go by. Judging by that alone, she thought he might be around thirty years old.

"What occupation is that?" She asked.

"I guess you could say I'm a sociology professor of sorts." As he spoke he shrugged his shoulders, then with his right hand he touched his temple with his index finger and gave it a little rub.

Kya stared at him, her brow furrowed and mouth slightly agape.

"I can't take away the pain, but is there anything I can do to help you?" The man asked after a moment of silence. There was a jovial tone to his question that was also somehow sincere.

Kya laughed in a less than happy way. "Not unless you have enough money lying around to buy me some Supers."

Tapping his chin, he tilted his head to its side slightly. "You know what's funny?" He didn't wait for a response before continuing. "In all my time as a sociology professor, I have learned time and time again one inalienable truth about humanity." He folded his arms and nodded as if he was satisfied that his point was already made.

Kya shook her head and stared at him. She waited several seconds, her breath baited while she still clutched her middle. "And, what is that?"

"We always want what we don't have, and we never fully appreciate what we do have."

Kya stared at him with her mouth closed, unsure how to respond.

The man sighed slightly, and then began pacing back and forth slowly. The alley was silent for several moments as the man gestured wildly. As if he came to a conclusion, he stopped, turned and threw his hands up in the air. "What if I knew a way that you," he pointed directly at Kya with both hands, "could get powers that didn't involve the Black Market or any of the conventional means?"

Kya raised an eyebrow. The world melted away as her mind became fully focused on the stranger in front of her. "I'm listening."

"Of course, it isn't without catches."

"Of course not," she commented dryly.

"You would be given a random set of powers and only as many and of a variety that your body will naturally tolerate. At least that is what past examples would lead me to believe." He shrugged again, then walked over to the red brick wall to Kya's left and began tracing his finger along the mortar lines.

"What's the cost?"

"No money crosses hands. All you would have to do is find out all you can about the history of Supers and then let others know what you find. If you are willing to do that, I will consider the trade to be fair."

"Okay..." Kya rolled her eyes. "Look, man, I have had a really stressful time of it recently, and I really don't know what you're playing at.

"What's your name?"

"Kya."

"Kya, I'm not playing at anything. I'm immune to Supers. They could inject me with the whole rainbow, and none of them would take. But I am, for lack of a better term, a carrier. My genes carry the mutations for pretty much every ability, but none of them manifest in me."

"Sure." Kya said and took a step away from the man. She found that it was easy not to believe someone with such an odd appearance and a love for being melodramatic. However, she couldn't force herself to leave. She had hoped, in some small place deep inside of her heart, that there was a chance to get what she wanted - what she felt she needed - to help herself and her friends.

He opened his hands wide, and spread his legs shoulder width apart, as though he was giving Kya an opportunity to get a good look at him. "I keep myself covered, so I don't accidentally give any unwanted gifts to an unsuspecting passerby. You see, one touch from me is all it would take to give someone superhuman powers as well as the limitations I talked about before and two more biggies. Anyone I touched would, like me, be immune to the Supers injections."

Kya stood firm, more than a little intrigued by his story.

"And any child of said person would also, like me, be immune to Supers and be a carrier."

"How do I know you're not just some crazy drama student or some other whack job?"

"You don't." He shrugged. "But if you think that Supers will help to solve your problems, and you are willing to do as I ask to find out all you can about Supers and tell others your findings…" With his left hand, he began picking at the material at his right wrist, and a moment later Kya watched as he began to unravel the fabric from his right hand. The skin underneath shone white as if it had never seen the sun before, pale and soft-looking. His nails were clean and trimmed short. "This is your choice, Kya. If you want to, touch my hand." He looked around and then stretched out his palm to her.

Kya thought for only a moment before she reached out with both hands, her heart racing in her chest.

His skin was warm and soft. There were no calluses on his hand, but it felt strong and powerful. Kya stared at their hands and saw nothing. There were no dazzling colours filling her veins, no rush of energy, and thankfully no sensation of pain. She felt nothing other than the warm touch of a stranger. A normal hand.

Kya bent and squinted, hoping to see underneath his hood to see his face, but even at arms length away, she found him to be covered in shadow.

He shook his head. "Hey! Not yet. You will see my face soon enough I'm sure. But not yet." There was still an expression of happiness to his voice that resonated with Kya. "When you're ready, see Everly. She's at the diner to the west of the last stop on the South Street bus line. It's before the turnaround. You'll know it when you see it." He gave her a thumbs-up with his right hand and then began to wrap it up again.

"Um, thanks." Kya said, sticking her hands in her pockets.

CHAPTER 17

Kya returned to her apartment, and she wanted to feel different. She dug deep inside herself and tried to pull out something amazing or super, but instead she just felt a tinge of pain from the injury that Frank had given her in the alley. She began to think the mysterious man she had met was truly just a whack job. Her chest still sore, and her body weak, she leaned against the apartment door and opened it.

The common space was dark. She dropped her keys in the dish and slipped off her shoes before she stumbled deeper into the apartment. It didn't take long for Kya to realize that Sam wasn't home. Usually at this time of night he'd be in the living room watching something on the wall mounted television, while also using his tablet and phone. A bevy of lights would be blinking and flashing as the room would be lit only from the various displays and not the half-dozen lamps and light fixtures scattered around the room. This time, however, the only lights that Kya could see were those bleeding through the shut curtains, coming from the busy city streets beyond.

Kya went into her room and shut the door behind her before she sat on her bed. Despite the emptiness of the apartment, she still felt most at ease when she was safe inside her bedroom with the door closed. For the entirety of her bus ride home, she thought she had tasted blood, and so she went into her bathroom to inspect the damage from Frank's fist. She lifted her shirt and with the bright bathroom light. She could easily see that there was already a deep, circular bruise forming. Taking a sip of water, Kya looked into the mirror and saw her own bloodshot eyes staring back at her. She swished the water and spat into the sink -no blood.

"Long day, wasn't it?" She said to her reflection. She turned off the washroom light and walked back into her room. She grabbed her laptop from her dresser and sat on her bed. As she opened it, a notification appeared, letting her know that she had received a dozen messages while she was gone. Most of the emails were related to newsletters she had subscribed to or companies she had an interest in, but one stood out: a message from Sam. A feeling of hope mixed with anger hit Kya when she saw his name, and remembered their last exchange. She held her breath as she read his message.

Hi Kya, I just thought you should know about this employment opportunity that a friend mentioned to me. Seemed like it might be something you'd enjoy. Be back tomorrow. - Sam

Kya was shocked at his ability to be so helpful and considerate after their argument, and she made a mental note to find a way to make it up to him. She wondered how someone so young could have such an endless amount of patience and understanding, especially when hers seemed to run out so fast.

At the end of the email was a link to an advertisement for an associate at a small, local bookstore and publisher. The requirements all seemed to fit Kya's experience, as it would allow her to use her degree in English Literature and it didn't require a Super. The listed pay seemed reasonable, and it was specifically for someone who enjoyed fiction. A rush of excitement coursed through Kya as she filled out the online application. She took time to craft a custom cover letter explaining her interest in fiction, the books she had recently read, and comparisons to movies. After an hour tweaking it, she read her application one more time, carefully analyzing her submission in hopes that she could sell her passion to whoever was going to read it.

It had been more than a few years since Kya had submitted a resume, and she felt a bit of anxiety as she completed her application. Pressing Submit on the online form, she wiped a thin film of sweat from her forehead and crashed backward into the pile of pillows on her bed.

The next morning, Kya found a response from a job she had applied for a few days earlier. Out of a dozen different places she had sent her resume to, a small, discount clothing store was the first to reply. She opened her e-mail, half expecting to find out she had gotten the job and half hoping she hadn't, only to find a very short message.

Hello Kya,

We regret to inform you, after speaking with your previous employer that you are not the candidate we are looking for at this time.

The words *previous employer* stood out and began to repeat endlessly in Kya's mind. It didn't take long for her brain to concoct a theory about what had happened. She hadn't thought about potential future employers contacting her previous boss and didn't know what to do to resolve the situation. Kya's mind raced as she thought about what might happen if the bookstore contacted Starlife Technologies and Don was able to smear her to them.

For a moment, she felt sick, but then she shook it off and tried to put the negative email out of her mind. She thought about the job she applied for the night before, the one Sam had found, and she began to feel a bit confused. She couldn't understand how Sam could be so nice to her when she had been so angry with him. She still felt betrayed by him, but a seed of curiosity had been planted within her, and she couldn't ignore it as it grew. *Samson Hart,* she typed into the search field, and once again the screen flooded with results. She stared at them trying to decide where to start. She scanned for the earliest dated article she could find and clicked on a link dated thirteen years earlier and read through the entirety of the article, word by word.

Hart Matriarch First Public Citizen to Get Supers

Multibillionaire Victoria Hart has signed on to be the first, of the general public, to purchase what the government has called "Supers". Earlier this year, a genetic manipulation technique, long since used for military and police, entered the third generation of testing and yesterday the technique was given the green light for administration to the general public. Victoria Hart, wife of Vincent Hart, and co-founder of Heimdal Energy was at the door of the first of many clinics where Supers will be administered. She was granted access before its doors were officially opened and placed the $5500 cash payment at the service counter before requesting a Super called Flight.

Mrs. Hart received an injection that will rewrite her genetic code to enable her to fly. The power should begin to take effect within a week. She is quoted as saying, "I can't wait to see all the possibility Supers will bring to the world, and I can't wait for others to join me."

It is presumed Mr. Hart will also likely undergo a procedure soon. Their son, Samson Hart, will have to wait three more years, as the government has imposed an age restriction so that Supers can only be obtained by persons over the age of eighteen.

Other restrictions on Supers include that each Super must manifest fully before another can be administered, and that a limit of five Supers can be obtained by one person. There is also an extraction technique in the works in case someone wishes to swap out one power for another.

The article went on to list the side effects of Supers and the predicted popularity of them. Kya sighed and clicked on another result. *World's First Flying Woman* was a link to a short video of a woman taking a very unsteady flight across a beach while a man and a blond haired boy watched. The caption under the video read *Victoria Hart shows off her new skills for her husband and son, Samson.*

Kya returned to her search results and clicked on a title she had read the last time she had searched Sam's name.

Hart Family Tragedy

Today the world mourns the death of the first Super Hero. Victoria Hart was a true pioneer, the first person to receive a Super. She received the injection that would rewrite her DNA to enable her to fly only twenty-six short days ago. Her bravery and sense of adventure started a frenzy for Super powers. It was this same power that took her life.

The article linked to a video of Victoria's final flight. Kya let her cursor hover over the link for a moment, but she could not bring herself to watch the video. The article explained that Victoria had flown too high, and passed out due to oxygen deprivation and plummeted to her death, leaving behind her husband and son, Samson Hart.

Her heart broke as she realized how inconsiderate she had been to Sam. Kya realized that in all the time she had lived with him, she never really asked about Sam's past. She couldn't remember a time when he needed her to be there to support him emotionally, or to give him advice, despite her unintentional habit of calling on him for such things. She mentally chided herself for being so selfish and thought back through all the conversations where she basically beat him over the head with her dreams of Supers.

Thinking about her interactions with Sam led Kya to analyze all of her friendships, and it quickly brought her to Amelia. Mentally dusting herself off, she grabbed her phone and sent a quick message to Mattea.

>*Hey, Mattie, You free?*

>*Kya! Oh, am I ever glad to see your name! What were you thinking?*

>*Look, Mattie. I need to find Amelia.*

>*Did you go where you said you were going to go?*

>*Yeah, but the answers I got just led to more questions. And I won't be going back there.*

>*So what are you going to do now?*

>*The next stop is Amelia's place. Can you drive me there, please? If I'm going to find her, I'm going to need help... More than just a car and someone to drive it.*

>*I will definitely help you, but it will have to be tomorrow, is that okay?*

Kya let out a deep sigh and paced her room. She felt the walls closing in on her. She could feel the seconds screaming by.

She pictured Amelia fighting against her Supers for her life. She desperately wanted to look for her friend, but she could not imagine going back to the apartment alone.

>*If it's gotta be tomorrow, it's gotta be tomorrow.*

Thank you.

> :-)

As Mattea's sedan pulled up to Amelia's worn down apartment, Kya took a deep breath and let it out heavily. She turned to her friend and, reading the look on Mattea's face; she couldn't help but comment. "Not what you were expecting, is it?"

"Not really, no." Mattea sighed in response. "I guess I just thought she'd live somewhere..."

"Nicer?"

"Yeah."

"Me too."

The girls traveled in silence as they parked the car in an underground, paid parking lot. The only one nearby where Mattea felt comfortable leaving her car behind. As they exited into the sun, Kya felt uneasy. She knew that she needed to ask around, talk to others that lived in Amelia's building, and putting herself out there, pushing herself to be social, with strangers, was difficult for her.

"So what's the plan?" Mattea said as they entered the run down building where Amelia lived.

The smell of garbage burned Kya's nose as they started up the stairs to Amelia's floor.

The door to Amelia's apartment was closed, and a printed notice was taped over top of the number. "Please contact me as soon as possible. Issac - Building Superintendent"

"I wonder if they fixed the horrible locks?" Kya said, more to herself than anyone else.

"Hello?" A strange voice came from down the hall.

A young man stepped out through the next door. He wore dark wash jeans, and stood taller than both girls, by a good amount. His t-shirt was tightly fitted, and his shoulder length black hair was well kept. He was both imposing and yet somehow had a disarming nature about him.

"Hi," Mattie said as she noticeably checked out the young man.

Kya felt slightly embarrassed and on the spot. She didn't know what to say, and she thought it funny that her married and pregnant friend found the stranger attractive.

"Do you know anything about what happened to the woman that lives here?" Kya said, stepping in front of Mattea.

"Nope. The building superintendent asked me that two days ago. Apparently, she hasn't paid rent. If she doesn't show up by the end of the month, I figure she'll probably be evicted. Or her stuff will at least." He excused himself and walked past them to the stairwell.

Kya turned to look at Mattea for a moment.

"You have a key?" Mattea asked.

"Nope," Kya replied as she placed her hand on the doorknob of Amelia's apartment and began wiggling it. Exactly like the previous time she had been there, the door opened.

"Well, that's safe!" Mattea remarked sarcastically.

Kya shrugged and looked around the apartment. It was unchanged since her last visit. A weight of sadness fell upon her and only then did she realize that she had been holding out hope, even after that exchange with the neighbour, that Amelia had been back.

"What now, Kya?" Mattea asked as she looked around the apartment, her arms wrapped protectively around her stomach.

"I have to find some information..." Kya said as she scanned the apartment again, not sure what she was looking for.

"How can I help?" Mattie asked, still taking in the scene.

"Just look for something that would help us find out where Amelia would go... What she would do." As Kya finished speaking, her eyes fell on Amelia's laptop. A small wooden desk with great detail of carved whimsical swirls sat near the window. Kya noticed the various scratches in the golden finish, looking more like an antique than something she assumed that Amelia would have purchased. A cheap, black task chair, with its coasters removed, sat on a small area rug next to the desk.

"Hey, maybe there's some information in a book somewhere. Like an agenda." Mattie said, wandering about the room and thumbing through the papers on the table, the magazines piled around the couch, and the half dozen books on a shelf next to various movies.

Kya flipped open the laptop and was greeted with a login screen that required a password. She sighed and rolled her eyes, wondering why Amelia needed a password when she lived alone, and what she would pick as a password. She had tried *Latte*, *latte* and *74tt3* before she noticed a small note sticking out from just under the lip of the computer. Pulling the paper from under the laptop, it listed a few websites Amelia frequented and helpful hints for her passwords. The hints were short clues that Amelia had written down to reduce her mistakes.

"Scatterbrained, much?" Kya said, smiling.

"Found something?" Mattea said as she craned her neck to look at what Kya was doing.

"Just a sheet of password hints that Amelia uses. Her laptop is locked down, and I didn't bring anything to help me gain access to it."

"Couldn't we just bring it with us?"

"I'm going to try to figure out the passwords that go along with the hints and see if I can get anywhere. Can you check her bedroom to see if she left anything behind?"

Mattie nodded and went into the small bedroom off to one side. Reading the first clue, *My favourite restaurant* Kya typed in *Coliseum* and the laptop sprang to life. "I knew you knew the name!" She said in a muffled tone to a room filled with Amelia's things.

Kya opened up a web browser and loaded the online email client that Amelia used. She read through the list of clues. She tried Coliseum first, but the service came back with an incorrect password message. She checked the next clue, *The Super I most want* Kya typed in *Telepathy* and Amelia's email loaded. The first twenty-six messages were all mailing list type emails from places like Noble Brew. The twenty-seventh was a quote from a reputable Supers clinic for different Supers.

After scrolling through a few pages of emails, Kya decided that it was a fruitless endeavour. She logged into the only social media site on Amelia's list and found that aside from a few contacts from her college days she had no *friends* and the account seemed to have gone unused for months at a time.

Kya was running out of options, and although she didn't want to invade her privacy any more than she already had, she began typing in the name of Amelia's bank.

"I found an old fashioned, printed address book." Mattea walked back into the room. "It was on a shelf by the bed. Not many entries, though." She said, thumbing through the pages.

Kya was flooded with relief that she might be able to use some of the information from the book to find a lead.

"Mom and dad are listed here," Mattea said. "But it looks like she tried to erase it."

Kya reached out her hand, and Mattea gave her the book. Written extremely faintly, with obvious eraser marks was *Mom and Dad, 1080 Solsbury Lane.*

Kya closed the banking tab and opened a new one

searching for *Bronsen 1080 Solsbury Lane*. The first result was a map showing where the address was in the city, the second was what caught Kya's eye, it was an article entitled *Couple Die in Terrible Car Accident*. Kya skimmed the article, knowing that she could not bear more loss and bad news. She gleaned enough from the article to know that Amelia's parents were dead and that her sister, Ainsley, was the only family she had left.

Kya checked the address book, but there was no entry for Ainsley Bronsen. She typed the name into the search field along with the numbers 411. It produced three results but only one close enough to contact.

Kya looked out the window; the sun was already long since set. She looked at Mattea.

"You free again tomorrow?"

"I have an appointment with the doctor in the early afternoon, but I'll pick you up after that, and we'll meet up with Ainsley Bronsen."

Waiting for Mattea was a type of torture Kya was becoming familiar with. Several times throughout the day she considered texting her friend and letting her know she would go alone. But every time she picked up her phone a crippling fear stopped her. She needed Mattea's calm nature to steady her and give her the courage she needed to find her friend.

Mattea drove to the address of the closest Ainsley Bronsen that Kya had found. Neither one of them spoke much on the drive.

Kya's mind raced with thoughts and worries about what she would say, how she would speak to Amelia's sister, and what they would find. Many other less concrete thoughts and worries swirled around, stealing her attention.

"I think this is it," Mattea said, just above a whisper, as she pulled over to the curb beside a nicely kept, suburban type home with a large two car garage built into the front of the red brick and white siding two story home. There was a mahogany stained wooden porch that stretched across the rest of the main floor of the house. Four hanging baskets of flowers hung at evenly spaced intervals along the overhang.

"Nice digs," Kya said, trying to ignore the sound of her heart beating fast and persistent in her ears.

"You ready to go up?" Mattea said. Her voice was still small, and she made no visible sign that she was going to leave the car.

"I guess so." Kya undid her seatbelt and slowly opened the car door, motioning to get out. Frantic, she closed the door until it was just a crack and turned her body back towards Mattea. "What do I say? How do I do this?"

"You go up, knock on the door, and then..." Mattea shook her head. "I don't know. But I know you are smart and caring, and I am sure you will figure it out. Do you want me to come with you?"

"Please."

Mattea and Kya, their hands clasped tightly together, walked up the patio stone path along the edge of the nicely manicured lawn and garden to the double door with large windows filled with a floral design of frosted glass. Kya let out a long guttural breath, and Mattea raised an eyebrow as if to ask which of them should ring the doorbell.

Kya raised her free, but slightly shaky hand to where the button for the bell was mounted beside the door. She closed her eyes and leaned her whole body into make her finger push the button. The bell rang melodically, and Kya opened her eyes to see a silhouette moving beyond the frosted glass. She leaned heavily on her heels, ready to turn and bolt from the stranger's house. Her discomfort was causing a slight, but noticeable cold sweat to form. As she waited, she couldn't help but count, an activity that helped her focus her mind and relax. She made it to fifteen before the door swung open.

Kya felt a huge smile burst across her face, and she nearly fell over with relief as she stared at the face of her friend. Amelia's regular straight black hair, her friendly smile, a healthy glow on her no longer sallow cheeks.

"Can I help you?" She asked, and the way she spoke, the lack of recognition, instantly broke Kya's heart. It was then she noticed the plumper cheeks, gentle wrinkles around her eyes, and thinner lips.

"Ainsley?" Kya could barely get the word out through the solid lump that had formed in her throat.

"Yes," She said, glancing suspiciously at the pair.

Kya couldn't speak, her mouth hung slightly open, completely dry inside. She simply stared at Amelia's sister, taking in her appearance and paying extra attention the differences between the two.

"Hi," Mattea interjected with a smile. "I'm Mattie, and this is Kya. We're friends of Amelia's. May we come in?"

The smile fell from Ainsley's face though she gestured to allow her new guests into her house. The house was painted with a neutral palette, and pieces of tasteful artwork hung on the walls. Ainsley led them into what seemed to be the formal living room. A fireplace with a wood mantle was set into the wall opposite the door. There was a window beside it that Kya assumed looked onto the brick wall of the house next door, only three feet away. To the left of the fireplace was the bay window overlooking the porch that Kya had briefly glanced at on her way to the door. In front of the window sat two matching beige armchairs, and opposite the fireplace sat a beige leather couch that matched the chairs. Kya and Mattea both sat on the couch. Ainsley sat in the armchair further from them.

"So," Kya said, finding her voice again. "Do you know where your sister is?"

Mattea shot her a reprimanding look.

Ainsley cleared her throat. "Can I get you, ladies, something to drink?"

They both nodded their affirmative.

"Just water for me please." Mattea clarified.

Ainsley left the room, her footsteps echoing as her heels tapped against the wood floor.

Kya found it odd to see someone wearing high heels inside their own house though she noticed that Ainsley was a well put together woman. It reminded her of someone that looked more prepared for a high fashion gala event than Ainsley's sister's normal barista attire.

"Kya!" Mattea whispered sternly. "You can't just say that!"

"I panicked!" Kya whispered back.

Ainsley returned with a shiny metal serving tray filled with drinks. She had a glass of water with ice and a slice of lemon in it, and two rather large crystal glasses filled with red wine. She placed the tray on the table and gave the girls a tight-lipped smile. She picked up the wine glass closest to her and took a large gulp.

"I don't know where she is," She said. "It's been weeks since she returned my texts."

Kya and Mattea each picked their respective drinks and sipped.

"We had gotten in a bit of an argument the last time we spoke, and I figured she was just mad at me. Well, at least until you two showed up at my door. You see, that's what we do. We fight."

Kya nodded, unsure of what to say. She tried to choose her words carefully. After a slightly uncomfortable pause, and another sip of her drink, she began to speak. "I'm sorry, and I don't mean to be rude, but do you mind if I ask what the fight was about?"

"It was about her stupid Supers. She showed up here. Literally just popped into existence in my kitchen. Made me break a plate. They were a really nice set of dishes."

Kya could see Ainsley's agitation rising.

"She was all proud of herself for paying some stranger in a back alley to mess her up. Then she comes into my house, showing off, as always! Making a mess and leaving me to clean it up."

"So, I'm getting the feeling you guys don't always have the best relationship." Kya said, and Mattie elbowed her in the side.

"Not since our parents died. They used to be able to rein us in and help us to see things clearer. Without them," she paused. "It's like we're two strangers." She took a gulp of her wine, nearly emptying the glass.

Mattea flinched and then pulled her phone out of her pocket. Leaning in close to Kya's ear, she whispered. "It's Rory. It's getting late, and he's getting worried."

"So you have no clue where Amelia is?" Kya asked.

"No. And I'm not about to go looking for her either."

"Really?" Kya said. "Why not?"

"Because." She folded her arms. "Amelia made her choice. It was a stupid decision and she has to live with the consequences."

"She could be dead."

"Then I guess I'll see you at the funeral."

"Kya," Mattea said, "I really gotta go."

"Okay," Kya said, standing up.

"Thanks for your help," Mattea said. Her tone both gentle and sincere.

Kya grit her teeth, turned towards the doorway and walked back to the front hall. As she walked out to the front porch, Ainsley's hand touched her shoulder and Kya turned.

"Look. I don't know if she would go there, but our family owns a cabin. Our parents left it to both of us to use as we see fit, but I haven't been there in years. It's north of the city by about two hours. We used to spend a lot of time there. It held a lot of good memories, but for me at least, they've all been ruined now. I could write the address down for you if you'd like to go see if she is there."

Kya nodded.

Kya walked to the passenger side of Mattea's car and opened the door. She climbed into the sedan, her mind racing with thoughts of Amelia. Her hand cramped slightly, and she noticed how tightly wrapped it was around the paper with the address to the cottage.

"I know Rory is missing you, but..." She let the sentence hang in the air and looked at her still clenched fist.

"Kya, you know I love you, and I want to help you find Amelia, but I have to get home."

Kya nodded. "I understand."

"Rory has been really protective since," she put her

245

ANNIE PERALTY & DAVID PERALTY

hand on her stomach, "the baby. And actually, I'm feeling it too. I don't want to risk losing this little one. So, I need to rest and take things slow."

"I get it," Kya replied in a kind and friendly tone. "Hey listen, why don't you drop me at the bus terminal? That way you can get home sooner."

"Thanks," Mattea said with a what Kya knew to be a genuine smile.

A few minutes later the car pulled up to the city bus terminal closest to Ainsley's house. Kya was grateful for all the time she had spent on the bus because despite never having been in the wealthier West end neighborhood before, she was certain that she knew the way back to her apartment.

Mattea shut off the car and got out as Kya did. She walked around the car to hug her friend. "I'll call you tomorrow, and we can work out going to the cabin, okay?"

Kya nodded.

"Take care of you," Mattea said as she climbed back into the car.

Kya waved as Mattea drove away. She then slowly walked into the terminal, paid her fare and found the correct route to take her home. She boarded the bus without it registering what she was doing. Her mind continued to reel with thoughts of Amelia.

With no family to speak of, except for a sister who didn't seem to care, and with no real friends that Kya had been able to track down, was anyone other than Kya missing Amelia?

People in her apartment building knew she was absent, but none of them seemed to be looking for her, if Kya gave up, would anyone continue the search for Amelia? Kya shut her eyes and rested her head against the back of the seat, feeling a weight of intense exhaustion and responsibility crush her.

CHAPTER 18

Kya's cell phone buzzed in a specific pattern that she knew was reserved for a special report being pushed to every mobile device. It was rare that Kya checked the broadcasts, but she felt a pang of concern that it might be about Amelia.

The screen illuminated her face as the bus continued its journey. Looking around, she saw that many others were also engaged in viewing the announcement.

A picture of Myles Redwood filled her screen, and large text scrolled along as words were spoken by a rather generic male voice. "Be aware, Myles Redwood is a dangerous class one fugitive. Call your local police department if you see him or have any knowledge of his whereabouts. Anyone able to subdue him will receive a reward."

At the end of the report, a button appeared asking the viewer to tap on it for more information. Kya thought about Sam, with his interest in Myles, and tapped the bright blue button.

A video started to load, buffering quickly as the data was sent to her phone, but Kya could already hear bits and pieces of it on the bus. Others were ahead of her and already playing the video. She focused her attention on her phone and listened intently as the introductory news corporation logo was replaced with a reporter sitting at his desk, a blue-tinted room surrounding him.

A tall, thin man filled half of the screen, and Kya recognized him as the reporter from Myles' accident. A computer graphic faded in below his head, reminding her that his name was Jason Lu. He smiled at the camera as he spoke while seated at a large slate desk. "We have found evidence that leads to the incomprehensible fact that Myles Redwood has received seven Supers now. He has received two Supers since his public Extraction. These additional Supers, place him one over the allowed five and have caused him to have a psychotic break that has led to his current erratic behavior." He paused, organized the papers on his desk and let his words sink in.

The reporter continued, in his calm and somewhat overly pleasant tone. "It is said that he has now murdered three people and evaded the police in multiple confrontations today. He has destroyed over ten million dollars in property and has threatened to destroy the entire city if he is not *'left alone.'* Doctors are now saying that his psychosis will only get worse until the authorities end his life, or he takes his own life."

The camera angle changed, and Jason's head swiveled to look once again at the camera, an eerie grin still plastered on his face.

Kya couldn't remember the last time something like this happened, and hoped it wasn't a common occurrence. She knew that all of the facilities had government oversight that limited the number of Supers you could get and that they likely had both records and tests to confirm how many Supers a person received.

"It is likely that Myles Redwood received his powers through bribing staff at Invista Medical, the same company that originally gave him the Strength Super that was used in the murder of Newton Wilson last month."

Kya shut off her phone, ending the video as the bus pulled around the corner that lead to her apartment. She felt a tingle rush up her spine as though something important had changed, but she couldn't put her finger on it. Despite all that she had seen regarding Myles Redwood, thoughts of Amelia continued to circle around in her mind, stealing all of her focus.

As Kya entered her apartment, she noticed Sam focused on his various devices. The television illuminated the otherwise dark room. Without drawing his attention, Kya quickly slipped off her shoes and went into her room. She didn't feel social, nor ready to talk to anyone about the recent events that she barely made it through. Tossing her jeans aside, she slipped under her covers and stared blankly up at her ceiling waiting for sleep to find her.

Kya's mind buzzed with thoughts of Amelia and her own experience with Frank. She found herself replaying everything from when Amelia first went missing, through her experience with the stranger, and finally her conversation with Amelia's sister. A hopeless feeling washed over her as exhaustion finally set in. As her eyes finally slammed shut, the first thought to enter her mind was about the cottage. *Will I find Amelia, or is this another dead end?*

Kya didn't feel as though she had slept at all. Her morning alarm on her phone buzzed and beeped endlessly as she swatted at her nightstand. Forcing her left eye open, the one that felt to be the less dry of the two, she noticed her phone wasn't in its dock, nor anywhere on her table. She paused and took a moment to listen, to try to detect where the noise was coming from, only to realize that she had left it in her jeans the night before.

As her feet hit the ground, Kya found it difficult to push herself up. It was as though she spent the night being punched. Her whole body ached, and her muscles seemed weaker than normal. A large stretch did nothing to improve the situation. Kya grabbed her cell phone, turned off her alarm, and set it to its charging station.

A notification of a text message was also on her phone, and it took Kya a few moments longer than normal to check what it had to say. Without removing the phone from the dock, she opened the messenger.

>Hey, just wanted you to know that I have time this afternoon if you wanted to go out to the cabin. Let me know.

Kya closed the message without responding. Through the night, she had come to terms with the fact that she had to go to the cabin alone. Somehow she had found the courage inside herself and, despite the nervous pain in her stomach and the constant stream of 'what if's in her mind, Kya was determined to get herself to the cabin as soon as possible.

Awkwardly, as her phone was still charging, she swiped over to the bus schedule application and pulled up the route needed to get her to the cottage. As she stretched again, she started to feel more alert and focused. It didn't take long for Kya to get all of her things together for the long trip to chase down another lead.

The bus dropped Kya off over an hour walk away from the cottage, but it was the closest stop, and she didn't have the money to pay for a taxi. The walk gave her time to clear her thoughts, and fight any expectations that were trying to creep into her mind. Kya didn't want hope to rise up within her as she approached the large wooden structure sitting amongst the heavily treed property atop a small hill. She didn't want to feel anything so that she could feel prepared for everything.

Amelia's cottage was more like a small mansion. It was made of large, dark wooden logs, with a pristine red shingle roof. Large glistening windows faced towards the road and the cobblestone path that lead up to the garage. Old trees were scattered around the property, and the lawn was noticeably manicured. It looked like someone was keeping the cottage in perfect condition.

As she arrived at the front door, Kya knocked, only to barely hear any resonance from her tapping. The door, solid oak, didn't translate the noise of her rapping into the cottage. She lifted the small metal knocker, and let it fall on the door, and a near-deafening noise echoed outwards. The birds nearby stopped singing for a moment, likely from shock, as Kya waited to hear any stirring inside.

After a few moments of waiting, her ear pressed against the door, Kya let the metal knocker slam into the door once again. She quickly counted to three in her mind, and then grabbed the doorknob and pushed on the door.

Unlocked, it opened with surprising ease, and the heavy door swung open revealing the sunlit interior of the cottage. An unfamiliar and unpleasant odour caught in Kya's nose and she stifled a wretch. Her head spinning as she took in every detail, her eyes quickly noticed something on the ground. Lying, unnaturally still, in a blue sun dress was a body, with pale skin and dark hair, tangled and messy. A small amount of blood, dried on the hardwood floor drew Kya's attention next.

Kya pulled on the door with both hands, and the sound of it slamming echoed through the air around her. She tried to take a step, and her legs gave way beneath her. She crumpled to the ground. She heard a ringing in her ears, and the world shifted in and out of focus, her skin exploded with goosebumps, and she started to sweat. She fought the sudden urge to vomit. Kya closed her eyes, but her mind's eye was focussed on what she had just seen. She forced her eyes open wanting to see anything other than the image burned into her mind.

Around her were beautiful trees and flowers in bloom, new life growing in the sweet late spring air. Birds were singing, and the sky was blue with a few puffy white clouds. It seemed a terrible mockery that the world wasn't darkened by the weight of Amelia's fate in the way that Kya herself now was.

I should go in and see if she's alright - she's not alright. I should go in and see if I can help her - I can't help her. Kya pulled her knees up to her chest and breathed deeply. She pushed her hair out of her face and rubbed her forehead with her hand. A hand she could no longer see. Kya blinked rapidly and stared at where her hand should be. She put both of her arms out in front of her and they just ended at her wrists. She could see her shirt's long sleeves and beyond that was the grass and the trees.

"My... My hands!"

She shook her hands and could feel them, blood still flowing, her fingers felt attached as she willed them to move. She blinked slow and hard, and her hands faded back into existence.

"I think I'm losing it," She said aloud to no one, as a numbness washed over her.

Kya put her hand in her pocket and pulled out her phone. She used the emergency call function.

"Fire, police, or ambulance?" A gentle sounding female voice said through the phone.

"Ambulance."

The lady asked Kya for the details of where she was, and Kya answered as accurately as she could.

"Help is on the way," The woman said after gathering all relevant information.

Kya ended the call, and as her thumb touched the *End* key, it seemed to flicker in and out of existence. Kya shuddered.

She closed her eyes, and felt her eyelids close, but she could still see the world around her. A scream escaped her. She dropped her phone and reached her hands up to her face. She touched lightly, exploring and expecting to feel the moisture of her eyes and the discomfort of touching them, but instead she felt her closed eyelids, completely transparent, still where they were expected to be.

"Oh, oh, oh help me!" Kya said as a cold panic wrapped itself around her. "What is wrong with me?" The world faded away to darkness, and for a moment Kya had thought she was blind. Relief filled her as she opened her eyes and she was able to see the world normally once again. She exhaled deeply, unsure of what was happening to her.

Kya picked up her phone and selected Mattea's number from her list of recent calls.

"Mattie, answer. Please, Mattie." She repeated as the phone rang.

Kya heard Mattea's voice say "Huh" before she immediately broke into a frantic rant.

"Mattie! You have to come get me! I'm at the cottage Ainsley mentioned. I came by myself. I'm really freaking out here. Amelia... Amelia's here... but she's not good. I'm losing it. Like, I'm barely here too! Literally, disappearing!"

"Kya!" Mattea yelled. "Stop!"

Kya shut her mouth, clenching her jaw.

"Breathe."

She took a deep breath through her nose.

"Is Amelia okay?"

Kya shook her head and closed her eyes. Blessed darkness once again. Tears cascaded down her cheeks as she tried to imagine herself back at her apartment in bed.

"Kya?" Mattea said calmly.

"No," Kya responded in barely more than a whisper. "No, she's not okay."

Over the phone, Kya could hear Mattea take a deep breath.

"Oh, Kya," She whispered. "I'm coming to get you."

"Thanks," Kya said and ended the call. She stared into the distance at the trees and flowers and grass, refusing to turn and see the cottage behind her.

Time seemed to tick by more and more slowly until it had completely stopped. The clouds in the sky appeared not to be moving, and the songs of the birds seemed first to slow, and then fade away. The sheer enormity of the space around Kya crushed her. A loneliness more profound than she had ever felt before paralyzed her. It would be at least an hour for help to arrive, and Kya could do nothing but wait.

Confusion wormed its way into her mind, twisting into her thoughts and leading her to reflect on how much and how badly things had changed in her life and how quickly it had all happened. As much as she tried, Kya couldn't outrun thoughts of how obsessed she and Amelia had been with Supers and the lengths they had been willing to go to get them. She reflected on how adamantly against them Sam had been, and in the end, how Sam had been right. She thought of Elliot's broken body and how long it had taken for him to be found, and now Amelia.

Every thought that entered her mind was harder to face than the one before it, but there were no distractions that could pull her out of her deep reflection, and Kya surrendered to the torrent of her thoughts.

CHAPTER 19

Sirens could be heard in the distance and the flashing lights cut through the trees as two cars approached. A police car and an ambulance rushed up the laneway throwing a thick cloud of dust up into the air as they hit the cobblestone path that lead up to the cottage.

Kya's eyes were completely dry as she stared, unblinking, at the two vehicles. One police officer and two paramedics rushed from their respective vehicles. The officer, a middle aged but extremely fit woman, came straight to Kya as the paramedics, both young men, went around to the back of their large white ambulance.

As the officer opened a small pouch, a silver sheet unfurled, and she stared solemnly at Kya as she approached.

"Ma'am. Are you okay?" She said before wrapping the metallic blanket around Kya's shoulders. "I know you've been through a traumatic experience, but I need you to walk me through what happened."

Kya noticed the officer's badge, engraved into a star-shaped piece of metal was a single word, likely her last name: Wells.

Officer Wells sat next to Kya, her back pressed partly against the door, and partly against the brick exterior. She took a small tablet from her pocket, and opening its leather cover, the device illuminated. "I'm going to record our conversation. Is that okay?"

The Police officer didn't seem to wait for Kya to respond, not that Kya felt like saying or doing anything. There didn't seem to be any point to anything, and Kya continued to stare, unendingly at the world in front of her. A slight wafting of floral scent hit Kya's nose as the direction of the wind allowed her to smell the officer's perfume. For a moment, Kya was once again paying attention to what was at hand, and she turned her head to face the officer, but a quick comparison to the scent of Amelia's perfume, and then the smell of the cottage dragged Kya back into the cycle of pain and sadness that ravaged her mind. She turned her gaze back out toward the trees.

The two paramedics, having retrieved a stretcher from their ambulance, brought it to the front door, where Kya was still sitting and blocking their path. Kya noticed as Officer Wells pointed at them. She made emphatic hand gestures before one of them let out an audible groan, and they both proceeded around the side of the building.

Officer Wells tried again to attract Kya's attention. "Miss Roberts, I'm sorry for what happened, but can you please explain how you came across this scene today?"

The words were all registering, but Kya felt frozen

within her body, unable to string together a response, afraid if she opened her mouth, that she would start screaming and never stop.

The officer leaned towards Kya, pressing into her side. "I could always just read your mind if that's your preference," she said. Her tone was noticeably stern, and the softness of her earlier comments was gone.

Not caring if the officer read her mind, Kya continued to sit perfectly still. Her mind was reeling as she was bombarded with thoughts from the recent events in her life. Behind her, she could hear the two paramedics inside the cottage. Inside her mind, she cringed at the thought of someone touching Amelia's body.

The sound of a car approaching reached Kya before she could see it as the sedan appeared through the trees she recognized it as Mattea's. Even before the car had stopped moving, the passenger door was open, and Mattea was undoing her seatbelt to exit the car. A moment later the car had stopped, and Mattea ran to Kya. Rory emerged as well, after turning off the engine.

Mattea came up the steps and gracefully landed on the porch in front of Kya. She wrapped her arms around her friend without saying a word.

"Pardon me, Ma'am, but-..." Officer Wells began speaking to Mattea.

"I'm Mattea. I'm Kya's friend. We have been looking for Amelia together. She called me to come." Mattea let go of Kya and sat back on the porch. Her hands reached for Kya's and held them tight.

"We are starting a serious and delicate investigation here." Officer Wells continued, her voice calm and soft, yet authoritative.

"Please." Kya squeaked.

Both the officer and Mattea turned their attention to Kya.

"Please, Mattie. Stay?"

The officer's eyes seemed to brighten, and a noticeable look of relief washed across her face. "Alright, you can stay. Now, please, what series of events led you here today."

Kya stared into Mattea's eyes, pleading without words for her help. The idea of putting any of her thoughts into words was more than Kya could tolerate. Her jaw clenched tight she continued to stare.

Rory placed his arm around his wife protectively. His dark brown hair moved slightly in the breeze as it caught the waves and loose curls. His face, one of worry, showed signs of neglect as the scruff of a quickly growing beard started to hide the clef on his strong chin. His large piercing brown eyes had visible dark circles beneath them, and his thick eyebrows were raised towards his forehead in concern. His long black wool coat swam slightly on his frame, and his jeans also looked too large for his size.

Officer Wells frowned at him. "This is a sensitive matter, and I must ask for as few outside parties as possible."

Mattea studied Kya's face, the way Kya's whole body shook, the coldness of her hands. "I'm sorry, officer, but I think this isn't a good time to get answers from my friend. Kya has been through a lot, and the person she found inside is one of her best friends."

Kya let out a sob as a new wave of anguish crashed over her. Still, no tears spilled from her eyes.

"Do you have a card we can take? Alternatively, can we give you our numbers to call? I really think it is best for Kya that we get her home. She needs time to process all that has happened, and I don't think you will be getting any answers today."

"It is important that I complete my investigation. I can read her mind if I can't get answers any other way."

"I understand that you have Supers, and I am aware that you can and do use them in your job as an officer of the law," Mattea said politely. "I also know that for you to legally use Telepathy on an individual, you need their consent. Kya is not in the proper state of mind to be giving consent."

"Mattie," Rory whispered, "please don't overdo it. Think of the baby."

The officer nodded and waved her hand at them in dismissal. "Sir, after you get these ladies to your car, please return to me with adequate contact information for each of you. You can *all* expect to hear from me within forty-eight hours."

The back seat of Mattea and Rory's car was warm and soft, and it hugged Kya as she climbed in on the passenger side.

"There you go. Just keep taking deep breaths and we will be out of here in a minute." Mattea said as she shut the door and walked around behind the car. Mattea hopped in the back as well, on the driver's side.

Rory sat in the driver's seat started the electric engine, and they drove away from the cabin. None of them looked back to see the still flashing lights of the emergency vehicles that were reflecting on the windows and mirrors of the car.

"Do you want to talk about it?" Mattea asked after an extended silence.

"I'd rather just listen." Kya groaned, staring out the window at the trees, as they rushed past in a blur.

"What would you like me to talk about?"

Kya shrugged. The cool breeze from the car's air conditioner calmed her nerves and helped dry the sweat from her body. She felt less uncomfortable, and a little less sick to her stomach.

Rory craned his neck and looked back at the pair of women. "Mattie, please, don't stress yourself."

"Rory, do you really think that talking is going to jeopardize the safety of the baby?" Her high pitched, defensive tone echoed through the cabin of the car.

Rory exhaled loudly but said nothing.

"It's like he thinks I'm made of something weaker than

glass these days." Mattea changed her tone to one more light and calming, but Kya could still hear an undertone of something like annoyance or resentment. "Granted, I am technically supposed to be on bed rest... It is a high-risk pregnancy, but so are ninety percent of the pregnancies out there." Mattea said projecting her voice at her husband as she finished her retort.

A deep voice quickly exclaimed from the driver's seat, "But those other ninety percent aren't my wife."

"It's this whole Fertility Crisis." Mattea continued, ignoring Rory's comment. "Genetic engineering and rigorous hormone therapies to get pregnant, and now I'm on more hormones to keep me that way. One large needle, three times a day."

"Every day," Rory said, driving his point home.

Mattea nudged Kya. Slowly Kya turned to look, at her friend.

A slight grin widened along Mattea's face. "He's just annoyed because he has to give them to me. I'd rather do it myself, but the sight of the needle is enough to make me vomit these days."

Kya tried to twist her mouth into a smile.

Mattea's expression softened into an unmistakable look of pity. "You look so tired." Mattea slowly brushed a piece of hair out of Kya's face and back behind her ear.

Unable to reciprocate, or appreciate the attention, Kya returned to staring out the window. She felt odd but tried to stay focused on the moment. She wanted to let her friend know that what she was doing was appreciated, but Kya felt she needed to lock down all emotions, good and bad, to be able to stay sane.

When they arrived at Kya's apartment, both Mattea and Rory got out of the car to escort Kya upstairs. Every step that Kya took felt heavy with exhaustion. Walking down the corridor to her apartment, it felt like she hadn't been there in years. The hallway seemed longer and darker than ever before. The floor felt unyielding, and an odd, unfamiliar smells permeated the air. An invisible weight pulled on her eyelids, but she refused to close them, afraid of the images her mind would force her to see.

Mattea used Kya's key to unlock the door, and Kya walked onto the apartment to see Sam sitting on the couch. The only light in the apartment coming from Sam's displays. Kya felt a minuscule moment of normality as Mattea blindly searched for a light switch to illuminate the front hall.

"Hey, Kya," Sam said smiling before turning to stare at the trio. His smile quickly dropped and his brow knitted in obvious confusion. "What's up?"

Mattea moved swiftly to Sam, who was now standing by his couch, and she began filling him in on recent events. Kya stood still at the front entrance. Her body limp, it was only Rory and the wall that were holding her up. Kya heard distant sobbing and with a great deal of effort, she turned her head to try to pinpoint the source before realizing that it was her.

After hearing only a piece of the whole story, Sam

rushed over and wrapped Kya in a hug, pushing Rory out of the way slightly in doing so.

Kya's legs dropped out from under her, and she was being supported completely by Sam's embrace. After a few moments of being squeezed by him, the warmth and familiar scent helped her find the comfort to lift herself up.

With her footing regained, he pulled away but still keeping an arm around her to support her, Sam led her to the couch, and she stood in front of it, staring blankly out the balcony window.

"Man, I'm sorry to drop all this on you," Rory said, "but I have to get Mattie home. She's supposed to take it easy with the baby, and today has obviously not been easy."

"Mmm hmm." Sam's lips were pursed so tightly that they were white. He did not take his eyes off Kya for a moment.

"I'm so sorry, Sam," Mattea said. "I'd stay if I could."

"Mmm hmm," Sam repeated.

Kya heard the door close, and then black fingers crawled across her vision from the outside corners, and the world slipped away from her.

Kya woke up in her bed. The morning sun was shining through her window, and birds were singing. She was fully clothed, including her shoes, and her head pounded. She sat up as slowly as she could, her every motion brought new ripples of pain through her head. Unable to remember how she got in bed, energy shot through her body. As she rotated her hips, her feet dangled above the floor, and she slipped off her shoes. One at a time, they hit the small area rug with a dull thud.

She stretched her arms upwards, relieving some of the tension in her shoulders and neck before sliding off of her bed. Her body once again revolted, and her stomach flipped and churned. Kya could barely think straight as she stumbled towards her bedroom door. She opened it and with no grace, stomped slowly towards the kitchen.

"So, you're awake," Sam said. His voice was curt, and he didn't meet her gaze as she approached.

She felt the bite to his words, but couldn't think of what she had done to deserve it. Still feeling like her emotions were being effectively bottled up, she tilted her head slightly in confusion. "Sorry?" She said.

A scowl took over Sam's normally kind face. He turned away from Kya, took a sip of his coffee, before hanging his head. "I know you are going through some horrible stuff right now, but that doesn't make you any less of an idiot."

"Pardon me?" Kya spat out.

"What were you thinking?" Sam turned to face Kya and leaned his hands on the kitchen counter behind him. Steam rose from the full coffee cup beside his right hand. "If you were even thinking at all." He paused and stared at Kya. The colour of his face shifted ever more red.

"Sam, I don't know what I did to you. I really don't understand what's going on." Kya said. Her heart pounded in her chest, and she fought the urge to run back into her room.

She quickly considered her previous evening, searching for something that might have made Sam angry, but came back to the current moment without an answer.

"You disappeared yesterday after your friends left!"

"What do you mean? Where did I go? Did I black out?"

Sam laughed, but it was a cold, hard, empty laugh.

"Look, Sam, it's not fair for you to throw this much hostility at me when I have no idea why. I am going through so much right now, and I need a friend, someone that can help me. Amelia is dead." Kya felt the heat in her cheeks, and her body buzzed with an energy that she had never felt before. Her mind reeled slightly at her verbal admission of her friend's death. Somehow, by saying it aloud, it felt more real.

Sam nodded and cleared his throat. He wordlessly picked up his coffee cup and walked to the living room.

CHAPTER 20

Kya took a seat opposite Sam on the couch. She sighed deeply and heard Sam do the same. The apartment was chilled, like normal, as the mid-morning sun shone directly through the window. It was rare for Kya to be sitting in the living room during the day, and she suddenly wondered why Sam was home on a Thursday. She didn't dare ask as they sat in silence.

She noticed little details that she never really paid attention to before. The small framed pictures next to the television were of Sam and a large group of children. It was likely from the first class he taught. She looked at the fake plant in the corner, and its long, wide leaves were a dark green with yellow highlights and, as with the rest of the apartment, it looked clean and dust free.

Sam opened his mouth as if to speak then closed it and let a deep breath out through his nose. After a moment, he began again. "I'm talking about Supers, Kya." He looked her straight in the eyes. His gray eyes seemed to pierce into Kya's soul. "I'm talking about how your Invisibility Super manifested yesterday."

A small involuntary smile twitched the right corner of Kya's mouth as one thought filled her head *I'm not crazy!* "That explains what happened at the-..." she cut herself off.

A fresh blade of grief sliced her heart. She couldn't let her mind wander to the previous day for even a moment. She swallowed hard then opened her mouth to speak, but Sam chimed in first.

"Look, I get the draw of Supers, but you know I'm against them."

"Because of your mom."

Sam flinched, and she wished she could take the words back as soon as they had left her mouth.

"It is more than that." Sam paused. "I mean, that does contribute to it, but I also believe that Supers are wrong on a bunch of different levels. They're unnatural to the extreme. I feel like they ruin society. They harm people. We've just replaced one type of class warfare for another, and I don't want to be part of such a broken system."

Sam's passion hit Kya like a slap in the face. This was the most engaged she had ever seen him, and it was all surrounding a point of contention that was no longer something she could fix. She tried to take in what he was saying, but Kya knew that she still lacked complete understanding regarding Sam's hatred for Supers. "I didn't get mine from any of those companies if that's what you mean."

"Kya, genetic engineering is wrong. It changes people. It

gave the world something beyond money to strive for, and though it was the stuff of dreams, it killed inspiration and hard work. It divided us all. How is that a good thing?"

"I've never thought of it that way."

"Well, it's hard to think rationally about something that is marketed to the world more than energy drinks, medications or loans." Sam shifted in his seat, and his posture became more relaxed. "To understand, I'd have to tell you a bit about my life, especially how it changed after my mom died."

"Okay," Kya said. She couldn't help but feel nervous about what she was going to hear. She worried that he was going to be able to convince her Supers were bad, and wondered what consequences such a conclusion might hold for her.

Sam grabbed his coffee and took a long, slow sip. As he took it away from his face, Kya recognized his contemplative look. "You know how my mom died, right?"

"Yes."

"And why she was important?"

"Yes. I finally got curious and did research." Kya felt her cheeks turn red.

"Alright, so, after mom died, my dad got a little crazy. He felt like we needed to save face with the world, and show that we were still worthy of public adoration. He wanted to make sure his investments continued to do well." Sam picked up his coffee and took another drink.

"Right," Kya interjected to fill the quiet.

"He was too afraid of getting the Supers injections himself. He was part of their creation, and he never told me what happened, but he was adamant that I get them as soon as I turned eighteen to show how safe they were."

"Did you end up doing it?"

Sam coughed slightly. Putting on his teacher's voice, he continued. "I'll never get through this story if you keep interrupting Kya."

"Sorry," She said, feeling the heat in her cheeks return.

"I told him that I didn't want Supers. And who could blame me after what had happened to my mom?" Sam paused, taking another sip of his coffee.

Kya could see that Sam was trying to swallow his emotions while he drank the dark, bitter drink down. He returned the now empty cup to the table.

"More coffee?" She asked gently as she reached out to take his cup. It slid into her open hand, and Kya blinked in shock. Her heart began pounding loudly in her ears, and she looked at Sam, who seemed not to have noticed. She refilled the cup and returned to the room.

Sam continued speaking. "It didn't help that in dad's social circle everyone was signing up and getting Supers, despite the accident. My father quickly felt like the elite class was going to remove him from their ranks if he didn't have someone to act as a bridge for him. Even though he was still too afraid to undergo the procedure himself, just before my eighteenth birthday he pushed once again for me to have them. He told me that if I didn't get Supers, he'd cut me off."

Things were coming into focus, and Kya began to connect the dots. She remembered the news articles she had seen and knew that Sam was still incredibly wealthy. "It all turned out, though, right? You didn't get Supers, and your dad couldn't cut you off from the family money?"

Sam groaned and ran his fingers through his hair. "Kya, money isn't everything. I loved my family. I loved my life. Then I lost my mom. My dad chose social status over my well being. It sucked. It still really sucks. It doesn't matter what I do. He doesn't want to know anything about me. The man I've become."

"I know what it's like to have a family who doesn't care," Kya said. She stared at her hands clasped together, and they flickered out of existence. She gasped, blinked rapidly and they came back. She touched each of her fingers to her thumb, confirming they were still solid and attached. "My parents only really care about their son. My brother is the *Golden Child*. You've been more like family to me than them."

Sam both sighed and smiled at her reveal. "Then why didn't you come to me with everything that was happening with Amelia? Or with getting Supers? Even if I don't agree with what was happening, I have experience with Supers and their side effects. I could have helped."

Her neck and shoulders felt tense, as though the weight of the world was sitting on them. "Well, you haven't exactly been around." Kya pointed out.

"True," Sam said with a frown. "But I'm here now, so tell me everything that's happening. Please?"

Kya started with Amelia's erratic behaviours, her texts and then her disappearance. She told Sam about Amelia's apartment and finding the Black Market contact.

Sam sat on the edge of his seat, listening intently to every detail. "Wait. Please tell me you didn't buy your Super from that Frank guy." Sam said, in a weary tone.

"No. My Supers are different."

"Sup*ers*?" Sam emphasized the plural.

"I don't know how many I have."

Sam raised an eyebrow. He took a deep breath, and Kya could tell he was trying extremely hard to keep his temper and restrain any judgement. His whole body became noticeably rigid as he shifted back and pressed himself into the couch.

"After my run in with Frank, I was helped out by a guy dressed all in shades of dark gray and black. He was wrapped in fabric from head to toe. I couldn't see his face or any of his skin. But he had a kind voice. He said he was a Sociology Professor. He was a bit of a weird one, I guess." As Kya spoke she was struck by the absurdity of her words, and how reckless she had been.

"Kya... What?" Sam stared at her, and his face was both frustrated and confused. It twisted in odd but ever more familiar ways.

Kya felt like she was telling the principal about her

mistakes, or her own father about how she had sold cows in trade for magic beans. "He said he could give me Supers with a touch of his hand. Only as many as my body could naturally tolerate and only of a variety best suited to me. He said they would make it impossible for me to get Supers any other way. I didn't actually believe the guy, but..." She extended her arm outwards for a throw pillow just beyond her reach, and it jumped into her hand.

"Can they be extracted?" Sam asked in a higher tone than normal, his brow wrinkled in worry.

"I don't know."

"How did he transfer the powers to you?"

"I don't know."

"Are there any side effects?"

"I don't know. None that I can remember anyway."

"Are you scared?"

"Honestly?"

Sam nodded.

She paused, trying to understand her emotions and the erratic waves of them that were stirring within her. "Terrified." Her mouth went dry.

The cupboard where they kept the glasses rattled on its hinges, and both Kya and Sam jumped at the sound of shattering glass. Kya rose from the couch and went to the kitchen, as she neared the sink the faucet turned on. The cupboard door opened and a glass shot out, hitting Kya in the chest. She caught it with both hands before it smashed on the floor as well.

"What's happening?" Sam wailed.

"I... I think I did it," Kya said. "I'm thirsty, and I was thinking about getting a drink of water."

Kya filled the glass with water and turned off the tap. "I think I'm going to lay down before..."

The pillow she had picked up before hit her square in the face, causing Kya almost to drop her drink.

"Did you throw that?" Kya asked.

"Nope," Sam said. "That was you too." Kya felt Sam's anxiety and stress. He looked at her like she had a strange disease. "Yeah, go to bed before you break something else. I'll clean up the glass."

Kya looked around her bedroom, and it was in shambles. More so than usual. Things were strewn about everywhere. The only saving grace was her well-made bed. Her pillows covered the first third next to the headboard, and her comforters were flat against the mattress. She closed the door and leaned against it. Images of Myles Redwood and Amelia flashed in her head, and she began to shake. Slowly she slid to the floor and began to weep. "What have I done?"

The moments ticked by slowly as she allowed herself to feel the full weight of her situation. Finally, she took a deep breath and rose to her feet, walked to her bed and climbed onto her soft queen sized mattress. Grabbing her laptop from her bedside table, she instantly felt more at peace. A quick mental note about cleaning the rest of the room was added to the long list floating around in her mind.

With her laptop in hand, Kya opened it and checked her e-mail. She knew that there had been notifications on her phone, but she always preferred typing on a full sized keyboard. Most of the messages were, as normal, advertising and spam, but three stood out as responses to her attempts to get a new job.

The first was a quick note saying that they went with another candidate, but the second let Kya know that her references didn't check out after they had taken it upon themselves to contact her manager at Starlife Technologies. Kya wondered if the first response had been about the same issues with Don Georgetown telling the world about how useless he felt Kya was.

Frustrated, she opened her resume and looked it over once again. It didn't list Don Georgetown as a reference, nor did it provide any direct contact information relating to her position at Starlife Technologies. Kya's mind reeled slightly as she realized that any job she was going to apply for was likely to contact her most recent employer to find out why her employment ended before she secured a new position.

Hesitant, she looked at the details of the next message before opening it. The reply was from the job that Sam had found for her at the bookstore and publisher, Classic Communication and was entitled *Employment Response*. Kya couldn't help but consider all of the potential responses she would receive, and prepared herself for the worst as she clicked on the email and slammed her eyes shut. It was a childish response, as she knew it could not change the content of the email, and she was only delaying the inevitable, but her nerves took hold. Despite everything else happening in her life, she was hoping for the opportunity to work, make money, and improve her own feelings of self-worth. Slowly, she opened one eye and looked at the screen.

Kya, we appreciate your application, and your passion has definitely resonated with us here at the Classic Communication bookstore and publishing house. We would love to have you come in for an interview next Friday at three in the afternoon. Please let us know as soon as possible if this is an issue.

Sincerely, Joanne Roddenberry-Roth

"Yes!" Kya screamed, and items jumped off her shelves as she flailed about, unable to sit still.

Kya opened a response. She didn't realize she was making small gleeful noises until she pressed the send button on her short message to let Joanne from Classic Communication know that she would be there and that she was looking forward to it. She went over the message a dozen times in her mind, hoping that she wrote the right words in the right way to continue to convey her excitement and passion. She wanted to tell everyone about the interview, and as she went through a list of people in her mind, a fleeting moment reflecting on Amelia crushed her excitement. Tears streamed down her face, and her gleeful noises were replaced with heavy sobs.

She had to admit to herself that she had been trying to block Amelia's death from her mind. The imagery came pouring back in, and it was hard to hold back the waves of grief from overwhelming her. With her pillow squeezed in hand, she placed it over her mouth and let out shrill screams and sad moans as she tried to let out all of the sadness.

CHAPTER 21

Over the next few days, Kya found herself emotionally rafting through whitewater rapids, every moment fearing she may either drown or momentarily celebrate her survival. Her powers of invisibility and telekinesis surprised and frightened her with their continued unpredictability. As excitement over the interview gave way, she was, once again, able to grieve over Amelia and fear how a reference from Don Georgetown could tear away any job opportunity. Her saving grace through it all was Sam. His calm support, even where his understanding failed, acted as an anchor for her.

On Sunday, after another quick conversation with Sam about how much life had changed recently, which ended in a few more tears, Kya returned to her room. Still in her pajamas, she found her phone half covered with the blinking light of a waiting text message. Before she had a chance to cross the room, the phone shot from the bed into her hand. The text was from Mattea.

>Doc put me on bed rest. Silly body doesn't know what it's

doing.

>Wow, Mattie. That sucks. Anything I can do for you?

>I wouldn't object if you wanted to come by and keep me company. Rory's at work. If you can't or whatever, I completely understand.

>I'll be there soon.

Kya smiled at her phone and began to get dressed. It was nice to be able to help her friend. She was also happy for the distraction. But as she thought about seeing Mattea, a memory of Amelia at the Noble Brew cast a shadow over her. With that fleeting thought of her lost friend, Kya felt the sting of tears in her eyes, and the familiar black tendrils crossed her vision. There was some comfort in the darkness. It let her know that even if someone were to enter her room, no one could see her cry. She shuffled her feet as she blindly tried to move towards her bedside table, where she knew a box of tissues awaited her. The dampness of her tears rushing down her face and her sinuses opening up made her uncomfortable. Kya had to guess at her bearings, and as a sharp object hit her shin, she tumbled over her laundry basket causing her desk chair to roll as she hit it on her way to the floor. She flickered back into existence to find little drops of blood blossoming from her leg, and her baby finger bent at a strange angle. With her good hand, Kya grabbed her shin and put pressure on the scrape. A chill emanated from her hand to her leg, and when she removed her hand, the scrape had vanished and so had the pain. While still half sitting, and half lying on the floor of her room, her hands both shook as she grabbed hold of her injured finger and attempted to place it back into the proper place. The same coldness seemed to pass from her good hand into her finger, and the pain immediately subsided.

The room seemed to spin around Kya as she tried to understand what had just happened. She sat on the floor, her mouth agape. She wheezed slightly as she reconciled her situation and quickly did a self-check making sure nothing else was injured.

"Kya?" Sam was standing at her door and looked down at her. "Is everything okay? I heard a crash." As he finished speaking, his face turned red.

Kya realized that in all of the time that they had lived together, Sam had never seen her in her underwear. "Yeah, I'm fine." She stood slowly, slightly embarrassed, covering herself with a nearby blanket before shrugging. "Blind invisibility is a stupid power."

Sam laughed. "Yep."

Kya stood in her doorway with the blanket wrapped around her as he walked towards the kitchen. He grabbed a bottle of beer from the refrigerator. "Can I get you a beer too?" Sam shouted, his head still behind the large black fridge door.

"No thanks, I am heading out to Mattie's." Kya moved back into her room, kicked the door slightly more closed as she entered. She grabbed some clothing from her closet and tossed it on in a hurry. She slipped out of the apartment, closing the door only a moment after she heard Sam shut the fridge. The bus came moments after Kya arrived at the stop, and she hopped on, sitting in her usual spot, a small grin on her face.

The bus stopped in front of the grocery store near Mattea's house, and Kya got off. The sun setting in the distance and a chill already in the air, she waited for what felt like hours for the traffic light to change so she could cross the street. The streetlights were already on as she walked down tree lined streets. Mattea's house was one in a long line of similar bungalows on the street. The front of Mattea's house was a mixture of red brick and white stone slabs. A big window was on one side of the front door, and a porch with two wooden deck chairs and a table was on the other side. Three separate gardens hugged the front of the house and looked like they were tended by someone who didn't much enjoy gardening. The driveway was noticeably missing Mattea's car.

Kya knocked on the already unlocked front door as she opened it. "Hey, Mattie. I'm here."

Mattea was laying on the oversized beige couch in her living room. The pale blue walls and the dark orange curtains contrasted heavily against the plain wooden shelves and furniture. Mattea was propped up with large pillows, and she was facing the powered-off television on the far wall. A throw blanket with an antique map of the world covered her legs and slightly protruding belly.

Mattea looked up from the book in her hands. "Oh, I'm so glad you're here!" She said with a grin. "How are you doing?" Her expression changed quickly from one of joy to one of concern.

"You know," Kya shrugged. "I've had some distractions."

"Please, tell me all the details." Mattea patted the chair next to her as an invitation for Kya to take a seat.

"Well, did you see my power of invisibility when you picked me up from the cottage?"

"Yeah, I can't believe you went and bought a Super after everything that happened with..." Mattea trailed off. "Well, you know."

"I didn't buy a Super." Kya paused, taking a deep breath. Recounting her experiences and, of course, the situation that lead up to them wasn't something she was looking forward to. "In a dark alley, I touched the hand of a mysterious guy that called himself a sociology professor. He was wrapped all in black and dark gray. He-"

"A sociology professor?" Mattea broke in.

"He was probably lying about that but, yeah, that's what he said he was. Anyways, he offered me a random group of Supers through a single touch of his hand. He said he was a carrier, and in exchange he wanted me to find out all I can about Supers and share what I find."

"That's insane. A carrier?"

"Yep. But it worked." Kya started to ramble ever faster. "I have Invisibility, but if I make my face invisible, I can't see. Well, actually it's my eyes. If my eyes are invisible, I'm blind. If my eyelids are invisible, I can't see them but I can see through them. If my hands are invisible I can't see where they are, only feel. I can make my clothes invisible... Basically, anything touching my invisible skin is invisible."

Mattea nodded. Staring at her friend with her mouth closed, expressionless. She rubbed her stomach slowly in small circles.

Kya felt joy as she unloaded on Mattea. She wanted to brag to someone about her Supers. She wanted to feel interesting and special, and she knew Mattea would be interested in a way that Sam, the only other person in her life at this point, just could not. "I also have Telekinesis. If I think about something specific, I can pull it towards me. Well, as long as it's not too big or too far away. Pillows, cups, books, my laptop. I can turn on taps or lights too. It seems that my Telekinesis works on anything light enough for me to carry with my own two hands, and I can move it about as far as I'd be able to throw it."

"Okay," Mattea said, still showing no emotion.

"I also think I might have Healing. It only showed up today. If it has limitations, I don't know what they are."

"So what have you done to hold up your side of the deal?" Mattea said. A slight edge had formed in her tone.

"Nothing yet."

"What happens if you don't keep up your side of the bargain?"

"I don't know."

"What are the side effects?"

"Well, I won't be able to get Supers from injections now, and if I had kids, they'd be carriers."

"Are those the only side effects?"

"I don't know."

Mattea opened her mouth wide and took a deep breath. Kya knew she was winding up for a motherly lecture.

"I have an interview next Friday," Kya said quickly, in an attempt to change the subject.

Mattea took the bait. "Oh, really? Where?"

Kya grinned. "It's at a bookstore and publishing house."

"That sounds like a great place for you."

"Yeah, I guess they haven't checked references yet since I have a feeling Don Georgetown has been bad mouthing me every chance he gets." Kya ran both of her hands through her hair, feeling frustration well up inside of her. "I just know he'd screw this up for me. He's got it in for me bad."

"Have you thought about talking to him?" Mattea asked in a gentle voice.

"Yeah, like he'd listen!"

"You never know unless you try. On the other hand, they might not even contact him." Mattea smiled kindly.

Kya's phone buzzed in her pocket. She shrugged and checked the message. It was from Amelia's sister.

>*Kya? This is Ainsley. The funeral for Amelia is tomorrow at two at Martin's Funeral Home.*

Kya's heart caught in her throat, and she couldn't help but sob openly.

"Kya?" Mattea said. "Come here." She opened her arms

offering a hug and Kya crumpled into them.

CHAPTER 22

There was something so final about attending a funeral. Kya knew she couldn't avoid her feelings any longer. She looked at the clothing laid out on her bed. It was layers of dark dress clothing that she had purchased on credit, special for the day. The idea of buying funeral appropriate clothing, and wearing it for anything else seemed strange, and as she put on her selections, everything felt uncomfortable. Her pants felt too tight, and the shirt felt scratchy. Her socks were itchy, and her shoes attempted to give her feet instant blisters. It was as though her clothing knew it was going to be a miserable day and wanted to add to her discomfort.

Once Kya was completely dressed, she looked at her reflection in her bathroom mirror and was struck for a moment by how much it reminded her of the man she had met in the alley. A flash of curiosity was piqued inside of her mind. She made a promise to herself to follow it and keep her end of the deal with that man. It was enough to give her a momentary reprieve from the dour thoughts that she wanted to hide from.

"All set?" Sam said from beyond the door.

Snapping back into the moment, Kya grabbed her new small black purse. She checked to make sure it had tissues, her wallet, cell phone and keys. "I think I am."

Kya was floored by what she saw as she exited out into the front hallway: Sam was dressed in a black suit.

"I don't think I've forgotten anything, so we can go whenever you're ready," Sam said. He tried to smile lightly, but his eyes betrayed his worry.

Kya was happy that Sam had decided to attend the funeral with her though he didn't give her much choice. When Kya had come home, Sam made sure she filled him in on the details and made himself available. He was also a strong shoulder to cry on as Kya came to terms with the words written in the text from Amelia's sister.

"Thank you again for doing this." She tried not to cry. She tried not to let the discomfort of her outfit frustrate her. She tried not to think about the day ahead. Instead, Kya focused on breathing deeply and taking each minute as it came.

As they pulled into the church parking lot, Sam found a spot and turned off his car. He reached across Kya to open the glove box then handed her a small box of tissues.

At first, she felt slightly offended by his gesture, feeling that it was a sexist commentary on women always crying, but that notion passed in an instant when she looked into Sam's face. Concern poured from his eyes that were locked on hers.

Kya placed the box in her small black handbag and took a deep breath. The sun almost blinded her as she exited the car. It felt like a cruel joke that the weather didn't reflect the mood of the day, as though it wasn't important enough for the universe to show respect for her lost friend.

The main area of the church, a long room with high ceilings, stretched outwards making Kya feel very small. She walked across the room, and it felt like it took an eternity. Sam took Kya by the arm, and in doing so, steadied her slow march towards the front of the room. A rainbow of sunlight from the stained glass windows poured down on the rows of wooden pews. Kya slid into a nearby seat and noticed that Amelia's sister Ainsley was absent. There were only a dozen people scattered in small clumps around the church. It looked empty compared to the hundreds of people that it could potentially hold. The sheer lack of people surprised Kya. She looked around and saw none of Amelia's co-workers from the Noble Brew, nor anyone else that she recognized. It angered her that so few people cared.

After a space of time that could have been an hour or only a few minutes, a procession of a handful of people entered the church. Amelia's sister, Ainsley, held the hands of two small children, presumably her son and daughter. They followed two men in suits who pushed a simple, unadorned wooden casket to the front of the church. All of their faces seemed emotionless.

"No pallbearers," Sam mumbled under his breath.

"Hmm?" Kya said mindlessly.

"Never mind."

Dazed and confused, the time spent in the church passed in a haze. Kya stumbled as she came back from the swarm of thoughts and emotions that had consumed her. She realized she was standing in the small graveyard behind the church. In front of her was the casket, a priest was in the middle of saying a few words, and a gentleman along the edge of the small group began to hand out long-stemmed red roses.

Kya turned to her left, and then quickly to her right, searching for Sam. Her startled movement attracted his attention, and they looked at each other.

He looked at her solemnly and pointed his right index finger at his cheek.

At first, Kya was confused but then realized that her face was wet. She opened her purse and retrieved a handful of tissues from the packaging. They came out in a clump, but it wasn't a priority for Kya to sort them out. Wiping her face, she started to feel like it was difficult to catch her breath.

A few people began placing flowers on the casket, and Kya was not one holding a flower.

As the last of the flowers handed out were placed, Kya inched forward and closer to the two larger men that she stood behind.

Sam bent down and whispered into her ear, "Go if you want to. No one will stop you."

Kya felt that there was an endless torrent of tears flowing from her eyes, but Sam's words propelled her forward, and she pushed through to the front of the small crowd. Grabbing one of the roses still on the ground, Kya placed it on the casket and stepped backward into the crowd. She turned and continued back towards Sam's car, unable to stop. She wanted to escape. She wanted to yell. She wanted to pound on the casket and tell her friend to stop being dead. Standing by the car, she tried to open the door, but it was locked. A moment later, she heard the telltale click that let her know that it was unlocked. Kya opened the door and sat inside.

Less than a minute later, she was joined by Sam. "Are you okay?"

Kya tried to stifle her crying and held her breath. She stared out the window and saw dark tendrils crawl across her vision.

"Uh, are you still there?" Sam's concern was palpable.

Kya gasped and felt better. Her sight returned, and she held up her hands and looked at them. A wad of tissue still in her right fist, she took another deep breath. "Yes. Sorry." She wanted to explain herself, but the words didn't come to her. She leaned back into the seat and closed her eyes. "Can you please take me home?"

Sam turned on the car and began to leave the church. As they pulled away, they could see the small cluster of people still standing around the graveyard, some talking to each other, others holding each other for consolation.

Kya broke the silence as they stopped at the first set of traffic lights. "I think I'm going to find out more about the guy that gave me my powers. I think I'm going to track him down tomorrow." Perhaps there was a way he could take back his *gifts*.

"Okay." Sam paused as the light changed, and the car sped up once again. "That might be a good idea."

CHAPTER 23

True to her word, Kya woke up and as soon as her eyes were clear, grabbed her laptop. She began to search out information on darkly wrapped figures, passing on Supers by touch, and mysterious men. All of her searching had led her to strange places on the Internet written cryptically about First Gens and with strong warnings about government involvement. Something seemed very wrong, and many of the online bulletin boards had no responses to messages asking if the original posters were still alright. One reply on such a thread that Kya had found had a message that simply stated, *"there goes another one."*

Annoyed by what little information she could find, Kya grabbed her purse and her jacket and put on her shoes. She knew that she needed to focus on a new mission. A mission to find the mystery person that gave her the Supers she now had. She remembered what the figure wrapped in dark gray had told her to do when she was ready. She decided she was ready.

As she boarded the bus, she checked the map on her

phone to see where the last stop on the South Street bus line was. She had never been to that part of the city. The strong, ever quickening thud of her heart rattled her chest, and her knees bounced rapidly up and down. She checked her phone again, seven more stops. Outside the city rolled on. The buildings seemed darker here, a lower quality of build, and shorter. The tallest building was no higher than ten stories. Everything was still densely packed. Strangely, it looked like care was being taken to maintain it.

Splashes of colour painted on the sides of the buildings caught her eye. Vivid blues and purples as well as deep grays and blacks contrasted the red bricks and aging off-white vinyl siding. The graffiti from building to building seemed to have a very similar and consistent motif. A section of the painting was extremely detailed, and in the center, a humanoid shape with non-distinct edges. They were devoid of any detail or structure, like a shadow. Some shadow figures seemed to be dancing or praying while others had wings and were reaching out to detailed people. Dozens of pieces all seemed to celebrate the mysterious figures. The murals reminded Kya of the other graffiti works she had seen throughout the city, but what struck her now was how these murals focused on the shadowy figures. The others Kya had seen all seemed to keep the mystery man in the background, like her favourite one of the girl in the dress that changed colours.

Kya remembered the man who had given her powers, and for the first time she wondered if these familiar figures were meant to be people like him. She wondered if they were the ones preserving this part of the city, an area that seemed like it had originally been slapped together in haste.

"Last stop!" The bus driver called, reviving Kya from her musings.

"Thank you." Kya stepped out of the bus into the sunshine. She looked to the west and saw some closed shops, but down about a block there was a sign lit up with an older, oddly coloured light that cut through the glare: *Gennie's Diner*.

As she stood underneath the neon sign for the diner, Kya nodded to herself. The man in gray had been right, just by the name she knew that this was the place she needed to be. The large glass panes from waist height to the ceiling of the restaurant were scratched and had a discoloured plastic film on them. The orange metal panels below the windows were faded, but surprisingly clean from any graffiti.

Kya looked at the double doors, with their large metal handles dividing the otherwise glass door as they went diagonally from two feet off the ground to the top of the opposite corner. She pulled open the door and was surprised at how light it was as she flung the right one wide, hitting a cracked rubber stopper that prevented her from potentially damaging it.

Inside, pictures of classic, old school celebrities were hung over each of the seating areas, and almost everything felt like it was pulled from several decades earlier. The floor was covered with large black and white tiles, both with a noticeable wear pattern. A quiet but upbeat song was playing in the background, creating a nice atmosphere.

Kya knew that she probably wouldn't be able to hear it if the diner was full, but the only person she saw in the entire restaurant was the tall woman behind the counter.

The lady, whom Kya assumed was probably less than a decade older, stared at her with a smile on her face as she wiped down the long metallic counter. Half a dozen large red stools were bolted to the floor in front of her.

"Come in and sit down. Is there anything I can get for you, Kya?"

"Wait, how did you know my name?" Kya said.

There were slight creases in the woman's skin, and Kya couldn't help but notice some lines forming around her mouth and brown eyes as she grinned. "You would be surprised the things I know."

Sitting on the stool directly across, Kya looked the woman up and down. She inspected her clothing. It was just simple blue jeans, and a t-shirt, nothing like what she had expected. Her hair was a natural-looking dirty-blonde, pulled back into a messy ponytail. Despite not seeing anything that should make her apprehensive, Kya couldn't shake the feeling that she should be on guard.

"My name is Everly."

A flicker of recognition shot through Kya's mind at the name.

Everly slid a tall glass under a drink dispenser and pushed a button. Quickly, a dark liquid filled the glass. "Root beer?"

"If you're Everly, who is Gennie?" Kya shot an offending look at the drink before turning her gaze back to Everly.

"I'm hurt!" Everly said with a chuckle, her voice had a raspy yet melodic tone to it, like someone who liked to sing her heart out. "I was sure you'd be looking for me."

On impulse, Kya shrugged, unwilling to volunteer too much information to this woman until she was given reason to do so.

Everly walked to the edge of the counter and flipped up a piece of it, sliding through and closing it behind her. She walked to the front door and flipped over the small paper sign from *open* to *closed*. As she locked the door, she turned to Kya and began to walk back. "When Callidus gave you your gifts he told you to come and find me. That's why you're here." She smiled again and tilted her head to the side a bit. "Isn't it?"

"Who is Callidus?"

"Oh, that's right. You never asked his name!" Everly laughed melodically. "Don't worry, it wasn't high on my priority list either."

An uneasy feeling crept into Kya's body, and she wrapped her arms around her stomach in hopes of settling herself. Her vision flickered in an all too familiar way, and darkness surrounded her.

"The Supers aren't quite what you expected, are they?" Everly asked gently.

Even though her lack of vision let her know she could not be seen, Kya shook her head reflexively.

"It's alright. it gets better."

"How would you know?" The tone of Kya's words was hard and on edge, betraying her feelings.

"You'd be surprised-"

"Try me." Kya's vision returned, and she glared at Everly.

"What did your searches reveal about First Gens?"

"Almost nothing." Kya blurted out before she could stop herself.

"Just more questions?"

Kya nodded once, then stared out the window.

"Come with me. I'm sure Callidus will be eager to see you."

Despite the strong desire to run away, Kya set her jaw, clenched her teeth, and followed Everly to the back of the diner.

"You really would have liked that root beer," Everly said. She opened a door at the far end of the kitchen, and it led out to an alleyway that was mostly clean. And again On the wall, there was a ten foot tall mural of a shadow figure. She stared at the details, the hood, the wrapped fabric. This figure was definitely like the man who had given Kya her powers, Callidus. The hood of the man in this mural was down showing shaggy hair and green eyes. The rest of his face was still covered in a scarf, but in the still image he was part way through unwrapping his hand. Each of his fingers turned a different colour as Kya walked by.

The alleyway ended at a large street. Large shrubs and

bushes lined the far side of the street with trees beyond. As Kya followed Everly across the four-lane street, her heart rate started increasing.

As she stepped up the curb on the opposite side, Everly turned to look at Kya her expression hard. "We have to be careful past this point. There shouldn't be a patrol for the next ten minutes, and the security cameras can't see this spot. But around here it's always best to be on guard."

"Patrol?"

"Yep." Everly glanced around. "There isn't a whole lot of love in these parts."

The bushes quickly got thicker as they went off of the beaten path. Beyond a row of evergreens, there was a chain link fence, three times taller than either woman, and it was partly pressed into the branches.

Kya watched as Everly grabbed the fence and pulled herself towards and then along it, her entire body coming in contact with either tree branches or the metal fence. "Are you coming?"

"Where are we going?" Kya pulled herself towards the fence and continued to follow Everly as they sidestepped slowly along it, crawling under branches. A small opening in the fence appeared only a few meters away, thanks to a strong tree that likely pushed it to its breaking point. Kya realized that no one could see this opening from outside of the thick forest of trees, and she followed Everly through.

After only a few feet, the forest cleared, and they were at the top of a steep hill. Kya looked down into a small valley.

"Bet you didn't know this was here?" Everly said. Her breathing was strained, and the rasp in her voice was far more noticeable.

Feigning confidence, Kya stood up straight and took in her breaths as normally as she could. "Do that often?"

"You'd-"

"If you tell me I'd be surprised-"

"You'll hit me? We both know you won't." Everly took a deep breath through her nose. "I like it here. It feels more like home than anywhere else I've been."

Kya looked down at the walled encampment below. A tall, thick stone wall surrounded over a dozen small single family houses. A large main building that reminded her of a school or a hospital was nearer Everly and Kya while a large planted vegetable garden and a baseball field were further away. Despite being fairly bright, several spotlights lit up both the interior and exterior of the walls and swept from side to side. Kya could see a few people along the wall, their uniforms were black and red, and they looked to be carrying assault rifles. "What is this place?"

"The public think that it is a quarantine zone. The military calls it *1GNE*, but the people that live here call it New Eden."

The sun continued to crawl across the sky as Kya and Everly stood looking down on the settlement. Kya realized that she knew of a few parks with government signs on the outskirts of the city, but she never had a reason to go looking for them. She also knew that the buses wouldn't bring her near any of them. She wondered if those government parks could conceal other communities like the one below. As she turned and looked at Everly, Kya noticed that Everly had a pleased look on her face that radiated a great deal of pride.

"Why New Eden?" Kya asked.

"I didn't name it." Everly shrugged; a grin still plastered on her face.

The two women walked down the hill towards the buildings, and Kya could hear the faint sounds of guitar music and the laughter of children. In nearly every way, it seemed like a small town, hidden away from society and trapped behind prison-like walls.

"So how do we get in?"

Everly chuckled slightly as they arrived at the edge of the light cast by the spotlights. "Just keep following me, but no more talking until we are safely on the other side."

Everly stepped forward, and Kya followed suit. Strangely, when any light even slightly illuminated Everly, it shut off. Arriving at the edge of the wall, a thick but tattered rope ladder fell.

Kya's heart was racing to the point where it was all she could hear. The rapid thumping in her chest drowned out all other noises, and the rope appearing from above only served to make it worse. Everly took the first rung and began to climb while Kya continued to follow her lead.

As they dropped down on the other side, Kya stumbled into a woman playing acoustic guitar on a front door step and a man carrying a basket of vegetables.

"Smooth," Everly said, she wiped a small bit of dust off Kya, while the woman, nearly unphased, smiled and started playing music once again. The woman wore a floral dress in earthy tones that came to just below her knees and had short sleeves, her feet were bare.

"You two okay?" The man said as he righted himself.

"Yeah, just her first time coming to visit."

Kya felt her heart rate slow as the man with the basket shot her a disarming smile. His clothes were heavily worn in spots, but still very functional. A light orange button-down shirt, sleeves rolled and with the first few buttons undone showing off his collar bone and a few strands of chest hair on his tanned skin. He also wore a pair of Khaki pants with the cuffs rolled to keep them off the ground and a dusty pair of work boots. Kya was surprised by his appearance. The clothes didn't cover every inch of his body, nor were they the dark gray she expected to find. There was nothing, beyond the worn quality and dated style, which deserved any extra attention.

"Sorry about that," Kya said. Her knee felt a little bruised from her stumble, but she knew her embarrassment was really what was shining through.

Everly grabbed Kya's arm and pulled her. "Come on. We can't stay here too long, or we will start attracting attention."

Following Everly, Kya looked around, trying to take in everything she saw. Various people went about their business, seemingly uninterested in Kya. All were wearing similar clothing to the man and woman that she had bumped into when descending the rope ladder. The three houses along the street all looked well kept, with small, well-maintained gardens. The sidewalks and roads were in disrepair and looked unfit for driving on. That didn't seem to matter though as there were no garages or cars to be seen. New Eden smelled of wood stoves and fireplaces mixed with a faint aroma of the forest outside of the walls.

After reaching the end of the street, Kya spoke up. "You would never know that there was a huge city just outside of here."

"Nope, and I bet you didn't know there was a small camp here."

Kya shook her head. Despite Everly's iron grip on her arm, Kya was trailing a few steps behind her, so she doubted that her response was noted.

"That's strange. I would have expected to see him by now." Everly said.

"Who? Callidus?"

"Yes. I thought he was supposed to be here this evening. Stay here. I'm going to check something."

Before Kya had a chance to respond, Everly released her grip on Kya's arm and jogged off to a nearby house. As she entered and disappeared from view, Kya started to feel exposed and out of place.

A moment later Everly rushed out of the house and back towards Kya. "Follow me," She said without another word.

Kya turned and rushed after Everly, who was increasing in speed to a near jog.

"He isn't here, but he should be back soon. We're going to try to meet up with him as we leave. It'll be safer to talk in the brush than in New Eden anyways."

Questions swarmed in Kya's mind. She hoped that they would be answered before they burst from her, unable to stop.

The wall felt easier to climb the second time, and Kya found her footing with ease. As they walked up the hill, three figures, dressed similarly, exited the forest and began to run towards New Eden.

The spotlights near Kya and Everly shut down again as they began to walk. "I know someone else with an Electricity Super."

Everly shot a puzzled look at Kya. "I'm not sure what you mean."

"The lights, that's you turning them off, right?"

Everly pointed behind her towards the wall. "That's Scott. He works for the group that keeps them here, but helps us with getting in and out."

Kya turned and watched as Scott flipped large breaker switches on a control panel on the wall around New Eden.

The three figures stopped only a matter of feet short of Kya and Everly, and at first, Kya just wanted to go invisible and run away, but her curiosity kept her in place.

"Kya, I am so glad you're here." The voice from under the hood sounded out of breath, yet familiar.

Based solely on the voice, Kya quickly was able to figure out that this man, wrapped in shades of gray and black, was the one who had given her Invisibility, Telekinesis, and Healing all from a touch of his hand. She opened her mouth slightly, expecting words to come out, but only a few short, incomprehensible sounds squeaked out before she closed it again.

"Don't worry, it's normal to be speechless in this kind of situation," Everly said in an attempt to be reassuring. She turned to Callidus. "She has a million questions for you like-"

"Would you please stop doing that?" Kya growled through clenched teeth. "I can speak for myself!"

Callidus removed his hood, revealing a mop of curly black hair that flopped around his head, curling around his ears, and striking green eyes that seemed to sparkle. "I see you met Everly." He nodded at Everly and then started unraveling the scarf at his neck revealing a long pointy nose and full pink lips. A wide smile revealed charmingly crooked white teeth. "She's come a long way, but she's still learning appropriate uses for her powers."

Everly shrugged, and the corner of her mouth twisted in a small smile.

"Anyways, Kya, welcome to New Eden."

"What is this place?" Kya asked, staring straight into Callidus' electric green eyes.

"That," he grinned, "is a complicated story."

"Yeah," Everly cut in, "She'd like to know why it's called New Eden. I wouldn't mind knowing too."

With a threatening glare from Kya, Everly shrunk back.

His attention never wavering from Kya, Callidus took a deep breath. "That is a story that needs the other story to make sense." As he spoke, he gestured wildly as he had in the alleyway. Kya could now see that his face was just as animated as the rest of his body.

"I think I have time," Kya said, noticing the shadows creeping in as dusk approached.

Callidus sat at one end of a fallen log and motioned for Kya to sit next to him.

"You know those buildings you went through, in the city?" Callidus said. "That was where they housed the test subjects of a fertility treatment that was supposed to modify a person's DNA. The hope was that the treatment would be passed down to the children of the test subjects, ending the Fertility Crisis."

There was rustling in the nearby forest. Kya turned her attention to the trees. The shadows were quickly getting longer, and it was difficult to tell what was pushing its way through. She felt a pang of apprehension as she considered the patrols that Everly had previously mentioned.

"It's just more *sociology professors* coming home for the night," Callidus explained.

"Callidus, you aren't still using that silly title!" Everly laughed.

"Like anyone would really know what Shadow Striders do or what they're about. At least sociology professors say something about our mission. Shadow Striders makes us sound like a bunch of superheroes, and we are anything but that."

"We've been called Shadow Striders since before you became one." An older, but soft, voice came from the taller of the two figures standing off to the side.

Kya couldn't help but let out a small chuckle. She had considered Callidus the sole authority before arriving and had never considered there might be others more senior to him.

Callidus shrugged. "Audentia," he called to the other person from his group wrapped tightly from head to toe in black.

Audentia, the shorter of the two, approached and removed her hood. Kya was shocked when the long flowing raven locks and soft eyes of a young woman were revealed.

"Will you please go see that they're alright?"

Audentia nodded and swiftly disappeared into the forest.

"Where was I?" Callidus began.

"The buildings." The timidness in her own voice surprised Kya.

"Yes. They built this part of the city to house test subjects. They wanted to monitor the progress of the mothers throughout pregnancy, but also monitor the growth and development of their children, specifically to see if they were affected by the Fertility Crisis."

"It didn't work," Kya said, nodding.

"Well," Callidus raised his hands and pointed his fingers in the air, "it did, and it didn't." He stood up and began pacing. "The women did get pregnant, but there were complications. And the babies were viable, but there were side effects."

The other Shadow Strider, who had spoken before, sat beside Kya. "I love this story," He said from under his hood. By the sound of his voice, Kya got the impression that he was smiling.

Everly was leaning against a nearby tree, twirling a piece of hair that had fallen from her ponytail around her fingers. "Callidus loves pausing for effect. We might be here all night." She explained.

Callidus laughed. "Strange things started happening in that part of the city. Unexplainable events! People disappearing or appearing from thin air, people summoning objects."

"Supers!" Kya interrupted.

"Perfect timing." The man beside her said. "You make a great audience."

"Exactly!" Callidus pointed both index fingers at Kya and grinned. "The genetic manipulation techniques they were using rewrote the mother's genetic codes and gave them a random smattering of superpowers that the doctors weren't expecting. The powers had limits; these women could jump high, but not fly, lift things with their minds, but only what they could carry with their hands. Some could hear the thoughts of others, but only thoughts of intent, something the person was about to do or about to say, a decision they were in the process of making. Deeper thoughts remained hidden."

"That's what I got." Everly shot a large grin and wink at Kya.

Kya clenched her teeth and returned her attention to Callidus.

"The ability to read deeper thoughts, maybe it would have protected the women. Maybe it could have changed their fate."

The man beside Kya chuckled quietly. "Callidus is such a great storyteller," he whispered.

"Of course, the doctors and scientists saw the marketability in this turn of events. If only they could control the mutations, expand the limitations. What would people pay to be able to fly?" Callidus gestured to the heavens as if he was about to take off. "What would they pay for super strength?" He flexed his muscles and scrunched up his kind face into a scowl. "They'd pay anything!" He said sadly as he flopped down to sit cross-legged on the ground. He began unwinding the fabric from his hands. All of his attention focused on that task as he continued his story. "They lost sight of the people they were trying to help. These mothers, they had no idea what was happening to them, and it was scary! Some of them..." He put his still bound right hand to the side of his head like a fist and opened it outward in an explosive gesture with an accompanying "boom" noise. "Many died. Many husbands were widowers and many children were orphaned."

"I don't like this part of the story," the man beside Kya whispered.

Callidus continued, unwrapping his right hand. "As I said before, there were side effects for the children. They were born looking and acting like any other babies. In fact, to look at them, hold them, play with them; they were normal little human babies. But within a number of days of their birth, strange things started happening to those who had touched them. Genetic mutations spread like a virus. The babies were carriers!" Callidus looked up, both of his hands now free. "Oh! Where are my manners? Kya, this is Nitor."

Nitor nodded to Kya. She nodded back.

"Back to the story, Callidus!" Nitor clapped his hands as he spoke.

"The mutations were on the verge of becoming an epidemic! I mean, who doesn't want to hold a baby? And the onslaught of uncontrolled Supers was, well, unpleasant. There were a lot of deaths and even more orphaned babies. But now they were seen as untouchable. The government worked hard to shut them away, and built these camps specifically for them. Keeping them and any surviving parents or medical staff who had contact with them locked away from the city at large. That way, they could perfect their *marketable* Supers."

"So New Eden is one of these camps?" Kya said.

With a nod and a sigh Callidus continued. "The first people to be brought here named it New Eden in order to try and turn their prison into a paradise. We have been banished *out* of the larger world for nothing that we have done, which is kind of the opposite of the original biblical story of Eden."

At that moment Audientia came out of the bush, her face soaked with tears. "I-I've tried everything!" She sobbed. "He - Callidus, Facillis... Ohhhhh..." She placed her hands to her face and wept as she crumpled to the ground.

Callidus ran past her, and Kya followed. He stopped suddenly, and she bumped into him. A boy who looked to be in his teens was lying on the ground. His face pale, he struggled for breath. Kya noticed his head was exposed as his hood and scarf were being used as a pillow. Blood gushed from the wound on his stomach, his black and gray clothing in tatters, cut away, making the bullet hole easy to see.

CHAPTER 24

"What happened?" Callidus growled.

"He was shot as we scaled the wall at the South Street Turnaround. The cops found us leaving the alley on Seventh."

"You got pretty far," Callidus mumbled as his hands had found the wound in the boy's stomach.

"I'm going to die." The boy said, his green eyes staring into Callidus'.

"Facillis, don't talk like that," Callidus said, gently.

"I'm not afraid," Facillis replied.

Kya moved without saying a word. She knelt beside the boy opposite Callidus. She placed her hands on the bullet wound and felt the familiar cold sensation of healing. The sensations spread past her wrists, past her elbows, and up to her shoulders. The feeling was more intense that she had expected, and fear gripped her that she was pushing her power too far.

"What are you doing?" Callidus asked.

"Healing him," Kya said through gritted teeth. When she pulled her hands away, they were covered in the boy's blood. His clothes were drenched, and the ground around him had turned to sticky mud. The hole in his stomach was gone.

"Thank you," Facillis whispered, and he closed his eyes. The trembling in his body stopped. He fell limp.

"What happened?" Kya asked. Her body tingled with fear. Her ears started ringing. She looked at Callidus.

Tears burst from his bright green eyes as he blinked. He licked his lips and opened his mouth, but no words came out.

"What happened?" Kya asked again. "I healed him. Look! He's fine!" She pointed to his flesh where the bullet hole had been.

"I've seen it before. First Gen limitations." Nitor said, placing his hand on Kya's shoulder. "You can only fix so much. You can close the wound, but you can't replace the blood."

Callidus and Nitor walked ahead of the two Shadow Striders carrying Facillis' lifeless body. Unlike with Amelia, there was no smell of death only the evergreens that surrounded them.

Audentia shuffled along, devoid of any expression, at the back of the group. Everly and Kya supported her, her legs almost giving way beneath her as she stepped along the sloping hill. The group walked in silence the entirety of the way back to the walls surrounding New Eden.

As they arrived at the spotlights, they began to shut down once again, but no rope came falling from overhead. Nitor waved his arms in the air at Scott, who was still standing watch on the wall, and a section of the wall in front of them vanished.

Kya was surprised but followed the group as they passed through the hole. The stones all reappeared once they were through, as though nothing had ever been disturbed. She felt a strong urge to ask what it took to pull off such a feat, but the weight of all that had happened warned her to stay silent.

Callidus took Kya gently by the hand and led her into a nearby house. The door opened to a kitchen with a large heavy wood table that looked like it had been made by hand. Callidus took Kya to the sink in the corner. The room was a mixture of rugged, rustic, pioneer elements and worn down looking modern conveniences. It was as if the house hadn't received anything new in years.

"You can clean yourself up while I fetch you some new clothes." Callidus' voice sounded heavy, his whole body lacked its usual animation. He walked up the stairway and Kya began scrubbing her hands, noticing only then that her sleeves, the front of her shirt, as well as her pants were stained.

When he returned, his expression was unchanged. He handed Kya clothing that consisted of a hand-knit green sweater and a pair of worn black pants.

"They belong to Audentia. She won't mind. Especially considering what you tried to do for her brother."

"The boy, Facillis is - was," Kya corrected herself, and her voice caught in her throat, "her brother?"

Callidus nodded and pointed towards a nearby room. "You can change in there."

Kya shut the door behind her and as she changed she heard him presumably cleaning himself up. When she returned, she carried her clothes in a bunch. The metallic stench of blood, still damp wafted from her clothing and caused Kya to have a strong compulsion to wash her hands again.

"I can see about cleaning them."

Kya pushed her lips up, attempting to form a smile. "I think they're passed that point."

He nodded again, but it was strained. His head seeming to have difficulty raising before quickly dropping. Callidus found a wicker basket for Kya to put her clothing in and then pulled out a chair and gestured for Kya to sit. He walked around the table to sit opposite her. He had removed the wrappings from his arms, nearly to his shoulders, and his visible skin was clean. There was an almost tangible weight on his shoulders, pressing down on him, draining him of his youth.

Kya felt like she could see lines forming on his face, aging him, stealing away the Callidus that talked so passionately less than an hour before.

Placing his arms on the table, Callidus dropped his head into his hands. "That is the other side of New Eden and the life of the First Gens." His sigh was so loud that it echoed off the near bare walls. "Inside of this compound, we are relatively safe, but for those of us who choose to leave, there are risks. We all know them." He sighed again. Each sentence seemed a strain. Veins popped from his neck and forehead as he continued to speak calm and even. "The powers that be see us as a threat to the world they have created. If the powers we have were to spread it would undo the whole Supers business within a generation or two." He paused and looked around the room. He ran his hands through his curly black hair and his intense and mournful green eyes locked again with Kya's. "It's bitter-sweet inside these walls, we can be seen, we can be touched. We are cared about. When we die here, people weep."

Kya squirmed slightly in her chair. Her thoughts drifted, considering the weight of the situation she was now in. Despite all of the recent events in her life, today, more than any day, felt unreal.

Callidus continued, seemingly unaware of Kya's discomfort. "But within these walls we are prisoners. We make a choice to leave. Out there we are free to go where we may, but we can't be seen, we can't be touched, and the government and corporations celebrate when we die." He raised his still clasped hands to his mouth and blew into them. He lifted his index fingers and wiped beneath his eyes.

Kya was unsure of what to say. She stared at Callidus, sitting across from her, speaking so solemnly.

"Facillis only joined our ranks a month ago. I don't know why they took him to the alley on Seventh." He spoke more to himself than to Kya, his eyes drifting around the room. After a silence, his sparkling green eyes fell on her, and there was something missing. His eyes looked slightly dimmer somehow, and there was an energy of shame, frustration, and sadness pouring from inside of him.

Kya could empathise. She lacked insight into their relationship, but she could see that Callidus was taking the whole thing hard. Sometimes, Kya thought he looked at her as though she was the one who had died.

"I'm sorry," He whispered. "I'm so sorry this was your introduction to our world."

"I - I just wish I could have helped."

"You did." He nodded. "You did."

Kya knew a change of topic was in order. She dug around in her brain, still swarming with unanswered questions, and one floated to the surface. "What do you Shadow Striders hope to accomplish?"

"We want people like you, and so many others to know what the cost of the Supers Market was, and is. We want people to know how these Supers came to be, and that we are still here. We don't want to be swept under a rug and forgotten about. We don't want to be caged, in fear of what could happen if we leave."

"What do you expect me to do?"

"I hope that you will share our story."

"How?" Kya was surprised by her boldness. "Everything I have read about you online has been cryptic, and people go missing as soon, as they say, anything about First Gens. Look what happened here tonight. How do I know I'll be safe?"

"Look, we stand out." Callidus gestured at his black and gray outfit. "By the sheer fact that we try not to be seen, when they find us, they know who we are. You look like everyone else. There is no consequence for someone who bumps into you on the street. You're safe."

"What if I'm found?"

"The government has bigger problems these days. Their limitations are falling apart on their *limitless* Supers; the Supers are too strong, and it's too easy to get more than a person can handle. Look at that Myles Redwood guy. He's been causing mayhem, and he's murdered, but they still haven't caught him. I think you're safe for now."

A pit of worry had formed in Kya's stomach, and now it seemed to grow so large, she thought she would throw up. "Is there any way you could take back powers once they're given?"

"No, Kya. I'm sorry. It's a one-way street. There's no extraction for First Gen Supers. I thought I had explained that in the alleyway. But still I am sorry to have caused you so much fear and sadness. I know that you will find your way through."

Kya wanted to leave but didn't know what to say. She was relieved when there was a knock at the door, and Everly entered.

"I think I should take Kya back." Her eyes were bloodshot, and her voice rasped like she had been crying.

"I'll escort you guys as far as I can," Callidus said.

Everly and Callidus walked Kya back to the bus stop near Gennie's Diner. None of them said anything, and so the silence was only broken by the noise of their shoes hitting the pavement and echoing outwards into the empty streets.

When they finally reached the bus stop, Callidus nodded his covered head while facing Kya. His outfit was the same as Kya remembered from their first meeting. Even the wrappings on his arms and hands had been placed back perfectly. There wasn't an inch of skin showing anywhere. "Thank you for coming to see us. And thank you for what you did for Facillis" His voice came somber and heavy from under his hood and scarf.

Kya swallowed hard. No words came to her. Fear, sadness, confusion, and uncertainty wrapped around her, making it hard to breathe. She wanted to see into Callidus' eyes once more and feel his passion for their cause. She hoped that the discomfort she felt, having seen behind the dark curtain of the world, would fade away and that she could again feel happiness. Kya took a moment to try to think back to when she felt her life was happy, but couldn't pull out a moment from recent memory.

Callidus, with an extreme exaggeration in movement, opened his arms wide and bowed deeply as he shuffled back into the shadows of the nearby buildings and vanished from view.

Kya grinned at the sight. It was as though Callidus knew exactly what she had needed from him and did it in his normal, highly animated way.

"Yeah, that was for you." Everly said, and Kya knew that the woman had read hers and Callidus' minds.

Everly waited with Kya until the bus came. The two stood in silence, exchanging occasional glances and Kya noticed that only after she was safely on board did Everly start walking back to the diner.

From the bus, Kya could see the glowing sign of Gennie's Diner, and as she got further away from it, she felt more normal. It was similar to leaving an action movie at a theatre. She felt exhilarated, but also knew that there was something unreal about it all. The energy faded fast as the sun set, and she focused on looking for landmarks she recognized on her way home.

Twenty minutes from her apartment, her cell phone vibrated in her pocket. "I thought I had turned that off." Kya felt nervous as she looked at the display. She half expected it to be the government letting her know that they had seen what she had done. Thankfully, it was just an email message from another job she had applied to.

It took a moment for it to load, thanks to the slower connection speeds out at the edge of the city, but once it did, Kya felt her face turn red with rage. She held her breath, choking down a frustrated scream. The email message within let her know that the person they contacted at Starlife Technologies had helped them realize that she would not be a suitable candidate for their opening.

She growled, louder than she had expected, and in a deep rumbling tone, through gritted teeth she pronounced a short name, "Don!"

Kya knew that it was time to confront him, and not just for what he was doing to her, but for what he had done to Elliot.

Without Supers, she knew that he would have just crushed her, but now, with her own set of Supers, Supers she had no choice but to embrace and learn to control, she suddenly felt more confident. In her mind, she concocted a plan. She knew she would have to spend time training with her Supers so that she could use them as needed, and not just as a reaction or accident. When she felt confident in her abilities, she would go to Starlife Technologies and confront him for the wrongs he had done. Kya was feeling so confident, that she considered threatening Don. In her mind, she continued to play out the interaction that they would have. Kya's creativity was working at full speed coming up with imagined victory after victory.

"Wow," Sam said from his usual seat without looking at her, beer in one hand and tablet in the other with the big screen television on. "You're home late -" He cut his thought off as he glanced up at Kya. "What are you wearing?"

"It's a long and terrible story. But suffice it to say that my own clothes are gone, and these belong to a First Gen."

Sam raised an eyebrow, and the corner of his mouth twitched as if he were debating whether or not to smile.

"I don't want to talk about it," Kya said, heavily.

"Okay, well if you want to, you know where to find me."

She walked into her room, and took off the sweater, she threw it in the laundry basket, then headed to her washroom for a shower.

When Kya returned to her room, the phone was flashing letting her know she had an unread message. It was Mattea.

>*Hey, Kya. How are you doing?*

She paced back and forth in her room deciding whether or not to respond. Her fingers had typed the words before she was fully aware of what she was doing. She told Mattea about Everly and Callidus and her experience in and around New Eden, but she left out everything about Facillis. She just couldn't bring herself to acknowledge another death. With trembling hands she finished.

>*Callidus says my abilities are permanent, but that I'll be safe. He says the government and corporations have more to worry about, but I can't help but feel afraid. This whole system is more sinister than you think.*

Kya held her phone, sitting on her bed. It seemed to take an eternity for Mattea to respond. Despite having her still damp hair twisted into the towel on her head, a single drop of water ran down the back of her neck, causing a chill to rush up her spine.

>*I had a feeling, from my research, that Supers and the Fertility Crisis were connected. I ran into the same dead ends you did. I saw the same types of disappearances. I don't know what to tell you. I guess, just take comfort in the fact that Everly from the diner is still around. It sounds like she has probably been doing this for a while. I wish I could help more.*

It was nearly an hour before Kya emerged again into the living room where Sam still sat.

"Better?" He asked gently.

Nodding slightly, Kya flopped onto the couch, and glanced up at the large screen. She was expecting some light, fluffy sitcom or reality television show, but instead she saw a news reporter. Beside the reporter was a picture of Myles Redwood from before he received his first Super.

A news ticker flickered at the bottom third of the screen and Kya knew that she had caught the start of it. Words slowly crept across the screen, revealing themselves to her one at a time, and she read them in her mind, over and over. *Justice has been served. Myles Redwood is dead.*

Kya's jaw fell, her mouth hung wide open. The words felt like a saw ripping through her brain. She turned her body slowly and looked directly at Sam. His face had a look of surprise as well, but when his eyes turned to her own, his expression changed.

"What's wrong?" Sam said.

"What happened to Myles?" Kya's mouth went dry. "He's dead?"

"Yeah, pretty unbelievable isn't it?" Sam's attention drifted back to his screens, and his eyes scanned quickly as he spoke. "They've been playing it on the news all afternoon. They have had a little more information during each of the news reports, and apparently the Chief of Police is going to speak on this broadcast."

Kya shifted her whole body back towards the display. The muscles in her neck were so tight her head was unable to swivel. Her jaw started to shake uncontrollably as she watched the news report.

An older woman, with silver hair, stood behind a podium, a dozen microphones were aimed at her. Her face was stern, and the deep lines on it only emphasized her scowl. "Myles Redwood was an exceptional case. He broke the law on several occasions, and although his *entertainment value* was great, his unpredictable and dangerous behaviour were a greater threat. As you all know, actions were taken early on, including an extraction process, in an attempt to keep the young man safely in line." The woman paused, taking a deep breath. "These tactics, however, were unsuccessful in controlling the larger problem: Myles Redwood was a rogue Super. Several attempts were made to settle the matter peacefully, but he was too far gone. He was completely out of control and a risk both to himself and others. It was with a heavy heart that I gave the order to have him neutralized." The woman's hard eyes stared into the camera and seemed to pierce right into Kya, turning her stomach.

"Doesn't sound much like she has a heavy heart," Kya commented on the cold, robotic tone of the silver haired woman. Kya pictured this woman giving the order to have her neutralized. A chill ran down her back.

On the screen, a younger man stepped up onto the stage and stood directly beside the older woman.

"Thankfully," the woman continued, "in combination with the police, special forces from Enhance were able to find Myles and after a risky engagement, they were able to bring him to justice."

A loud chattering could be heard as she finished her statement. Hands shot up everywhere, covering portions of the video feed.

"We owe a huge debt of gratitude to organizations like Enhance that help keep our society safe." A graphic faded in at the bottom of the screen, identifying the woman as the *Chief of Police, Margaret Hall*. She turned and shook the hand of the young man, presumably from Enhance.

The young man then leaned forward towards the wall of microphones attached to the podium, and Margaret moved back. "I want to thank the Police for allowing us to assist them in this matter. We at Enhance never want to see society at risk as a result of Supers. I also want to assure the public that we have made enhancements to our security and safety procedures so that an event like this never happens again. You can be sure, however, that we are always prepared to help the Police with whatever issue they might be having."

The lower half of the screen helped to identify the young man as well with a graphic that showed his name to be Pietro Peters.

With her neck still locked in place, her jaw still trembling, and her heart racing, Kya felt like the walls were caving in on her. The thought that she could be their next target made her blood run cold. She thought back to what Callidus had said about being safe because the Police couldn't even catch Myles, and now she saw the lower third filled with text, slowly scrolling by were the words that she had first seen when sitting down: Myles Redwood is dead.

"Kya?" Sam asked with concern, but Kya ignored him.

Rushing from the living room, and almost tripping over her own feet, she moved awkwardly towards her bedroom. She slapped the door in a hurry, and it slowly creaked closed. Her vision blurred, but unlike going invisible, she could still see, though everything was heavily distorted and swimming. She also started to feel like her stomach was filled with acid. Placing her hand on her forehead, she felt both sweaty and cold. She had a strong feeling regarding what was going to come next and rushed into her bathroom. The lid of the toilet was tipped up only seconds before she emptied her stomach into it.

Immediately afterwards Kya felt physically better, but the worry still nagged at her. She felt angry as if she knew she was going to be cheated out of the life she deserved. She thought for a moment about the job she wanted at Classic Communication and how she might not get to live to enjoy it, and then her thoughts focused in on Don Georgetown. The fact that Myles had been caught only increased her drive to confront him. If it was the last thing she could do before being neutralized she needed to stop Don from ruining the lives of others.

Having Supers was one thing, but Kya knew that knowing how to effectively use them wasn't going to be easy. She also knew that Don was well versed in his own Supers and that she would need to practice before confronting him.

"Are you okay in there?" Sam yelled.

"Yes. I'm fine. Thanks." As she responded, her voice was sweeter and higher pitched than normal. She knew Sam would know she was not fine.

As she left her washroom and sat on her bed, she focused on trying to become invisible. Kya held her breath and the tendrils of darkness that she had become so used to crawled along her vision. The blackness they caused blinded her, but she was fairly certain she was completely invisible. Still holding her breath, she focused on trying to only make her head visible. At first, nothing changed, but upon releasing her breath, the tendrils faded away. Kya looked down at herself, only to realize she was completely visible once again. She gritted her teeth, growled in frustration and tried once more.

Time passed quickly as Kya tried to master her powers. She tried testing the limits and accuracy of her telekinesis. When she became frustrated and threw her lamp against the wall, she bent down and with a shaking hand picked up a piece of the glass. She closed her eyes and groaned as she squeezed the glass, forcing it to puncture her skin. She opened her palm and looked at the beads of blood blossoming there. With her other hand, she touched the wound and waited for the cold sensation of healing. It didn't come. Kya kicked open the washroom door and grabbed a bandage.

"They'll work right when I need them," She said as an affirmation, repeating it to herself so many times the words lost all meaning.

An alarm on her phone turned her focus to her next immediate challenge. The message flashing on her screen was one she had set hours ago, *"Are you prepared for your interview with Classic Communication tomorrow?"*

CHAPTER 25

Kya checked herself out in the washroom mirror one last time before leaving for the interview. She was wearing a blue dress shirt tucked into a black pencil skirt that she had found in the back of her closet, black tights and dressy black flats completed the outfit. She had put on a bit of eye makeup and had her hair pinned back. A little of the faded purple streaks were showing.

"Okay, body. Listen up. None of this Supers business when I'm in the interview. No grabbing random things. No disappearing-" Kya saw familiar black lines crawling along her vision, extending towards the center. She looked at the bathroom mirror, her pulse quickening, but before her vision blackened completely, she saw a glimpse of herself semi-transparent and fading away.

"Like that." She said, and her sight immediately returned. "None of that."

A knock at the washroom door startled Kya slightly.

"Hey, Kya." Sam's voice came muffled from the other

side. "You all right in there?"

"Yep. Just a pep talk before the interview." Kya replied as she opened the door.

"You look great!" Sam said, with a wide smile. With his hand, he reached out and touched the purple streak in her hair.

"Yeah. I decided I'll be honest about it and let Joanne know that if they don't like it, I'll change it back to brown."

"Bold choice." Sam smiles approvingly.

Kya grinned. "I hope it's the right one."

After a brief silence, Kya continued. "Well, wish me luck."

"You got it, and much more," Sam replied.

Classic Communication wasn't very far from the apartment, so a quick walk the three blocks over made the most sense. Kya found the air was already shifting warmer, and she could feel a bit of humidity taking hold. The streets were packed with people, despite it being before most jobs let out for the day.

She took a moment to inventory herself as she waited for the first crosswalk to notify her it was safe to cross. A spike of nerves hit her as she looked through her purse. Her phone, which held a digital version of her resume, and a neatly folded printed version were both where she expected them to be. Locating her keys and wallet, she breathed a sigh of relief.

Inside the entrance to the skyscraper was a large digital

directory, and Kya selected Classic Communication. With over fifty floors for both businesses and residences, Kya felt a little let down that the store and offices were all on the first floor behind the elevators. As she passed the chokehold in the hallway, there were two large wooden doors each with a word engraved on it. The left said Classic, and the right said Communication. They were beautiful, intricate, solid carved wood doors, and the character of them struck Kya as odd. Surrounded by stark gray and beige hallway walls and carpet, steel doors, and buzzing fluorescent lighting this entryway felt magical.

"You must be Kya." A kind voice exclaimed from behind her. A woman, standing as tall as Kya, approached; her hand out and a warm smile on her face. The woman was maybe five years older than Kya, though unlike most women she had a smattering of gray strands through her brown hair that was tied up in a loose bun. She wore no makeup but had a porcelain complexion. She wore a green blouse that tied at the side, a beige skirt that came to her knees, and green sandals. Kya found her to be quite pretty.

"Yes, I was just heading in. Are you Joanne?"

Quickly shaking hands and nodding, Joanne proceeded to open the right door and enter the store.

Straight rows of bookshelves were arranged in a semicircle like rays emanating from the main desk. At the end of each row was a large stained glass window, casting brilliant colours onto the shelves. An immense glass and metal atrium arched above their heads and domed the whole area and letting the sunlight in. Kya followed a beam of light down to the floor where a red carpet lead from the door to the large desk.

ANNIE PERALTY & DAVID PERALTY

"Welcome to Classic Communication," Joanne said as she walked quickly towards the front desk.

Kya followed, and after a tour, they arrived in a small office off to one side. There appeared to be two offices, but neither of them was very private, as they were inset into the wall, with no dividers from the open bookstore space. As they sat, Joanne poured two large glasses of water.

"Have you ever been here before? What do you know about us?" Joanne said in a chipper but direct way.

At first it caught Kya off guard, and her mind spun for a moment, trying to find traction and come up with an appropriate answer. "I actually have never been here before."

Joanne smiled, and Kya felt that she approved of her honesty.

"I order most of my books online and read them on my tablet."

"As technology is such a constant in our lives, reading printed books is really becoming more of a nostalgic hobby. But one of the great things about classically printed words is that once they are on the page, they can't change. Online things are edited, rewritten or removed entirely. But books remain constant, the only way to change them is to destroy them." Joanne paused and smiled. "But I digress. Here are a few things that you need to know about us." Joanne explained, handing Kya a document from the top of the desk. "Our clientele tends to be Normals of varying financial states. We tend not to have many Supers come into the store as they have other options available to them. Are you equally comfortable with highly

332

educated business types and those that are more," she paused as if searching for the right words, "run of the mill?"

Kya smiled confidently. "I definitely can be friendly and approachable with a wide variety of people."

"Now, this is customer service, so you will likely have to deal with ornery customers from time to time."

Kya thought about Don Georgetown. "Oh, that won't be a problem. I can definitely let hostility roll off my shoulders. It would take a lot before I would crack."

The interview continued, all the questions blurred together in her head. She smiled and tried her best to answer honestly and positively.

"Any questions about the open position for me?" Joanne asked at the end of the interview.

"Just one that I can think of."

Joanne raised an eyebrow. "Oh?"

"I currently have some purple streaks in my hair."

"I noticed."

"If that will be a problem I have no problem dying them."

"No need. But, if you dye them darker they'll stay vibrant longer." Joanne smiled.

Kya couldn't believe how easily she felt like she fitted in with the owner of Classic Communication. She tried to keep her excitement in check as the interview wrapped up. Streams of coloured light bounced around the wide open, high ceilings from the stained glass windows. The room filled her spirit with a calm and happy energy.

Joanne finished her glass of water, and Kya noticed that she had barely sipped from her own. Not wanting to be rude, she grasped her glass and took a long, deep sip of the water. As she drank it down, Joanne grinned.

"Great stuff, isn't it? We have all the taps on a reverse osmosis filter system. I just can't get enough of it." Joanne stood up, and Kya followed suit. "So, we will contact you in around two weeks after we finish interviewing the other candidates, and checking references."

Kya's heart began to race slightly at the mention of references. She thought they had already completed a reference check and hadn't contacted Don Georgetown. She tried to search for a way to politely ask Joanne not to contact Starlife Technologies, but the moment to interject was over before she got a word out.

"You'll hear from us either way," Joanne said, ushering Kya through the large wooden doors. "I really appreciate you coming in today." She extended her hand for Kya to shake, with a kind and genuine smile on her face.

The door closed behind Kya, and as she walked back to the apartment, she tried to focus on the positive aspects of the experience and in doing so, she was home in what felt like an instant. There was an excitement, a vibrant energy, surrounding her as she entered her bedroom and fell on her bed face first.

She kicked off her shoes and started to pull off the interview clothes she was wearing. Breathing deeply, with her face still embedded into her pillows, she felt the weight of the makeup on her face. She lifted her head only to see some of the colour she had put around her eyes smeared onto her pillow.

"Ugh." She moaned, and decided to wash her face. She stood and walked to her door, making a mental note to put the pillowcase in her next load of laundry. The pillow smacked into the back of her head. "You know, I really hate you sometimes."

"Hmm?" Sam said, from somewhere else in the apartment.

"Telekinesis."

"Ahhh."

Kya washed her face, recounting each question and answer she had given during the interview while being grateful that none of her Supers had made an appearance while she was out.

CHAPTER 26

Kya's phone started buzzing early in the morning. Thanks to her curtains being pulled back, the sunlight was streaming in through her window, and the light illuminated floating streaks of dust. Slamming her fist onto her phone, and realized what her plan for the day was going to be. Instantly, a rush of anxiety filled her mind, coursed through her veins and caused her entire body to tense up. She had contemplated what was going to happen, spending all night tossing and turning in her bed before finally passing out. But before this moment, it had all just been imaginary. Now she was going to make it real.

She checked the weather app on her phone and decided to layer because it was unseasonably cold outside. She threw on a thin, long-sleeved shirt and over top her t-shirt that said *GEEK* across the front in large bold letters. She brushed her hair, and pulled the top half into a ponytail, boldly showing her purple streaks. She was going to go into Starlife Technologies proudly looking like herself. Checking how she looked in her mirror, Kya saw the scared face of a much younger version of herself. The black tendrils of invisibility started in her peripheral vision before completely blocking it out. She breathed deeply, her eyes open, waiting to see her reflection again. Kya exhaled sharply, and both her vision and her reflection faded back into existence.

Once in the common area of the apartment, she realized Sam had already left for work. A paper was on the counter nearest her room. It was a quick note from him.

Hey Kya, we should hang out tonight. I'll be back around seven, and we can eat dinner together if you are up for it. I feel like we haven't really hung out lately.

It was as though his words struck a nerve. Kya felt like she was going to cry. Tears welled up in her eyes, but swallowing hard, she forced her emotions back down and re-focused on the task at hand. She knew that today, she was going to change her life, and finally be rid of Don Georgetown.

The bus ride to Starlife Technologies seemed so familiar, yet so different, as though she was remembering a previous life. Tidal pulses of calm routine and panicked uncertainty washed over her. As the bus arrived at her old workplace, she found it difficult to leave her seat. There was a small part of her mind that wanted her to run away, rather than prepare for a fight.

She pushed through the large glass doors of the building and walked inside. She was greeted by a young security guard standing firm at the front desk. Dozens of people were walking in and out. A few people that worked the night shift were still leaving, and others who started early were already heading out for their first break.

"May I help you?" He asked.

"I'm here to see Don Georgetown," she said with a smile. "I used to work here. I just need to tie up a few loose ends." Kya stood in silence as the security guard looked at his tablet computer, scrolling through a list of names. A bead of sweat formed on Kya's brow, and she wiped it away quickly. The thought of her plans coming to an early end because of a security guard was not something that she had planned for.

"Kya?" A familiar voice came from behind her and sent a chill up her spine.

"Leonard!" She said in a friendly, though surprised voice. She forced her lips to turn into a tight smile.

"Wow! Look at you. Really rocking your unique style." He grinned at her. He was dressed in a blue dress shirt, with a gray pin-striped vest and a matching pair of slacks.

Kya nodded. "I'm dressing for the job I want," she said in what she hoped would be perceived as a friendly tone. She looked down at her jeans, sneakers, and layered shirts. She felt even more out of place now surrounded by all of the suits and dress clothing rushing around her. The shirt she had chosen, the wording on it marking her as a geek, now felt like a sign announcing that she was an outsider and didn't belong.

"So, what brings you here then?"

"Don-" She trailed off, unsure how to proceed.

"Hey, Walt," Leonard said, turning his attention to the

security guard, "she's cool. She's with me."

Leonard swiped his keycard and led Kya through the door. "Hoping for a reference from Mr. Georgetown?" He asked, leading Kya through a corridor she had never been down before.

"Something like that," she mumbled, taking in her surroundings.

"Things haven't changed much since you left, but I'm sure you already knew that. You still have friends that work here, right?"

Kya felt Leonard's words pierce her deeply. She knew he didn't mean it in a derogatory way, but she almost felt physical pain as he said them. "No, I don't have any connection to this place anymore."

The information technology area was a bustling hub of activity. The department hadn't grown or shrunk since Kya had left, but the newly remodeled area felt like it lacked a special something. As she arrived, she could hear Don Georgetown in his office.

"I'll check to see if he's busy if you want." Leonard gestured towards the opaque glass door.

"I can handle it from here. Thanks."

Kya knocked on the door, and she heard Don's chair thump as he got up. She could hear each of his steps, the footfalls almost shaking the walls. Kya turned and looked around, but Leonard had already left and was talking to someone a few cubicles over.

As the handle twisted, Kya's heart pounded rapidly, her palms became clammy. She felt as though she wanted to go invisible, and it took all of her willpower to stand her ground, and not run away.

The door creaked open, and Don's imposing figure filled the entire door frame. "Well, look who we have here. Everyone!" Don raised his voice to draw attention. "This is one of the only people I've ever met that went obsolete."

Kya swallowed hard but because of her mouth being completely dry, she had a difficult time with it. "Can we speak in your office?"

"You have ninety seconds, Kendra. My time is too valuable to waste on you."

His words felt like physical strikes in her brain and Kya was roused out of her reluctance. She threw her shoulders back and raised her head high. "This won't take long," she said in a strong and authoritative voice.

Kya noticed Leonard's head pop up from the cubicle and give her one last glance and nod as she entered the office. The look on his face seemed to be one of both shock and support.

Don walked across his office and sat in his chair, leaving Kya to close the door.

"Take a seat," Don demanded.

"No. I'm fine." Kya stood behind the two office chairs set-up for guests in his office. She felt taller than Don and, for some unknown reason, it added to her courage.

"So, what's this about?"

"I want you to stop saying bad things about me. What gives you the right to try and ruin my life? You already took this job from me; now you're stopping me from finding a new job. You need to stop."

"Why should I stop? I'm just telling the truth. You were a horrible employee, and you don't deserve a job that requires any responsibility."

Kya began to grind her teeth as each word fueled her rage more and more.

"There is nothing you can do about it," Don said. A smug look spread across his face, and Kya could tell that he felt victorious over her.

A feeling of heat spread across Kya's cheeks. She forced herself to stand as straight as possible. In her mind, she dug deep and mustered up as much confidence as she could. She wanted her next words to be powerful, despite a small voice inside of her providing a reminder that nothing good could come of what she was about to do. "You have no right to go bad mouthing me behind my back!"

"You!" Don Georgetown yelled, his deep voice causing Kya to flinch involuntarily. He took a breath and continued quietly. "You came in here dressed-" He waved his hand at her as though he was pausing to try and find the right words. "Like a child. Streaks in your hair that you knew were against the dress code. Did you think that we couldn't see them? Jeans or sweatpants, showing up late, and improper documentation. Everything you did was to spit in the face of the corporate image. You rebelled every chance you got. You were a liability. I am looking out for the welfare of any company considering you as an employee." Don's face went red as he completed his rant, seeming both winded and satisfied; he stopped.

"I don't need to take this," Kya said coldly. "You never gave me any respect, why should I-"

His voice changed and became eerily calm. "You never earned any respect." He traced his finger along the surface of his mahogany desk, looking at his hand as he did so. "You know Leonard started the same time as you. He was always early for shifts, always dressed to impress. He followed the job description to the letter. He went above and beyond what was asked of him."

A sarcastic laugh escaped Kya's lips. "He went above and beyond alright!"

Don lifted his head and raised an eyebrow at Kya. He shifted in his chair, leaning forward. His upper body seemed to rest heavily on his extended gut.

"I know he only got a promotion because of Elliot."

Don flinched at the name in an almost imperceptible way. It was mostly his eyes that changed, displaying unhappiness. It was only for a moment and then his hardened, confident exterior returned. "What?" He asked in an aloof tone.

"I know what happened to Elliot. Leonard only got his promotion because he helped you get rid of the evidence."

"Elliot?" Don said in mock confusion. "Elliot who?"

"Elliot Shepherd," Kya said, frustrated.

"Who?" A smile crept across his face and then he began to laugh. He turned his attention to his computer and after a moment turned the screen towards Kya. "Go ahead. Hack away! You'll find no record of an employee named Elliot Shepherd. No security videos, entry logs, pay stubs. Nothing."

"Because Leonard helped you cover it up!" Kya's anger was almost at its breaking point. She wanted to strike out, to make him admit what he had done. His smug confidence grated on Kya's nerves.

"How do you think I got this office? My people skills?" His grin made Kya's skin crawl. "I know more than a few things about computers. I didn't need Leonard's help. The Director of I.T. saw Leonard's work and his work ethic and promoted him. I won't say the positive reference I gave him didn't help, though."

"You admit you removed Elliot from the database? I know what I saw, you killed him. You covered it up."

"There's no point trying to convince you otherwise. You know what you saw, and I know how seriously the authorities will take the word of a desperate and unemployed Normal with no evidence and a good motive to want to ruin her ex-boss." He smiled again.

"They'll listen."

"Elliot was an old man, set in his ways, nothing to show for it. No one cares about him."

"I care."

"You're no one!"

Deep rage overflowed and the pulsing ringing in her ears became so loud that she couldn't hear anything else. Kya could feel her throat rumbling as she breathed in and out. She knew it was likely an audible growl. Don waved his finger at her, a disgusted look upon his face, and without fully being aware of what she was doing Kya leaped swiftly over his desk, and slid inches away from his face. There was no will or thought fueling her actions, only anger. Her arm pulled back and swung forward hitting Don Georgetown square in the jaw.

Kya heard the dull thud of her fist hitting his face and felt a twinge of pain shot through her hand and up her arm and into her shoulder.

Instead of seeing shock, anger or pain, Don's expression was one of smug victory, and Kya could tell her assault had done nothing. He stood up from his chair and towered over Kya, who was still kneeling on the edge of his desk. Don pushed up his sleeves, exposing his hairy, thick arms. His grin widened as he pulled back his right fist and Kya caught a gleam of excitement in his eyes. He paused for a moment, his eyes locked directly on Kya. "Don't forget who started this."

Kya knew what was coming next. She clenched her whole body in anticipation, squinting her eyes and preparing herself for retaliation. She watched as black tendrils crossed her vision, and as much as she wanted to take comfort in her invisibility, she knew that it wouldn't save her.

"Oh, well look at that!" Don said. His tone was snide,

but Kya could hear the undertones of surprise in his comment.

She shuffled backward, hoping to get away from him without completely giving away her location. Papers, pens, and other office supplies slid under her hands as she repositioned. Unfortunately, the next thing she felt was agony rippling from her cheek and then soon after, the back of her head as she hit the hardwood floor. Kya knew she was no longer invisible, as she could see once again though her vision was distorted with flashes of light and pain. She tried to slide backward towards the door and realized that the chair she had been sitting on earlier was flipped over on her leg, slowing her movement.

"Thought you could hide from me? Being invisible doesn't stop you from being hit, or bleeding." Don pointed at Kya's face.

Kya touched her cheek, and it felt raw. Inside her mouth, she could taste blood, and it felt as though a few of her teeth had knocked loose. With her head swimming, she pushed the chair off of her leg and put her hand to her cheek again and concentrated. A pulse of cold washed over her face, and the pain she felt subsided. As she swallowed another mouthful of blood, she could tell inside her mouth was no longer bleeding.

"Some kind of healing, too? How much can you heal? If I crush your chest, can you fix that too? What happens if you pass out?" Don's tone was giddy as his words became a life or death challenge.

Kya went from feeling like she was going to achieve victory, to knowing that she just wanted to live. A quick inspection of her surroundings gave her the ammunition she needed to try to turn the tables. Dozens of pens, manuals, and even Don's computer started lifting into the air and repeatedly assaulting him. A few of the pens tried to dig their way into his skin, but it wouldn't give, no matter how hard Kya pushed with her mind.

A huge belly laugh came from Don as Kya continued her assault. "You are just as useless with Supers as you were without."

Kya tried to focus once again and made herself invisible. She tried to continue to push things towards where she thought Don was as she opened the door and slipped out of the office. She could hear Don's angry shout as she shut the door, popped back into existence and ran like her life depended on it towards the exit.

Before leaving the information technology area, she turned and looked back at the office filled with people standing and staring at Don Georgetown's office. Using her back to push through the door, Kya exited Starlife Technologies.

CHAPTER 27

With the tall glass building behind her, Kya took a deep breath and considered what had occurred. She was still enraged, thinking about the mediocrity of her Supers and Don's insistence that she had been such a horrible employee. As the throbbing in her head subsided slightly, she began to replay the entire confrontation in her mind. In doing so, she had to reflect on what Don said. It stung that it was her worst enemy, but Kya couldn't help but wonder if he might have been, at least a little bit, right about her.

Before she had a chance to dissect everything in detail, she heard a booming voice yell from Starlife Technologies. "You didn't think I'd let you leave after I saw what you could do, did you?"

Don Georgetown was moving along the ground, speeding up slowly, like a freight train. His weight seemed to slow how fast his momentum built up, but each step shook everything not bolted down in the front courtyard of Starlife Technologies.

In all of her planning, Kya never thought that having Supers would make her a person of interest to Don. She never planned anything out, assuming only that she would be successful or victorious. She mentally chided herself for not going to the police and using her Supers as a way to coerce them to investigate Elliot's death. Her heart began to race again. Don still had a lot of ground to cover, but he was closing quickly.

Kya could swear she felt his steps through the concrete slabs and the half wall that she was holding onto for support. His feet hit the ground like sledgehammers, cracks snaking away from each imprinted footfall as he propelled himself forward. She looked around at the nearby buildings. The bus was still minutes away, and even though she was in broad daylight, in a busier area, she didn't want to risk seeing what would happen if Don caught up with her.

Rushing into the alley between two large skyscrapers, there were many places to hide, and it was mostly shielded from the daylight. The alley smelled like garbage, and vents from the sewers exited into the area, making the sour smell worse. Kya crouched down low and hid behind a small pile of cardboard boxes beside a set of concrete stairs leading into a nearby building.

As she held her breath, she closed her eyes tight. She didn't wait for any signs that her power was working but hoped that she couldn't be seen.

"You can't hide from me!"

The booming voice sent a shiver down her spine. Kya continued to hold her breath and considered what she would do if she were found. Kya forced her eyes open. She looked at a large shadowed figure. His silhouette nearly filled the width of available space, and Kya, for a split second, had to hold in a snicker at the ridiculous idea that her ex-boss might get stuck between two buildings.

Don picked up one of the nearby steel trash bins. He held it high over his head and launched it down the alley. It bounced off the walls of the buildings, denting the can into an unrecognizable shape. Kya ducked down further into the boxes and peered out through a small gap between them.

The noise reverberated down the corridor, and Kya quivered. The can had not come anywhere near her, but she could feel the strain in holding her breath. Frozen in place, lungs beginning to burn, she watched Don throw another metal trash can down the alley.

Again, the can bounced around but didn't come near the area that Kya was hiding. At this point, she could see Don's frustration. He had moved much closer but was still looking around, spending time quietly listening for any noise.

Don shoved the various boxes, garbage cans and dumpsters out his way. He threw random bags of garbage down the alley and continued to walk around. Every few attempts, he would stop, and listen intently. Kya watched in horror as he walked within inches of her.

Suddenly, she realized that if she could see Don, that meant she was visible, or at least partly so. It took a great deal of concentration to let her aching lungs exhale slowly and quietly before refilling and once again holding her breath. She concentrated, focused on becoming invisible. Darkness covered her vision again, and there was a small sense of relief before realizing she had to wait, in darkness, for whatever would happen next.

She heard a noise right next to her as Don kicked the boxes she was hiding behind. She knew if her invisibility failed now, Don would see her and kill her.

Kya clamped down, swallowing down the buildup of carbon dioxide in her lungs. Her body was aching, her muscles twitching. She imagined what it was like to breath, and tried to meditate. After few excruciating moments, Kya heard a noise further away as Don continued his search.

"Come on out!" Don said. His voice was a deep bellow of frustration and anger. Kya listened to him continue his path of destruction through to the back of the building, heading back towards Starlife Technologies.

Kya exhaled loudly and saw her body instantly appear. It felt as though something was caught in her lungs, and so not wanting to attract attention, she had to cover her mouth and cough deeply. Her whole body felt weak. Each breath was a struggle against the pounding of her heart. She wiped the streams of tears from her face, trying to pull herself together.

Kya jogged down the street, her will propelling her forward in a way that her body was nearly unwilling to do. Sweat poured from her face and body. She rounded the corner a few blocks away from the office. Her mind was clouded with panic and fear. She couldn't be sure that Don wouldn't go to her place to look for her there. He knew where she lived; it was on her employment records.

An image of New Eden flashed into Kya's mind, and she knew that Don wouldn't find her there, but how long could the First-Gen colony keep her safe? An image of Facillis flashed inside her head, and a chill went down her spine. Kya was not ready to go back there yet.

She slowed to a walk and kept checking around for signs of trouble. She imagined this was how an animal felt when it was being hunted. She took out her phone to text Mattea.

>*Can I stay with you for a bit, and lay low? Things went BAD at Starlife.*

Kya read over the message before sending it and decided to delete it. How could she hide with Mattea? How could she potentially endanger her friend and her friend's unborn child?

A startling revelation struck her like a lightning bolt rushing through her mind: what would happen to Sam while she was running away? What if Don went there looking for Kya? Sam needed to know what was going on. With the next bus still half an hour away, Kya turned another corner and hailed a cab. She directed the driver to their apartment building. Phone still in hand, she began another message to Mattea.

>*Mattie, I saw Mr. G. It went BAD! I'm alright for now. I don't know exactly what to do next, but I will figure it out. Right now, please just give me space. I don't want you or the baby to get hurt. I'll check in when I can.*

She took a deep cleansing breath and hit send.

Kya didn't pay attention to the meter as she paid the cab driver and got out at her apartment building. She pushed through the front door and rode the elevator up. As she pulled out her keys to open the door, her phone buzzed in her pocket. It was Mattea.

>*Take care of you.*

With everything that Sam had done for Kya, she felt a strong need to get to him quickly. She had no proof that Don was going to be an issue and track her down, but if he did, she didn't want anyone else to get hurt.

The apartment door was locked. As she pulled her keys from her pocket, she felt a new wave of concern. She considered that Sam might have been intercepted. An imaginary scenario played out in her mind where Kya would have to trade her life for his. She shuddered and opened the door.

"Sam?" She called out.

No one answered.

Immediately, she locked the door behind her and looked around to see if there was a note or anything to indicate where Sam was. She saw nothing. Her heart was pounding in her ears, as she knocked on his bedroom door.

"Sam?" She asked.

No reply.

Her hand dug into her pocket and retrieved her phone. She typed out a message to Sam.

>*Hey Sam, where are you? Please let me know. Thanks.*

With her free hand, she pushed her hair back from her face. She walked into her room and wrapped herself in the covers of her bed. Time seemed to slow down and nearly stop as she waited to hear back from her roommate. Her mind tormented her with involuntary and unsolicited thoughts of Amelia and Facillis. A knot grew in her stomach as she worried that Sam may suffer a similar fate.

Her phone vibrated, and she was shocked to see that only three minutes had passed since she sent her message.

>*I'm at work. What is wrong?*

Relief washed over her, and Kya laughed in spite of herself as she read Sam's reply. She quickly typed a response.

>*My meeting at SLT went sour, and I made an enemy out of Mr. G. How did you know something was wrong?*

>*I know you too well. How sour? How much of an enemy?*

Kya stood and began pacing her room as she frantically typed out a series of messages explaining her experience inside her old work, ending with Don's rampage of the alleyway and her narrow escape.

>*Kya that's not good. What are you going to do now?*

>*I don't know. But I think you should stay away from the apartment until it's safe. He knows where we live, and I've seen what he's capable of.*

>*I'll crash at friends. Don't worry about me. BUT you have to take care of this, Kya. Neither one of us can hide away forever.*

She knew Sam was right. Throwing a few essentials in her backpack, Kya left the apartment with a new sense of determination and hailed another cab.

The cab stopped in front of police headquarters, and Kya felt apprehensive. She wondered if the sensor waved over Sam's hand on their previous visit would show that she was now a Super. She also wondered if this was where Don was planning on intercepting her. It was his idea to come here and report him.

Her entrance to the police station was unmarked by conflict, and despite a rising level of nervousness, she found herself stuck inside her imagination, wondering how events were going to unfold.

"Hi, I'm here to report a crime," Kya said. Standing there, she couldn't remember getting to the small window where an officer, with an expression of disdain, etched into his aged face, was sitting. Even her words slipped out before she had a chance to reconsider them.

Slowly, he raised his eyes and looked at Kya. She noticed the deep creases in his face; the skin looked leathery and his eyes tired. "Please wait." The man disappeared, and the door to her left opened. The officer, standing only as tall as Kya, walked towards her with the scanning device in hand.

Sweat poured from Kya's brow as the officer waved the device over her outstretched palm. The light on the top went green, and the officer's expression changed. He seemed lighter, more alive. There was an increase in energy that took Kya by surprise. It was as though he was standing at attention, and awaiting her orders.

"What can I do for you, ma'am?" He said in a polite tone.

"Well, a friend of mine was murdered by a Super, and I'd like him to be arrested." Kya feigned confidence as she stood firm, holding herself up, the energy from the officer providing her with drive and motivation.

"Do you have any evidence of this crime?"

"No, the evidence was destroyed, but I saw a recording of it before it was destroyed, and I'll testify." It was as though the words spewing forth were not her own. Kya couldn't imagine putting herself in a situation where she would potentially have to tell the world that she had Supers. What if someone found out where she got them?

"Follow me please." The office opened the door he had come from, pocketed the scanning device, and walked into a sea of cubicles on the other side.

Kya followed quickly, staying only two steps behind. "Where are we going?"

The officer pointed at a door at the far end of the building. "We have a Psyker in our department. He can read your mind, see your memories, and that is considered trusted evidence."

She knew that if the officer read her mind, saw what she saw, then maybe, finally, Don Georgetown would get what he deserved. Thoughts of Elliot finally getting justice also illuminated a large piece of her heart.

The door opened, and a thin man sat in a darkened room. He sat with his hands folded, resting on a wooden desk. He was sickly thin, and his skin looked untouched by daylight. His short, black hair matched his fitted black shirt, and he continued to stare at the wall, unmoving, despite the interruption.

Inside the room there were no windows, the walls were painted in a blue-grey tone. There was something eerie about the man, and Kya entered the room before noticing that the officer who had escorted her wasn't just holding the door open for her to enter, but also closing it behind her.

Kya took her seat and sat across from the thin man. He wasn't wearing a police uniform, and there were no personal belongings that Kya could associate with him. After a few moments of silence, she looked directly at him and plastered a knowingly awkward smile on her face. "Hello?"

"Hi. Do I have your consent to read your mind?"

"Um, well… How does this work? Do you see everything or just the crime?" Kya wished she could have made a joke, in hopes of drawing any attention away from all of the secrets in her life, but she remained quiet.

The officer took a piece of paper from his desk and slid it and a pen over towards Kya. His face was expressionless, and his breathing was slow. "Sign this, please, if you give consent. I will only be viewing your thoughts on the crime. We will not use anything I see against you, and you are pardoned for anything illegal you may have done in helping bring this criminal to justice."

Picking up the pen, Kya signed the form. "So now what do I-"

She began to relive the moments leading up to watching the video of Don and Elliot's confrontation. She watched the whole scene unfold in her mind and sat through the experience of checking the parking lot logs and then the eventual towing of Elliot's vehicle. Once it was over, she gasped for breath and reached out to the table as a wave of dizziness overcame her. She saw the slim man sitting in front of her once again.

The thin man, still sitting idle across from her, nodded slightly as her stomach started to settle. "What was that?" Kya said.

"It'll wear off in a second. That's how this Super works. I've seen what you have experienced, and I agree that Don Georgetown killed your co-worker. You may go."

Kya didn't feel comforted. She tried to stand, but the world seemed to sway slightly, and it took more effort than expected to move towards the door. "Okay, so what happens now?"

In response, the man gestured with a small wave of his hand toward the door.

As she grabbed the handle of the door and opened it, the officer that had escorted her was waiting to the right, standing with his back against the wall.

"Everything work out okay?" The officer said as peered in through the open door.

Kya instinctively turned and saw the thin man nod.

"Well, young lady, you can head home. We shouldn't have any further need of you." The officer started to walk towards the exit and Kya followed him, feeling better as the moments passed, but still struggling to completely regain her composure.

"What happens now?"

Ignoring Kya's question, the officer continued, "if you are concerned that the suspect may try to hurt you or otherwise retaliate before we are able to apprehend him, you should stay with a friend or family member. Please leave your contact details with Lisa," the officer pointed at an older, silver-haired woman sitting off to the side of the sea of cubicles. "And if you need anything else, don't hesitate to contact us."

"Thank you," Kya said. She felt as though she had a ball of iron the size of her fist sitting inside of her stomach. The dizziness, nausea and stiffness all faded by the time she had walked over to the cubicle pointed out by the officer, but her stomach was still very uncomfortable.

"Name?" The older woman said without even glancing in Kya's direction.

"Kya Roberts."

"Is this you?"

Kya looked at the screen, and her information

populated. She noted that it included her social media accounts, email accounts, phone number, address and last known occupation.

"Yes, that's correct, but I don't work at Starlife Technologies anymore."

"That's fine. You can go. We will contact you if we need anything else." Her voice was shrill and full of disdain. Kya could tell that Lisa had no love for her job.

Stumbling from the Police Precinct, Kya walked over to a nearby bus stop. Her whole visit seemed too easy. She thought back to her previous experiences at the police station, and the sour taste that it had left her mouth, and now, thanks to her Supers, she was finally getting respect. The whole thing angered her slightly. Kya knew that everyone should receive the same respect that she just had. She knew that the law should work for everyone. "How easy would it have been to scan my thoughts before and bring those thieves to justice?"

A nearby woman waiting for the bus looked at Kya in shock.

"Sorry. Long day."

The bus arrived, and Kya hopped on and took her usual spot. Looking at her phone, she was saddened to see that there were no new messages. It wasn't long until the bus was pulling into the main transfer point, and Kya knew she would have to pick a destination. The thought of returning to the apartment while Don was at large, or even worse, being hunted by the police, caused her stomach to churn, reminding her of how upset it still felt.

As she completed her thought, a bus pulled in that she recognized as the route that went to the edge of town and the area where Callidus and the other Shadow Striders lived. Kya wondered if she would be allowed to hide out there until Don was caught? With the decision to go and ask made, she changed buses and waited until the now familiar route was near the diner.

CHAPTER 28

Kya walked towards *Gennie's Diner* she was not looking forward to seeing Everly again. As she approached the diner, her thoughts focused on Everly's Super. The way Everly could read her mind, even if only thoughts of intent, just made Kya's skin crawl. She reached out her hand to push the door of the diner open, and Everly pulled it from the inside at the same time.

"Hey, Kya," she said with a smile. "I heard you coming."

Kya nodded solemnly and said nothing.

"I know you don't like my Super," Everly said, her smile fading. "I sometimes forget that I'm using it. I'm really sorry."

Kya opened her mouth, but before words could come out, Everly began to speak again.

"It must be hard."

"Please, Everly, let me speak," Kya said, heavily. "My best friend, Amelia, she could read minds too."

Everly nodded knowingly.

Kya rubbed her forehead in frustration and took a deep breath. The diner smelled of fresh apple pies, and despite being empty, the restaurant seemed more welcoming this time. She refocused on attention on Everly. "I know you're aware of what I intend to communicate, but could you please pretend like it's brand new information as it leaves my mouth?"

Everly took on a neutral expression. "Sorry, I'll try."

"Her Supers were wild and uncontrolled. Before she died," Kya paused and licked her lips, her mouth suddenly dry.

"You don't have to do this." Everly's tone was soft and compassionate.

"Before she died, my conversations with her were erratic. She would read my mind and finish my sentences or respond to things I didn't say, things I barely even registered thinking. It was insane! And it drove her insane. So seeing you, it sucks." She wrapped her arms tight around herself. "It's like sometimes I see her."

Everly put her hand on Kya's shoulder, comfortingly. "I'm sorry."

"Thanks."

"Can I get you a slice of apple pie?"

"Sure. Then can you take me to New Eden?"

"Of course!"

Kya felt lighter for having said what she did. The pie

tasted delicious, and Everly made polite conversation and tidied up the diner while Kya ate. Kya told her that she had run into a bit of trouble and that she would have to lay low for a while.

Everly nodded, and Kya knew that she knew more than what Kya had said aloud. "New Eden is a good place to lay low. I'm sure they'll welcome you for as long as you need to stay."

With Kya's pie eaten, Everly closed up the diner, and the two women walked toward New Eden.

The sun had already set as Everly led Kya to the First Gen village. As they shimmied along the fence, the entrance was even harder to find than before. They arrived at the wall at the same time as a trio of Shadow Striders.

"Callidus?" Kya asked the three covered figures.

"No." A female voice responded. The girl slid her hood off of her head, revealing the sad eyes of Audentia.

A pit formed in Kya's stomach, as seeing Audentia made her think of Audientia's brother, Facillis. Kya had tried to bury his death in her memories along with the others she had experienced recently. And seeing Audentia had brought them all to the surface. Her emotions were still so raw, she forced the memories back down, taking a breath as she did so.

Beside Kya Everly visibly shifted her weight from foot to foot, swaying awkwardly.

"Welcome back, Kya," Audentia said kindly. The corners of her eyes crinkled in what appeared to be an almost happy way. The lower half of her face still covered by her scarf left Kya uncertain.

Audentia and the other Shadow Striders accompanied Kya into the city and led them into a nearby house for dinner. It was small and cozy. Sitting in the warm and rustic dining area with a fire, for both cooking and warmth, roaring in the hearth, Kya suddenly realized she hadn't eaten all day. Her stomach growled in acknowledgment.

"What brings you back so soon, my friend?" A man asked, and Kya immediately recognized his voice.

She smiled and turned. "Nitor!"

Nitor smiled broadly. The wrinkles around his eyes stood out in the firelight, and the silver of his hair seemed to flicker like the flames. He opened his arms and bent to wrap Kya in a hug.

It took Kya a moment to respond. She was not used to such outward signs of affection being given so freely.

"Nitor!" Everly interrupted, "people in the city aren't so huggy. Remember?"

Nitor let Kya go. "Sorry about that. Because it doesn't affect anyone here, it's kind of what we do."

Kya nodded. She could feel the heat of blushing in her cheeks. A few others joined them in the room, sharing around a loaf of bread and a deep bowl of salad.

Over dinner, Kya recounted the events that led her back to New Eden: her confrontation with her boss, going to the police, and needing a place to stay until something was done about Don Georgetown.

"You are welcome here anytime." Nitor affirmed.

One of the First Gens that Kya had not been introduced to started playing his guitar as the dishes from the meal were cleared. Kya sat and listened. She felt so calm, so relaxed. There was a special energy to New Eden, and through the music, she felt like she was tapping into it.

"Welcome back," Callidus said from the doorway as he entered the house. He was dressed in an oversized plain beige top and a pair of brown pants with wear marks in the knees. Kya stared at him in his First Gen clothes.

She had expected him to be surprised that she was back, but in looking around, she realized that Everly was standing behind him. "Hey, Callidus," She said, swallowing back a fluttering of nervousness. "Um, can we talk? In private?"

"Sure." Callidus took a step back outside the house and extended his hand out and away, inviting Kya to walk outside with him.

A slightly offended looking Everly passed by the pair and back inside the house, where she took Kya's seat.

Slowly walking down the sand and gravel path, the sound of the guitar faded. It wasn't long until they turned a corner and were three houses down from where Kya had eaten. Her stomach growled at the thought of the food. The meal helped fight her hunger, but it wasn't enough to satiate her. She had hoped for something more substantial but quickly came to terms with the idea that she would just have to tighten her belt.

Callidus walked at a leisurely pace, his hands casually tucked in his pockets. "So, what would you like to discuss?"

"Why me?"

Callidus stopped walking, removed a hand from his pocket, and ran it through the curls of his black hair as he sighed.

"Why me and not Amelia? Why me and not some other random? Why did you pick me, Callidus?"

"I didn't exactly pick you, Kya." He now had both of his hands out of his pockets and held them palm up in front of him as he shrugged. "You were just the right kind of person."

"What does that even mean?"

"It means, you have a hunger inside of you. A fierceness."

Kya stifled a laugh.

"You might not see it yet, but I know that you do. You asked questions, and you wanted answers. You called that bonehead, Frank, out on how what he had done to your friend and how it was wrong."

Kya folded her arms across her chest. She wanted to say something, but she didn't know where to start.

"You craved Supers, right?"

Kya nodded.

"Why?"

Kya opened her mouth, unsure of what would come out. "Because the world is not fair without them! Because it's like people without Supers, don't even matter. Because I was tired of being ignored. Tired of not being good enough."

"Did you want to fly?"

"I don't know."

"How about to teleport? Telepathy? Strength? Did you have a list of Supers that you wanted?"

"Not really. I had toyed with some ideas, but..." Kya ran her hands through her hair and sighed in frustration, "no, I didn't."

"Exactly." He pointed both index fingers at her and grinned.

Kya raised an eyebrow.

"You wanted to be treated fairly. You wanted safety, and you wanted the truth. That was what I saw in you. That is what made you the right kind of person." Callidus began pacing. "We have this ability, Shadow Striders I mean, and most of us in New Eden. We could touch everyone, and give them random Supers. We could spread it like an epidemic, touching everyone, and then it would die out as each child born to one of those parents would be born with the power of a Shadow Strider, immune to all Supers. Because of that, we are treated like lepers. You are a person who, I believe, will stand up for the fact that we are treated so unfairly."

Kya stared at Callidus, a mixture of frustration and understanding washing over her.

367

"I touched you so that you can help us and hopefully help non-Supers as well."

"But my Supers don't even work right!" Kya's voice sounded more like that of a whining child than an adult woman. "Invisibility makes me blind, Telekinesis is no easier than using my hands, I can't even heal right. And they all get shoddy when I'm nervous!"

"So?"

"So!" She screeched. She took a breath to compose herself. She began again in a more controlled voice. "So, what am I supposed to do? I can't even be a proper Super."

Callidus sighed. His face drawn in sadness. "That's not the point, Kya." His shoulders dropped, and he turned around and began walking towards where they had started. When he spoke again, his voice seemed tired. "Supers have never been the point."

CHAPTER 29

There was a large board in the main building that listed where each person had a bed for the night, and Kya noticed that she would end up floating from house to house based on what was available. She scanned the board for patterns, and it looked as though only a few people seemed to stay in the same spot. Another thing that caught her eye was that the strangest names, which she determined must be Shadow Striders, weren't always on the schedule each night.

Everyone shared rooms, and bunk beds were in nearly every spot that could fit them. Despite the lack of privacy and the idea of ever changing roommates, Kya somehow felt comfortable and had no trouble falling asleep.

In the morning, she stumbled down the stairs to the kitchen and was greeted by a kind looking older woman, with round and gentle features. She stood a full foot shorter than Kya and wore very vibrant clothing. It was as though she was the opposite to the Shadow Striders, and wanted to be noticed. Her hair was white and done up in such a way that it framed her apple cheeks. She smiled and handed Kya a cup of coffee.

"Hi, Kya, I'm Sarah. I am one of the original First Gen mothers, and I was among the first to come to New Eden."

"Nice to meet you," Kya said in a gravelly voice as she accepted the cup of coffee. "What time is it?"

"We don't look at clocks around here, but it's just after sunrise."

"I'm never up that early." Kya mused.

"The commotion must have woken you." Sarah smiled and spoke gently. "And that's a good thing. While you're here, you'll be expected to act as a part of the community."

Kya nodded.

"Excellent. Everyone in the community helps handle some part of the communal meals and everyone, from child to adult, is responsible for helping tend the gardens. One of your chores will be to assist with dishing out supper in the mess hall."

"The mess hall? I have only ever eaten in houses here. Last night-"

"Last night you got in late," Sarah said in a gentle but matter of fact tone. "You ate with the last of the Shadow Striders."

Kya nodded though she was still confused.

"We make two communal meals in the mess hall three times each day. Aside from that people may choose to eat alone or in a small group in one of the houses, and there is always a warm meal made for the last shift of Shadow Striders. But most of the time we eat together in the mess hall for breakfast, lunch and dinner."

"Okay," Kya said. "I get it."

"Your other chore will be weeding a small section of the garden."

Kya smiled, despite the fact that she had never had to weed anything before. "Sounds great." She took a big swig of her coffee and grinned again at Sarah. It was hard for her to be frustrated with the work she was assigned while being provided with meals and a bed to sleep in and being safely out of the reach of Don Georgetown.

"When you're ready, I'll walk you to the mess hall."

Kya nodded and finished her coffee quickly so that she wouldn't keep Sarah waiting.

Kya took in the sights around her. Every house was full of life despite the earliness of the hour. People were about doing chores, music and singing drifted in on the breeze as well as laughter and friendly voices. A smile found its way to Kya's face. "This place is amazing."

Sarah nodded, but there was sadness in her eyes. "It wasn't always."

"You've been here right from the start." Kya mused. "Would you mind telling me?"

Sarah took a breath and walked a little slower. "I had a son. His father and I named him Derek. He was such a beautiful boy. He wasn't even a month old when I was widowed - a teleportation accident - and we were forced to come here. I gave birth to one son, but here I had so many more children. Not many of the families that came in here were whole, and over the following months, as we tried to gain control of our unwanted powers, there were many more casualties. It became clear that traditional home setups wouldn't work for us as children were orphaned and mothers and fathers were left alone. Back then it looked more like what it is: a prison. We had food rations, passed through the gate with no contact with the outside world. It took all the power in me not to succumb to the despair. I don't know when it happened but as the years went by, things changed. We realized that, although we were trapped, they could only take our hope if we let them. The children became curious about their surroundings and how we got here. Derek became one of the very first Shadow Striders. He was my son, and he is gone. But I have so many children here." Sarah wiped a stray tear off her cheek and glanced at Kya. They walked the rest of the way in silence.

A week passed quickly, and Kya easily lost track of the days. It didn't take long for her to feel like she was already making some close friends. She spent almost her entire afternoon in the garden, chatting and weeding far more than the little patch that she had been assigned. As she walked back down the main road through the village and heard the familiar sound of music wafting through the air, she was struck by how tired and how good she felt. It helped to have Henry by her side, carrying the heavy tools, after insisting multiple times.

He was strong, tall and easy to be around. It didn't hurt

that he had piercing blue eyes, and fiery red hair. The day old stubble he always had on his face only added to his masculine charm.

"Thanks again, Kya. I really appreciate the help," Henry said. He tipped his baseball cap towards her, nodding slightly.

"No problem."

Kya enjoyed Henry's company. Sarah had made sure that Henry and Kya would meet, and it had been an awkward set-up. Despite the rough beginning, their friendship only served to make it harder for her to imagine leaving the community she was now part of.

"Will you be coming to first supper this evening?"

Kya knew that the first supper was usually the better of the two. The food was fresher, and she was assigned to help serve on the second supper. "I hope to. I have to clean-up, and then I'll try to make it."

Kya wiped dirt from the garden off her hands onto an apron she had tied around her waist. Her hair was tied back with a piece of string, and she could feel the warmth of a slight sunburn across her nose and cheeks. She felt like she had been in New Eden for ages, and she thought she was beginning to look the part. She smiled at Henry.

"I'll save you a seat," he said, grinning back at her, and Kya noticed a smudge of dirt on his cheek.

As she went off to clean up at a nearby house, she reflected on what she had experienced. Everyone was so sincere, and always so complimentary, and polite. Being away from the outside world hadn't seemed to do much harm to those trapped within the walls of New Eden.

The house had three large bathrooms, and while they were always in high demand, they were also the one place in New Eden where you could get some privacy. Kya looked in the mirror and saw some dirt from working in the garden had been smeared on her forehead. She noticed the same dirt still caked on her hands. It was easy to tell that she had transferred it when wiping her brow but felt a little embarrassed that Henry had never mentioned it. Then she laughed remembering the dirt on his face that she had also said nothing about.

Her phone, which always seemed to have a nearly drained battery, thanks to the lack of cell coverage, buzzed in her pocket, rousing her from her thoughts. Despite always having it with her, she had almost forgotten about the device. It was an email from Classic Communication.

Hi Kya,

I hope this message finds you well. I have considered your application, and I am happy to say that you are the candidate that we want. Please stop by my office at nine in the morning next Wednesday for orientation. I look forward to having you as part of our team.

Sincerely, Joanne Roddenberry-Roth

Kya stared at the message, her mind began to spin. She was so excited about getting the job, but how could she return to her life in the city with Don Georgetown still on the loose? She ran her hand through her hair and noticed the dirt under her fingernails. Her thoughts turned to New Eden and to the friends she had made there. This place felt like home, and her heart hurt at the idea of leaving. She opened the calendar on her phone to find that the current day was Wednesday, so she had exactly a week to figure everything out.

A bundle of clean clothing from the community was waiting in the room Kya was assigned. Her jeans and *GEEK* labeled t-shirt were folded on top. As she had done so many times before, she moved them aside. She chose a moss-green skirt with a slightly tattered hemline that went to her knees, a beige tank top and a plum coloured long sleeve shirt that wrapped around the front and tied at the side. She brushed her hair, and then pulled back the strands around her face. She looked in the mirror and was happily surprised by the version of herself staring back at her. Sun-kissed skin, well rested looking eyes, a faint smile at the corners of her lips. She went to meet Henry and the rest of her new friends in the mess hall for dinner.

"Kya!" Henry called with a wave when she entered.

The room was long and narrow, but it looked more like a school gymnasium from half a century ago than a room that was originally designed for communal eating. Over three dozen chairs, many of different sizes or construction surrounded the two long rows of tables. Off to one side was a small group of tables with large metal trays of food. Behind each tray was a server, smiling to each person as they doled out a serving.

Henry was sitting with two guys and two girls that Kya knew from the village. They were all in their late twenties or early thirties, and they were singing along while one played the guitar.

The one with the guitar had dark curly hair. Kya remembered his name was Jeremy. He had a rather pointy nose and the same sparkling green eyes as Callidus. He had a deep singing voice, and the only time she had seen him without his guitar was when he was working.

Kya sat and was greeted by smiles all around. Brooke was short, skinny, absolutely covered in freckles and had blond hair that was always tangled. The boys sometimes teased her about it, but she did not seem to care. Leslie was tall and reminded Kya of a swan, with a long neck and graceful features and sleek straight brown hair. She could spit and swear with the best of them, though. Gabriel was quiet, he was the smallest of the three guys and had mousy brown hair. He had a quicker wit than anyone Kya had ever met.

As Kya greeted her new friends, it struck her that her time in their world would be temporary.

"You okay? Leslie asked.

"Yeah, I'm good," Kya replied, intentionally smiling.

Henry gestured for her to sit beside him. She smiled and accepted.

"You clean up nicely," He said.

"Thanks," Kya replied.

The wide double doors at the end of the mess hall swung open, and a small group of Shadow Striders entered. Kya was fairly certain that leading the group was Callidus, but with such a similar set of outfits, and an air of confidence surrounding all of them, it was hard to know for certain.

"Hey, Jer. When are you gonna drop your guitar and join the big boys?" Callidus asked, confirming Kya's suspicion, before clapping Jeremy on the back. Callidus removed his face coverings revealing a playful smile.

"When every last string I can get my hands on has worn out, and all the rest of you big boys are gone," Jeremy said, playing a quick little tune. "And even then, I'll only head out to get more strings."

"Face it, Cal. Your brother's an artist. He's gonna change the world with his songs." Esurio said with a smile. Esurio was tall, lanky, and if the woven leather and bandages added any appearance of bulk at all, Kya swore he would be transparent underneath. Removing his hood revealed fair skin, high cheekbones, and a shaved head. His eyes were small, almond shaped, and recessed, hiding under the shadow of his heavy brow.

"You're brothers?" Kya said, glancing between Callidus and Jeremy. She was suddenly embarrassed that she hadn't made the obvious connection on her own much sooner.

"Yep," Jeremy said, still playing a happy melody. "I remember when he was just my big brother Jonah."

Kya stared between the two brothers, confused. "Jonah?"

"That's what mom named him," Jeremy replied.

"Callidus is the name I assumed when I became a *sociology professor.*"

"Oh, Cal, let it go!" Brooke said with a friendly laugh.

377

Gabriel, keeping his head down, broke into the conversation, his voice came across as less confident than the others. "We've all seen what happens when you try to teach someone something, Callidus."

Everyone burst into laughter, and Kya had to stifle hers as Callidus shot each of them a look of mild embarrassment. The group of Shadow Striders, continuing their conversations, sat down next to Kya and the rest of the group. The area where the Shadow Striders usually sat to eat immediately seemed very far away to Kya.

When it was their table's turn to eat, everyone stood and lined up, grabbing a plate, cutlery, and napkin. Kya grabbed a small piece of chicken, a large heap of roasted vegetables, some salad, and some flatbread. A simple but filling meal. She couldn't help but notice that Esurio, who was next in line, had two plates of food, and each of them was overloaded.

"Hungry?" Kya asked.

"Always," Callidus had answered before Esurio had a chance to. "His chosen name literally means *to hunger*."

Everyone began to laugh again, and Kya felt her face slightly redden.

The conversation flowed easily over the meal, and Kya allowed herself to simply enjoy the experience with her friends.

CHAPTER 30

She didn't recognize the number but accepted the call immediately and placed it to her ear.

"Hello?"

"Hi, Miss Roberts?" A man's voice came through loud and clear.

"This is her. Who's this?"

"This is Detective Harrison. I have been asked to call you regarding an update on the status of your case."

"Okay," Kya said, uncertain of what they were going to tell her, she was unsure of how to respond. In an instant, her mind imagined dozens of different scenarios.

"We have arrested Mr. Georgetown. He is currently sedated pending a trial." The officer spoke in a firm monotone. The timbre of his voice was almost relaxing. "We will contact you if we need anything further from you, but I doubt that will be necessary."

"Um, okay." The world seemed to dance around Kya as she processed what the detective had said, and relief washed over her. "Thank you."

"If you need anything else, please feel free to contact us."

"Thank you."

The officer hung up the phone, and Kya took in a long, deep breath before she let it out slowly. She didn't feel like the same person who had been hunted in the alley, and then gone to the cops just a few short days ago. She turned and stared at herself in the mirror, and there was something about her reflection that looked different. She felt like the person staring back was a little older, wiser, and stronger.

Her phone still in her hand, Kya texted Sam.

>Sam, they caught DG. Everything is safe. I'll see you back at the apartment tomorrow. I'm so sorry again for all of this.

Her phone buzzed as Sam replied.

>Thanks for the head's up. I'll make sure I'm home tomorrow. I really think we need a chance to sit down and have a real chat. Just the two of us, if that's cool.

Kya read Sam's message over and over, trying to decipher his tone. She was fairly sure that he was not impressed with her for causing him to have to hide out for a few days, and she knew they had not spent much time together recently. She worried that he would want her to move out, and that was what he wanted to discuss. The notion of leaving the apartment felt like a lead weight inside her, dragging her down. Kya tried to push it aside and focus on getting ready for dinner.

Kya tried numerous times to say goodbye to them all, but the words just never came to her. The conversation focused on how the crops were doing, gossip about people wanting to join the Shadow Striders, and those looking to start families. Finally giving in, she just took it all in and enjoyed it. She tried to memorize everything and store it away in a special place both in her mind and in her heart.

When the meal was done, Kya excused herself and walked outside. The air was sweet and clean, and there was a bite to it that chilled her skin after the warmth of the mess hall. She breathed deeply and hugged her arms close.

Dawn signaled the start of a new day. Kya went to get ready, but instead of putting on the clothing given to her by the community, she wore the laundered clothing she had arrived in. It was finally time to leave New Eden and go back to the world she had left. She felt concerned. Kya had become used to being a citizen of the First Gen village, and she felt like she was needed.

Upon descending to the kitchen, Sarah was waiting, coffee in an outstretched hand. "I heard you are leaving us today." Despite being in a different kitchen than when they first had met, Sarah seemed completely at home. There was an ease about her that was comforting.

"Yeah, I have to get home and ready for my new job. I wish I could stay longer."

"Well, I hope you won't forget your time here. Never forget that you can always come back." Sarah's face softened, even more than normal, and Kya felt a warmth radiating off of the woman. Both women's eyes welled up, seconds away from tears.

Kya caught herself first and took a breath to stabilize herself. "Thank you. I appreciate that."

Sarah wiped the edge of her eyes and then shot Kya a wide smile.

Turning around towards the front door, Kya noticed Henry filling the frame of the open door. "You didn't think you'd leave without saying goodbye, did you?"

"It's such a cliché, but *goodbyes* have never been my strong suit." Kya chuckled lightly.

Henry moved his lumbering frame quickly, as though a magnet was dragging him along the ground. He smashed into Kya, almost knocking her down, but before she could fall, his arms held her in a strong embrace. Due to their height difference, she couldn't help but hear the rapid beating of his heart through the top of his chest.

Kya knew Henry's feelings were stronger than the ones she harboured for him, but she embraced him just as tightly. "I'll be back soon. I just need to get my life back on track. Then we can race again to see who can pick the most carrots."

As Kya left, without looking back, she heard what she knew to be Henry's voice, quietly pleading. "Your life could be here."

Uncertain if any of her outfits were a good choice to wear for orientation, Kya felt slightly nervous. She jumped off the bus two stops before her apartment where a wall of clothing stores were near closing for the day. One of the smaller shops had clothing for business women and didn't have any bright, offensive colours in its front displays.

Kya wanted to dress up. She wanted to show her new boss that she was professional and excited about the opportunity given to her. Upon entering the store, one of the sales attendants immediately snubbed her and went off to arrange clothing. The store was filled with black, gray and white clothing. There was very little colour to be found, and as much as it pained Kya not to wear colour, she knew that she wanted to make a good impression on her first day.

Picking out a long black skirt, and white button up blouse, Kya felt like she looked a bit more like a librarian. The clothing seemed to add to the new version of herself that she saw reflected back in the mirror. Her purple streak, mostly faded, still added that touch of colour and personality that Kya recognized as a key part of who she was, even now, after everything that had happened.

The cashier made eye contact with Kya, but only for a moment. "Will you be needing to set-up a payment account for your purchases today?"

"No." Kya felt slightly offended, but pulled her bank card from her wallet and tapped it on the sensor. It was now the principle of the purchase, to prove that she could. The poor service she received frustrated her, but she recognized their attitude as par for the course in her life.

The machine came back with a flashing message saying that the transaction had been approved. Kya felt triumphant.

The whole demeanor of the cashier changed. A smile flashed on her face, she stood straighter and looked directly at Kya. "Is there anything else you need? That outfit would look amazing with a belt."

Kya grabbed her purchase and rushed out the door. She knew that she would need to do more shopping trips if she was going to have a wardrobe of work clothing, but with a nearly empty bank account, she was going to have to be more thrifty with her other purchases.

From the hallway of her building, Kya could hear pots and pans rattling around from inside her apartment. She tried the handle before taking her keys out to unlock the door. The door opened, and Kya walked in. She set her clothing bag on the floor next to the table near the front door. She then placed her keys in the bowl and timidly entered the apartment.

"Hey, Kya." Sam's voice came muffled from the kitchen. His tone was low, and not very animated. "Come on in, I'm just making dinner."

She couldn't tell if he was concentrating or upset. She slowly inched towards the kitchen.

"What are you making?"

"Nothing too exciting, but it smells okay, doesn't it?"

Kya took a deep breath. "Yeah." She smiled slightly at

Sam, and he reciprocated.

"It's almost ready, why don't you grab yourself a seat and I'll be over with the food in a minute."

"Okay." Kya poured herself a glass of pop and walked to the table that had already been set for two. She sat in her usual spot, on the far side of the table facing the kitchen. Sam brought over the food, a pan of roasted chicken breasts and vegetables, and a pot of mashed potatoes.

"So, a lot has happened recently, wouldn't you say?" Sam served himself some food as he spoke, and Kya felt for a moment like she was about to get a lecture from her father.

"Yeah," She said, staring at her empty plate.

"You seem different. I mean for one thing, you have a sunburn on your face."

Kya touched the bridge of her nose, and her mind transported her back to working in the garden with Henry, Brooke, and the others.

"I have no idea what's been going on with you since..." Sam closed his mouth like he wasn't sure he should finish his sentence.

"Since Amelia's funeral." Kya finished it for him and nodded. "I've been dealing with a lot and taking the time to process it all. You're right, I am different. I have these powers, but more than that, there's something bigger that I can't articulate."

"If you want to talk about it, I'm here. But it seems like

I'm not the person you want to talk to these days. I hardly see you anymore, and when I do, it's not for long."

Kya's chest turned hot. Sam had been like family to her, closer even than her own family, and she was scared of what he was going to say next. Kya served her food without saying a word.

"Look, Kya, you know that I can carry the cost of this apartment on my own. If you don't want to live here anymore, I understand."

Her mouth went dry, and she took a big gulp of her pop.

"But if you want to stay, you are more than welcome to. I really do enjoy having you as my roommate, and if I can help you with everything that's going on, I'd really like that. I just don't want us to be strangers who live in the same house."

"I get that, Sam, I do. And I want to live here more than I can express. And I want to tell you everything." Kya grinned. She then shoveled potatoes into her mouth trying to alleviate her hunger.

Over dinner, they discussed in detail her experiences with the First Gens, and New Eden. They talked about Don Georgetown and her limited powers. She told him about her experience with the police, and for the first time, Kya spoke out loud about Facillis, and how she wasn't able to save him.

Sam listened and asked questions. Kya felt that he was trying hard to understand her, and help her understand herself.

When Kya had eaten too much, and the conversation was dying down, she felt content. Her night had gone better than she ever could have dreamed. She stood and grabbed her shopping bag from earlier.

"What's in the bag?" Sam said.

"I bought some nice clothing for my orientation at work."

"Smart move. I'm sure you'll do great."

Kya knew Sam was sincere, and she felt a warm glow surrounding her. "We should go out for shawarma soon."

"Definitely," Sam responded.

CHAPTER 31

The tall glass and steel skyscraper shone in the early days light. Kya felt excited as she approached the building. She smoothed out her blouse tucking it neatly into her skirt, making sure everything looked perfect. The doors to the building were constantly opening and closing as a wave of office workers flooded through the entrance. With her completed checklist still repeating endlessly in her head, Kya joined the masses and entered. The air inside the building was dry, and slightly warmer than the chill of the morning breeze.

Walking between the elevators, and around behind to the hallway, she saw the familiar solid wooden doors of Classic Communication. It was as though a fire was ignited inside her, one she knew she couldn't quell, and she would likely never want to.

She pushed open the door and entered. Sunlight poured through the windows into the open space. It was not as intimidating as it had been when she had sat through her interview.

"Kya! I'm so happy you made it. No issues getting here I hope?" Joanne rushed towards Kya, her tone chipper, a smile on her face.

"No, this place is within walking distance of my apartment," Kya replied, with an equal smile.

"That's great." Joanne looked Kya up and down. "I guess I should have mentioned that we are more of a casual place, eh?"

Joanne was wearing black slacks and a flower print t-shirt. Her running shoes were clean, and much more comfortable looking than the black dress flats that Kya had chosen.

Kya blushed slightly. "I wanted to make a good impression."

"If you hadn't, do you think I would have hired you?" Joanne moved in close, standing shoulder to shoulder with Kya. Both women faced the interior of Classic Communication, standing by the door. Light beams from the windows illuminated the solid wood shelving where thousands of books were stored. "You will be our front-line person. When people come in here, they will interact with you first. I want them to have an experience. I want them to feel welcome and comfortable. I want them to remember you, and consequently this store."

Heat filled Kya's cheeks as she knew her light blushing had been replaced with an entirely red face.

Joanne, not missing a beat, began to walk towards the large central desk and placed her hand on it. It illuminated, and the wooden top was hidden by dozens of computer applications. Without much thought, Kya followed at nearly the same pace.

"This will be your desk. From here, people will purchase books, or look at making appointments to talk to me. There are many things you will have to learn, and it might feel overwhelming at first, but I have faith that you'll figure it out in due course. Just let me know if I try to throw too much at you today."

"Okay."

"You should know that I started this company, and I have four people working for me, including yourself. I just recently promoted Cassie, who used to have your job, to be one of the editors of the book submissions we get. Feel free to ask her any questions as well."

Energy was bursting from Kya, in an almost uncontrollable way. She felt like her body was vibrating. "I can't tell you how excited I am."

"You don't have to," Joanne said with a kind chuckle. "Follow me, and we'll look at the print-on-demand system we have here. It is probably the neatest machine we own."

Kya followed her new boss down the rows of books to a small back room where several large printers sat. In the middle, on a pedestal, was a small, mostly metal object.

"What's that?" Kya asked, pointing.

"That is a scale miniature of a Gutenberg printing press. It is here as a symbol. It brought printing to the masses, sharing knowledge and passion in a way that hadn't been done before and that's my goal in life."

The rest of the day passed by in an instant. Joanne's passion only served to increase Kya's own. It was infectious. Over the course of the day, Kya helped print manuscripts with writers that were working with Classic Communication to publish their books. She was able to assist a customer in finding the book they were looking for in the thousands shelved within the store and helped a first-time writer organize an appointment to meet with Joanne.

There was a huge sense of accomplishment that she could hold her own and be so productive. Her mind was a hurricane, with facts, figures, information, and statistics. While she was exhausted by the end of the day, she also felt fulfilled.

"Good night, Kya. Great first day!" Joanne said as she turned off the overhead lights.

Kya exited the now quiet building and walked out onto the sidewalk. She didn't want to go back to the apartment yet, but wanted to share her day, and experiences with someone.

"Hey Mattie," Kya said when her friend answered her call. "How are you doing?"

"I'm good, I'm good. How are you?" Mattea's voice was melodic, and she sounded genuinely happy to hear from her friend.

"I'm good," Kya answered. "Listen, are you free? I'd like to see you in person if that's at all possible, even just for a quick coffee or something."

"Sure," Mattea said, and it sounded like she was smiling. "Rory's working late tonight, and I was just wondering what to do for dinner. Would you mind swinging by here? I can cook up something nice for us."

"That sounds awesome! Whatever you want to make is good by me." Kya grinned, and walked, almost skipping, to the bus stop. She sent a text to Sam to let him know her day went well and that she would be going to Mattea's for dinner.

>*Awesome! Have fun. I'll see you when you get home.* He sent back.

Kya greeted the bus driver with a friendly smile as she boarded and paid her fare, then moved to the back, donning her earphones to listen to music on the long bus ride to Mattea's house. As the bus wound its way through the city, Kya glimpsed graffiti murals of black hooded figures, which she now recognized as Shadow Striders, helping the poor and the weak out of the darkness. Kya smiled to herself. She looked around the bus at all of the people who didn't even seem to notice the graffiti, and it struck her how little most of the population knew about the world they lived in. How little she had known of it a few short months ago.

She got off the bus at the grocery store and walked the rest of the way to Mattea's house. Her feet hurt in her dress flats, but she still didn't mind the walk.

The porch light was on, at Mattea's house and the front door was open a crack. As Kya climbed the steps, the aroma of meat and black pepper wafted in the air and caused her to salivate. She entered and started talking before she could even see her friend. "Hey Mattie, is that stew? It smells delicious!"

"Yeah, I just opened a few cans," Mattea replied from the kitchen.

Kya kicked off her shoes in the front hall and rounded the corner into the kitchen. The dining room table had already been set for two.

"I got up to cook and realized I have, like, zero energy. I hope you don't mind."

"Not in the slightest," Kya said, wrapping her friend in a hug.

"Wow! You look nice!" Mattea said, taking in Kya's appearance.

"New clothes for work," Kya said with a nod. "Is there anything I can do to help? Shouldn't you sit down?"

"I'm okay. I'm not that pregnant yet. It just needs to be served into bowls."

Kya grabbed the bowls and served the food, directing Mattea to sit. She looked at her friend's bulging belly. There was something about knowing that there was a precious life growing inside of her friend that made Kya tingle slightly with joy.

"Okay," Mattea said with a heavy sigh as she sat at the table. "Tell me everything. How did it go at SLT?"

Kya brought over Mattea's bowl and stared straight into her eyes.

"Don Georgetown was right," Kya said, placing the bowl in front of her friend.

Mattea's brow furrowed, and her mouth fell open.

"About my job." Kya continued, grabbing her bowl. "I deserved to be fired. I was a terrible employee."

"Okay," Mattea said slowly.

"Don't get me wrong, Don Georgetown is a terrible person. He should never have had as much power as he did, and he got away with far too much for far too long. But he was right about me. I never gave my all. I never tried. My negative attitude held me back and made me a liability. My attitude was contagious, and I got the same negativity handed to me that I was dishing out."

Mattea raised her eyebrows. "Wow."

"It's time for me to grow up. To start pulling my weight." Kya paused for a moment to eat and couldn't help notice that the stew was pretty good. "Even today at Classic Communication, for the first time I felt like an adult. I still have a lot to learn about my job, but I feel like I fit. Do you know what I'm talking about?"

Mattea smiled and nodded, chewing on a mouthful of food.

"It's like the world can be a terrible place, and it's so not fair. But you kind of get what you give. The First Gens are forced to live in a prison, and can't be seen or touched in the larger world, but New Eden is..." Kya fought to find the words. "Full of music. It's a family. It's so full of life!"

Mattea grinned. "I wish I could see it."

"I've learned that you get what you give. I have been handed some amazing opportunities in my life recently, and I have to share my good fortune for the greater good."

Kya and Mattea chatted and enjoyed each other's presence for hours, and Kya cleaned up while Mattea rested.

"Hey, Kya, there's something I've meant to ask you," Mattea said as Kya was getting ready to leave. "Rory and I were wondering if you'd be willing to be our baby's godmother."

It took Kya a moment to find her voice. "I - I'd be honoured," she said in slightly more than a whisper.

CHAPTER 32

The sun hung high in the sky causing the shadows along the skyscrapers to be very faint. Returning from an early lunch, Kya felt satiated as her meal digested in her stomach.

"It has been a long time since I've gone to the Coliseum." There was a small pang of sadness that swirled in her mind as she thought about Amelia.

"It is a bit pricey, and not really baby friendly, but I thought it was appropriate somehow."

Kya carried Mattea's baby, Evan, in her arms while she walked. Mattea pushed the empty stroller.

As they entered Classic Communication, Evan started to make small noises of glee which caused Joanne to leap from her desk and rush over to the trio.

"Oh my, he's getting so big!" Joanne said. Her arms outstretched, looking to have a turn to hold Evan.

Kya was hesitant to pass off the baby to Joanne, but the

look of excitement in her boss' eyes was greater than the instinct to keep Evan for herself. She glanced at Mattea to get the okay and Mattea nodded.

Joanne faced Mattea's baby outwards, and he continued to smile and make joyful noises as she gently bounced him.

"It's hard to believe that he will be one in four more months," Mattea said with her eyes laser focused on her child. Pride beamed from her face.

Kya let Evan grip her finger. His large blue eyes focused on her face. He smiled, and his round rosy cheeks showed his dimples.

"I should get back to shelf reading," Kya said. She looked towards her boss, with knowingly sad eyes.

"Oh, there hasn't anyone in yet. I'm sure things will be fine for five more minutes." Joanne said before looking at Mattea. "Is he sleeping through the night yet?" She brushed her cheek against his soft, white blond hair.

"Oh, yeah. He's such a good baby." Mattea grinned. "But Daddy will be home soon," she cooed to the baby, "so Mommy shouldn't stick around too much longer."

Both Kya and Joanne chuckled.

"Babies turn adults into crazy people!" Kya cooed. "Godmama knows these things."

The large wooden door swung open behind the three women,

and a tall, thin man entered. He wore a black suit, black dress shirt, and a dark red tie. His black hair was slicked back on his head, accentuating his large forehead. He held a black leather briefcase in his left hand.

Kya noticed him first and walked over to intercept him as Joanne and Mattea continued entertaining Evan. There was something about the man in the black suit that didn't feel typical of a visitor to Classic Communication. Kya felt nervous as she stopped a few feet in front of him.

"May I help you?"

"I need information about an author." His voice was quite nasal and had an edge to it.

A pit of uneasiness twisted in Kya's stomach as she knew, somehow, that he was a government agent. She tried to focus on thinking about Evan and hoped that the agent wasn't one that could read her mind.

He set his briefcase on Kya's desk without invitation and opened it. He pulled out a well-used paperback, with the cover so beaten up it was almost unrecognizable. He slapped it on the wooden desk, and a loud noise reverberated through the open space. The man in the black suit kept his grip firmly dug into the paper.

Despite its appearance, Kya knew what book it was, and so she had to put on her best poker face.

"What's that?" She asked.

"It's a book," He said in an annoyed tone. He held it out for her to see.

"Who are you again?" Kya asked.

The man stood silent for a moment. "Agent Wells."

"Well Mr. Wells, I know it is a book." She raised an eyebrow and gave it a closer look.

"Do you have any copies of it here?"

"Yeah, we carry that title."

Just then, Kya noticed her boss, having handed back Evan to his mother, walking over.

"Hello," Joanne said with a smile and a friendly tone as she extended her hand for the man to shake. "I'm Joanne Roddenberry-Roth. Welcome to my store. I believe this is your first time at Classic Communication."

Agent Wells turned up his nose at Joanne's outstretched hand with a look of disdain. "Tell me what you know about Amelia Facillis."

Joanne cleared her throat and smiled again, showing off her straight white teeth. "I know that's the name of the author of the book in your hand. Beyond that, I know very little."

"I find that hard to believe."

Kya could hear that Evan was starting to get fussy. She looked over at her friend and saw Mattea signaling that she was going to go. Giving her a small nod and wave, Kya communicated that she didn't want to leave the conversation to escort Mattea out. Mattea nodded with a look of understanding.

"Kya, do you remember seeing who dropped off the manuscript?" Joanne asked in a very polite tone. Kya recognized it as the voice Joanne reserved for stubborn people.

"I don't remember. I think it came in the mail. We must get thirty or more manuscripts per day. Most of them in the mail. I just remember this one came with a note attached." Kya went around to the far side of the desk where her chair was. She tapped the tabletop activating the screen, typed in her password, and a few moments later, the output tray on the side of her desk had a few sheets of paper in it. "Here you go. We scanned it into our records in case anything came up." Kya handed the printed copy of the letter to agent Wells.

Joanne shot Kya a large approving smile before morphing into her more serious face as she turned back to the government agent. She turned slightly, so that she was squarely facing the agent, and stood up as straight as she could. "As I'm sure you can see, this note discusses what is to be done with the book. It asks that each store that receives it prints copies for those that want to purchase it and that all profits go towards the store. Nothing goes to the author, no contact information beyond the name."

He scowled at the page. "Don't you think it's abnormal that someone would write a book and then not want any of the profit from it? I wouldn't be here if the government weren't aware of the risks these countercultural ideas could pose to our society. You don't want your business to get messy, do you?"

Kya's boss responded using her most powerful voice. "Whatever the author's reasons, I still plan on selling it. Millions of people have purchased this book, and unless there are some legal grounds to prevent us from distributing it, I will continue to do so. I will not be the only bookstore in the city or even the country not selling this book. It has been a huge source of revenue for our company, and it has caught on like wildfire." She took a breath, smiled and allowed her voice to take on a more pleasant tone as she continued. "Besides, it is just a work of fiction, right?"

The agent seemed frustrated. Kya didn't know if this was stop one or one hundred on his journey to research the book still clenched within his spindly fingers. "Of course. Well, if anyone comes in claiming authorship, or you remember anything else about Second Class Supers, please contact me." The agent took out his phone and tapped it against the desk. His contact information appeared on the screen, and Kya tapped on the save button.

"We will be sure to do that," Joanne said as she turned and left towards her office.

Agent Wells slammed the tattered book back into his briefcase, spun on his heels, and marched out of Classic Communication.

Kya couldn't help but smile as she grabbed one of the copies she stored in her desk. She let out a sigh of relief. "They can't stop us now."